THE DEVIL'S RIGHT HAND

LILITH SAINTCROW
THE DEVIL'S RIGHT HAND

www.orbitbooks.net

ORBIT

First published in the United States in 2007 by Orbit,
Hachette Book Group USA
First published in Great Britain in 2007 by Orbit
Reprinted 2008, 2009

A CIP catalogue record for this book
is available from the British Library.

ISBN 978-1-84149-673-3

Printed and bound in the UK by
CPI Mackays, Chatham, ME5 8TD

Papers used by Orbit are natural, renewable and recyclable
products sourced from well-managed forests and certified
in accordance with the rules of the Forest Stewardship Council.

Mixed Sources
Product group from well-managed
forests and other controlled sources
www.fsc.org Cert no. SGS-COC-004081
© 1996 Forest Stewardship Council
FSC

Orbit
An imprint of
Little, Brown Book Group
100 Victoria Embankment
London EC4Y 0DY

An Hachette UK Company
www.hachette.co.uk

www.orbitbooks.net

For Kazuo, my best friend

Non satis est ullo, tempore longus amor.
—Propertius

Warlord: You are looking at a man who can run you through with this sword without batting an eye.

Monk: You are looking at a man who can be run through with that sword without batting an eye.
—old Korean folk tale

The last of the theories is the most intriguing: what if the Awakening itself was prompted by a collective evolution of the human race? Psionic talent before the Awakening was notoriously unreliable. The Parapsychic Act, by codifying and making it possible to train psionic ability, cannot alone account for the flowering of Talent and magickal ability just prior to its signing into law—no matter how loudly apologists for Adrien Ferrimen cry.

A corollary to the theory of collective evolution is the persistent notion that another intelligence was responsible. The old saw about demonic meddling with the human genetic code has surfaced in this debate so many times as to be a cliché. But as any Magi will tell you, demonkind's fascination with humans cannot be explained unless they somehow had a hand in our evolution, as they themselves claim.

For if there is one law in dealing with demons, it is their possessive nature. A demon will destroy a beloved object rather than allow its escape; in this they are like humanity. A second law is just as important in dealing with demons: as with loa *or* etrigandi, *their idea of truth is not at all the human legal definition. A demon's idea of a truth might be whatever serves the purpose of a moment or achieves a particular end. This leads to the popular joke that lawyers make good Magi, which this author can believe.*

In fact, one might say that in jealousy and falsity either we learned from demonkind, or they caught these tendencies like a sickness from us—and the latter option is not at all likely, given how much older a race they are. . . .

—from *Theory And Demonology:*
    A Magi Primer
    Adrienne Spocarelli

1

It's for you," Japhrimel said diffidently, his eyes flaring with green fire in angular runic patterns for just a moment before returning to almost-human darkness.

I blinked, taking the package. It was heavy, wrapped in blue satin, with a wide white silk ribbon tied in a bow. I pushed the large leatherbound book away and rubbed at the back of my neck under the heavy fall of my hair. Long hours of reading and codebreaking made my vision blur, the white marble behind him turning into a hazy streak. For just a moment, his face looked strange.

Then I recognized him again and inhaled, taking in his familiar smell of cinnamon and amber musk. The mark on my shoulder burned at his nearness, a familiar sweet pain making my breath catch. The room was dark except for the circle of light from the antique brass lamp with its green plasilica shade. "*Another* present?" My voice scraped through my dry throat, still damaged; I didn't have to worry about its soft huskiness, alone with him. The tattoo on my cheek twisted, and my emerald spat a single spark to greet him.

"Indeed." Japhrimel touched my cheek with two fingertips, sending liquid fire down my back in a slow, even cascade. His long dark high-collared coat moved slightly as he straightened, his fingers leaving my cheek reluctantly. "For the most beautiful Necromance in the world."

That made me laugh. *Flattery will get you everywhere, won't it.* "I think Gabe's prettier, but you're entitled to your opinion." I stretched, rolling my head back on my neck, working out the stiffness. "What's this?" It was about the size of my arm from wrist to elbow, and heavy as metal, or stone.

Japhrimel smiled, his mouth tilting up and softening, his eyes dark with an almost-human expression. It looked good on him—he was usually so fiercely grim. The expression was tender, and as usual, it made my entire body uncomfortably warm. I looked down at the package, touched the ribbon.

The last present had been a copy of Perezreverte's *Ninth Portal of Hell* in superb condition, its leather binding perfect as if it had just been printed in old Venizia over a thousand years ago—or been sitting in a stasis cabinet since then. The house was a present too, a glowing white marble villa set in the Toscano countryside. I'd mentioned being tired of traveling, so he presented me with a key to the front door one night over dinner.

My library breathed around me, deep in shadow, none of the other lamps turned on. I heard, now that I wasn't sunk in study, the shuffle of human feet in the corridors—servants cleaning and cooking, the security net over the house humming, everything as it should be.

Why was I so uneasy? If I didn't know better, I'd say the nervousness was a warning. A premonition, my small precognitive gift working overtime.

Gods, I hope not. I've had all the fun I can stand in one lifetime.

I rubbed at my eyes again and pulled at the ribbon, silk cool and slick against my fingers. Another yawn caught at my mouth—I'd been at codebreaking for a full three days and would need to crash soon. "You don't have to keep giving me—oh, *gods* above."

Satin folded away, revealing a statue made of perfect glassy obsidian, a lion-headed woman on a throne. The sun-disk over her head was of pure soft hammered gold, glowing in the dim light. I let out a breath of wonder. "Oh, Japhrimel. Where did you..."

He folded himself down into the chair opposite mine. Soft light from the full-spectrum lamp slid shadows over his saturnine face, made the green flashing through his eyes whirl like sparks above a bonfire. His eyes often held a green sparkle or two while he watched me. "Do you like it, Dante?" The usual question, as if he doubted I would.

I picked her up, felt the thrumming in the glassy stone. It was, like all his gifts, perfect. The funny melting sensation behind my ribs was familiar by now, but nothing could take away its strangeness. "She's beautiful."

"I have heard you call upon Sekhmet." He stretched out his long legs just like a human male. His eyes turned dark again, touching me, sliding against my skin like a caress. "Do you like it?"

"Of course I like her, you idiot." I traced her smooth shoulder with a fingertip, my long black-lacquered fingernail scraping slightly. "She's *gorgeous*." My eyes found his and the mark on my shoulder pulsed, sending warmth down my skin, soaking through my bones, a touch no less intimate for being nonphysical. "What's wrong?"

His smile faded slightly. "Why do you ask?"

I shrugged. A thin thread of guilt touched me. He was so gentle, he didn't deserve my neurotic inability to trust anything simple. "A holdover from human relationships, probably. Usually when a guy gives a lot of presents he's hiding something." *And every couple of days it's something new. Books, the antiques, the weapons I barely know how to use—I'm beginning to feel spoiled. Or kept. Danny Valentine, Necromance and kept woman. Sounds like a holovid.*

"Ah." The smile returned, relieved. "Only a human suspicion, then."

I grimaced, sticking my tongue out. The face made him laugh.

"Oh, quit it." I was hard-pressed not to chuckle, myself.

"It pleases me to please you. It is also time for dinner." He tilted his head, still wearing the faint shadow of a smile. "Emilio has outdone himself to tempt you away from your dusty papers."

I grimaced again, setting the statue on the desk and stretching, joints popping. "I'll get fat." *This code seems a little easier than the last one. Probably a Ronson cipher with a shifting alphanumeric base. I hope this journal has more about demon physiology—I can always use that. The one treatise on wings was invaluable.*

I had never before known what a tremendous show of vulnerability it was for a Greater Flight demon to close the protective shell of his wings around another being.

"You think so?" His smile widened again. "That would indeed be a feat. Come with me, I need your company."

It abruptly warmed me that he would admit to liking

my company, let alone *needing* it. "Great. You know, I've gotten really fond of this research stuff. I never had time for it before." *I was too busy paying off my mortgage. Not to mention chasing down bounties as fast as I could to keep from thinking.* I stretched again, made it into a movement that brought me to my feet. I scooped the statue up, wrapping it back in the blue satin, and offered him my hand. "I suppose you're going to try to talk me into dressing for dinner again."

"I so rarely see you in a dress, *hedaira*. The black velvet is particularly fine." His fingers closed over mine as he rose, putting no weight on my hand. He stepped closer to me and slid his hand up my arm, my shirtsleeve giving under the pressure. I wore a silk T-shirt and a pair of jeans, bare feet. No rig, no weapons but my sword leaning against the desk, its Power contained. It rarely left the sheath anymore, except during sparring sessions.

I still kept my hand in, unwilling to let my combat reflexes go rusty. I probably shouldn't have worried—demon muscle and bone would still keep me quicker and tougher than any human. But I've spent my life fighting, and that isn't something you just lay aside no matter *how* safe you feel.

The idea that he was right next to me and my sword was just out of arm's reach didn't make me feel unsteady or panicked like it used to.

Go figure, the one person on earth I trust while I'm unarmed, and it's him. I leaned into Japh, my head on his shoulder. Tension slid through him, something I hadn't felt since our first days of traveling away from Saint City. The only thing that would soothe him was my nearness, I'd learned it was better to just stay still once in a while and let him touch me, it made things easier for both of us. I was getting used to the curious feeling of being practically unarmed around a demon.

A Fallen demon. *A'nankhimel*, a word I still had no hope of deciphering.

"You're talking about the black velvet sheath? Half my chest hangs out in that thing." My tone was light, bantering, but I let him hold me.

Bit by bit, his tautness lessened, drained away. "Such a fine chest it is, too. The very first thing I noticed." His tone was, as usual, flat and ironic, shaded with the faintest amusement.

"Liar." *The first thing you noticed was my annoying human habit of asking questions and being rude.* I rubbed my cheek against his shoulder to calm him. It had taken a long time for me not to care what his long black coat was made of. I was getting better at all of this.

"Hm." He stroked my hair, his fingers slipping through the long ink-black strands. I often had wistful thoughts of a shorter cut, but when he played with it I always ended up putting off the inevitable trim. At least I no longer had to dye it, it was black all the way through naturally now. Silken black.

The same as his. Just as my skin was only a few shades paler than his, or my pheromonal cloak of demon scent was lighter but still essentially the same.

"Japhrimel?" The huskiness that never left my voice made the air stir uneasily. My throat didn't hurt anymore, but something in my voice was broken all the same by the Prince of Hell's iron fingers.

"What, my curious?"

"What's wrong?" I slid my free arm around him and

squeezed slightly, so he'd know I was serious. "You're...."

You're in that mood again, Japh. The one where you seem to be listening to something I can't hear, watching for something I can't see, and set on a lasetrigger that makes me a little nervous. Even though you haven't hurt me, you're so fucking careful sometimes I wish you'd forget yourself and bruise me like you once did.

"What could be wrong with you in my arms, *hedaira*?" He kissed my cheek, a soft lingering touch. "Come. Dinner. Then, if you like, I will tell you a story."

"What kind of story?" *Trying to distract me like a kid at bedtime. I'll let you.*

It didn't often show, how old he was; I suspected he deliberately refrained from reminding me. Perfect tact, something I'd never known a demon could exercise. They're curiously legalistic, even if their idea of objective truth often doesn't match a human's. Another pretty question none of the books could answer. How close *is* legalism to tact?

He made a graceful movement that somehow ended up with him handing me my sword and turned into a kiss—a chaste kiss on my forehead, for once. "Any kind of story you like. All you must do is decide."

Emilio had indeed outdone himself. Bruschetta, calamari, soft garlic bread and frésh mozzarella, lemon pasta primavera, a lovely slate-soft Franje Riesjicard, crème brulee. Fresh strawberries, braised asparagus. Olives, which I didn't like but Emilio loved so much he couldn't imagine anyone hating. We were, after all, in Toscano. What was a meal without olives?

The olive trees on the tawny hills were probably older

than the Hegemony. I'd spent many a late afternoon poring over a solitary Magi's shadowjournal written in code, Japhrimel stretched out by my side in the dappled shade of a gnarled tree with leathery green-yellow leaves, heat simmering up from the terraced hills. He basked like a cat as the sky turned into indigo velvet studded with dry stars. Then we would walk home along dusty roads, more often than not with his arm over my shoulders and the books swinging back and forth in an old-fashioned leather strap buckled tight. A schoolgirl and a demon.

I had basic Magi training, every psion did. Since the Magi had been dealing with power and psychic phenomena since before the Awakening they were the ones who had the methods, so the collection of early training techniques was the same for a Magi as a Necromance, or a Shaman or Skinlin or any other psion you would care to name. But actual Magi nowadays were given in-depth magickal training for weakening the walls between worlds and trafficking with Hell. It was the kind of study that took decades to accumulate and get everything right— which was why most Magi hired out as corporate security or took other jobs in the meantime. Japhrimel didn't stop me from buying old shadowjournals at auction or from slightly-less-than-legal brokers, but he wouldn't speak about what being Fallen meant. Not only that, he wouldn't help me decode the shadowjournals either...and good luck apprenticing myself to a Magi circle, if any would take me while Japh was hanging around. They would be far more interested in him than in me, even if I could convince one to take on a psion far too old for the regular apprenticeship.

Dinner took a long time in the high, wide-open dining

room, with its dark wooden table—big enough for sixteen—
draped in crisp white linen. I was happy to savor the food,
and Japhrimel amused himself by folding some of my
notes—brought to the table in defiance of manners—into
origami animals. I always seemed to lose some when he
did that, but it was worth it to see him present them almost
shyly after his golden fingers flicked with a delicacy I
wouldn't have thought him capable of.

Emilio, a thick, round Novo Taliano with a moustache
to be proud of, waltzed in carrying a plate with what
looked like...it couldn't be.

"*Bella!*" His deep voice bounced off warm white stone
walls. A crimson tapestry from the antique shop in Arrieto fluttered against the wall, brushed by soft warmth
through the long open windows, my sword leaned against
my chair, ringing softly to itself. "Behold!"

"Oh, no." I tried to sound pleased instead of horrified-
and-pleased-plus-guilty. "Emilio, you didn't."

"Blame me." Japhrimel's lips curved into another rare
smile. "I suggested it."

"You suggested Chocolate Murder?" I was hard put
not to laugh. "Japhrimel, you don't even *eat* it."

"But you love it." Japhrimel leaned back in his chair,
the origami hippopotamus squatting on his palm. "The
last time you tasted chocolate—"

Heat flooded my cheeks, and I was glad I didn't blush
often. "Let's not talk about that." I eyed the porcelain plate
as Emilio slid it in front of me. A moist, heavenly chocolate brownie, gooey and perfect, studded with almonds—
real almonds grown on trees, not synthprotein fooled into
thinking it was almonds. Nothing but the best for a Fallen
and his *hedaira*.

The thought made me sober, looking down at the still-hot brownie mounded with whipped cream and chocolate shavings, cherries soaked in brandy scattered in a flawless arc along one side of the plate. I could smell the still-baking sugars, could almost taste their delicate balance of caramelization. "Oh," I sighed. "This is *fantastic*, Emilio. Whatever he's paying you, it isn't enough."

He waved his round arms, his fingers thick and soft, not callused like mine. Our cook didn't take combat training, nobody wanted to kill a rotund Taliano food artist who wore stained white aprons and spoke with his plump hands swaying like slicboard wash. For all that, he was very easy with me—one of the few normals who didn't seem to fear my tat. *"Ch'cosa, s'gnora*, I don't cook for him. I cook for you. Take one bite. Just one."

"I'm almost afraid to, it's so beautiful." I picked up the fork, delicately, and glanced at Japhrimel, who looked amused. The hippo had vanished from his palm. Emilio waited, all but quivering with impatience. "I can't do it. You have to."

Emilio looked as horrified as if I'd suggested he cut up his own mother and chew on her, his mustache quivering. I offered him the fork.

"Please, Emilio. I really can't." I blinked, trying not to look like I was batting my eyelashes. "You made this, it's beautiful, you deserve to break it."

He shook his head solemnly. "No, no. Wrong." He waved a blunt finger at me. "You don't like the Chocolate Murder?" His voice was laced with mock hurt—he was *so* good at laying on the guilt. His accent mangled the Merican; I still hadn't learned Taliano.

I laughed, but an uneasy frisson went up my spine. I glanced at Japhrimel, who now studied me intently.

His eyes were almost human, dark and liquid in the light from the crystal chandelier hanging overhead. "Thank you, Emilio. She loves it, but she simply can't trust a gift. It's in her nature to be suspicious."

I let my lip curl. Even a demon had a better time of dealing with normals than I did. "I never said that." To prove it, I broke through the pristine whiteness of the whipped cream, took a scoop of brownie, and carried the resultant hoverload of sinful k-cals to my mouth.

Bittersweet darkness exploded, melting against my tongue. I had to suppress a low sound of pleased wonder. No matter how many times Emilio made this, I was still surprised by how bloody *good* it was. It's supposed to be a cliché, women and chocolate, but damn if it didn't have a large helping of truth. Nothing else seems to satisfy.

"*Sekhmet sa'es.*" I opened my eyes to find both Japhrimel and Emilio staring at me as if I'd just grown an extra head. "That's *so* good. What?"

"Thank you, Emilio." Japhrimel nodded, and Emilio, satisfied, bounced away out of the dining room. My eyes strayed to my pile of notes. Japhrimel's fingers rustled among them. "I shall make you a crane. A thousand of those are said to buy a space in heaven."

That managed to spark my interest. "Really? Which heaven?" Warm wind blew in from the Toscano hills, making the house creak and settle around itself. The shielding—careful layers of energy applied by both demon and Necromance—reverberated, sinking into the walls as Japhrimel calmed the layers with a mental touch.

The sense of him listening to something I couldn't hear returned, and I watched his face. "Elysium? Nirvana?"

"No. Perhaps I am wrong, and it only buys good fortune." His mouth turned down at the corners. "Is it good?"

"Have some." I balanced a smudge of brownie and whipped cream on my fork, managed to scoop up a brandied cherry as well. "Here."

He actually leaned forward, I fed him a single spoonful of Chocolate Murder. I don't know what Emilio called the dessert, but I'd called it *murder by chocolate* and Japhrimel found it amusing enough the name had stuck.

He closed his eyes, savoring the taste. I examined his face. Even while he concentrated on the dessert, his fingers still moved, folding the paper into a crane with high-arched wings. "That's very pretty." I took the fork back. "I had no idea you were so talented."

"Hm." His eyes flashed green for just a moment, a struggle of color losing itself in a swell of darkness. "Inspiration, *hedaira.*"

"Yeah." I took another bite, the siren song of chocolate ringing through my mouth. "The man's a genius," I said when I could talk again. "Give him a raise." *Since we don't seem to be hurting for cash. I'd ask you where it comes from, but demons and money go together. Besides, you'd just change the subject, wouldn't you. As usual.*

"For you, anything." But he looked grave. The crane was gone. "Days of poring over Magi scribbles seem to have taxed you."

"If you'd just tell me, it would be a lot easier." I took another bite, adding a brandied cherry to the mix. He was right, it was heaven. Took a sip of wine, sourness cutting like a perfect *iaido* strike through the depth of chocolate. "What does *hedaira* mean, anyway?" *Just one little clue, Japh. Just one.*

Demons wouldn't talk about *A'nankhimel*, I guessed it was an insult to imply they could Fall. Asking a demon about the Fallen was like asking a Ludder about genesplices: the whole subject was so touchy with them that precious few demons—if any—were capable of discussing it rationally. Japhrimel was highly reticent about it even with me, and I was the reason he was where he was.

I wondered if I should feel guilty about that, tried not to ask him. Couldn't help myself. It was like picking at a scab. He never stopped me from researching, but he wouldn't provide anything more than tantalizing hints. If it was a game, the point of it was lost on me.

"*Hedaira* means you, Dante. Have I told you the story of Saint Anthony?" One coal-black eyebrow lifted fractionally, the mark on my shoulder compressing with heat as he looked at me. "Or would you prefer the tale of Leonidas and Thermopylae?"

I stared at the remains of the brownie. It would be a shame to waste it, though my stomach felt full and happy. I was pleasantly tired, too, after three days of slogging through code. *Why won't he answer me? It's not like I'm asking something huge.*

It was always the same. I had a real live former demon living with me, and I couldn't get him to answer a single damn question.

I used to be so good at finding things out. I scooped a brandied cherry onto the fork, chewed it thoughtfully while I watched him. He was busy looking through my notes. As if they could tell him anything he didn't already know.

The paper rustled, a thin, familiar sound. "Shall I make a giraffe for you?"

"They're extinct." I laid my fork down. "You can tell me the one about Saint Anthony again, Japhrimel. But not now." Silence fell between us, the wind from the hillside soughing in through the windows. "Why won't you tell me what I am?"

"I know what you are. Isn't that enough?" He ruffled through my notes again. "I think you're making progress."

You know, if I didn't like you so much, we'd have a serious problem with your sense of humor. "Progress toward what?" Silence greeted the question. "Japhrimel?"

"Yes, my curious?" He folded another small sheet of paper, over and over again, the spidery ink scratches of my notes dappling the paper. The mark on my shoulder throbbed, calling out to him. I was tired, my eyes strained and my neck aching.

"Maybe I should go back to Saint City. The Nichtvren Prime there has some demonology books, he and his Consort invited me to stop by anytime." I watched his face, relieved when it didn't change. He seemed to be concentrating completely on folding the paper again and again. "It'd be nice to see Gabe again. I haven't called her in a month or so." *And I think I might be able to go back to Saint City without shaking and wanting to throw up. Maybe. Possibly.*

With a lot of luck.

"If you like." Still absorbed in his task. It was uncharacteristic of him to concentrate so deeply on something so small while I spoke to him. That look of listening was back on his face, like an unwelcome visitor.

Night breathed into the room through flung-open windows. Uneasiness prickled up my back. "If something was wrong, you'd tell me, wouldn't you?" *I sound like an idiot girl on a holovid. I'm an accredited Necromance and a bounty hunter, if something's wrong I should know, not him.*

"I would tell you what you needed to know." He rose like a dark wave, his coat moving silently. Green flashed through his eyes. "Do you not trust me?"

That's not it at all. After all, who had rescued me from Mirovitch's deadly *ka* in the ruined cafeteria of Rigger Hall? Who had I left Saint City with, who had I spent every waking moment with since then? "I trust you," I admitted, softly enough my voice didn't break. "It's just frustrating, not knowing."

"Give me time." His voice stroked the stone walls, made the shielding reverberate. He touched my shoulder as he passed, pacing weightlessly across the room to stare out the window. His long dark coat melded with night outside. I caught a flash of white—did he still have the animal he'd made out of my notepaper? "It is no little thing, to Fall. Demons do not like to speak of it."

That did it. Guilt rose under my ribs, choked me. He had Fallen, though I had no idea what that meant beyond a few hints gathered from old, old books. He'd shared his power with me, a mere human. Never mind that I was more than human now, never mind that I still *felt* human every place it counted. "Fine." I pushed my plate away, gathered up my notes. "I'm tired. I'm going to bed."

He turned from the window, his hands clasped behind

his back. "Very well." Not a word of argument. "Leave the plates."

I stacked them in a neat pile nonetheless. It doesn't pay to be sloppy, even when you have household help. I've washed my own dishes all my adult life, it feels wrong to leave them to someone else. When I spoke, it was to the ruins of the brownie. "If there's something you're not telling me, I'll find out sooner or later."

"All things in their proper time." Damn him, he sounded amused again.

Dante, you're an idiot. "I hate clichés." I brushed my notes into a scarred leather folio and crossed the room, carrying my sword, to stand beside him as he looked out onto the darkness of the hills under a night as rich as blue wine. The smell of demon—amber musk, burning cinnamon— rose to cloak us both, the deeper tang of sun-drenched hills exhaling after nightfall making a heady brew. "I'm sorry, Japh. I'm an idiot." Easier than an apology had ever been, for me. Which meant that it only hurt like a knife to the chest, but didn't claw its way free.

"No matter. I am a fool, as any Fallen is for a *hedaira*'s comfort." He forgave me, as usual, and touched my shoulder. "You mentioned being tired. Come to bed."

Well, that's another sliver of information. For a hedaira*'s comfort.* "Give me back my notes, and I will." I sounded like a kid throwing a tantrum for an ice-cream cone. Then again, he was much older than me. How old was he, anyway? Older than the hills?

Lucifer's eldest child, Fallen and tied to me. *As any Fallen is for a* hedaira*'s comfort.*

Did that mean there was something so terrible he was actually doing me a favor by not telling me?

He made a single brief movement, and an origami unicorn bloomed in his palm. I took it delicately, my fingertips brushing his skin. "Where did you learn to make these?"

"That is a long story, my curious. If you like, I will tell it to you." He didn't smile, but his shoulders relaxed and his mouth evened out, no longer a grim thin line. The listening look was gone, again.

For once, I opted to take the tactful way out. "Sounds good. You can tell me while I brush my hair."

He nodded. The warm breeze stirred his hair, a little longer over his forehead since I'd met him. "Heaven indeed. Lead the way."

Now what the hell does he mean by that? He knows this house better than I do, and I'm the one always following him around like a puppy. "You know, you get weirder all the time, and that's saying something. Come on." I reached down, took his hand. His fingers curled through mine, squeezed tight enough to break human bones. I returned the pressure, wondering a little bit. It wasn't like him to forget I was more fragile; he was usually the very first to remind me. "Hey. You all right?"

He nodded. *"A'tai, hetairae A'nankimel'iin. Diriin."* His mouth turned down again as if tasting something bitter, his fingers easing a little.

"You're going to have to tell me what that means someday." I yawned, suddenly exhausted. Three days locked in a library. Scholarship was heavier than bounty hunting.

"Someday. Only give me time." He led me from the dining room, my hand caught in his, and I didn't protest. I left the folio behind on the table. Nobody would mess with it here.

"I'm *giving* you time. Plenty of it, too." Behind us, the sun-flavored night crept in through the windows. What else could I do? I trusted him, and all he asked for was something I had plenty of nowadays. So I followed him through our quiet house, and ended up letting him brush my hair after all. Once again, he'd distracted me from asking what I was—but he'd also promised to tell me eventually, and that was enough.

2

I woke from a trance deeper than sleep, a dreamless well of darkness. I had been unable to sleep for almost a year while Japhrimel was dormant; it seemed now I was making up for it by needing a long, deathlike slumber every few days. He told me it was normal for a *hedaira* to need that rest, during which the human mind gained the relief it needed from the overload of demon Power and sensation. I'd done some damage by pushing myself so hard. Now, each time Japhrimel soothed me into blackness I felt relieved. Every time I woke, disoriented, with no idea of how much time had passed, he was there waiting for me.

Except this time.

I blinked, clutching the sheet to my chest. Moonlight fell through the open floor-length windows, silvering the smooth marble; long blue velvet drapes moved slightly on a warm night wind. Here in Toscano the houses were huge villas for the Hegemony rich. This one was set into a hillside looking over a valley where humans had farmed olives and wheat for thousands of years and now let the olive trees grow as decorations. My hair lay against my back, brushing the mattress, silk slid cool and restful against my skin.

I was alone.

I reached out, not quite believing it, and touched the sheet. Japhrimel's pillow held a dent, and the smell of us both hung in the room, his deeper musk and my lighter scent combining. My cheek burned as my emerald glowed, and I saw the altar I had made out of an antique oak armoire lined with blue light. I turned my head slightly, and the spectral dart of light from my emerald made shadows cavort on the wall.

I slid out of bed naked, my fingers closing around the hilt of my sword. The blade sang as I pulled it from the lacquered sheath, a low, sibilant sound of oiled metal against cushioned and reinforced wood. More blue light spilled on the air, runes from the Nine Canons—the sorcerous alphabet that made up its own branch of magick—sliding through the metal's glowing heart. Jado had named the blade *Fudoshin*, and I rarely drew it.

I had nothing left to fight.

It had been a long time since my god spoke to me. I approached the altar cautiously, sinking down to one knee when I reached the invisible demarcation between real and sacred space, rising and stepping into the blue glow. My hair moved, blown on an invisible breeze as blue light slid down my body like Japhrimel's touch.

Where is he? Does he leave while I sleep? He's always here when I wake up. I discarded the thought. If my patron psychopomp wanted me, I was safe enough, and it didn't matter yet where Japh was. I had never seen him sleep—but I didn't care. This was private, anyway.

I stood in front of the altar, my sword tucking itself

back behind my arm, the hilt pointing down and clasped loosely in my hand. The metal's thrumming against my arm intensified as the katana's tip poked up past my shoulder. My cheek burned, the emerald sizzling, the inked lines of my tattoo shifting madly under the skin.

The new statue of Sekhmet glowed, set to one side of my patron Anubis—all I had left of the altar I'd set up in my old house in Saint City. Anubis, dark against the blue light, nodded slightly. The bowl set before him as an offering was empty, the wine I'd poured into it gone. I reached up, touched my cheek with my fingertips, felt my skin fever-hot, hotter than even a demon's blood.

Then the blue light took me. I did not quite fall, but I went to my knees before the gods, and felt my body slide away.

Into the blue crystal hall of Death came a new thing.

I stood upon the bridge, an oval cocoon of light from my emerald anchoring my feet to the stone. I wore the white robe of the god's chosen, belted with supple silver like scales. My new sword, glittering with fiery white light as if it too lived, was clasped in my hand for the very first time.

I had not ventured into this place since Jason Monroe's death.

The fluttering crystal draperies of souls drew very close around me. I was used to it—I was, after all, a Necromance—but the one soul I sought I did not see. No unique pattern that I would recognize, no crystallized streak of psychic and etheric energy holding the invisible imprint of shaggy wheat-gold hair and blue eyes.

I looked to find him, and I was grateful he was not there. If he was not there I would not have to face him.

Instead, my eyes were drawn irresistibly to the other side of the bridge, where Death stood, His slim dog's head dipping slightly, a nod to me.

Behind my god stood a shadowy figure, flames crackling around the shape of a woman, Her lion's head surrounded by twisting orange. A rush of flame and rise of smoke dazzled me for a moment, I lifted my sword blindly, a defense against a Power that could burn me down to bone.

Coolness rolled along my skin, dispelling the heat. The blade glowed fierce white instead of the blue I was used to. Steel shivered as Power stroked its edge and the mark on my shoulder flared with a deep bone-crunching pain I had not felt in years, sending a stain of twisting-diamond demon fire along the cocoon protecting me. Even here in Death I was marked by Japhrimel's attention, though my god didn't care.

Anubis knew I was His. Even a demon could not change that. I am Necromance. I belong to Death first, and to my own life second.

The god spoke, the not-sound like a bell brushing around me. Yet I am the bell, the god puts His hand on me and makes me sing.

Anubis bent, His black infinity-starred eyes fixed on me. He spoke again. This time the sound was like worlds colliding, blowing my hair back, the edges of my emerald's glow shivering so for a moment I felt the awful pull of the abyss beneath me. My fingers loosened on the hilt, then clutched, the sword socking back into my grip.

—a task is set for you, my child—

Comprehension bloomed through me. The god had called; I was asked to do something. This was warning and question both, a choice lay before me. Would I do as He asked, when the time arrived?

Why did He ask? I was His. For the god that had held me, protected me, comforted me all my life, it was unnecessary to ask. All You must do is tell me Your will, *I whispered soundlessly.*

The god nodded again, His arms crossed. He did not have the ceremonial flail and hook, nor did He wear the form of a slim black dog as He usually did. Instead, His hand lifted, palm-out, and I felt a terrible wind whistle as my skin chilled and my ears popped.

Then She behind him spoke, rushing flame like a river, the dance of unmaking the world taking another stamping step. I fell backward, my knuckles white on the sword's hilt, a long slow descent into nothingness, waiting for the stone to hit my back or the abyss to take me, the words printed inside my head, not really words but layers of meaning, each burning deeper than the last, a whisper of a geas laid on me. A binding I could and would forget until the time was right.

3

I surfaced, lying on my side against chill, slick marble. Warm sunlight striped my cheek. I'd been out a long time.

Hot iron bands clamped around my shoulders, lifted me. "Dante." Japhrimel's voice, ragged and rough as it had only been once or twice before. "Are you hurt? *Dante*?"

I made a shapeless sound, limp in his hands. My head lolled. Power flooded me, roaring through my veins like wine, flushing my fingers with heat and chasing away the awful, sluggish cold. I cried out, my hand coming up reflexively. Steel fell chiming as Japhrimel twisted my wrist. He was so much stronger than me, I could feel the gentleness in his fingers as well. So restrained, careful not to hurt me. "Easy, *hedaira*. I am with you."

"They called to me." My teeth began to chatter. The chill of Death had worked its way up past my elbows, past my knees, turning flesh into insensate marble. How long had I been away, on the bridge between here and the well of souls? "Japhrimel?" My voice cracked, a child's whisper instead of a woman's.

"Who did this?" He pulled me into his arms, heat closing around me, his bare chest against mine. My back was brushed with softness—he had opened his wings and pulled me in. I shivered, my teeth chattering, more Power burned down my spine from his touch, warmth pulsing out from the mark on my shoulder. "What were you doing?" He didn't shout—it was merely a murmur—but the furniture in the room groaned slightly as his voice stroked the air. It didn't sound like my voice, the tone of throaty invitation. No, Japhrimel's voice loaded itself with razorblades, the cold numbness of a sharp cut on deadened skin.

"The g-g-gods c-c-called—" My teeth eased their chattering. He was warm, scorching, and he was *here*. "Down for a long time. Gods. Where were *you*?"

He surged to his feet, carrying me. I felt the harsh material of his jeans against my hip, heard the clicking of bootheels as he carried me to the bed and sank down, cradling me. My sword rang softly, lying on the floor.

Japhrimel held me curled against him like a child, warmth soaking into my skin. "What were you thinking? What did you do?"

It had been a long time since I'd felt the cold of Death creeping up fingers and toes, sinking into my bones. "You were gone." I couldn't keep the petulant tone out of my voice, like a spoiled child with a hoarse, grown-up voice. "Where were you?"

"You're cold." He sounded thoughtful, rubbing his chin against my temple, golden skin sliding against mine, a hot trickle of delight spilling up my back. "It seems I cannot leave for even a moment without you doing yourself some mischief. Stay still."

But I was struggling free of him. "You left me. Where were you? What did you do? *Where were you?*"

"Stay *still*." He grabbed my wrist, but I twisted and he let me go, my skin sliding free of steel-strong fingers. I arched away, but he had my other wrist locked, an instinctive movement. It didn't hurt me—he avoided pressing on a nerve point or locking the rest of my arm, but it effectively halted me, making me gasp. "Just for a moment, be still. I will explain."

"I don't want *explanation*," I lied, and pushed at him with my free hand. "Let *go*."

"Not until you hear me. I did not want to leave you, but a summons from Hell is not ignored. I could not put it off any longer."

My heart thudded up under my collarbone, and I tasted copper. "What are you *talking* about? Let go!"

"If you do not listen I will make you listen. We have no time for games, *hedaira*, though I would gladly play any game you could devise. But *the Prince has called*."

The words didn't mean anything for the first few seconds, like all truly terrible news. Most of the fight went out of me. I slumped, and Japhrimel's arm tightened. He released the wristlock and I shook my hand out, my head coming to rest on his shoulder. He pulled me closer, his wings brushing softly against my shoulder and calf. It was incredibly intimate. I knew enough, now, to know that a winged demon—those of the Greater Flight that had wings, at least—did not suffer those wings to be touched, or open them for anything other than flight or mating.

Lucky me. Lucky, lucky me. Dear gods, did he just say what I think he said?

"Do you hear me?" he whispered into my hair. "The Prince has called, *hedaira.*"

I have been unable to contact him in the usual manner. Lucifer's voice purred through my head. That had been during the hunt for Kellerman Lourdes and Mirovitch, the Prince of Hell sticking his elegant nose into my life again. In the mad scramble of events afterwards, I'd forgotten all about it. Psychic rape and the death of one of your closest friends can do that to you.

Japhrimel was telling me that life was about to get very interesting again. I raised my head, hair falling in my eyes, and looked at him.

His mouth was a tight line, shadows of strain around his dark eyes, a terrible sheen of something that could be sadness laid over the human depths I thought I knew.

My hands shook. It had taken a long time for me to stop seeing Mirovitch's jowly face printed against the inside of my eyelids, a long time before the aftermath of facing down my childhood demons of Rigger Hall faded to a nightmare echo.

It still wasn't finished. My entire body chilled, remembering the *ka*'s ectoplasm shoving its way down my throat and up my nose, in my ears, trying to shred through the material of my jeans while Mirovitch's spectral fingers squirmed like maggots inside my brain, raping my memories. The only thing that saved me was my stubborn refusal to give in, my determination to strike back and end the terror for everyone else.

That, and the Fallen demon who held me, who had stopped the *ka* from killing me. Who had searched until he found me, and burned my childhood nightmares to the ground simply because I *asked.*

I looked at Japhrimel. The morning sunlight didn't reach the bed, but reflected golden light was kind to his high balanced cheekbones and thin mouth. A terrible, paranoid thought surfaced, and I opened my big mouth. "You're leaving me?" I whispered. "I...I thought—"

His eyes sparked green. "You know I would not leave you."

It was too late. I'd already said it, already *thought* it. "If the Prince of Hell told you to, you might," I shot back, struggling free of his arms, my feet smacking the floor. He let me go. I scooped up the fallen scabbard and made it to my sword, steel innocent and shining in the rectangle of sunlight from the window. Scooped up my blade and slid it home, seating it with a click. "What is it this time? He wants you back, you just go running like a good little demon, is that it? What does he *want*?"

My shoulder flared, a tugging against the mark branded into my flesh. I ignored it.

"You misunderstand, my curious." Japhrimel's voice was terribly, ironically flat. "The one the Prince seeks audience with is *you*."

4

I turned so quickly my hair fanned out in a loose arc. Sunlight warmed my hip and knee, pouring in through the window. Japhrimel had stood up, and his long dark Chinese-collared coat was back, wings folded tightly as if armoring himself.

As if he was the one who needed the armor.

He watched me, his hands clasped behind his back again. "It seems that once again I am to ask you to face the Prince, Dante. There is ... terrible news."

I swallowed dryly. "Terrible? When you say that, I suppose it means something different than when I say it." Then the absurdity hit me—I was standing here naked, my entire body gone cold and tense with foreboding, talking to a demon. How did I get myself into these things? "Am I allowed to get dressed, or does Lucifer want to see me in the buff?"

"If you wish to present yourself as a slave, I can hardly stop you." The edge to his voice glittered and smoked like carbolic tossed across antigrav. "Try to rein your tongue for once. If I have meant anything to you, you must *listen* to me."

Slaves are naked in Hell? Yet another demon custom I don't know about. The mad urge to giggle rose up inside of me and died away again. My jaw set itself like plasteel. "You have no idea what you mean to me," I informed him, just as flatly as he'd ever spoken to me.

"And vice versa. You are a selfish child sometimes. It could even be your particular brand of charm."

I lifted the sword slightly. "Do you want a sparring match, or do you want to explain to me why you left me while I was unconscious? And defenseless, I might add?"

"I cannot imagine you defenseless." Japhrimel stepped forward once. Twice. He approached me slowly, as if I might bolt at any moment. I stood trembling at the edge of the sunlight and let him come near, my hand with the sword dropping. "I gave up my place in the Greater Flight of Hell for you. I am of the Fallen, and I have chosen to bind my fate to yours. Remember that."

The mark on my shoulder sent a burning tingle all through me. His hand brushed my elbow, slid up my arm to polish the bare skin of my shoulder, then slid under my hair, curling around my nape. He didn't have to pull me forward, I leaned into him like a plant leans toward a window. "I have fended off the polite requests Lucifer has sent for your presence, and I have parried his less-than-polite requests. He has stopped asking and started summoning, *hedaira*, and he is an enemy we cannot afford to make. Not if we expect to keep living, and I find I have grown fond of life with you. Even this pale world has its beauty when seen through your eyes." He dropped his face, spoke the last sentence into my hair. He inhaled, a slight shudder passing through him. My sword dropped the rest of the way, my arm hanging slack, the scabbard resting in my hand. "At the very least, I ask you to come and listen. Will you?"

The lump in my throat made it difficult to talk. "Fine," I rasped. "But don't expect me to be happy about it. I hate him, I *hate* him, he killed you and I hate him."

The tension running through him drained away. "He did not kill me. I am here."

I couldn't argue with that, so I let him pull me back to the bed and run his fingers through my hair. I let him kiss my shoulder, my cheek, and finally my mouth. I sighed as he folded me in his arms and spoke to me the way I understood best—the language of the body, an instinctive semaphore used to tell me once again that he was real. His mouth against mine, his body against mine, and the rough hungry fire of my own desire swallowing me whole—but tears slid down my cheeks as I gave myself up to him.

I should have known things wouldn't stay perfect forever.

5

It took a long time for my heartbeat to return to normal. I lay in his arms, my eyes closed, feeling the weight of his body against mine. The Magi say that demons invented the arts of love, and after years of living with Japhrimel I didn't just believe it—I *knew* it, all the way through my veins.

It was too bad he couldn't have been human in the first place. Would I have loved him so much if he was?

I propped myself up on my elbow, my hair sliding over my shoulder as he threaded his fingers through and pushed it back, tucking it behind my ear. The silky strands clung to his fingers, unwilling to let go. "All right," I said, my legs tangled with his. "Time for you to come clean. What's going on?"

He shrugged, his touch trailing down my arm and skipping to touch my ribs. As usual, slow fire followed, unstringing my nerves, soothing me. His eyes, half-closed, still held sparks of green circling in their depths. "You have been buried in your books, my curious. While you have done so, there has been unsettling news. The air is full of ... disturbance. For Lucifer to request a *hedaira*'s presence is a thing unprecedented in the history of Hell. The Three Flights—Greater, Lesser, and Low—now know of Vardimal's rebellion. A demon escaped Hell and lived among humans for fifty mortal years, and even created an Androgyne. Now they think it is possible to leave Hell unremarked—and they think perhaps Lucifer is weakening, or his grip on Hell is slipping. Mutters of discontent rise everywhere. The fact that Lucifer lost his assassin to a human woman does not help."

"I'm missing the part where that's my problem," I muttered.

He brushed my cheek with his knuckles, a gentle, careful movement. "If Lucifer loses control of Hell, do you think demons will cavil at settling old scores with me? We have notoriously long memories." A swift snarl crossed his face. A long time ago, it would have frightened me. "Not to mention that it is the Prince's will that keeps demonkind from meddling further with your world. *That* is something you should be devoutly grateful for." His pause sent a chill down my back. "Our kind play cruel games."

That makes sense. Too much sense to be comforting. I sighed and sank down into the pillow, untangling my legs from his and turning on my back. The rectangle of mellow sunlight moving across the room reminded me I should be in the library. I could only acquire shadowjournals from the estates of solitary Magi, since circles burned shadowjournals when a member passed, or kept them in heavily guarded libraries that were destroyed if the circle died out.

Each solitary Magi had a different code, and each text required months of patient work to break that code and strip-mine whatever information the Magi let slip about demons, hoping for a word about the Fallen. It was slow, frustrating, difficult going, and now I might never finish.

Japhrimel's hand slid down to spread against my belly. It reminded me of claws digging into my guts, the sick leprous light of Mirovitch's *ka* burning the air, my own helpless screams. My skin had healed without a scar. I had no scars left except the fluid twisted glyph on my shoulder, the mark of my bond with him. "So what does Lucifer want with me? I'm no use to him."

"My guesses are unpleasant, and it is better not to guess where the Prince is concerned." Old bitterness shaded his voice. He didn't like to talk about his life as Lucifer's Right Hand; I might have understood more if he'd told me even a little about it.

"So when you told me nothing was wrong, you were lying? Like when you didn't tell me you helped Santino escape from Hell?" I closed my eyes, staring into the mothering dark behind my eyelids. Japhrimel's aura swirled, black diamond flames sliding through the trademark sparkles of a Necromance, showing I was linked to him. *Dante, for the sake of every god that ever was, don't do this.*

"I did so under the Prince's direction." Was it me, or did his voice sound even more bitter? "I had no *choice*. Not until I Fell, and you freed me by completing your bargain with him."

I blew out another long, frustrated breath. "So he wants to see me. Posthaste."

"We have until nightfall. Then I will take you to the meeting place. I was told we will meet a guide there who will take us to a door into Hell. Once we pass into Hell, you will be required to do the speaking for us."

Another arcane custom? "I am *not* ready for this." A new thought struck me. "Lucifer wants a bargain?"

I could feel his eyes moving over me, the weight of his gaze like amber silk and honey against my skin. "I would assume so."

Does this mean I have a chance of.... "Then I can bargain for Eve?"

Japhrimel froze, his hand tensing. He made a slight sound, like a bitter snort of laughter. After a long pause, his fingers gentled against my abdomen. "It would be most unwise, Dante. *Most* unwise."

"He *took* her. She was Doreen's. He had no *right*." *Plus he almost strangled me, and he killed you. The Devil owes me, and if he needs something from me I'm going to make him pay with interest.* It was hollow bravado at best. I had no illusion of being able to win in any game involving the Devil. Humans just don't win when they tangle with him.

But I had Japh on my side, didn't I? That had to be worth something.

"How would you have raised her, Dante? You do not even truly understand a demon, let alone an Androgyne. He took her for a reason." His tone was soft, reasonable, and did not mollify me in the least.

I don't care why he took her. "He nearly strangled me in the process, Japhrimel. Or did you forget?" *If I don't understand demons, whose fault is that? You won't tell me anything!*

"You survived, did you not? For him, that passes as a light warning. Must I beg you to be cautious?" His hand tensed again, his thumb moving slightly, a light caress.

"I'm *plenty* cautious. Especially where demons are concerned. Last time I didn't come off too badly, did I?"

"I was pleasantly surprised." Levity, his own particular brand of dry humor. We both knew how close it had been.

I sighed, opened my eyes, saw the blue velvet canopy flutter. How many times had I awakened to this bed? How many times had Japhrimel soothed me out of a nightmare, stroked my back and shoulders until I could stop trembling? How many times had I sobbed out the names of my failures and listened to his calm voice making everything better?

If Japh needed me to, I'd take on the Prince of Hell and more. What else *could* I do? "All right. If you want me to, I'll meet the Devil again."

I hadn't realized how tense he was until he relaxed, the silent crackling static of his attention swirling out of the air. I took a deep breath of the scent we made together—amber musk, burning cinnamon, something spicy and overwhelming to a human but the equivalent of a shield for a demon; a defense against the mortal world and its pervading odor of dying. It was also the equivalent of an air bubble, climate control and some indefinable gas making breathing easier. I used to think the smell of a demon wasn't physical. Now that I was part-demon it was all *too* physical.

"I will protect you, Dante." His tone was low, a promise. "Never doubt that."

Silence rose between us. Before, quiet had been something shared. Now it was dangerous.

"What aren't you telling me?" I swallowed the next

question: *Do you mean it when you say you're staying with me?*

I wouldn't have been surprised if he'd heard it anyway. I did some quick mental calculations. It had to be months that we'd lived here, quite how many I didn't know. Time got away from me nowadays, especially when I was in the library.

However long it had been, I hadn't doubted a single word that crossed his lips until now. "And how long has Lucifer been asking for me?" I added.

"Since I was resurrected, my curious. We have had more time than I ever thought possible. You needed it." He stroked the curve of my hip, rounder now since I'd put on a little weight. Not much, but a little.

"You *lied* to me." Flatly. I shouldn't have been so upset. Even as I said it, I knew I shouldn't have.

You forgave Jace, didn't you? He lied to you about Santino too. My conscience, of course, piped up loud and clear. But Jace had stayed with me, putting up with my grief and my inability to stop moving, pushing his aging human body to its limits to keep up with me on bounties, watching my back. I *had* forgiven him. He'd earned it. Danny Valentine, the woman who swore that even one lie was a treasonous offense, had forgiven Jace everything, even if I couldn't be what he wanted or needed.

But Japhrimel...was different. The thought of Jace lying to me had filled me with untinctured rage and contempt at the time; the thought of Japhrimel hiding something from me, no matter the reason...hurt. As if my heart had been replaced with a live coremelt. Tears rose behind my eyes, I pushed them down. Blinked furiously. *Why does it hurt like this? What's wrong with me?*

He sighed, tracing the arch of my rib without tickling. I almost wished he would tickle me—that would end up in a wrestling match, and *that* would mean I wouldn't have to think for a while. "What would you have done, had you known? You were a shadow. Whatever ghost I rescued you from crippled you. I feared you might die of despair, and if you locked yourself in the library at least you were not grieving." His fingers were so gentle, he stroked my skin delicately, soothing. I had never been touched so carefully by a human lover; even Doreen's comfort had lacked the deep softness of Japhrimel's. Who would have thought a *demon* could be so gentle? "To know that Lucifer was asking for you was a burden you were not ready for."

It wasn't so much the chain of his logic as the infuriating tone of reasonableness and *I-know-best* he used that made me spitting mad. The fresh anger and irritation was like a tonic against the clawed pain in my chest, fear sparking fury as a defense.

All in all, I was taking the news rather well.

"I'll decide what I'm ready for," I snapped, rolling up and pushing his hand away. "You should have told me." I gained my feet, scooping up my sword, and strode for the bathroom. If I was going to meet the Prince of Hell again, there were things I had to do first.

The mark on my shoulder warmed, a prickling of heat.

"What of *your* secrets?" His voice rose from the tangled bed behind me, a silky challenge. "What of the dead you bear such guilt for? You grieved for me while living with your human paramour, and I have never asked you to explain *that*."

I actually stumbled. I hadn't believed he would throw

Jace at me, especially since it was salted with the pinch of truth. I took in a deep breath, my head down, tendrils of my hair slipping like living things over my shoulders. Then I lifted my head, regaining my balance. "At least Jace didn't lie to me," I flung back over my shoulder, and slammed into the bathroom before he could reply.

It wasn't quite true. Jace never told me he was Mob, and part of the Corvin Family to boot. But I'd flung it at Japhrimel. Now who was the liar?

6

_I_f I was going to visit the Devil, I wanted to be fully armed. So I opened up the huge dresser in the corner of the bedroom. Japhrimel was nowhere to be seen. I knelt on naked knees, my hair drying in a thick braided rope against my back. Pulled out the lowest drawer and saw with faint surprise everything was still there.

Well, why wouldn't it be there? You put it there. You're being ridiculous, Danny. Get moving.

Trade Bargains microfiber shirt, sheds dirt easily and doesn't smell no matter how long you wear it, thanks to antibacterium impregnation. Butter-soft, broken-in jeans, cut to go over boots and treated to be water and stain resistant, patches tailored in to accommodate holsters and with the crotch inset so side-kicks are possible. The old explorer's coat, too big for me because it was Jace's—supple tough Kevlar panels inset in canvas, one pocket scorched where a silver spade necklace had turned red-hot and burned its way free. The rig, still oiled and spelled, not cracking like regular leather. Knives, main-gauches and stilettos, and the two projectile guns, cartridges neatly stacked off to the side. And in its deep velvet case, the necklace Jace had given me in the first days of our affair. I'd worn it all through the last job—tracking down Kellerman Lourdes. Even after I'd finished, that job had almost killed me

I could admit as much now, if only to myself.

The necklace was beautiful. Silver-dipped raccoon baculums on a fine silver chain twined with black velvet ribbons and blood-marked bloodstones as well as every defense a Shaman knew how to weave, all twisted together in a fluid piece of art. He hadn't given any other woman something like this—at least, not that I knew of. He had spent months making it, a powerful mark of his affection for me.

If I went into Death again, if I used the necklace he'd worked so hard on or the sword twisted with his death to call his apparition up, what would he have to say to me?

Maybe something like "I loved you, Danny, and I was human. Why couldn't you love me*?" Maybe something like that. Or maybe "Why did you let me die?" Or "What took you so long to come find me?"*

Any or all of those questions were equally likely, and equally viciously hurtful. Which one would I pick to answer, if I could?

"I'm not brave enough to find out," I whispered, and picked up the necklace with delicate fingers. I fastened it, and spent a moment arranging it so the baculums hung down, each a curve of silver against my golden skin, knobbed ends pointing out. "Or am I?"

I felt as if a shell had been ripped away, as if my skin was hitting the air for the first time. I'd spent so long living on the edge of a sword, taking one bounty after another, jobs other Necromances wouldn't touch, honing myself into a weapon to still the voices whispering in my head. *Not good enough, not strong enough, not brave enough, not tough enough.* Now, instead of feeling properly terrified, I felt a type of giddy glee. Soon I'd be facing down some new kind of danger, feeling as if my heart was going to explode from adrenaline. I had said that all I wanted was a quiet life, to be left alone.

I'd actually believed it when I'd said it, too.

Under the necklace were my rings, chiming as they tangled together. I lifted them one by one—amber rectangle, amber cabochon. Moonstone. Plain silver band. Bloodstone oval, obsidian oval. Suni-figured thumb ring on my left hand. They began to glow, sullenly at first, then brighter as my Power stroked at them. I sighed, feeling the defenses and spells caught in each stone rise to the surface, tremble, and settle back into humming readiness.

I dressed quickly, my fingers flying as they hadn't for a long while. Buttoning up my shirt, my jeans, finding a pair of microfiber socks. My boots were a little cracked, but everything still fit. Living soft hadn't made me fat yet, though I'd lost the look of being starved. A demon metabolism, every girl's best friend.

I picked up the rig with trembling hands. Shrugged myself into it, buckled it down. Tested the action of the knives. They were still sharp. The plasgun went into its holster under my left arm. The projectile guns rode easy in their holsters. I slid clips in them both, chambered a round in each, and found the little clicks comforting to hear.

The only thing left was my tattered canvas messenger bag—the bag that had gone into Hell with me, back to the nightmare of my childhood with me, the bag I'd carried on every job since Doreen had bought it and sewn in the extra pockets and loops of elastic to hold everything down.

I scooped up the bag and the six extra clips, paced over to the bed, and dumped everything out. Scraps of paper, containers—blessed water, salt, cornmeal mix, my lockpick set, extra handkerchiefs and ammo clips and my athame, still glimmering with Power inside its plain black leather sheath. The chunk of consecrated chalk—my fingers trembled, touching its dry surface. I'd been searching for it desperately in the abandoned cafeteria of Rigger Hall with Lourdes chasing me, carrying the poisonous remnant of Mirovitch inside his brain like a cancerous flower. A silver Zijaan lighter with a cursive-script *CM* etched into it. A battered paperback copy of the Nine Canons—the runes that Magi and other psions and sorcerers had been using since before the Great Awakening—that I'd had since the Academy. My tarot cards in a hank of blue silk. Rough bits of quartz crystal, a few more bloodstones, some chunks of amber. More odds and ends.

My hands knew what to do. I laid Jace's coat down, my fingers moving, checking, stowing everything in its proper place. I picked up the bag, gave it an experimental shake, and let it settle. I ducked through the strap and settled the bag on my hip, under the holster carrying my right-hand gun. I rolled my shoulders back as everything settled in, then shrugged into Jace's coat. Picked up my katana.

"Ready for anything," I muttered.

The house was oddly quiet. I listened and heard nothing, not even servants moving. I realized how used to the sound of human hearts beating I'd become. The maids didn't talk to me—I didn't speak Taliano, and they didn't speak much Merican, so I let Japhrimel translate and was grateful none of them looked askance or forked the sign of the Evil Eye at me. None of them set foot in the library unless it was to dust while I was sleeping or to leave a box of new books inside the door. Only Emilio seemed completely unafraid, both of me and of the demon who shared my bed.

I stood for a few moments, the room resounding with small sounds as my attention swept in a slow circuit, brushing the curtains of the bed, sliding along the walls, caressing the framed Berscardi print above the low table where Japhrimel kept a single lily in a fluted black glass vase. The lily was gone, the vase dry and empty. The curtains fluttered. I sighed.

I turned on my heel, my boots clicking, and strode out of the bedroom, down the hall. The doors rose up on either side of me, never-used bedrooms, a small meditation room, a sparring room with a long wooden floor and shafts of light coming in every window.

The sparring room almost quivered with the echoes of sessions between Japh and me, combat as intimate as sex, his greater strength and speed giving me the ability to push myself harder, faster—I didn't have to worry about hurting him, didn't have to hold back. The only times I'd ever fought as hard were in Jado's *dojo*, training to take on the world.

I found the door I wanted unlocked, hit it with the flats of both hands. It swung inward silently, banging against the wall. Dust flew. This wasn't a place anyone entered often.

The room was long, a wooden floor glowing with lay-

ers of varnish. At the far end, barred by two shafts of sunlight, stood a high antique ebony table, and on this table
lay a scarred and corkscrew-twisted *dotanuki*, its hilt-
wrappings scorched.

Jace's sword. Still reverberating with the final agonized throes of his death.

A blot of darkness hunched on the floor in front of the
table. Japhrimel, on one knee, his back turned to me, his
coat lying wetly against the floor behind him.

Of all the things I expected, that was probably the
last.

He didn't move. I strode up the center of the room
and came to a halt right behind him, my boots sliding on
the floor. I dug my heels in—going too fast. It seemed I
would never learn how to slow this body down. My rings
spat, swirling with color, each stone glittering.

I waited. Japhrimel's head was down, inky hair falling
forward to hide his face. His back was utterly straight.
He didn't speak. Sunlight fell like honey, but the sun was
sinking down in the sky. We were going to go find this
door into Hell soon.

I finally settled for stepping close and laying my hand
on his shoulder. He flinched.

Tierce Japhrimel, Lucifer's assassin and oldest child,
flinched when I touched him.

I didn't choke with surprise, but it was damn close.
"Japhri—"

"I have been here, asking the ghost of a human man
for forgiveness." His voice slashed through mine. "And
wondering why he has more of your heart than I do."

It was the closest thing to jealousy I'd ever heard from

him. I closed my mouth with a snap, found my voice. "He never did," I finally said. "That was the problem."

Japhrimel laughed. The sound was so bitter it dyed the air blue. "Are you so cruel to those you love?"

"It's a human habit." The lump in my throat threatened to strangle me. "I'm sorry."

Even now, saying *I'm sorry* didn't come easily. It tore its way out of my chest with razor glass studded along every edge.

Japhrimel rose to his feet. I still couldn't see his face. "An apology without a battle. Perhaps there is hope."

I knew he was using that black humor again, like a blade laid along the forearm to ward off a strike. It still hurt. "If I'm so bloody bad why don't you go back to Hell?" *Great, Danny. Lovely. You're really on edge, aren't you? This is really adult. No wonder he treats you like a little kid.*

"I would not go back, even if Hell would have me. I seem to prefer your malice." He turned on his heel, away from me, the hem of his coat brushing my knee. "I will wait for you."

My voice had turned ragged, but even that couldn't stop the dripping sweetness along its edges. "Don't run away from me, dammit."

He paused. Stood with his back to me still, his shoulders iron-hard. "Running away is your trick."

You little snot of a demon, why do you have to make this so fucking hard? "You're an arrogant son of a bitch," I informed him. The air turned hot and tight, the twisted corkscrewed sword lying on the table ringing softly, its song of shock and death cycling up a notch. Catching the fever in the air, maybe. We were both throwing off enough heat and Power to make the entire room resound like an echo chamber.

"I am what you make of me, *hedaira*. I will wait for you outside the door." He strode away, every footfall a clicking crisp sound. Anger like smoke fumed up from his footprints. His coat flapped as if a wind was mouthing it.

"Japhrimel. Japh, wait."

He didn't pause.

"Don't do this. I'm sorry. *Please.*" My voice cracked, as if Lucifer had just finished strangling me again.

Two more steps. He stopped, just inside the door. His back was straight, rigid with something I didn't care to name.

I folded my arms defensively, the slim length of my sword in my right hand, a bar of darkness. "I'm *frightened*, Japh. All right? I woke up, you weren't here, and you drop this on me. I'm fucking terrified. Cut me a little slack here, and I'll try to stop being such a bitch. Okay?" *I can't believe it, I just admitted being scared to a demon. Miracles do happen.*

I thought he'd continue out the door, but he didn't. His shoulders relaxed slightly, the hurtful static in the air easing. It took the space of five breaths before he turned back to me. I saw the tide of green drifting through his eyes, sparks above a bonfire. His mouth had softened. We looked at each other, my Fallen and I. I tried to pretend I wasn't hugging myself for comfort.

"There is no need for fear," he said finally, quietly.

Yeah, sure. We're about to go meet the Devil, for the third time in my life. I could have done without ever meeting him at all. He's probably got something special planned for us, and the Devil's idea of a little surprise is not my idea of a good time. "You've got to be joking." I sounded like I'd lost all my air. The mark on my shoulder turned to velvet, warm oil sliding along my skin from his attention. "It's the *Devil*." *I don't think he's likely to be in a good mood, either.*

He came back to me, each footfall eerily silent. Stopped an arm's-length away, looking down to meet my eyes, his hands clasped behind his back. "He is the Prince of Hell," he corrected, pedantically. "I will let no harm come to you. Only trust me, and all will be well."

I've trusted you for a long time now. "Is there anything else you haven't told me?" I searched his face, the memorized lines and curves. He had his own harsh beauty, like a balanced throwing-knife or the curve of a katana, something functional and deadly instead of merely aesthetic. Funny, but when I was human I had thought him almost ugly at first, certainly not *beautiful* by any stretch of the imagination. The longer I knew him, the better he looked.

He shrugged. Gods, how I hate demons shrugging at me. "If I told you what I guess, or what I anticipate, it would frighten you needlessly. Until I am certain, I do not wish to cloud the issue with suppositions. Best just to go, and to trust in your Fallen. Have I not earned as much?"

Goddamn it, I hated having to admit he was right. Even *I* knew that anticipating something from the Prince of Hell was likely to end in a nasty surprise. Japh had never let me down. "I do." My voice dropped, the soft ruined tone of honey gone granular soothing the last remains of tension away. "Of course I trust you. Don't you know that?"

I thought he'd be happy about it. Instead, his face turned still and solemn as we looked at each other, the mark on my shoulder pulsing and sending a flood of heat down my skin. "Cut it out." I could hardly get enough air in to protest. It was as intimate as his fingers in my hair, as intimate as his mouth against my pulse. "Let's just get this over with."

A single sharp nod, and Japhrimel offered me his hand. I let him take my right hand, my sword hand; it made me nervous as hell to know that he could very easily keep me from drawing just by tightening his fingers a little.

I don't want to do this. I don't. Japhrimel led me out of the room, and the doors closed behind us, silent on their maghinges. *But if I have to face down Lucifer, at least I've got Japh with me.*

It wasn't as comforting as I'd thought it would be, since Lucifer had killed him once before. Dead, or driven him into dormancy—gods, I didn't want to try to figure out the difference again. Even with Japh on my side, seeing the Prince of Hell was likely to be hideously unpleasant.

Still, I'd do it. What you can't run away from, you have to face. Living with the ghosts inside my head had taught me that much, at least.

I just hoped facing this would leave me alive.

7

The town of Arrieto has dozed in the middle of wheat fields and olives for centuries, drowsing in southern sun. We caught a transport in the town square, a piazza still picturesquely cobbled with worn-down stones. Here in a historical preserve of the Hegemony, there was no urban sprawl and no great flights of hover formations—but every sunbaked house had a bristling fiberoptic array and invisible security nets humming. Slicboards were racked outside cafes, and a Necromance was still local news.

By the time we lifted off, me in the window seat and Japhrimel in the aisle, I had already had enough of stares and whispers hidden behind hands. I've walked the streets of Saint City, one of the biggest metropolises in the world, and had my armor hold up. But this little town's obvious fear got to me. Normals always think psions want to read their deep dark secrets, or use mental pressure to force them to do something embarrassing. Not one normal seems to understand that to a psion, touching a normal's mind is like taking a bath in a festering sewer. Messy thoughts, messy emotions, messy fantasies all stirred to-gether, randomly emitting and decaying; a normal mind was the *last* place a psion wanted to find herself in. The psions that *did* take advantage of normals very quickly found themselves subject to bounty hunters and dragged in to answer felony charges.

I should know. I've dragged more than a few in.

Still, all the holovids are full of evil psions and occasional psion antiheros, taking down the bad guys while crippled by their own talents. The fact that psions don't work in the holovid biz only makes it worse.

None of the normals could tell what Japhrimel was, but I had a tat on my cheek, the emerald flashing, and my sword. Only an accredited psion can carry edged metal in transports and guns on city streets. Only an accredited psion or the police, that is. So I stuck out, and Japhrimel blended in.

Sort of. It's kind of hard to hide a tall, golden-skinned demon in a long black Chinese-collared coat. To normals he probably looked like he'd only been genetically augmented, which was a little odd but not way out of the gravball court. A genescan would show him as a different species but no weirder than a werecain or kobolding. No, it would take a psion to see the twisting black-diamond flames of his aura. They would know what he was. But there were no other psions on the transport.

I leaned my head back against the seat. The flight was quiet, only ten people—we had plenty of empty seats around us in every direction. Nobody would want to crowd me; Necromances have a reputation for being a little twitchy. "So we're going to get a guide, and go through a door," I said.

"Yes."

I wanted this all *very* clear. "You'll negotiate our

passage, but you're not going to talk—once we pass *through* the door."

"No." Japhrimel's eyes were closed. He leaned back into the seat, his mouth a straight line, his hands cupped and upturned in his lap.

"Because that would look as if I was weak."

"Yes."

"If you don't speak and you stay behind me while we're in Hell, you're just a bodyguard—and not responsible for anything impolite I do." *Which is bound to be something, since I have the worst manners in the world. Don't think I'm going to make a special effort for Lucifer either.*

"Yes."

"Don't touch anything, don't take anything from the Prince, and especially don't eat or drink." I looked out the window. The whine of hover transport settled against my bones. I hated it, my back teeth grinding together before I could make my jaw unloose. "And you don't know what he wants me for. Won't even venture a guess."

"I have my guesses. None of which are pleasant."

I couldn't help myself. "Care to clue me in?"

That earned me a quirk of a smile. "If we go to meet death, I would prefer it to be a surprise for you. I do not want you dreading it and becoming distracted."

I couldn't tell if he was joking, for once. His sense of humor was a little strange, when it wasn't mordant black wit or irony it was a particular brand of macabre I was beginning to recognize as purely demon. "Oh, how comforting." I tapped the sword's hilt with my fingernails. I'd been painting them with black molecule-drip polish for so long the polish was starting to maintain itself on my nails. I knew how to make my fingers into claws now, I was stronger and faster than any mortal.

Fat lot of good it would do me against Lucifer. Every culture has its stories about nonhuman beings—beings whose beauty didn't conceal their essential difference, beings who didn't necessarily believe in the human idea of truth. The fact that we can separate them into *loa, etrigandi,* demons, or what-have-you doesn't make them any less dangerous.

The Old Christers had called Lucifer the Father of Lies. I was beginning to think they'd had the right idea, even if their conception of gods was so narrow as to be laughable in this day and age.

"Japhrimel?"

He moved slightly, restlessly. "What is it, my curious one?"

"If I died, what would happen to you?"

One eye opened a fraction of an inch, glanced at me. "There is little cause to worry, *hedaira.* Even Fallen I am still the one who was Lucifer's assassin, and that is your safety. There are not many demons who would challenge me, weakened as I am."

I shouldn't have felt guilty. I hadn't *asked* him to Fall. If he'd told me what he'd intended to do I would have done everything possible to dissuade him, including drawing my sword or lighting out to track Santino on my own. I hadn't had the faintest *clue* of what he'd intended when he'd changed me.

Still…I did feel guilty. Right up under my breastbone and slightly to the left, the place where my heart still kept steady time. "I'm sorry. That you're…weakened."

I watched, fascinated, as his right hand curled into a

fist. My own right hand had been spoiled and knotted for a good year or so after I'd killed Santino. I'd been unable to draw another sword until Gabe called me in to work on the Lourdes murders.

That thought sent another hot prickle of guilt up my spine. She'd sent some news clips about the murders and some other messages through my datpilot, and I called her as frequently as I could stand to. The conversations were usually short. *Hi, how are you. Not bad, Eddie's good? Oh you're busy? Sorry about that. Okay, well, catch you later.*

Ghosts of the words we could never say to each other crowded the phone line, robbing us both of breath. She tried to apologize for bringing me in on the Lourdes case, I didn't let her. Each time she started, I would tell her not to.

I would try to thank her for performing a Necromance's duty at Jace's bedside. She would tell me not to. Everything that lay between us stopped the words in both our throats.

Why was it so damn hard to talk to the one person I could have said anything to?

I wished now that I'd spent more time on the phone with her. I would have given a lot to call her, maybe even use my datpilot's fiendishly expensive voice capability. But she didn't even know Japhrimel was alive. I had, for the first time, lied to her when I'd left Saint City. Even if only by omission, it was still a lie told to the one person on earth I should never have misled. Gabe had gone through hell for me.

You can't do anything about it now, Dante. Focus on the task at hand.

I raised my left hand, threaded my fingers through Japhrimel's. It took some doing—he didn't fight me, but his fist was clenched. I finally pried it open, and the touch of his skin on mine rewarded me. "Talk to me," I said, so softly only a demon's sensitive ears could have heard.

He let out a quiet breath. His anger could blow the transport to pieces, but no whisper of it escaped. Except for the mark on my shoulder, burning as it twisted its way more deeply into my skin.

"You are cruel and gentle, in the manner of your kind," he said finally. "You have never treated me as anything less—or *more*—than human. As one of your own."

I thought about that for a moment. I had fallen into the habit of treating him just like another human early on in the hunt for Santino and never quite grown out of it. Was that what he was talking about? "It wouldn't be fair otherwise."

"Fair?" His hand relaxed slightly. His eyes were closed, but I would have bet hard credit and the emerald in my cheek that he knew the location of every person on the transport and had them evaluated down to the last millimeter. "Life is not fair, Dante. Even demons know this."

"It should be," I muttered, looking at my swordhilt.

"I dislike the pain you inflict on yourself." He stroked my wrist with his thumb, an intimate touch making me catch my breath. "We will arrive exactly nowhere if we do not reach an agreement."

Memory rose around me. He'd said the same thing in my kitchen, all those years ago, during the first stages of the hunt for Santino. One terrified Necromance bent on revenge and a demon without the sense to keep from falling in love with her, and the Devil pulling all the strings behind the scenes.

"An agreement? How about *I* try to be a big girl and keep my mouth shut, and *you* try not to keep things from me from now on?" *I'm pretty sure I can keep my half of that bargain if you can manage to keep yours. What do you say, Japhrimel?*

His thumb stroked the underside of my wrist again. My breath hitched. "There." He sounded less tense and more like the Japhrimel I knew. "That is the Dante I know."

I could have laughed at the parallel thoughts. Instead, I studied my swordhilt. Jado-*sensei* was an old crafty dragon, and I wondered if he'd given me a blade that could cut the Devil himself. Yet another thing I missed— Jado's nut-brown wrinkled face framed by long pointed ears. Maybe I *did* want to go back to Saint City.

The thought made my heart pound. I took a deep breath. "Japhrimel?"

A slight, subtle shift, he leaned toward me in his seat. "What?"

"Don't hide things from me. Even if you think it'll scare me."

"You're persistent."

It was like one of our sparring sessions. During the first few I'd held back, afraid of hurting him because he so rarely used a weapon. It was only after the third time he took my blade away from me without even seeming to try that I started to get angry—and I hadn't held back since. The same sense—of slashing at an opponent who simply melted away from my strikes then blurred in to take my weapon away—was there in our conversation.

"Don't change the subject." I kept my temper by a thin margin. "Please."

"Even if it is for your own good, *hedaira*?"

I scowled at my sword. *Even then, Japh. I'd rather be scared than have you hide something from me.* "Who are you to decide that?"

"Your *A'nankhimel*, Dante. The one who Fell through love of you."

"I didn't ask you to." *I didn't make you Fall. I just treated you like a person. Was that so wrong?*

He moved again, still leaning toward me. "And yet, it happened. Enough. I will tell you truth, but I will not bother you with trifles or distract you unnecessarily."

It was no use. He wasn't going to budge. *It's going to be goddamn hard to get through this if you don't tell me little things like "Oh, Dante, the Devil keeps calling and wants to talk to you." That kind of sounds like need-to-know information to me, Japhrimel.* I bit the inside of my cheek to keep the words from spilling out. I was already in a hell of a bad mood.

Not the best way to meet the Devil at all.

8

$\mathcal{V}$enizia lay atop its lagoon, shimmering gilt and pearl. Once, long ago, the city had been at the mercy of a rising sea. Climate control, antigrav, and reactive had changed all that. Now the entire city was mythically beautiful, its buildings arching over canals gleaming crimson as the sun died its daily, fiery, bloody death.

After the failure of the celebrated Gibraltar Locks Project, the Hegemony had funded a massive retrofit to keep Venizia afloat. Everyone was mildly surprised when the Locks architect (an Academy Magi dropout-turned-engineer named Todao Shikai) was assigned to the task, and slightly more surprised when he actually pulled it off. He collapsed and died of a massive cerebral hemorrhage six months after the retrofit was finished. Rumor was he had called up a particular imp after the Locks project failed and bargained away his life for a career success. I'd always discounted the old story—but I was on my way to my second official meeting with the Prince of Hell.

Meeting the Devil does tend to change the way one looks at gruesome old legends—the more gruesome, the more thought-provoking.

The transport floated down, hovercells whining as it held steady above the water for a few moments before gliding onto the dock and landing with barely a thump. Whoever the pilot was, he or she was highly capable. AI decks can't land without jolting everyone aboard; it takes a human touch.

I sat looking out the window, as everyone coughed and shuffled off the transport. Japhrimel, his fingers warm against mine, said nothing. There was a time when I would have fought tooth and nail to get *out* of the damned transport as quickly as possible, but for now I was content to let everyone else go their merry way first. Well, maybe not *content*. Maybe I just didn't want to get out of the hover.

"We must go, Dante," Japhrimel said quietly. His thumb touched the underside of my wrist again, the heat flushing through me and washing away sharp cold fear. The man was dangerous to my pulse. "I would ask you something."

"Hold that thought." I blew out between my teeth and stood up. He moved too, without relinquishing my hand. We went down the central aisle, my bag bumping against my hip. He had to bend slightly, a little too tall for a human transport. His coat rustled, sounding like soft cloth-leather; he must have been agitated for all his face was calm and his aura perfectly controlled.

We stepped off onto the dock washed with sunset light. I glanced into the sky, looked across the dock to where water glittered and foamed under the antigrav. Shikai had done a good job—the retrofit was seamless; Venizia was now truly a floating city. Unfortunately, that much antigrav meant that the whole city whined with a sound inaudible to most normals. Most psions can't stand the sound of hovers for long, it settles in the back teeth and rattles the bones. I sighed. My shields swirled, taking in the quality of the Power here—people and stone and reactive, a taste like sour oily water on the back of the throat, overlaid with coffee fumes and synth-hash smoke. What would have taken me hours before I met Japhrimel—acclimatizing to a new city's Power well—was done in seconds, my almost-demon metabolism shifting through the necessary adjustments. "I bet there aren't a lot of psis here," I muttered, then looked up at him. "What is it you're going to ask me?"

Japhrimel finished scanning the dock, his eyes glittering and that look on him again—the look of listening to something I couldn't hear. His jaw was set, golden skin drawn tight over his bones. I wondered what it felt like to him, to be going back into Hell. Then again, he'd gone last night, right?

I wondered what it was like, seeing what he'd given up for me. Hell was no place to party if you were a human—but he wasn't, and it was his home. Was he homesick?

Then he looked down, and that rare smile lit his face. I couldn't help myself—I caught my breath, smelling pollution-dyed water and sunwarmed stone, and a thread of synth-hash smoke. The pilot and copilot of the transport had just come out of their cockpit access hatch, the gold braid on their uniforms twinkling. The pilot had a synth-hash cigarette dangling from her lip.

"I ask you again to trust me, Dante. No matter what befalls us. And I ask you not to doubt me."

"I'm here, aren't I?" I hunched my shoulders, a faint breeze off the Meditterane touching my braided hair. As usual, a lone strand had come free and fell in my face. It seemed the longer my hair got, the more of an independent consciousness it possessed.

"You are." The smile faded from his face. "*A'tai, hetai-rae A'nankimel'iin. Diriin.*" It might have been a prayer, the way he said it, but it wasn't a prayer I knew. He had only taught me a little of the language demons used among themselves, saying it wasn't fit for my tongue, and anyway we had time.

Now I wished we had more time.

"What does that mean?" I searched his face as the sun finished its slow slippage under the horizon. I took a deep breath—the wind off the sea was warm, but with a promise of later chill. Lights flickered in the city atop the lagoon. The antigrav made the ground feel as if it was thrumming underfoot, like the deck of an old ship or a balky slicboard.

"Promise me. Say you will not doubt me, no matter what happens."

"It would be a lot easier if you would tell me exactly what's going on," I said irritably. "Are we going to get this over with or not?"

"Promise me." He wasn't going to budge. Stubborn demon, stubborn human woman—only I wasn't fully human anymore.

I set my jaw and glared at him. "I promise." *After all, who do I have left, Japhrimel? Tell me that. You and Gabe, and Eddie by extension. That's all.*

I'm damn near rich, having even that much.

"Say you will not doubt me, no matter what."

And he called *me* persistent. "I promise I'll trust you and I won't doubt you," I chanted as if I was back in primary school. "No matter what. Now can we get this *over* with?"

"I will never understand your tendency to hurry." But his face had eased. Now he looked thoughtful and almost relaxed. It was only a millimeter's worth of difference or so in the lines around his mouth but it shouted at me. At least I knew him well enough for that.

If I have to do this, I want to get it over with. Then you and I are going to have a little chat about our relationship. It's high time we got a few things straight. My heart leapt into my throat, I lifted my sword slightly. "I'm armed and ready to face the Devil, Japhrimel. Let's go."

I wish I could say I saw more of Venizia. The city is a treasure trove of pre-Hegemony art and artifacts; its architecture alone is worth a lifetime's careful study. As it was, I looked down at my feet, barely marking the turns we made and fixing them into a mental map, letting Japhrimel navigate me over bridges and through darkening streets not big enough for even single-passenger hovers. The people here used narrow high-prowed transports on the canals—some of them open-air transports, which gave me a shudder—and slicboards to get around. The fourth time I got tagged by the wash from a slicboard's localized antigrav I made up my mind to draw my sword the next time one came near me.

I almost did it too, but Japhrimel closed his fingers around my right wrist, a bracelet as gentle as it was inexorable. "You *are* out of sorts," he murmured, making me laugh. The sound sliced through the street, rattled away against the hoverwhine pressing against my back teeth.

"I'm going to smashtip the next kid who buzzes me right into the canal," I said through gritted teeth.

"No need. We're here." He halted in front of a soaring pile of stone, I tilted my head back—and back, and back.

The cathedral rose in spires toward the sky just beginning to take on the look of a city at night, reactive and electrical light and freeplas all conspiring to wash the vault of heaven with orange. I saw a round window, real glass repaired with bits of plasglass, in the shape of a rose that would glow red inside when the sun hit it. "The entrance to Hell is in a temple?"

"No." He shook his head, his eyes flaring with runic patterns of emerald green for a moment. "This is simply where I was told to meet our guide. Though most temples are very good places to find a door into Hell." He led me up the steps, and I ran the fingers of my right hand over the waist-high iron railing. The hand that had killed Santino—it had twisted into a claw after I had driven the shards of my other sword into the scavenger demon's black heart.

I touched my swordhilt, lifting the slim scabbarded blade in my left hand.

Did Jado give me a blade that can kill the Devil?

I hadn't thought to ask him at the time, too busy thinking about Rigger Hall and too sick with mourning Japhrimel. Besides, how could I have known the Prince of Hell would start messing with my life again? I thought he'd had enough of me the first time around. I had certainly emphatically had enough of *him*.

I looked at Japhrimel's back as he paused at the double doors, one golden hand lifting to touch them. I'd thought him dead once.

Dead and gone. Grieving for him had almost killed me. So he'd said nothing about Lucifer asking for me, trying to protect me. He was right, if I'd had to deal with Lucifer *and* the echoes of Mirovitch's papery voice rustling in my head, I might have gone gratefully, howlingly insane.

No extenuating circumstances, my conscience barked. *What happened to the old Danny Valentine, the one nobody would dare lie to?*

I did something I'd never done before—tried to shut that voice up. It didn't go gracefully.

"Japhrimel."

He turned his head slightly, keeping both me and the door in his peripheral vision.

"I never would, you know. Doubt you." *I've violated one of my biggest rules for you.* I couldn't bring myself to say the rest of it, and hoped he understood.

His lips thinned, but the mark on my shoulder was suddenly alive with velvet flame, caressing all the way down my body. I took a deep breath, bracing myself.

He pushed the door open, glanced inside, and his shoulders went rigid for half a breath. Then he turned back to give me one eloquent, heart-freezing look, warning me something was wrong, and stepped inside. He paused just inside the door, his attention moving in a slow arc over the church's interior. I waited.

He finally moved forward. A heavy fragrance boiled out of the opened door, and my heart rose to lodge in my throat again like a lump of freeplas. Smoky musk, fresh-baked bread, the indefinable smell of *demon*.

Not just any demon, either. I knew that smell. Had hoped to never, *ever* smell it again.

I stepped into the church, Power brushing along my

skin, teasing, caressing. My mouth had gone dry. My heart fell down from my throat into my stomach, somersaulted, then started to pound in my chest, my wrists, my neck. I even felt my pulse in my ankles, my heart worked so hard.

Well, would you look at that. The doors slid along the floor behind me, closing of their own will—or *his*. Ranks of pews marched all the way down the cathedral's interior, but on the altar was a massive Hegemony sunwheel; other gods had their own niches in the halls going to either side. Candles flickered in the dimness, I smelled the faint tang of kyphii. My nose filled with the heatless scent of generations of worship, guilt, and fear, and the later tangs of Power: Shamans and Necromances and *sedayeen* and Ceremonials coming to make offerings, dyeing the air with energy all mixed together to make a heady charged atmosphere.

Most old temples and later cathedrals were built on nodes, junctures of ley lines. During the Merican Era churches had stopped being built on nodes and started to spring up like mushrooms. After the Vatican Bank scandal and in the beginning of the Awakening, the old churches started turning back into temples; the process only accelerated after the Seventy Days War and the fall of the Evangelicals of Gilead. The Parapsychic Act and the codifying of psionic abilities meant that only temples and cathedrals on nodes survived, others were inelegantly torn down to make way for urban renewal.

This place had been reverberating with Power and worship for a very long time. And there at the altar rail was a tall, black-clad figure with a shock of golden hair glowing with its own flaming light. A figure slim and beautiful even from the back, and obviously not human.

We hadn't needed a guide into Hell after all, despite all Japh's careful preparations.

Anubis et'her ka. My throat closed. For one frantic moment I wanted to scramble back for the doors, wrench them open and *run*, anywhere was fine as long as I could get *away*; the feel of Lucifer's steely fingers sinking into my throat rose like an old enemy, taunting me. This was the last chance I had to bolt. I almost made it, too, my body straining against horrified inertia.

Japhrimel half-turned, caught my arm, pulled me forward. He ended up walking just behind me and to my left, to protect both my blind side and my back. The mark on my shoulder flared with heat again. I choked back what I wanted to say and instead moved up the central aisle, each booted footfall echoing along stone and harsh wooden edges. Just like doing a slicboard run through Suicide Alley in North New York Jersey; the only thing you can do is hold your breath and go full throttle—and hope it doesn't hurt too bad on the way through.

I stopped at the front pew. Lucifer stood at the rail, his golden hands loose at his sides. My heart thudded.

I thought we were going into Hell to meet him. The frantic idea that I might almost have preferred the trip into Hell just so I could have a few more moments before I had to face down the Devil made a gasping, breathy laugh rise up in my throat. I killed it, set my jaw so tightly I could feel my teeth squealing together. A worm of suspicion bloomed; I didn't want to think that my gentle Fallen, the lover who had nursed me through the double blow of Mirovitch's psychic rape and Jace's death with more patience than anyone had ever shown me, could still be on the Devil's side.

It's not possible, Danny. It's just fear talking. Just stupid, silly fear.

I said nothing. Japhrimel went still as a stone behind me, radiating a fierce hurtful awareness. I had rarely felt this kind of pressure and tension from him. It was the same feeling—him listening to a sound I could not hear, seeing something I could not see—only magnified to the *n*th degree.

Finally—probably after he thought I'd stewed enough—Lucifer turned slowly, as if he had all the time in the world.

He probably did.

He was too beautiful, the kind of androgynous beauty holovid models sometimes have. If I hadn't known he was male, I might have wondered. The mark on his forehead flashed green, an emerald like a Necromance's only obviously not implanted, the skin smoothly turning into a gem. Lucifer's radioactive, silken green eyes met mine, and if I hadn't had practice at meeting Japhrimel's green gaze—and later, his dark eyes so much older than a human's—I might have let out a gasp.

Instead, I stared at the emerald. He might think I was looking him in the eye if I focused on the gem. The emerald grafted in my own cheek burned. I tried to remind myself it wasn't like his; my emerald was a mark of my bond with my personal psychopomp, the god whose protection I carried, the mark of a Necromance.

It didn't work. I still felt nauseated.

Silence stretched between us, humming. Japhrimel was tight as a coiled spring next to me, and I felt a little worm of traitorous relief inside my chest. As long as he was on my side, I might conceivably get out of this alive.

Still, I wished I could talk to him. I wished I could turn and look at him. My curse—I was so fucking *needy*. I wanted constant reassurance. My big flaw when it came to relationships—questioning the loyalty of anyone crazy enough to date me. After all, I was damaged goods. Had *always* been damaged goods.

You're being ridiculous, Danny. Keep your wits about you. This is Lucifer you're dealing with. You show any weakness, and he'll eat you alive.

I concentrated on staying quiet.

Lucifer said nothing. *I'll be damned if I give the Devil the first word.* I tightened my left hand around the reinforced scabbard.

Power blurred, singing in the air, a physical weight against heart and throat and eye. The demon part of me wanted to drop to my knees; the human part of me screamed silently, resisting with every single fiber of stubbornness I could manage to dredge up from my stubborn, painful life.

I suppose I should have been grateful I'd had practice in enduring the unendurable.

It was close. *Very* close. I had no time to worry how Japhrimel was staying upright, I was too busy keeping my own knees locked, mentally digging my teeth in, *resisting*. My rings spat golden sparks, defiant.

Finally, the Prince of Hell spoke.

"First point to you, Dante Valentine." The voice of the Devil, stroking, easing along every exposed inch of skin, a flame so cold it burned. "I have left Hell, I have come alone, and now you force me to greet you. You must be certain of yourself."

Irritation rasped under my breastbone, lifesaving irritation. It broke the spell of his eyes and bolstered my knees. "Goddammit," I rasped, my voice as hoarse as if he'd just tried to strangle me again. "I don't play your little games. I didn't even know you wanted me until today." I met his eyes, then, something inside my chest cracking as their deep glow burned against my face. "Just get to the point, *Prince*. Use small words, and can the goddamn sarcasm. What do you *want*?"

Lucifer regarded me for a hair-raising moment, during which I had time to curse my big fat mouth.

Then he tipped his head back and laughed, a sound of genuine goodwill raising my hackles. My right hand closed around my swordhilt, Japhrimel's hand came down on mine, jamming the sword back into the sheath, stinging me. His hand vanished as Lucifer looked back down, and all of a sudden I was glad, deeply glad, that I hadn't drawn steel. The thought of trying to cut him, this being so much older and more powerful than anything short of a god...no. *No*.

"I think I have missed your unique charm, Dante." He sounded almost as if he meant it. "I want your service, Necromance, and I am prepared to pay any price necessary."

Go fuck yourself. I don't work for the Devil. I learned my lesson last time. My mouth was dry as a barrel of reactive. "What do you want me to do?"

"You are most honored among humans, Necromance," Lucifer said slowly, his mouth stretching in a shark's grin. "I need another Right Hand."

9

I blinked. I couldn't help myself—I glanced down at the end of his right arm and counted his fingers. Five. Just like a human. Or four fingers and one thumb if you wanted to get really technical.

"You seem to still have yours," I cracked, and the smile fell from Lucifer's face so fast I was surprised it didn't shatter on the stone floor. The cathedral rang with soft sound—whispers, mutters, laughter. Nasty laughter, the type of laughter you hear in nightmares.

"Do *not* taunt me, Valentine." The emerald in his forehead sparkled, a gleam that reminded me of Japhrimel's eyes back when I had first met him. The meaning caught up with me—Japhrimel had been Lucifer's Right Hand. His eldest son, trusted lieutenant—and assassin.

Right Hand? What the hell? I can't live in Hell. A fine edge of panic began curling up behind my thoughts.

Then someone laughed.

I almost didn't recognize Japhrimel's voice. It boomed and caromed through the entire cathedral. Dust pattered down from the roof, I heard stone groaning. One of the pews rocked back slightly, wood squealing under the lash of sound. The mark on my shoulder blazed with fierce hurtful pleasure, as if his hand was digging into my flesh, keeping me still as his voice tore the air.

I froze, keeping Lucifer in my sights. The Devil looked past me to his former assassin, and the snarl that crossed his features was enough to almost send me to my knees. "You find this funny, *A'nankhimel*?" His voice scraped through the air, cutting across Japhrimel's laughter.

I found my own voice again. "Leave him alone," I snapped. "You're bargaining with me."

He could turn on a red credit's thin edge. The snarl was gone, his eyes so bright they all but cast shadows on the floor. "So we're bargaining now?" His sculpted lips curled up in a half-smile. He was so goddamn beautiful it hurt to look at him, actually *hurt* the eyes, like looking into a coremelt, stinging and blinking against the glow humans were never meant to see.

I tore my eyes away from him. Looked over at Japhrimel, who had stopped laughing. Funny, but he didn't look amused. Instead, his eyebrows were drawn together, examining Lucifer as if a new kind of bug had scuttled out from underneath something and Japh wanted to give it his entire attention.

Then Japhrimel's eyes slowly, so slowly, flowed over to meet mine. The mark on my shoulder eased, sending a wave of heat down my body.

Relief and fresh faith burst inside my chest. Japh was with me. What could Lucifer do, with his assassin on my side?

Oh, be careful, Danny. He could still do plenty. You know he can.

Japhrimel's gaze held mine.

I quirked my eyebrows slightly, a silent question.

He gave an evocative shrug, little more than a fraction of a millimeter's lifting of one shoulder. He couldn't tell me or he didn't care, either way. Then he tipped his head back slightly, raising his chin. *I am with you, Dante.* His mental tone was gentle, laid in my brain like one of my own thoughts.

Had he always been able to do that? Given the depth of the bond between us, it wasn't unlikely. The mark on my shoulder pulsed insistently, a taut line stretched between us. At the moment, it was a good thing, a way to confer with him without Lucifer hearing.

Or at least, I hoped Lucifer couldn't hear him.

I swallowed and looked back at Lucifer, who watched this exchange with a great deal of interest.

"What do you need an assassin for, Prince?" My tone came out flat, not as powerful as his or Japhrimel's, but still something to reckon with. The Hegemony sun-disk ran with a sudden random reflection of light.

He doesn't own me. Anubis owns me; the Devil can't do anything but kill me. The thought wasn't as comforting as it could have been. Death never is, even if you're a Necromance.

"Four demons have escaped Hell. The others I can deal with, but these are of the Greater Flight, and I wish their capture or execution to be both swift and...public. It will go a long way toward easing the...unrest...in my domain. Who better to hunt my subjects than my former Right Hand and the woman who killed Vardimal and returned my daughter to me?"

That did it. My temper snapped. For him to claim my murdered lover's daughter, to act like he hadn't half-strangled me and left me to deal with the fallout after playing his little game and getting control of the Egg and Hell back in one neat stroke—fury smashed through the fear, a familiar anger at injustice, held back and choked for most of my life.

"*Your* daughter?" My voice rose, the sun-disk rocking back on its stand, squealing. "*Your daughter?*"

"Mine," Lucifer replied silkily. "The human matrix means nothing, Dante. Only the Androgyne matters."

She isn't yours. She's Doreen's, and you stole her. "You arrogant son of a bitch," I snarled. "No way. Go fuck yourself, Lucifer, if it will reach." I spun on my heel, static gathering on the air, and would have stalked away with my back exposed if Japhrimel had not caught my arm.

He said something to Lucifer in their demon tongue, sliding consonants and harsh, hurtful vowels. I stared up at Japhrimel's face, his hand burning on my arm—he didn't squeeze, but his grasp was firm enough that I knew he meant business. He wouldn't have broken my arm, but he would have kept me there, and an undignified struggle in front of the Devil wasn't something I wanted.

What the hell was he saying? I didn't even know what *hedaira* meant. All I knew of demon language was Japhrimel's name and the hissing sibilance of their word for *no*. And, oddly enough, the word for *sunlight*.

Lucifer made a reply. Not even his golden voice could make that language sound good.

Japhrimel asked something else, the intonation clearly a question.

Lucifer's reply was brief and pointed enough that I looked from Japhrimel back to him, craning my neck.

This went on for a few minutes, question and reply; the horrible sound of that tongue crawling along my skin with prickling venomous feet. Finally, Japhrimel said something quietly, and the Prince of Hell's lip curled. He nodded, once, curtly. His eyes were bright and avid, resting on me. I felt the weight of that gaze like a load of coldly poisonous sedation, flooding my veins and making me shiver.

Japhrimel looked down at me, his eyes flaring green again for a moment. "Very well," he said quietly. "A moment to speak to my *hedaira*, Prince."

"Granted." Lucifer eyed both of us, then turned away to look back up at the sun-disk. He wore a very slight, very *nasty* smile that dried up all the spit in my mouth.

Japhrimel dragged me down the aisle a few steps, his coat separating in front, then spread his wings slightly and drew me in. He rested his chin atop my head. *Dante.* It was a calm, quiet sound in the very middle of my head, a thread of meaning. *We have no choice.*

Bullshit. We had a choice. There was always a choice. I closed my eyes, rested my forehead against his bare chest. Fine tremors walloped through me, each successive wave beating at the cocoon of Power Japhrimel held me in. My sword hilt dug into my ribs, I held the blade with creaking knuckles.

Japh's voice continued, inexorable. *Either we bargain with the Prince, or we make an enemy of him as well as of the demons that have escaped his control. At least if we bargain with him we have a chance of continuing our life together.*

I didn't want to "bargain." I wanted Lucifer to leave us alone. I got the distinct impression that if I made *any* bargain with the Prince of Hell, I'd come off as badly as I had last time—crippled, barely alive, and possibly with another long, despairing time of trying to resurrect Japhrimel on my hands. Or the whole thing could end up with *both* of us dead, and no way was I in the market for that.

Then let me negotiate. I have, after all, bargained before.

I swallowed, let out a soft breath against his skin. Felt his sudden attention as his arms tightened, pressing me against his body. His fingers traced up my back through my clothes, a wave of familiar fire curling through me. He was taller, his shoulders broad, and with his wings around me I was completely enclosed. The small shudder of response—the proof that I affected him—comforted me much more than it probably should have.

"Fine," I whispered. "You go ahead, then." We weren't in Hell, the rule about him not talking probably didn't apply. Besides, he was more likely to come out ahead when it came to fencing verbally with the Devil.

He nodded, his chin moving against my hair. "Courage, *hedaira*," he said very softly, mouthing the words. I shivered.

I have plenty of courage. I just don't have any assurance Lucifer isn't going to turn on us both.

Japhrimel led me back to the altar rail and waited until Lucifer faced us, green eyes sliding over us both. I saw a flash of something odd on the head demon's face, just a flicker, his eyes darkening and his mouth turning down.

What the hell was that? Did Lucifer actually look guilty? Or envious?

Actually, I was betting on *enraged*. Or *murderous*.

Danny, your imagination just works too well.

"Five years of service," Japhrimel said. "The full control of Hellesvront. Your word on your Name that you will protect Dante with every means at your disposal, forever."

The Devil's eyes closed slowly, opened again. Some essential tension leaked out of the air. Now it was a bargaining game, cat and mouse, bartering for my life. Well, last time I hadn't been able to bargain; it had been pretty goddamn simple. *Do what I tell you, or be killed.* This was a step up.

Not really.

Lucifer countered. "Twenty years, with a meeting to discuss renewal. Full control of Hellesvront, and my friendship to Dante Valentine as long as her life lasts."

"Seven years, full control, and swearing on your Name to protect her until eternity ends, Prince. *That* is nonnegotiable."

"What else?" The Devil didn't look amused now. As a matter of fact, he looked sour. It didn't mar his beauty, but it fascinated me.

Japhrimel paused for only a moment. He said something in their language again, something very slow and distinct.

What the hell? I looked up at Japhrimel, then over at the Devil. *What the hell is he doing?*

Lucifer's eyes glowed. I set my jaw, trying not to feel as if I was burrowing into Japhrimel's side. *Anubis, et'her ka,* I prayed. *Lord of Death, watch over me.*

"You *dare*?" Lucifer snarled, his face suffusing with rage. If I could have made any sound at all I might have whimpered. I'd never seen the Devil truly angry before—and I didn't want to. "*Abomination.*"

Japhrimel shrugged. "I learned too well from you. You should not have offered me freedom, Prince—even if you never intended to fulfill that offer."

Oh, Anubis, don't piss him off. I don't want to see the Devil in a really *bad mood.* Japhrimel's arm was tight and reassuring over my shoulder. He'd been the Devil's assassin. If Lucifer lost his temper would Japh be able to get me out of here alive? I certainly hoped so. The entire temple vibrated with Lucifer's anger, stone groaning and air swirling, freighted with a soundless fiery static. One of the pews cracked down the middle, the sound loud as a gunshot. I didn't jump—but it was close.

Damn close.

"I would not have, if your service had not been exceptional." Lucifer bit off the edges of the words. Then he darted a look at me, and I would have sworn his green eyes lit up with *glee*. The Power cloaking him swirled once, spread out to haze through the cathedral. "Well, Dante. What do you think of your Fallen now?"

I waited for Japhrimel to warn me not to reply, but he did nothing, standing curiously still. I cleared my throat. "I trust him a *hell* of a lot more than I trust *you.*" That, at least, was unequivocally true.

That made the Devil's eyes light up. Was he actually looking mischievous? Wonders never ceased.

Then again, the Devil in a mood to play with his prey was not something I ever wanted to see, either. I was suddenly fiercely glad I wasn't completely physically human anymore, for the very first time. A human would never have been able to stand the welter of razor-toothed Power in the air or the way Lucifer's eyes suddenly drifted down to touch my throat. My heart gave an unsteady leap.

"Well-matched, the pair of you. Very well, Tierce Japhrimel. Seven years, full control, and my protection sworn on my own ineffable Name for the miserable Necromance, for eternity. I accept your other terms." His voice was brittle as glass. "Is there aught else?"

I could have left it there. I *should* have, Japhrimel's arm tightened around me. But I couldn't help myself. "Eve," I said.

Lucifer's entire body tensed. "Be very careful," he warned me, in a chill, beautiful, hurtful voice. "You do not know what you say."

I cleared my throat. If the Devil truly needed me, I had a way to erase at least one name from my long list of failures. "Freedom for Doreen's daughter, Lucifer. That's *my* condition, on top of Japhrimel's." My lips skinned back from my teeth. There comes a point past which terror gives you a crazy type of courage; maybe I'd reached it.

His eyes blazed. He took a single step forward, the shadows in the cathedral suddenly pulling close, red eyes glowing in the dimness, the susurrus of flame or wings beating in the vaulted space.

I didn't see Japhrimel move, but he was suddenly a little in front of me, his shoulder pushing me aside and back. That put him mostly between me and the Devil, and my heart thumped sickly against my ribs at the thought of him facing down Lucifer. "Enough, Prince." His voice cut through the thunderstorm of Power. "Have we reached agreement?"

"Seven years. Full control. Protection for *her*. And you,

Japhrimel, restored to your place of pride in the Greater Flight. I agree."

My heart slammed into my throat. I couldn't help myself. I looked up at Japhrimel, who was utterly still, pale under his golden skin. *What the fuck?* The full meaning of the words slammed home.

"Done." Japhrimel's jaw tightened after the word. His eyes flared, angular green runic shapes sliding through the darkness.

"Done," Lucifer repeated. His eyes turned to me.

Oh, gods. Gods, no. He's going back to Hell, I thought numbly. *What did he just do? But Eve—*

"I am waiting for your agreement, Necromance." Lucifer's voice turned silky. "I counsel you to take this bargain; it is the best you will receive from me."

"Done," I said, tonelessly, shocked. I had no choice— Japhrimel had already agreed, and if I pushed it, he might not be able to keep Lucifer from ripping me a new spleen or two.

Trust me, Dante. Do not doubt me.

The first rule of dealing with nonhumans: their idea of *truth* isn't the same as ours. Maybe Japh had grown tired of hanging out with a damaged human, maybe I'd pushed him too hard. He'd maneuvered me into agreeing, played me neatly as a synthesizer. Eve's freedom wasn't a part of the bargain.

It hit me again, like a thunder-roll after lightning. Japhrimel was going home to Hell for a while, and I was sold to the Devil for seven years.

Great.

Lucifer's elegant lip lifted in a sneer. "Send her away, Tierce Japhrimel. I will wait."

I didn't struggle, but Japhrimel had to drag me away, my boots scraping the floor. The last I saw of Lucifer, he had turned back to the altar, his golden hand resting on the rail again. His black-clad back rippled, as if some force streamed away from him. "Fools," he hissed, and I wondered if he meant humans in general, or demons, or just me.

10

Japhrimel closed the cathedral door behind us, hauling me into the smoky dark of a Venizia night as if I weighed nothing. The whine of hovercells settled against my bones again, not only because of the city but because a sleek black hoverlimo was now waiting, a plasteel stepladder flowing down from the side entrance to touch the cathedral's steps.

Oh, look. Mad glee bubbled hot and acid in my throat. *The boys send Dante home in style. Pack the human off until we need to use her again.*

"Go home," Japhrimel said. "Wait for me."

"Wait for what? You're coming back?" I asked numbly. Or maybe I just thought it, a roaring filled my head. My bag bumped my hip, and I was glad I'd suited up. If I'd had to deal with this without my weapons I would have started to scream. "Wait a second—*Japhrimel*—" My fingers tightened around the sword. If I drew it now, what would he do? What could *I* do?

"There is no time for explanations, Dante. Do as I say."

"You asked to go back to Hell? Is that what happened?

Are you coming back?" This time I was sure I'd spoken, but I didn't recognize the small, wounded voice as mine.

He made a short sound of annoyance and dragged me down the steps. Something hard and clawed rose in my throat, I closed my teeth against it. Denied it.

I'm not *going to cry. It doesn't hurt. I am not going to cry. It doesn't hurt.*

Number one rule for anyone who practices magick, *don't ever lie to yourself.* I knew, with miserable clarity, that I was breaking that rule. "You *bastard.* Are you going back to Hell? For how long? What's going on? At least say it out loud if you're not coming back, at least *tell* me, the least you could do is *tell* me—" Instead of sounding angry, I only sounded tired. Curious numbness spread through my chest. Numbness like metal must feel when a blowtorch kisses it.

Japhrimel stopped. He caught my shoulders, and before I could back up he pressed a hard, closed kiss on my mouth. I would have struggled, would have tried to break free, but his hands were like steel claws.

"*Listen* to me." His voice held none of the plasgun-charge of Power he'd used inside. Instead, he sounded carefully restrained, almost human. His eyes were full of green sparks, dancing in their depths like fireflies. "I will come for you. I will *always* come for you. Wait for me at home, do *not* open the door to anyone. I will be with you soon. Now *go.*"

What could I say to that? I simply stared at him, my fingers nerveless-tight around my sword.

He shoved me up the steps and into the hover. "Go, and wait for me," he repeated, then leapt back down from the steps. I collapsed on the pleather seat, all the strength running out of my legs. The door closed, I heard the whine-rattle of the hovercells beginning to take on flight frequency.

What just happened in there? If he goes back to Hell and leaves me alone, how long will I last against four Greater Flight demons? What did he really ask Lucifer for? I thought he couldn't go back! The thought rose like bad gas in a reactive-painted shaft. I let out a choked sound that rattled the glasses in the rack over the wet bar.

The driver didn't speak. I wondered for a lunatic moment if it was one of Hell's human agents or just autopilot.

He's going back to Hell. For how long? When will he come back? Soon, he said. What's a demon's idea of soon?

Abandoned. Again. All my life I've been left behind— by parents, lovers, friends. I'd thought this time was different. Would I *ever* learn?

I scooted over as the hover rose, pressed my forehead to the window. I had one glimpse of Japhrimel, his face upturned like a golden dish, standing on the cathedral steps and watching as the hover rose into the night sky. His black coat fell down, melded with the shadow lying over the steps, then he was gone.

Vanished. Back into the cathedral.

Back to Lucifer.

Back to Hell.

I collapsed back against the seat. The trembling got worse, running through my bones like hoverwhine.

"Gods," I breathed, and closed my eyes.

It wasn't numbness burning cold inside my chest.

It was a pain so immense I immediately drove my

fingernails of my left hand into my palm, squeezing my hand with every erg of demon-given strength. My rings popped and snapped, a shower of golden sparks filling the air. Panic. I was panicking. *Stop it. Ride the pain, Dante; come back, get a grip on yourself. Get a goddamn grip. You're alive. You're still alive.*

For how long? The smell of my own black blood rose to assault my nose. I opened my eyes, lifted my blood-slick hand, dragged it back over my hair to wipe it clean. The nasty ragged half-moon marks from my claws sealed themselves away, closed seamlessly.

The hover banked, turning to go over land. So I wasn't going to be dumped in the sea.

Good to know.

As soon as I realized the thin keening sound was coming from me, I swallowed it. The hole in my chest got bigger. The mark on my shoulder flared with heat, one last caress burning all the way down my body. I'd lived without Japh for a little under a year last time, when he was ash in a black lacquer urn, waiting for me to figure out how to resurrect him. I *never* wanted to do that again. It hurt too goddamn much.

I moved again on the seat, and paper rustled.

What the hell?

I looked down. There was a brown-paper package on the seat I was sure hadn't been there before.

"Well," I said out loud. "That was interesting." My voice broke.

I will always come for you. Don't open the door.

"Gods." Seven years, was that what I'd agreed to? Seven years of working for the Devil. Not just a hunt like last time. Lucifer was probably sitting in Hell right now laughing his immortal ass off. Seven years of working for the Devil, and if Japhrimel went back to being in Hell where did that leave me? Was I going to turn back into a human, without him around? Would I like it? I hoped the process wasn't too painful.

Goddammit, Dante, wake up. You saw the Devil again and lived through it. You should throw a party. A big one. With lots of booze. Fireworks. And a goddamn military marching band.

Only who would show up? Who would even care?

I reached down with shaking fingers and touched the package. It was tied with twine, wrapped in brown paper, bigger than my clenched fist. I picked it up as if dreaming.

The twine and paper fell away.

It was a wristcuff made out of oddly heavy silver metal. Etched into its surface was a complicated pattern that reminded me of a Shaman's accreditation tattoo, thorns and flowing lines twisting through each other. The inside was smooth and blank except for two daggered marks that looked like fangs. It had the slightly alien geometry of something demon-made.

Great. A party favor? An afterthought? What was this?

I touched the cuff with one finger, feeling smooth silver. I traced one etched line.

Oh, what the hell. Nothing can get any worse. I winced at the thought—thinking that was the surest way for some new and interesting twist of awfulness to show up. Any Magi-trained psion knows better than to tempt Fate, even if only inside one's own head.

I picked it up, slid it around my left wrist, twisting

so the open part of the cuff lay upward, the flat demon-carved surface along the underside of my arm. It settled against my skin as if it belonged there, a little higher than my datband. It looked barbaric—I've never been one for jewelry, despite my rings. I like all my accessories to have lethal capability.

He knew I wanted Eve free. He knew it. Why did he back away from pressing for Eve? What did he really say to Lucifer? Why did he ask to go back to Hell? Does that mean he's tired of me? He said he would come back. Even told me to lock the doors at home.

Home. Like it's home without him.

Had he wanted to be free of me? Had all the presents just been a way to tell me so?

Sekhmet sa'es. I was even disgusting myself. If he wanted to break up with me, there were better ways of doing it. He'd given me presents because he wanted to. *You know him, Danny. He'll come back.*

But what then? I hadn't the faintest.

"Gods," I whispered. "Anubis. *Anubis et'her ka. Se ta'uk'fhet sa te vapu kuraph.*" The prayer rose out of me with the ease of long repetition. *Anubis et'her ka. Anubis, Lord of the Dead, Faithful Companion, protect me, for I am Your child. Protect me, Anubis, weigh my heart upon the scale; watch over me, Lord, for I am Your child. Do not let evil distress me, but turn Your fierceness upon my enemies. Cover me with Your gaze, let Your hand be upon me, now and all the days of my life, until You take me into Your embrace.*

I crumpled the paper in my fist and tossed it across the hover, a passionlessly accurate throw. Sparks popped from my rings again.

Japhrimel gone back into Hell, to return as gods-only-knew-what, gods-only-knew-when. And me, sent home to wait for further orders, and working for the Devil again.

To hell with tempting Fate. "It can't get any worse," I said out loud, and curled up, bracing my heels against the edge of the soft cushioned seat. My bag shifted and clinked against my side. I wrapped my arms around my legs, buried my face in my knees, and struggled to stop hyperventilating.

It took a while.

11

The house was still, dark, and silent. The hoverlimo let me off on the landing pad; clearly it was on autopilot. As soon as I jumped down from the side hatch, my boots thudding on concrete treated to look like flat white marble, the whine of hovercells crested and the sleek black gleaming vehicle rose, circled the house once, and drifted away very slowly, far more slowly than it had carried me home.

I stood, and shut my eyes. A Toscano summer night folded around me, warm and soft, the kind of night I could spend in the library, my eyes glued to the page. Or a night I could spend curled against Japhrimel's side in the comfort of our bed, listening to his quiet voice as he told me stories of demons and history, sometimes true, sometimes only rumors. My own voice would answer his, a lighter counterpoint, and sometimes a soft laugh would break the silence.

No more. Lucifer had stopped all that.

I set my shoulders, walked down the steps between the masses of fragrant rosemary growing on either side. The flagstone path to the front door was there, dark and inviting. *Stay inside, don't answer the door, wait for me.* But for how long?

I was grateful none of the servants were there, especially Emilio. Japhrimel must have quietly and efficiently taken care of sending them away, maybe guessing he wouldn't be back tonight.

Did he want to go home? What the hell does Lucifer need me *for, if Japh's going back to Hell?* I shook the thought away, it was useless. What the Devil wanted, the Devil got, and he wanted both of us for some reason.

I pushed open the front door. The security net recognized my datband and genescan; the shields—Japhrimel's careful demon-laid work and my own trademark Necromance shields, layers of energy rippling over the place we called home—parted to let me through.

The mark on my shoulder was quiescent, not throbbing in time to Japh's heartbeat or burning with his attention to me. I did not reach up to touch it. If he was in Hell, I didn't want to see through his eyes. I just hoped the awful empty feeling in my chest would go away sometime soon.

I made my way through silent halls and death-quiet rooms, my bootheels clicking against marble or sinking into rugs. I tried not to look at any room Japhrimel might have walked through. *Gods, Danny, can't you just calm down? Just wait for him. He'll be back. You know he will.*

Most of me knew he would. A small, critical, half-buried part of me still wasn't so sure. The part of me that trusted no one, believed no one; the hard, cold streak of stubborn doubt I hated myself for. I was always waiting for someone to hurt me, maybe because most of the people I'd loved or trusted—or who had power over me,

especially when I was a child—had either died or misused
my trust. Betrayed me. Hurt me.

Abandoned me.

I finally reached the double doors. Pushed them open,
gently. They whispered across the floor.

The long room, dappled with low light, looked just the
same. I paced down the middle of the floor, put my palms
together, and bowed slightly to Jace's sword. *Why the hell
am I in here? What am I doing?*

The sword rang softly, a slow low song of distress
from the death of its owner still reverberating in the steel.
I wondered sometimes if the shards of my old katana,
rusting in frigid ocean depths with rotting bits of Santino, sang with the same aching agony. Only I hadn't died,
just been crippled—and lost Japhrimel as well as my own
humanity.

I reached up with my free hand, touching the slim,
hard shapes of silver-dipped raccoon baculum. The protections wedded to the necklace hummed and shifted, a
gentle touch closing around me. Between the necklace,
the cuff, and my rings, I was beginning to feel quite the
fashion holoplate.

*I have been here, asking the ghost of a human man
for forgiveness. And wondering why he has more of your
heart than I do.*

Did he really think that? Had he really thought I was
that petty or disloyal? I *had* loved Jace. Loved him and
been unable to touch him, unable to return his own affection for me. He had been one of the last links to the person
I was before Rio, before I'd ended up half-demon and tied
to Lucifer's assassin.

I'd loved him. But I *needed* Japhrimel, the way I'd never needed Jace.

"I'm doing okay with this," I said out loud to the dim dappled half-light and the twisted, blackened sword's moan of agony. My voice startled me, I almost jumped. My heart settled into a fast high pounding. *Japhrimel. Japh. Where are you now, what are you doing? How long am I going to wait here?*

"As long as it takes." My voice startled me again. I shook my head, the thick braided rope of my hair bumping against my back. My fingers gentled on the scabbard, losing a bit of white-knuckled panic. I took a deep breath, turned on my heel, and stopped dead.

A shadow melded with the gloom at the other end of the room. My heart hammered, leaping wildly. I tasted copper.

Blue eyes glittered. A shock of golden hair—gone. The dust in the air swirled, coalesced into a thorn-twisted Shaman tattoo before a stray breath of air smashed through the delicate pattern. I knew that tat as well as I knew my own, as well as I knew Gabe's.

"Gods," I whispered. A breath of warm night wind blew through the room.

Stop it. You're imagining things. You're in shock. You've just had a nasty experience and you're wishing someone, anyone was here. Quit imagining. That's deadly, for a Necromance to start hallucinating.

But the air was full of the scent of tamales, and blood— and the smell of midnight ice and wet ratfur.

Chills rilled up my spine. My right hand blurred to my swordhilt, and I drew the blade free in one fluid motion. Blue fire began to flow along the metal's edge, dappling the floor with reflections as the sword slanted slightly up in first guard, the position so habitual and natural I barely realized I'd drawn steel.

The smell of tamales and blood and Power was Nuevo Rio, Jace's hometown. But the other smell gagged me, made my hackles rise and a thin gleam of light jet from the emerald set in my cheek. The tattoo shifted under my skin, my cheek burning. My rings boiled with sparks for a moment, gold spangles drifting down to touch the floor and wink out.

Ice and wet ratfur was the scent of a demon I'd indisputably killed, with a huge helping of luck and a lot of berserker rage. I'd torn through his throat, plunged the shards of my blade through his heart, and shredded what muck remained of him into the ocean, that great cleanser. Japhrimel had assured me Vardimal was completely dead.

Of all the times to be haunted by a dead demon, it just has to happen when Japh's not here to help.

Rage rose up inside me, a red sheet of fury crackling along my skin, popping sparks off the edge of my blade. I lifted the scabbard in my left hand, held along my forearm with about three inches protruding from my fist for striking at an enemy's vulnerable point. I lowered myself slightly, almost crouching, my back to the wall behind the ebony table. I slid along the wall, backed into the corner, and waited.

The most nerve-racking part of any attack is the waiting—for both attacker and defender. Once Jado and I had held our positions across the tatami mats of his sparring room for a good half an hour, neither of us moving except to blink. I am never the most patient of fighters, preferring to attack and turn the enemy's incipent force back on itself—but that didn't mean I *had* to attack.

Quite frankly, right now I didn't feel in my best fighting shape. I felt like my heart had been ripped out and stabbed—my eyes blurring with tears and my chest aching with swallowed sobs. I *missed* him, a horrible sinking feeling of missing him boiling up inside my chest.

I heard the whine of hovercells too. Was someone coming to visit me?

Take a number, I'm busy with another enemy. Japh told me to stay inside, am I going to have to fight a guerilla action inside my own house?

Cold fury dilated inside me, blue light sliding over the walls, lighting the long room clearly. I inhaled again, filled my lungs. The smell had disappeared—both the smell of Nuevo Rio and the smell of Santino/Vardimal.

It isn't Santino. I killed Santino. It's something like Santino maybe, or something playing a trick on me.

The outer edges of my shielding thinned. Nothing could get in here, could it? Not through Japhrimel's shields. Not through mine.

Right?

Japh told you to come here. He insisted on it. He wouldn't have done that unless it was safe. Right?

Of all the times to have a thought like that, now was the worst.

Settle down, Danny, a soft male voice I never thought I'd hear again said inside my head. *Don't second-guess yourself. You smelled it, and your body knows what's up. Just stay put a minute, just wait.*

It was good advice, even if it came from a dead man. Fine time to think of Jace Monroe now, wasn't it?

I waited, my heartbeats thudding off time. Premonition itched under my skin. I wasn't at all sure the house was a safe place to be right now. After all, *someone* had to know we were living here. Being where your enemy expects you is not good tactics.

Why would he tell me to wait here, then? He was very clear about it.

I saw it as the whine of hovercells returned more loudly; a shadow flitting along the window—*outside*. Too quick to track even for my demon-acute eyes, but I was already moving, even as the shields shivered under an assault that threatened to throw me to my knees with the backlash. I let out a short cry, pumping available Power from the reserves below the house and a generous portion of demon Power into a flare that knocked whatever-it-was off. Had to be physical, no magickal assault would feel quite so thumpingly real.

Japhrimel had told me to stay inside, but if someone crashed a hover into the house I didn't want to stick around to see it.

No route like the short route. I gathered myself and leapt. The crash and tinkle of breaking plasglass filled the air, I landed cat-silent, cat-quick, and streaked along the wall of the house, making for the corner. It was a relief to have something to fight at last.

I rounded the corner and saw it, a low black vaguely humanoid shape moving with blurring speed. I let out a short, sharp curse just as it twisted away from the wall of the house, which was resonating like a struck bell, stone singing with the stress of the Power wedded to it *stretching*. Another magickal attack, and I'd gotten out of the house just in time. The shields sang a low feedback squeal

I didn't like at all, the night suddenly alive with half-heard chittering and shrieking. I heard a terrible glassy growl float from the front of the house just as the shields shuddered from that direction, taking another massive impact and going hard and crystalline, locking down.

The thing I was chasing bolted across the field on the west side of the house. I jabbed my left hand forward as I ran, making a complicated nonphysical gesture. The bloodstone ring on my left third finger shot a single bolt of thin red light. I'd sunk four or five trackers into this ring, little runespells meant to latch onto a bounty, an unshakeable magickal bloodhound. I was secondarily talented as a runewitch, able to use the runes of the Nine Canons with more accuracy and ease than most; I could make my own trackers rather than buying them from a Shaman or a Skinlin dirtwitch.

I gathered myself and hurtled forward, following the thin smear of red light, using every iota of demon speed. Heard the whining sound as the tracker slammed home. Then, something *shifted*.

POW!

There was a massive sound like every bell in the world struck at once. I dropped to my knees, all speed gone. Reflex took over, earthed the Power, red crackling along my skin in rippled lines. The Power meridians along my skin burned, subsided as I shook my head, my hair slipping forward over my shoulders. My braid had come loose. I sat there on my knees, blinking, my sword gone dark since I no longer needed it.

The thing, whatever it was, had done something...strange. Just popped out of existence and thrown the tracker back at me.

Nothing human could do that. The trackers were meant to hang on to even a combat-trained human psion. I should have been able to follow that thing to the ends of the earth.

We're not dealing with earthly things here, Danny. Get with the program, will you?

I levered myself to my feet, reflexively. If I'd still been human, the backlash would have knocked me out, possibly even burned me physically along my Power meridians. As it was, I shook the stunning sound out of my head, gained my feet, and took a deep breath, my almost-demon body taking a split second to deal with the burning from the snapped tracker. I cocked my head. "What the bloody blue *fuck*?" I barely even realized I was whispering aloud.

The whine of hovercells crested with an abused squeal of antigrav, and a massive shattering sound slammed into me. I was tied to the shields on the house, so I felt a sharp pain, like a tooth yanked from its socket, as the layers of energy, both mine and Japhrimel's, imploded. It would take unimaginable force to break those shields, even with both Japhrimel and me away. Only one thing could supply that kind of force.

Well, two, actually. A god, which was unlikely—gods just don't attack people like that. They have other ways to make their displeasure known.

Or a demon. If presented with a choice like that I wouldn't even lay odds on it; there wasn't any point.

This just keeps getting better.

I sheathed my sword again, and turned to look back at the house just as fire lanced the sky.

For the second time in as many minutes, my legs spilled

out from under me. A white-hot column of flame boiled up from the house.

Holy shit. I laid on my side as the shockwave rolled over me. *That's reactive and plas!* Blood slid from my nose in a painless gush, my body trying to cope with this new demand. I waited for the aftershock, half my face tingling where it was exposed to the scorching air. The smell of cooking grass simmered in my nose, I felt another wave of fruitless rage rise up.

Jace's sword. My altar. My books. Goddammit. Heat boiled over me, then aid hovers began to wail in the distance.

My brain started to work again.

Someone had just seriously tried to kill me.

Lucifer, or one of the demons he said he wanted me to hunt? Which would mean they already know the Devil's hired me—which means I'm not going to survive for long without Japhrimel around.

Four of the Greater Flight of Hell, and I'm Lucifer's new little errand girl. All on my own, without Japhrimel. Who told me to stay in the fucking house and get killed. Goddammit. I spared myself one grim smile and shook my head, rolling onto my stomach and bringing myself up to hands and knees, my sheathed sword braced against the earth in my left hand.

I made it to my feet in two tries. There's a limit to what even my body can handle. If Japhrimel's return to Hell and reclaiming his place as a demon undid my change and made me human again, I was looking at a very short, exceedingly uncomfortable lifespan.

The mark on my left shoulder tingled faintly. I closed

my eyes against a wave of dizziness. Then I patted myself down.

Bag, knives, gun, plasgun, sword. Everything there. Including all my fingers. Hallelujah.

I looked at the inferno my home had become, suddenly glad none of the servants had been there. The stone itself was warping and twisting, the structure of the marble weakened by the interaction of reactive and plas fields, the very molecular bonds broken down. This was why you never discharge a plasgun near reactive, why shooting a plasgun at a hover isn't used even as an assassination technique. The interaction of reactive paint and a plasfield creates a chain reaction that propagates at roughly half the speed of light, burning and warping molecular bonds, leaving giant scars on the earth unless contained and decontaminated. Even after that, the effects linger in living things, trees grow brittle and other plants wither and die. It's a hugely messy way to kill someone, but pretty effective if you don't care about being fined for contamination and ecological irresponsibility.

And if you were pretty sure *you* could outrun the shockwave.

"Anubis," I breathed. My statue of the god, the obsidian statue of Sekhmet Japhrimel had given me, Jace's sword—probably gone. Had the vision of a dead Shaman been a warning, one my god knew I would heed? "Thank you, Lord Death," I whispered. "For saving my life."

The first of the aid hovers from Arrieto crested the rise, lights flashing. I looked around for cover. They would dump plurifreeze on the flames to keep them from spreading and damp the reaction field, then stamp out any grass fires. I didn't think any of the attackers would stick around after this, they would think they'd trapped me when the house shields went into lockdown. Gods alone knew what had been loosed inside the house when the shields broke, the reaction fire consuming all evidence and mopping me up if I'd survived.

Wait in the house, don't answer the door. As advice goes, Japh, that was terrible.

I faded into a small stand of olive trees, leaning against one, my hand resting on warm bark. There would be a scar on this hillside until the plant life recovered from stresses in cellular structure caused by the reaction and the heat. More glowing aid hovers crested the hill, some of them already beginning to release a fine silvery mist of plurifreeze. Decontamination from a reaction fire this big would take a while, two days at least. The books Japh had bought me were gone, and gods alone knew if anything else might survive. It wasn't likely.

I blew out through my teeth, my free hand coming up to touch the necklace. If his sword was destroyed, this was all that was left of Jace except his ashes, kept safely in Gabe Spocarelli's family mausoleum as a favor to me.

Anger rose in me, sharp and hot. Useless fury that I had to turn into cold clarity if I expected to get out of this mess alive.

I didn't even know who was trying to kill me yet. The list of suspects was getting longer by the hour.

Stay in the house. Lock the doors.

Yeah. Right.

I sighed, gauged the distance between me and the aid hovers, and disappeared into the night.

12

The first train I could catch from the station rocketed across the landscape on its cushion of antigrav, part of a rail network so old the banks on either side of the tracks have risen to overshadow the sleek trains in some places. That bounced the antigrav back at itself and made everything feel queer and light, but it was a quick way for me to get out of Toscano and to a major Hegemony city—in this case, the great hub of Franjlyon. Once in a big city, I was confident I could hide—but out in the Historical Preserve I stood out like a black-market augment at a Ludder convention.

In Franjlyon I could catch transport for anywhere and start plugging into the bounty-hunter network. If I could find a few Magi, I might have a fighting chance of staying alive for a little while; I also had a fighting chance of staying out of sight for a few days. If I could find a Magi—circle or solitary—I could persuade to part with a few trade secrets, my chances would get even better. Screw decoding old shadowjournals. I wanted to find out what I was and if I would turn back into a human once Japh was a full demon instead of *A'nankhimel*.

I was getting to the point of not being too choosy about how I extracted that information, either.

I settled myself deeper into my seat, wishing I could find a way to make the carriage a little darker. I wasn't exactly inconspicuous, with the tat on my cheek, the emerald glittering there too, my sword and guns, and the flawless lovely architecture of my face. I had grown a little more used to seeing a holovid model's face in the mirror, but it was still a horrendous jolt if I wasn't ready for it. Lots of normals did double- and triple-takes, as if I was a holovid star gone slumming. Or as if I was a psion. Ha ha.

It wasn't so much the overlay of demon beauty that bothered me. It was that every time I caught sight of my face in the mirror, I had a weird double image—my old human face, tired and familiar but *changed*, turned into loveliness even I had trouble looking at. I hated even catching glimpses of myself in windows, like I was doing now.

I focused out the window, seeing nothing but strips of orandflu lighting and the meaningless smear that was the ghost of my face. Orange stripes blurred together, telling me the hovertrain was gliding along with no trouble at all in the reactive-greased furrow we still called "tracks" even though no train had run on tracks since about twenty years after the discovery of reactive and antigrav.

That's great, Danny. Think about historical trivia instead of how you're going to stay alive past tomorrow. If demons are looking for you, the world gets really small really quick, and I'm not exactly inconspicuous. I even smell like a demon—good luck hiding.

Nobody else was in the compartment. I'd been alone

since I boarded the train. Not many tourists took the red-eye from Turin Station to Franjlyon.

My eyes dropped to the silver cuff on my left wrist. It sank into my skin, and the gap between the curved ends seemed smaller. I couldn't believe I'd fit even my wrist through there. When I'd been human my wrists had been big, corded with muscle from years of daily sword drill. Now they were thinner, looking frail even though they held a great deal of strength in their flawlessly powerful demon bones and claw structure.

The cuff felt good, though my left hand was frozen around my scabbard. I reached over with my right hand, touched the fluid etched lines. It was beautiful. Japhrimel had never given me an ugly present. Was it from him, or was it something I shouldn't have picked up? One of Lucifer's little jokes?

I wondered if it was a tracking device. But it felt so impossibly right, snugged against my wrist as if made for me. I couldn't quite bring myself to take it off, despite the uneasy idea that perhaps the bracelet was *growing* closed around my wrist.

I looked out the window again. Rested my head against the back of the seat. The black demon blood I'd wiped in my hair smelled like perfumed fruit, absorbing back into black silky strands.

The trouble with traveling like this was that I had too much time to brood.

I sat there mulling over the situation and not coming up with anything fresh for a good two hours. The train bulleted through a mountain tunnel, the peculiar directionless sense of being underground raising my hackles. I needed a quiet stationary room and some time to myself—and some food. I was beginning to feel a little strange, light-headed, as if I was going into shock. The world was going gray, color leaching out of the orange strips outside the window, the blue pleather seat across from me losing its shine, a sort of fuzz creeping over my vision.

I closed my eyes but that made it worse.

The train rocketed out from under the mountain, and the mark on my shoulder began to tingle.

There was no sound but the whining lull of the train and a faraway murmur of other minds, *human* minds full of the random stink of normal human psyches. I reached up with my right hand, touched the mark through my shirt, rubbed at it. If I touched it with my bare fingers I would see out Japhrimel's eyes. It was very, very tempting—though if I looked out his eyes and into Hell, would I come away from the experience quite sane?

The thought that the scar might burn off my skin if he became a demon again was unpleasant, to say the least. I racked my brain for demon sigils and magickal theory but couldn't come up with anything that applied even vaguely. I didn't have a clue what would happen, and that was uncomfortable. To say the least.

I blindly trusted him the same way I'd blindly trusted Jace. But Jace had been human...and Jace had ended up giving up his life for me. Japhrimel had given up his power as a demon, shackling himself to me, and there was a time when I could have sworn he didn't care.

Maybe going back into Hell without me last night had made him care again. The more I thought about it, the more I wondered.

How quaint. I'm pretty much a dismal failure at rela-tionships with two species now.

No. He'd said he would come back. He had promised. I was just going to have to wait and see.

Wonderful. My favorite kind of magickal riddle: one where you just sit and wait for the unpleasantness to begin.

I wasn't an idiot. I knew I had trust issues. Plenty of bounty hunters do. You don't go into bounty hunting without being a little paranoid, and if you survive you get even more paranoid. My parents had left me before I was ten days old, my social worker had left me for Death's country, my friends—when I made them at all—either betrayed me or died as well. Except for Gabe.

Always excepting Gabe.

And let's not even talk about my lovers. I'm overreacting. Who wouldn't overreact, when Lucifer starts playing with them? Japhrimel will come back, Dante. He promised.

Still, I wondered. I *doubted*.

I rubbed at my shoulder through my shirt, rubbed it and rubbed it. The buzzing, prickling tingle in the mark intensified.

Then it gave one incredible, crunching flare of pain that ate right through the gray blanket of shock. I sat bolt upright, four inches of steel leaping free of the sheath, disappearing as I shoved the sword back home. There was no enemy to kill here—just one flare after another of deep grinding pain in my shoulder.

What if the mark vanishes? What will I do then? I tried to focus on my breathing, deep and serene.

The trouble was, I felt less than serene. My entire body ached for Japhrimel. I knew I wouldn't be able to sleep; in fact, I'd probably go insane from lack of rest. I'd survived almost a year without him before, but the bond between us was too established by now. My research, fragmented as it was, told me one thing for sure, *I* certainly couldn't break it.

But with a demon's power, *he* might be able to.

Will you stop it, Dante? He'll come back for you. It's just when *we have to worry about.*

The pain in my shoulder eased little by little. I tucked my chin, reached up, and pulled my shirt away from my chest. Ropy lines of scarring twisted in the golden-skinned hollow of my shoulder, looking decorative rather than scarlike. They also flushed a deep, angry red.

An amazing, searing bolt of Power hit the mark, spreading down my skin like oil. My hips jerked forward as my head snapped aside and I gasped, suddenly glad there was nobody in the compartment with me. The hovertrain rocked slightly on its cushion, I gulped down stale recycled air, panting. It felt like I'd just slammed a hypo of caffeine-laden aphrodisiac, pleasure spilling and swirling through my veins, tautening my body like a harpstring.

The cuff on my wrist reacted, etched lines suddenly swirling with green light. I tipped my left hand over and stared at the design, fascinated, as the lines moved on the metal, shaping themselves into patterns I could almost recognize. They looked like demon glyphs, mutating and twisting, as beautiful as they were alien—and as beautiful as their language was hurtful.

What's it doing? I probed at it delicately with my non-physical senses, felt nothing. Was it just a decoration, a pretty but useless thing? If it kept glowing I was going to have problems—it would be hard to hide.

I tipped into a half-trance, looking at the colored lines

sway and slide over the metal's surface, still probing at it. For all magickal intents and purposes, it was invisible. That in itself was strange, as most things have a psychic "echo" of one kind or another.

The Power continued pulsing down my skin, each successive wave deeper and warmer. It was nice, I supposed—but *why?* Was Japhrimel reaching for his mark on my skin, trying to locate me? Did that mean he was out of Hell and feeling frisky?

I will always come for you.

Was he looking for me? I hoped like hell he was. But staying one step ahead of demon assassins might also make it hard for him to find me.

This drowsy, dreamy thought occurred to me as I stared at the cuff's little lightshow. I blinked.

When I looked again, the lines were frozen into a single symbol.

Hegethusz, one of the Nine Canons. Shaped like a backward-leaning angular H with a slash through it, a simple stark rune of a simple stark nature.

The Rune of Danger.

There was only one door. I rocked up to my feet, reached it in two steps and slid it aside, pressing the lock-lever. Any transport employee would have the keycode for the outside lock, so it would be easy to pick out of an unprotected brain. Just one more reason why people feared psions. If you didn't mind getting a wash of uncoordinated jumbled filth with any usable information, a psion could probably do all the things normals were so afraid of. The thought of the effort it would take to clean out my mind after pickpocketing something from a normal's head made my skin crawl.

The corridor between the windows on the other side of the train and the blank plasteel walls broken by doors into individual compartments was barely wide enough for an anorexic techna-groupie to get through. I turned my back to the windows—I was fairly sure any incoming fire wouldn't be coming from there, we were going too fast—and stuffed my sword in the loop on my rig. The corridor was too narrow for swordplay, and if I had to do knifework I didn't want to do it here.

So it was guns. I slid the two projectile guns out of their holsters. A plasbolt might interact with any reactive paint on the outside of the hovertrain, and I had no desire to see another reaction fire up close. I was glad the train was all but empty. Collateral damage was *not* something I wanted happening if I could help it. Silly of me to worry—demons were sneaky, powerful, and not overly concerned with loss of human life. I was already playing under a handicap and worrying about casualties would make it worse.

I edged down the train toward the back, one gun on either side, my arms stretched out. If any normals came out I was going to look silly—and if anything else showed up I would shoot it. *Please don't let anyone out. Let them all stay in their compartments. If I have to shoot please don't let me hit anyone innocent, Anubis witness my plea, please don't let me hit anyone.*

The mark on my shoulder pulsed again, another soft wave of Power sliding down my skin, burrowing in toward my bones. Why? What was happening?

I couldn't afford to holster a gun and reach up to touch the mark. If he could track me through the scar, could another demon do so too? I shone through the ambient landscape of Power like a demon myself, but without the heavy-duty shielding Japhrimel carried. Stuck between two worlds, too strong for human psions and too weak to combat demons, I was just powerful enough to be visible and not powerful enough to protect myself if a serious demon came gunning for me. And this was the second attack in twelve hours.

I was really racking up the score in this gravball game.

My feet shuffling soundlessly, I covered both ends of the train, looking back and forth, wishing I had eyestalks like the Chery Family bodyguards were all augmented with. It would have been good to be able to see both ways at once.

I felt it, then. A quick fluttering brush against my shields, retreating almost as soon as it occurred. Training took over, clamped down on my hindbrain as adrenaline flooded my system. Too much adrenal juice and I'd be a jittery mess. Other trained mental reflexes locked down the direction, complex metaphysical calculations and intuition all slicing in an arc that pinpointed the location.

That smell again—ice-cold moonlight, wet ratfur—assaulted my nostrils. The thing that had thrown my tracker and disappeared—or something that smelled like it—was now on the train. Probably just appearing out of thin air, the way demons had a nasty habit of doing that according to the demonology texts. Especially the Lesser and Low Flights. The Greater Flight liked more dramatic entrances.

At least some of my grueling, piecemeal demonology research was now useful. I knew that some demons could send the Lesser or Low Flight of Hell to do their bidding in the human world. If the demon had enough Power...or if the demon was given permission by Lucifer.

Lucifer's permission was invoked before every conjuration a Magi solitary or circle attempted to bring a demon through, and I got the idea from Japhrimel that there was a bureaucracy in place to handle the requests. Since Magi were traditionally so jealous of the methods they found to weaken the walls between the world and Hell to get their messages through, it sometimes it took years for the proper method to be found to reach a demon one could control or make a familiar. No Magi ever attempted to contact more than the very lowest echelons of the Lesser Flight. If a Greater Flight demon showed up in a Magi's conjuring circle, the practitioner was either especially lucky or incredibly painfully doomed.

Most likely the latter.

Demons weren't under that type of restriction. It was thought fairly easy for a Greater Flight demon to bring a Lesser Flight demon through, and even easier for them to bring one of the Low Flight.

Which all added up to bad news for Danny Valentine.

I turned my back to the rear of the hovertrain. Backed up one slow step at a time, the guns held steady, pointed down the front of the corridor, Power beginning to glow in my hands. The bullets alone might not do much against whatever this thing was, but hot lead wedded to fiery Power made a lethal combination for most things. It wasn't as elegant as blessed steel, and it was so messy and draining not many psions could do it—but I was no longer human, for however much longer I wore Japhrimel's mark. As long as I had the capability, I might as well use it.

I had almost reached the end of the train when it came for me.

Hovertrains are long flexible snakes, each plasteel carriage connected to the next by plasreactive cloth. This means that pleats of the material separate the compartments, rattling and flexing as the hovertrain twists, bounces, and curves its way through a shallow, reactive-laden groove that provides the necessary relief from friction and gravity. This *also* meant I was staring down a long corridor lit only with orandflu light and fluorescent tubes in thickly grilled floor divots, watching the tunnel stretch and twist like the digestive tract of some huge creature, when a small, pulsing movement alerted me.

It melted out of the shadows, crawling forward on hands and feet—and when I say *hands and feet,* I mean that its palms rested flat against the floor, fingers spread, claws extended. Its feet were flat on the floor too, which made its femurs rotate oddly in their sockets. Human bal-lai dancers would have sold their souls to have that kind of turnout.

It was vaguely human-shaped, white-skinned like the underbelly of a blind fish, with black diamond teardrops painted over its eyes making them into oubliettes. Its ears came up to high sharp points on either side of its oily bald head, and my skin went cold.

The face was different, thank the gods. It wasn't San-tino's face.

This was a ruined chubby dollface twisted up like a demented child's, with soft cheeks and pudgy lips. It wore the remains of a red robe, tied at the waist with a bit of what looked like hemp cord; but the robe was kilted up by its posture and I saw its genitals flapping loose.

Well, now we know where the expression "three-balled imp" comes from. The lunatic desire to laugh rose inside my chest as it always did. Why did I *always* feel the urge to laugh at times like this?

If I hadn't been studying what I could of Magi-coded demonology all these years, the resemblance to Santino might have made me start to scream. Instead, I held my ground, pointing the guns at it, thanking the gods again that the compartments around me were empty. I didn't want anyone caught in this crossfire.

It was a demon, a scavenger. One of the Low Flight, I was betting, since it looked like something I could possibly kill if I had a lot of luck. It stood to reason that if some of the larger demons had escaped, one or more of them might have brought a few friends.

No other demon was on the train, though. I would have bet my life on it—I was *going* to bet my life on it.

It was a demon, and I was only a *hedaira*—but I was *hedaira* to the Devil's assassin himself, at least until the mark faded—*if* it faded. I hoped that was enough to buy me my miserable life. I maybe overmatched the imp in Power, but it might have more speed—especially since it was born in a demon's body, and I still didn't have complete control over my inhuman-fast reflexes. The close quarters favored it, it was smaller. I would have preferred edged metal when dealing with this thing, but beggars can't be choosers.

All this flitted through my mind in less time than it takes an unregistered hooker to vanish from a Patrol. Then it coiled on itself, its terrible child's face twisting and slavering, and threw itself down the hall at me.

I squeezed both triggers, the recoil jolting all the way

up to my shoulders; Power tore out from me too, matching the physical velocity of the bullets. I had no time to care about stray fire catching anyone else now that the fun had started. Again, again, again, tracking the thing, it was unholy quick, throwing myself backward, *got to get enough speed got to get enough speed*—

The *kia* burst from me as my back hit the rear of the hovertrain. Metal squealed. Physics, insulted, took her due revenge, and I tumbled out of the speeding hovertrain with the imp's left-hand claws sinking into my chest.

13

*F*alling. Fire in my chest. Right-hand gun slammed back in holster, hand blurring.

I meant to reach for my sword, demon-quick reflexes just might save me yet—but the thing snarled and twisted on itself, bleeding momentum, and we crashed into the side of the hovertrain trough, all the breath driven out of my lungs. The tall banks on either side of the train-trough were hard clay dirt instead of stone, thank the gods, I coughed up blood as I slid downward. Cool night air touched my face, steam rising from my skin. I spat, clearing my throat, reflex forcing me clumsily up to my feet, almost overbalancing, hilt of my sword socking into my palm, blade singing free of the sheath as the imp snarled and chattered.

I almost understood the words.

It was definitely one of the Low Flight, incapable of anything other than demon speech. If it was trapped inside a Magi's conjuring circle I might have been able to force it to my will, but it was loose in the world, obviously told to come and make life difficult for me. Had I been a Magi I probably would have known something to do to trap it so I could question it, but I was a Necromance. Demons weren't my trade, for all that I'd been screwing one for a long time now and trying to decode documents about others.

It smacked down inside the hover trough and howled, leaping up as if stung. Blood trickled down my chest, hot and black and thick, too much blood. Why wasn't it healing the wounds?

The imp clung to the clay wall and yowled at me again, a sound like rusty nails driven through screeching nerves. I held my sword in second guard, scabbard reversed in my left hand—had I holstered my left-hand gun? I must have. Either that or dropped it, didn't matter. *I'm standing in a hovertrain trough with an imp yowling at me*, I thought, not without a certain macabre humor. *My life certainly gets interesting sometimes.*

I took a deep breath flavored with night air and the dry chemical reek of reactive, pain flaring through me as the thing's clawswipes burned deeper, whittling like hot blades. *Did it have poisoned claws? That would just cap the whole goddamn night, wouldn't it.* "Come on," I whispered, my sword dipping slightly as it shifted position. Here on open ground with my sword, I felt a little more sanguine. A little? No, a lot. There's just something about a bright length of steel that makes a girl feel capable of kicking ass. "Come get me, if you want me."

It howled at me, its baby's face distorted and reddened. But it didn't leap.

Great, I can stay here until another hovertrain comes along and pastes me, or I can try to climb up a fifteen-foot clay wall while trying to fend off this thing. What a marvelous choice.

Well, no time like the present. "*Come on!*" I screamed, stamping my foot. "*Come and get me!*"

It leapt, a marvel of uncoordinated fluidity, and muscle memory took over. I heard Jado's voice, as I often did in a fight—*Move! No think, move!*

The sword, given to me by my *sensei* to replace the blade I'd killed a demon with, carved the thing's head from its shoulders. Half-turn, the hilt of the blade floating up to protect me, the tip whipping faster than the eye could follow, a solid arc twisting like a Möbius strip. The imp's stomach cavity opened, noisome fluid gushing out. Another strike, lightning-quick as the last, and the thing's right arm fell too.

Panting. A few passes of true combat take more energy than any amount of sparring. I shuffled, ready to strike again if the shattered, sliced body should twitch. My feet slipped in the thick bouncy greasiness of reactive paint, a layer of rubbery stuff at least six inches deep giving resiliently under me.

The thing collapsed, twitching. Smoke rose up from its corpse. I watched as its skin and tissues interacted with the reactive, not looking away. Partly because if I looked away, I wasn't sure I would see it if it twitched again—and partly because of Jado. *Watch the death of your enemy if you can, for you have caused it. When you have killed, watch the consequences of your actions.*

It was a good thing I'd killed it, too. I didn't think I could take another pass or two of combat. I was savagely tired, the mark on my shoulder pulsing, another soft, warm wave of Power sliding down from it. That was beginning to get downright distracting. Was he looking for me?

I will always come for you.

How long did it take to turn an *A'nankhimel* back into a demon, back in Hell? What would happen to me if he found me, assuming he was even back in my world again? Could the genetic reshaping he'd done to me be undone? Last time it had taken a mixture of genetic shaping and tantric magick, a remaking from the center of my bones outward. I still wasn't sure of the extent of what it had done to my psyche, but as long as I was still a Necromance it didn't matter.

Maybe. But still, I wondered just how human I was anymore.

I waited until the imp was just a bubbling streak on the reactive before the point of my sword dropped slightly. I hadn't known reactive would do that. I wondered what it would do for other demons. It was cheap and easy to obtain, and maybe I could think of something to do with it that would make my life easier.

Like maybe plasgunning Hell? The thought made me chuckle grimly, pain from the clawmarks in my chest suddenly slamming back into my awareness as the one-pointed concentration of combat eased. The laugh turned into a half-gasp. I sheathed my sword, blew out a long, soft breath between my teeth. Hopefully the hovertrain would make it to the next stop; hopefully nobody would do anything stupid like fall out the hole in the back; hopefully nobody would even notice a huge gaping hole in the back of the train.

Yeah, right. And Ludders will suddenly start riding slicboards.

The sides of the trough began to vibrate, another train was on the way. I took a few running steps and leapt, my claws digging into clay. My chest tore open, I screamed, bit back the scream halfway. Forced myself up the bank, boots scrabbling, claws frantically grabbing at the hard-packed material. Something else ripped free in my chest and I whimpered. Why weren't the wounds healing?

Another hot flush of Power from the mark on my shoulder gave me strength to haul myself up over the edge of the wall. I collapsed and lay panting along the top, closing my eyes and blessing the gods. "Thank you," I whispered. "Thank you. Thank you."

The rumbling whistle of a hovertrain—antigrav and screaming air pushed too fast—began to mount. Another train coming; would it have another imp on it? I rolled away from the hovertrain track and half-fell down a gently sloping embankment, landing with a splash in something cold and wet.

Oh, great. I lay and listened to the rumblewhine.

My arms and legs were weighted with lead. The mark pulsed again, this time all the way down my left arm and out my fingertips. I coughed, turned my head to the side, and vomited an incredible mass of ice-hot writhing poison; it jetted out of my nose and mouth and I almost choked on a lunatic giggle thinking that it might blow out my ears too. It seemed to take forever, but when it was done, I immediately felt much better. Scrabbled myself over onto my other side, hooked my claws in the solidity under the wet slimy stuff I'd landed in—*please don't let it be slag*, I prayed—and began to struggle away from whatever I'd thrown up. My chest no longer burned.

I reached the top of another shallow slope and the scent of pines closed around me. I rolled, and ended up against something soft—tree branches drooping down to the ground.

They made a lovely little tent. I wriggled my way underneath, getting a confused impression of mountains and trees. It was as far away from the track and possibly being seen as I could get. I wanted to hide further away, but I couldn't manage the energy to move. I curled up into a ball and fell into a deathly doze.

14

$\mathcal{F}$our days later I made it into Freetown New Prague.

I wouldn't have chosen a Freetown. I was a Hegemony citizen, and even the Putchkin Alliance was safer than a Freetown. I would have been able to plug into the bounty net in a Putchkin or Hegemony town. In a Freetown, I'd have to depend on luck and wits, both severely strained by recent events. I'd come a lot further on the hovertrain than I'd thought, and striking out across open country seemed more dangerous than just following the hovertrain trough and finding a station where I could get a transport or buy a slicboard. I'd found a station all right. The only trouble was, I'd somehow gotten on a nonstop train that ended up in New Prague.

I came into the city tired and grainy-eyed, the mark pulsing softly on my shoulder, and found a room in the red-light district. I don't speak Czechi, but Merican is the trade-lingua in most Freetowns, so after a bit of pidgin-laced negotiation and the exchange of a handful of New Credit notes I found myself in possession of a few square feet among the bordellos and hash dens for a few days.

Strictly speaking, the bordellos and hash dens were my

type of places; I've hunted many a bounty down in whore-houses and bars. More importantly, the psychic turmoil of sex, synth hash, and—since it was a Freetown—real hash, Clormen-13 and other drugs, desperation, and violence would keep some of what I was hidden. Not for long—I'd have to live with being hunted for a while—but the longer I could stay alive, the more I could find out about the de-mons Lucifer wanted tracked down. Since I had nothing left to do and was already being attacked, hunting down four demons was where I was going to start. Better to face death on my feet doing what I could, I couldn't assume Japh would find me in time.

I warded the room well and dropped down on the nar-row bed, sinking into another type of deathly doze, sleep-ing just deeply enough to let the mind rest a little; not the deep velvet unconsciousness Japhrimel could lull me into.

Stop thinking about him. He'll find me. He said he would.

Yeah, but when? And what else might he have said to Lucifer when he was sure you couldn't understand? An-swer me that. I tossed and turned, fretfully.

Stop it. This doesn't do you any good. Rest.

I lay and tossed, tried not to think about it, failed mis-erably. The room was small—a pink-flowered rug on the floor, a retrofitted plas-powered radiator giving out heat I didn't need, a bed, a dresser I didn't need either, and a bathroom. It was a far cry from a villa in the Toscano hills.

I didn't need to use the toilet, but I did fill the bathtub and scrub the dirt off my skin. Then I soaked in the warm water, and then spent some Power on cleaning off my clothes. I *had* landed in slag after killing the imp, and if I was still human my skin might be burning with slagfever by now as my body struggled to cope with the aftermath of a cocktail of chemical sludge. It took a long time to get my clothes free of the stink.

Finally, clean enough to pass for human, I scanned the wards again. Nobody had noticed me, but I was still cautious. I didn't catch a whisper of anyone even *looking* at the thin, subtle glow of warding meant to keep away notice and guard my door.

I had one other thing to do. The only thing I had was a knife, and it took a long time of hacking at my hair before I managed to get most of it off. The resultant shaggy mass around my face was short enough that I wouldn't lose out on visibility, and nobody should recognize me right away unless they knew my tat. Only other psions were likely to be capable of distinguishing the fine differences between one psion's accreditation tat and the next, so it would make me a little less likely to be caught.

Or so I hoped. Then again, I looked like a holovid model and spread out through the psychic ether with the unmistakable flame of *demon*. But the people who knew my face might just know my *human* face, and a demon would probably simply be able to smell me. In any case, I'd have to risk it; it was the best I could do. I toyed with the idea of trying a glamour to change my appearance, or even buying some skinspray to alter my complexion; but a glamour would just attract the notice of more psions and demons. Besides, I didn't know how my dermis would react to skinspray. The last thing I needed was to break out in hives.

Though that might have been a good disguise strategy, too.

I slipped out through the third-story window and down the rickety iron fire escape, leaving the door locked—I had another day paid for—and I didn't leave anything behind.

The alley below was filthy, but I was relatively comfortable in my own bubble of demon scent. I found a mound of garbage and threw down the heavy mass of curling black hair, then used a very small bit of Power to spark the strands. They smoked and smelled awful, but they burned. I finally stamped the fire out and kicked garbage over it to hide the stench and the crisped ash. I tried not to feel victorious, but I didn't try very hard. I'd survived for five days—not bad when you're matched against demons.

I stepped out into the wilds of Freetown New Prague on a chilly afternoon just as the sky was beginning to cloud over. I decided to look around the bars a bit and see if I could get lucky. After all, everyone went to the bars to hook up, and I might be able to find a mercenary or bounty hunter I knew, either personally or by reputation. It was more than likely that someone I had met once or twice would be hanging around—New Prague was that kind of town. Once I found someone I knew, things would get a whole lot easier. I could hire someone to help me hide, or maybe find a Magi I could "persuade" to give me a crash course in what to do when demons were looking to kill you.

Six bars and one short, vicious fight in an alley later, I stepped into a dingy *pivnice,* a watering hole tucked under a bridge. I brushed at my sleeve—one of the group of normals who'd thought I'd be easy prey had bled on me. I hadn't killed any of them, but I'd been tempted. Human flotsam tends to collect in Freetowns. Sometimes their greed overpowers their good sense and they decide to find out if a psion carrying steel is combat-trained.

I can never understand why any accredited psion— someone legally allowed to carry anything short of an assault rifle on the streets—would *not* undergo combat training and stay in shape. Even non-accredited psions are allowed to carry steel and one projectile weapon, though non-accrediteds usually didn't go in for bounty hunting or anything else that would make a weapon necessary. Still...it doesn't make sense to me *not* to both carry steel *and* know how to use it. Life is just too dangerous, especially for a psion. Normals hate and fear us enough that the less law-abiding are often tempted to think of us as targets.

The silence that fell in the *pivnice* when I entered was enough to make me think I'd done the wrong thing. It was a low, smoky room, three steps down from the side-walk outside, a first floor that might have been at street level a hundred years ago but was now halfway to being a basement.

I scanned the place once. Normals, no shielding on the walls, and an atmosphere suddenly charged with fear and loathing. A deadhead bar. I would have backed out, but a familiar pair of almost-yellow eyes met mine.

Well, isn't this par for the course. Shock and unfamiliar fear slammed into my stomach. A queasy sense of unease boiled under my breastbone. Of all the people I expected to see here, *he* was the last.

But I'd been looking for someone I knew, and this was

better than I'd hoped for. *If* I could convince him not to try to kill me.

I paced away from the door, through the haze of synth-hash smoke and the effluvia of unwashed human. This was a rough place—for once I didn't look out of the ordinary with my weapons. Freetowns don't have the type of legislation covering who could carry what the Hegemony or Putchkin have; it's largely up to the ruling cartel of each town to make the rules and enforce them. So I saw projectile guns and shortswords, a few machetes, assorted other odds and ends. No plasguns.

That was a mark in my favor. I had a bounty hunter's license, and here in the Freetown I could carry whatever I wanted if I kept my nose clean and didn't interfere with Mob Family wars or cartel turf disputes.

Lucas Villalobos sat in a heavily shadowed back booth, a bottle on the table in front of him. I picked my way between tables, giving the bartender in his stained apron one glance when he opened his mouth. My tat shifted on my cheek, burning, my emerald spat a single green spark. I saw a few normals around me flinch.

Don't say anything. I really don't want to kill anyone today.

The bartender, a stolid heavy Freetowner with a long, drooping black moustache, closed his mouth and wiped his hands on his apron. I felt no gratitude or relief.

Lucas had his back to the wall. There was nothing I could do—I slid into the other side of the booth, my back prickling at the thought of the door behind me. It was an implicit gesture of trust. Lucas wouldn't get many clients if he let them get shot in the bars he frequented. He was known for taking difficult, complex jobs most generally involving assassination; if you had enough cash to hire him, he would kill whoever you asked. He only had one rule—*no kids*. He wouldn't kill anyone under eighteen.

At least, not unless they got in the way during a job. I'd heard unavoidable casualties didn't bother him too much.

His eyes met mine. A river of scarring ran down the left side of his narrow face. I shivered. Word was—now, this is only pure rumor, I don't know for sure—that he'd once been a Necromance, and committed some act so awful Death had denied him.

I couldn't imagine. To be a Necromance, to be protected by Death, and to have that protection snatched away; to be able to see other psions but unable to touch, unable to perform in that space where a Necromance is most fiercely alive…that would be torture. I could have pitied him, if he wasn't so dangerous.

He examined me, blinking slowly like a lizard. His almost-yellow eyes brightened a little, and his lipless mouth curled up slightly. "Well," he said, lifting one finger and tapping his ruined cheek. "You come up in the world, *chica*." He used the same whispery tone most professional Necromances adopt after a while. Or maybe it could have just been something wrong with his throat. Sometimes a whisper's more effective than a shout for scaring the blue lights out of people.

I felt a prickle between my shoulderblades. Did *not* look back over my shoulder, did not dare even shift my weight. "I wasn't sure you'd recognize me."

"I'd know that tat anywhere. You still move the same, too." His hair lay lank against his skull. He smelled, as usual, of a dry stasis-cabinet, and I realized it wasn't a *human* smell. Whatever he'd once been, he wasn't strictly human now. "You owe me."

I'd bargained with him in Nuevo Rio, while hunting Santino. "You turned down payment that time," I reminded him. Shivered at the thought of paying him what he usually asked of a psion. There was a reason most of his clients were corporations and Mob Families. I heard he even did secret work for the Hegemony sometimes. "You thought I was dead."

His face didn't alter in the least, his expression was blank uninterested boredom. "Ain't you? I don't see much of what you once was in your face, Valentine."

A hot plasburst of relief exploded in my stomach. So he *did* know who I was, he wasn't just bluffing. Or if he was bluffing, he'd bluffed right. "Every day is a death," I quoted, tapped my fingers on the table. "I've got a question and an offer for you, Lucas."

He looked at me for a long time. There was a time when I would have raised my sword between me and his gaze, a time when the demon Japhrimel had been melded to my shadow while I faced down Lucas and I'd been damn glad of the backup. Now I held his eyes, hoping he wouldn't see how desperate I was. I kept my thumb on my katana's guard and my right hand near the hilt, just in case. I might be almost-demon, but Lucas was truly dangerous. They don't call him the Deathless for nothing.

He finally scooped up the bottle, lifted it to his lips, took a swig. Set it down with a precise little click. "What you want, *chica*?"

Relief, sharp and acrid. I didn't let it show. He wasn't averse to bargaining, or being hired. Maybe I could pull this off. "Are you afraid of demons?"

That won a small whistling wheeze from him, Villalobos's version of a laugh. I watched his face crinkle, scarred flesh pleating. "They die just like everythin' else," he finally whispered.

I'm not even going to ask you how you know that. "All right. How would you like to work for the Devil, Lucas Villalobos? The Prince of Hell?"

He measured me for a long moment. "You're fucking serious?"

I held his eyes for longer than I would have thought possible. "I'm fucking serious. Pay's negotiable; the boss is a bitch, but you get to kill things the like of which you've never seen before." *At least I hope you've never seen them before. Or maybe I hope you have, and you know what to do to keep me alive.*

He thought about it. I hoped he was tempted, too.

Dante Valentine, alive despite demons for maybe a little while longer, tempting a man who couldn't die. I thought temptation was a demon trick.

Maybe I'd learned it from the best.

"Pay's negotiable?"

I set my jaw, stared into his eyes, and nodded. "Negotiable, Lucas. What do you want?"

The faint twitch at the corner of his eye warned me. I slapped his hand aside, locking his wrist, the knife buried itself into the table. I found myself sitting across from him, my slim golden fingers locked in a vise around his hand on the knife.

Lucas Villalobos smiled, the river of scarring down one side of his face wrinkling. He hadn't meant to attack me, just see if I was on my toes. His other hand was loosely clasped around the bottle.

I've never seen anyone human move that fast. If I squeezed, I could probably break a bone or two in his hand, and my fingers would sink into plasteel if I extended my claws.

His pupils dilated, turning his almost-yellow eyes a darker shade. "What's the job?" he whispered. His skin was dry and surprisingly fine, but I could feel the tense humming strength in his arm. No, he wasn't human anymore.

If he ever was. It's only rumor when it comes to him, Danny. Be careful.

I took a deep breath. "Keep me alive long enough to kill four Greater Flight demons, and be my eyes and ears." I quelled the urge to look behind me. The mark on my shoulder was soft heat now, wrapping around me, each pulse of Power sliding through my veins and bones. Distracting—but I could use the Power. Was Japhrimel tracking me even now?

Oh, gods, I hope so.

Lucas made that whistling, wheezing sound again, as if he was being slowly strangled. "You're never boring," he said in a low, choked voice. "Let's go out the back door."

Relief made me feel a little weak, but I didn't look away. "What do you want in return, Lucas?"

"The usual." His mouth twitched. "Or I'll think of somethin' else."

Oh, gods. Gods above. My skin seemed to chill. But here was an opportunity, and he was *definitely* the lesser of two evils. I was slightly nauseated at the thought of what I was about to agree to.

Slightly? *More* than slightly. But when it comes to a

choice between nausea and dying in some hideous way, I'll take a little bit of indigestion.

"Done." My voice husked through the word, like sodden silk dipped in honey. "One thing." I paused, my hand still clasped around his. The knife creaked in the tabletop, a muttering tide of whispers rising through the *pivnice*. The town would soon be buzzing with the news that Villalobos had found a new client. "What are you doing in New Prague?"

He rasped out a laugh. I wasn't sure I liked being the butt of Lucas Villalobos's humor. "Abracadabra." He pulled a wad of rumpled New Credits from his pocket and tossed a few on the table. "I was in Saint City way; she told me to go to New Prague and you'd find me. Bad news always turns up. I owed her a favor."

The Spider of Saint City wasn't quite a friend, but she wasn't an enemy either. We'd done each other some good turns in the past—and she had warned me about Santino and given me the direction to track him. So she'd used a favor to send Lucas to me, which meant I owed her now.

Oddly enough, I found myself not minding. And unsurprised that Abra knew I'd turn up in New Prague. I wasn't quite sure what she was, but she wasn't human either, and she always seemed to know far more than she should even with her thriving trade in information.

But there might be more to this. "What were you doing visiting Abra?" I loosened my fingers, and he worked the knife free of the tabletop and made it vanish back into his clothing. I watched, but he didn't so much as twitch toward another weapon.

"I drop in every twenty years or so. Nice to have a client that doesn't age." He stood up, and I slid out of the booth as well. Now I could see he was only about three inches taller than me (instead of the five-inch edge he used to have), and bandoliers still crisscrossed his narrow chest. He wore a blousy cotton shirt, yellow with age, and old broken-in jeans. The heels of his boots were worn down. "Let's go, Valentine. From now until the fourth demon's dead, I'm your new best friend."

I let out a sound that wasn't quite a sigh. Lucas was a viper, deadly and unpredictable—but if he said he was my man, it was a bargain. Villalobos didn't back down from his word. He still scared the hell out of me, but if you're facing down a clutch of demons you could do worse than have the Deathless on your side.

15

*W*hen you spend decades doing assassinations, it pays to have a bolthole in a major city or two. I was just glad Villalobos had one here.

I followed his shuffling feet and slumped shoulders through twisting narrow streets in the Old Town, marking each turn in a Magi-trained memory that has seen many cities; it's amazing how much they start to look alike after a while.

We ducked down an alley and into the sewers through the basement of a crumbling building that now housed a colony of slicboard couriers, Neoneopunk music pounding through the air and the sharp smell of Czechi cooking filling my nose, sparking hunger. I already had a good basic grasp of the shadow side of the city after my six-bar odyssey. Now Lucas took me underneath.

Here under the Stare Mesto, water dripped in chilly rivulets down stone, twisting its dark way from the rounded ceilings of the old sewers. Lucas pressed the scanlock on the round door, after making sure we weren't followed by doubling back a few times.

Claustrophobia filled my throat with acid and made

my heart pound. I didn't say a word. The door creaked open. I lose a lot of my sense of direction underground, but I was fairly sure I could make it to the surface and give anyone chasing me a good run. *If* I didn't expire of hyperventilation when the walls started to close in on me. I do *not* do well with closed spaces; most psions don't. I have memories that don't help either, memories of the Faraday cage in the sensory-deprivation vault under Rigger Hall, where the darkness was like worms eating the foundations of my mind and the air itself turned to solid glass, choking and slick.

Better claustrophobic than dead. I can live with an awful lot when demons are trying to kill me.

Beyond the door, mellow full-spectrum light played over wood and tile. I stepped through the round hole and let out a soft breath of wonder.

Lucas's lair in New Prague was in a long, vaulted chamber, well insulated from psychic or physical attack. If I knew Lucas, there would be a few little surprises hidden in the room, as well as quick ways to get out that didn't involve the front door. But for a moment, I simply stopped to admire as he closed the door behind us.

I saw two beautifully restrained maplewood tables with the distinctive den Jonten curve to their legs. A restrained red Old Perasiano rug, a Silbery lamp. A near-priceless Mobian print—a naked man sitting on a wooden table, his legs pulled up and head resting on his knees, a tattoo of a scorpion on his bicep straining against the skin—hung on the wall over two low, graceful Havarack chairs.

I remembered a different Mobian print, the one hanging in Polyamour's house in Saint City. A sudden, intense longing to see the noodle shop on Pole Street, or Gabe's house on Trivisidiro, or even Abra's pawnshop, stole the breath from my lungs. I'd lived in Saint City nearly all my life.

My *human* life, that was. Now that I had no chance of getting there, I found myself longing to go back.

Lucas paused behind me.

"It's beautiful," I said. "I like Mobian."

"Valuable," he returned dismissively. "Sit down. You hungry?"

I was *starving*. I was lucky to be able to fuel myself with human food instead of sex or blood, but I hadn't had the chance to eat as much as I'd've liked. "Yeah." *I don't think I've ever seen you eat, Lucas.*

"There's a kitchen through there. Help yourself. I'm going to go bounce through town and see if anyone's looking for you, pick up a few things." I heard him moving behind me, my back prickled. *Lucas Villalobos is behind me. I can't see what he's doing.*

I nodded, turning slowly to face him, telling the ridiculous jolt of panic to go away. He wasn't going to stab me in the back, or at least, I didn't *think* he would. Instead, he was planning on doing what I would have done if our situations were reversed, checking to see if there was any static on the new client. "Is there another exit?" I asked. "In case the front door's compromised?"

He studied me for a long few moments, his almost-yellow eyes empty of all expression. I suppressed a shiver. I was crazy, contracting Lucas to help me; still, a man who couldn't be killed was far from the worst ally when it came to dealing with demons. I had no *choice*.

Dammit, Dante, quit being such a whiner. Until Japh finds you, you're on your own.

He nodded. "Come over here."

Behind a painted Cho-nyo screen he showed me a small depression in the tiles, just big enough for a hand. It triggered a slice of the wall to swing inward, and if you were quick, you could drop down into another tunnel that would take you to the surface. Push the door closed from the other side, and nobody would be the wiser. "But be careful, it's slippery." It hurt to hear him talk. He sounded like he had a lung infection, wheezing out the words.

"Good enough. Thank you, Lucas."

He gave another whistling, snorting laugh. "Don't thank me, Valentine. I'm only taking this because I'm fuckin' curious."

"About what?" I followed him out from behind the screen and almost to the door. Our footsteps echoed, and I was suddenly cold, thinking of when he shut that door and I was alone. Underground. In a windowless room. *Oh, gods.*

"Maybe the Devil can kill me," Lucas Villalobos said, triggering the scanlock on the door. "The gods know I've waited long enough."

16

The kitchen was where he said it was, and down a short hall was a bathroom and—oh, Anubis—a tiny womblike bedroom. I looked longingly at the plain missionary-style bed, exhaustion weighing me down. It was the first time in my life I'd faced Lucas Villalobos without feeling almost too terrified to talk.

I suppose that possibly losing your ex-demon-soon-to-be-real-demon-again boyfriend and fighting off a three-balled imp behind a hovertrain—not to mention getting your house shattered and blown up—would make anyone a little too worn out to feel the proper fear when facing the man Death had denied. Besides, I was different now. Tougher than a human, capable of taking more damage.

For how much longer, though? If Japhrimel was a citizen of Hell again, was I going back to being a human? I wouldn't have thought a genetic remodel like mine could be undone, but demons have been tinkering with genetics for so long I wouldn't put much past them. Some people even say demons might have been responsible for humanity's evolution, but nobody likes to think about that particular theory. It leaves a bad taste in the mouth.

Japh had changed me in the first place, after all. Reversing the change might not be so big a deal to him. It might even happen just-because.

I sighed, rubbing at my temple with my right hand. This was getting ridiculous.

Ridiculous or not, you need to rest so you can think. So just settle down, sunshine. Relax. Wait for Lucas to come back.

My hunger was sharp, but Lucas's taste ran to heat-sealed meals. They taste like cardboard and sit in the stomach like bowling balls, not providing enough in the way of nutrition—especially for my metabolism. So I did the next best thing, dragged two blankets from the bed behind the Cho-nyo screen and propped myself up against the wall, my right hand loose around my sword-hilt. I closed my eyes, listening to the quiet. I rarely if ever heard complete silence, being a child of the urban age. Being underground meant the psychic noise of so many people was shut out. The only thing left was Power itself, filtering in through the ground like water, and the peculiar directionless static that meant "you're underground."

Maybe I'll have to go to ground like an animal for the next seven years. The prospect was alternately comforting and horrifying, depending on whether my eyes were open or closed.

I dozed in Lucas Villalobos's lair, feeling a little safer now. Time slid away as I tipped my head against the wall, the back of my neck curiously naked. I hadn't had my hair this short since Rigger Hall. I shivered, thinking of that place again. Afterward, in the Academy, I'd started growing my hair out almost immediately. It was messy to dye to fit in with Necromance professional codes—codes dating back to the Parapsychic Act, to present a united front to the world and make us instantly recognizable— but when Japhrimel had changed me, my hair had turned the same inky black as his.

I was back to Japhrimel again.

Stay inside. Don't open the door. Do not doubt me, no matter what.

I'd walked into that church and faced Lucifer with him. My mind kept pawing lightly at the memory—the speaking in their demonic language, the maneuvering me into the position of having to agree...and here I was, almost everything I owned in the world gone in a reaction fire and demons chasing me down. I was damn lucky that I'd only tangled with one imp so far—an imp Japhrimel hadn't attacked and exhausted first, like he'd done with Santino. I was *damn* lucky to be alive on both counts.

Some demon somewhere knew what Lucifer had bargained me into doing and was looking to get the first shot in. It was predictable—after all, I was the weakest link in the chain leading to the Devil, especially if Japh was a full-fledged demon again. If they killed me messily enough, like a Mob turf hit, it might be a statement to other demons looking to rebel. If Lucifer couldn't even keep one lousy human alive, his reputation would take a hit, and Hell might get even harder to control.

I felt cold at the thought of demons slipping out of Hell and causing havoc in my world. Like it or not, Lucifer was relatively well-disposed toward humanity, and I suspected it might be hard to contact demons mostly because he wanted it that way. The thought of a change in that status quo was enough to give anyone nightmares.

I thought of the temple and Lucifer's eyes on me,

his mischievous expression and the cold razor-mouthed beauty of his voice sending another shiver up my spine. I felt goosebumps trying to break through my sleek golden skin but not succeeding, a sensation like a phantom limb's pain. He had neatly outmaneuvered me, as a matter of fact. I hadn't even managed to stick up for Eve's freedom.

Eve. A little girl, her pale hair a shining sleek cap, her indigo eyes too wide and too calm with awful, chilling maturity. Doreen's daughter, birthed from Lucifer's genetic material and the marrow and blood Santino had murdered Doreen for. One of my biggest failures, one of a long string.

Why do I keep going from one subject I don't like to another? I shifted uncomfortably, rubbed my head against the chill tile wall. Since I was so much warmer than human now, it was nice to feel the coolness seeping into my skin.

Sometimes.

Of course Japhrimel will turn you back into a human, a little voice of self-loathing spoke up inside my head. I shifted restlessly again, tried to shut it up. *You're too cold, too hard, too damaged. You've locked yourself up with your books—he's said so himself—and you used Jace to taunt him, didn't you? No wonder he went back to Hell, it was probably more fucking fun than hanging around with* you.

The thought that perhaps Lucifer could be behind the blowing-up of my house or the imp attack wasn't comfortable either. But Japhrimel had made such a big deal of asking for my protection, and he'd told me not to doubt him. No matter what.

Stop it, Danny. Stop it. If you can't trust Japhrimel

you're dead in the water. Don't start doubting him now.
He's never let you down before; he'll come through.
Whatever happens, he'll do all he can to help you.

After a few hours of fruitless brooding, I opened my eyes and sighed again. I was just about to shift so I could lie down on the floor when my demon-sharp ears heard the sound of stealthy movement out in the tunnel leading to Lucas's door. I hadn't even realized I was listening so intently, straining my ears for any whisper of motion.

I froze, my left hand palm-up, clasping my sword. My eyes dropped to the almost-forgotten wristcuff. Its etched lines were moving again, and even under the full-spectrum lights they glinted eerie bright green.

I didn't need a demon-language dictionary to know that meant nothing good for me.

I let out a long soft breath through my open mouth, pushed up to my feet, and started hunting on the wall for the small depression.

17

$\mathcal{N}$ight had fallen when I reached the end of the long slick tunnel, the wristcuff held up to provide me with a little light. Demon-acute sight is a blessing in the dark, but even demon eyes need a few photons to work with; they're not like Nichtvren with their uncanny ability to see in absolute blackness. It was a long, slippery, stumbling walk. Even my preternaturally quick reflexes and sense of balance had difficulty. Imagining Lucas struggling up for the surface through this dark, slimy, slanting passage wasn't comfortable either. I heard squeaks, and once or twice saw beady little animal eyes.

I suppose it was silly to be worried about rats—or any other urban critter—when I was possibly being chased by homicidal demons, but I was getting sillier by the moment.

The wristcuff's glow was steady and green. I was beginning to wonder about this bracelet. Twice now it had warned me of danger. The shifting green lines came together, flowing like water over the smooth surface. I still couldn't feel anything when I probed it for magick; it was oddly invisible.

Was it a gift from Japhrimel? I'd assumed so. He'd told me to accept nothing from Lucifer, especially not food or drink but most importantly, to accept *nothing* from the Devil. Had I done something stupid by putting it on? But it had *warned* me. A backhanded gift from the Devil wouldn't stir itself to keep me alive, would it?

The thought that if I was hit it would mean trouble for Lucifer's prestige was comforting. Unless, of course, Hell wouldn't care about a human Necromance.

Then why would they look to kill me?

I wasn't *all* human either, was I? Not anymore. *Hedaira.* For how much longer?

Dammit, Danny, will you quit it? You're even starting to annoy yourself.

I found myself coming out under another heavily patched concrete and plasteel bridge, with a thin trickle of water sliding from the bottom of the pipe I had been bent almost double traversing. The pipe mouth widened until I could almost stand upright. I heard thunder rumble far away over New Prague, smelled incipient rain heavy and wet and chemical-laden against my palate. A staircase led up to the street, and I picked my way up the crumbling narrow stone steps cautiously, scanning the street above. It was deserted.

This part of New Prague looked bombed-out and deserted, but several ruined buildings had thin columns of cooking smoke rising into the night air. I scanned in a circle with eyes and other senses, my attention moving over the buildings. Nothing dangerous, no shimmer of bloodthirsty intent.

Now that I was aboveground I started to feel a little vulnerable. Who could find Lucas's lair? He was a professional, he wouldn't have led anybody back down to me. Would he? Certainly not willingly, unless he was a double agent. But that seemed paranoid. Maybe a demon could follow Lucas without his knowing?

Either way, the bracelet had warned me of the imp on the hovertrain, I wasn't foolish enough to disregard it now.

What if Lucas was really working for someone who wanted me dead?

Dammit, if that was it he would have leapt on me when my back was turned. I'm starting to get paranoid. Starting? No, I'm a full-blown flower of paranoia. A fucking garden full.

I heard the tooth-grating whine of hovercells, and my nape tingled.

Instinct took over. I ducked back down the stairs, my body moving with preternatural speed, and slid under the cover of the bridge just as a sleek black hover swept into sight from around the shattered hulk of what looked like an apartment building. Light stabbed down from its underside. I caught the bristle of relays on the bottom, like spines on a poisonous fish.

A search hover? I bit my lip as I watched, drawing back in the shadows and hoping they didn't have infrared. I'd show up like a Putchkin Yule Tree with my demon's metabolism radiating heat against the cool night air.

The hover swept the area again in a standard quartering pattern. I was tempted to scan it—but if I tried that, any psion aboard would feel my attention and tell I was close. Despite the interference from the deep well of New Prague's ambient Power and the fact that I was pressing myself into stone and willing it to hide me, they still might be able to tell my general location. It was good to have a share of a demon's Power—but it was not the most circumspect way to get around.

And let's face it, Dante, who knows how long it will last?

I told that voice to shut up and leave me alone. When the hover drifted out of sight I waited, then went slowly up the stairs again, and looked around. Underground. I had to either find a way to get underground again or find a way to contact Lucas.

What the hell am I thinking? I've got a big target painted on my back. If I stay alive long enough, Lucas will find me. Gods know there's only a limited number of places I can hide.

I closed my eyes for a moment, willing myself to *think*, and opened them to find another faint green glow coming from the wristcuff.

What's the one thing they would never expect? Just like that, the answer came.

You must decide to fight or flee, Jado's voice whispered in my head. When attacked, sometimes your enemy's force could be turned back upon itself, and I was rapidly running out of options. I needed to know exactly how the battlefield was arranged against me.

I planted my feet, my left hand curled around the scabbard, and centered myself. I inhaled, smooth and deep— and threw up a very huge, very *loud* burst of Power.

I didn't expect it to flame into the visible spectrum. It did, a sparkling crackling bolt of blue-green lanced up from my outflung right hand and arrowed for the clouds above. It would disperse over the city, but not before it was remarked. If Lucas was near, he'd come find out what the fuss was.

With that done, I ran for the abandoned apartment building. No smoke drifted from its broken windows, and it stood in the middle of a tumbled wilderness of concrete blocks next to an impressive crater hosting a few twisted scrub trees that had managed to grow amid the wreck.

In other words, a good defensible position. If I had to retreat from it, I'd have plenty of cover. Of course, anyone sneaking up on the building would have plenty of cover, too, but life couldn't be perfect.

I'd settle for just living through the night, really.

I heard the whine of antigrav before long, and the sleek black hover came back just as I shinnied through a space between two boards nailed to the broken windows. The hem of Jace's coat tore a little on ancient broken glass, real silica glass instead of plasglass, and I managed to bolt toward the side of the building that would give me a view of the hover.

Trash littered the bottom floor of the building, and a gigantic hole had been blasted through several floors. I could glimpse the sky as I gathered myself to *leap*, claws sinking solidly into crumbling concrete, every nerve alive, *twist* and throw the body upward again, landing cat-soft in my boots. Then I ducked and ran, blurring through the debris littering the third floor. I finally reached the side where I could see the hover and peered out through a broken window, sheltering myself behind a crumbling wall.

The hover yawed, strings tangling down from its underbelly. Had people bailed out on jumpcords? I'd missed something. The sleek black shape slid to the side as if something was terribly wrong, but there was no hint of *what.* It was oddly, eerily silent except for the whine of its hovercells and the stabilizers giving out a ratcheting overloaded squeal.

I looked below and saw dark humanoid shapes flitting through the broken cover. Some moved like humans.

Others did not.

They had to have been in the neighborhood, or came down the jumpcords from that hover. Did they see me coming in here? I thought this over, biting at my lower lip. The hover heeled alarmingly again, and a puff of bright green light showed from inside its tinted windows; quickly seen and just as quickly snuffed.

What the hell is going on here?

I decided a bit more altitude would be a good thing and retreated to the hole blown in the building, trying not to feel like I'd trapped myself. At least now I *knew* they were after me, and I was fairly sure I could fight my way out if I had enough cover to hide behind while I got close enough to conduct a little guerilla action. A few more leaps and I was on the sixth floor, levering myself in and rolling away just as I heard a shuddering boom.

I made it to the window just in time to see the hover grounding itself, throwing up chunks of dirt and stone, its plasteel sides ripped open as it smashed into the bridge I'd hidden under. The ground shook, the building swaying under my feet. I wished for a slicboard—I could get out of here fast with one. Instead, I skirted the gaping hole on owl-soft feet, fleeing for the more broken-down area of the building. It was dangerous since I was denser and heavier than a human, but I could also handle a higher fall.

So a hover had been downed, but not with a plasbolt. A

reaction fire would bring this whole damn building down and burn a scar into the city to boot. It had been downed quietly, all things considered, which probably meant some kind of EMP pulse, probably fairly unremarked since we were out of the main hover lanes. That meant, possibly, two groups of enemies tangling with each other.

Good for me.

Fight or flee? I heard Jado's voice yet again, calm and considering.

I found a blind corner and waited. I'd be able to see anything that moved on my floor, I'd be able to shoot anything that came up through the hole. It looked as if this place had been bombed, maybe even in the aftermath of the Seventy Days War or a local brushfire action. If I had to, I could drop out of the building and tear my way through a search ring or two, make enough time to lose myself in New Prague. I'd have the benefit of knowing who was after me and what resources they could scramble on short notice.

The air pressure changed, heaviness sliding against my skin. The cuff tightened, squeezing. I bit back a gasp and folded up inside myself, trying to stay as small and still as possible. The air turned hard and hot, and my throat stopped as I held my breath, unconsciously.

Below, I felt the arrival of something with an aura full of twisting diamond flame. The smell of heavy oranges and bloody musk filled the air.

Another demon. I trembled like a rabbit.

I hadn't felt this since the first time Japhrimel showed up at my door. The black, twisting diamond flames of demon Power warped through the building's physical space. I gauged the distance between me and the window.

Fight, or flee? There was no way I could take on a demon. But if it managed to trap me, I would have to see what I could come up with.

The soft, chilling voice echoed up from below. "Right Hand," it said in Merican, the words making the building quiver like a plucked string. "Kinslayer. I wish to speak to you. Come and face me."

What the hell? That answered a question—he wasn't babbling in Czechi, whoever he was. Speaking Merican meant he was probably after me.

The answer to a question like that is almost worse than having to ask that question in the first place. I had to swallow a wild braying laugh. Why did I always feel the urge to *laugh* at times like this? I had to breathe; took in a shallow, soft sip of air. Smelled the oranges and musk again, a heady scent.

I stayed where I was, waiting.

"I know you are here," the voice continued. Too deep to be female, full of an awful welter of bone-chilling, nerve-twisting Power. Japhrimel's voice had *never* been this uncomfortable. He had occasionally sounded furiously cold or threatening but never so...inhuman. "I can *smell* you."

Good for you. I'd give you a prize but I don't think you'd like it.

My right hand tensed around my swordhilt. *If a demon comes for me, I want it to be on my terms.* I was pretty sanguine about my chances against humans or even werecain, but I didn't know enough about this terrain to be comfortable facing something bigger. Now I knew there was at least one demon in New Prague, and that he was most likely looking for me.

And that he could smell me, mistaking me for Japh.

My mouth gaped, my breathing soundless. I gathered myself, centimeter by centimeter. Like a coiled spring. Japhrimel had taught me how to do it, conserve my body's need for motion, then explode into demon-swift action.

Don't think about him—think about getting out of here. Quickly. Now that you know what you're facing, get the fuck out of here.

Movement below. If it was easy for me to haul my carcass up here, it would be even easier for a demon. Especially one of the Greater Flight.

Stillness, a killing silence like radiation-burn. *Demon down there, and what else? What else is waiting to make my life miserable?*

The cuff tightened on my wrist again. Its glow had dampened, as if it didn't want to give away my location. I went so still I could imagine my molecules slowing down their frenetic dance. I could imagine the flashes between my nerves slowing down too. I could imagine too goddamn much, as a matter of fact.

"Show yourself." The voice mouthed along the dark well of the hole slicing through the building. "I come to speak of—"

The unthinkable happened.

Pressure crackled in the air. Another arrival. Just like a damn transport dock. *Gods above, this just keeps getting better.*

Chaos exploded underneath me. The noise was so instant and so huge I tore my sword out of its sheath, blue flame exploding along the blade.

I heard a howling snarl, then another chilling scream cut the air. This one froze all the blood in my veins and rather rapidly altered the entire situation. One demon who didn't know where I was I could handle. Two demons in a melee I could most definitely *not* handle, but it would give me enough cover to get the fuck out of here.

I barely thought, all the compressed energy in my body tearing loose at once. I bolted for the window and hit it with Power and flesh both. Wood exploded out, the momentum carrying me far, I braced for impact, tumbling through the air.

Plasgun fire streaked past, and the coughing roars of projectile weapons. I slammed down, my boots cracking concrete, the shock jolting all the way up to the crown of my head, and took the first two opponents with a clash. All things considered it was actually a comfort to have a clear-cut problem in front of me.

Mercenaries, human, each with guns and blades. It barely slowed me down, I didn't even kill the second one, just knocked him aside and streaked over smoking rubble, bowling over another two mercenaries. Plasgun bolts crisscrossed my path, I heard a rising scream I didn't recognize, a sound of lung-tearing female effort. Something brushed my cheek like a whip, a line of fire against my face. The screaming sound was mine, a howl pushed past all endurance and smashing aside crackling yellow plasbolts. They were firing at me because I was moving too fast to engage now.

I burst out into a street, deserted but lit with streetlights, flashes of buildings as I ran using demon speed, hearing the footsteps behind me, pounding. They sounded even swifter than mine—I had to do something quick, gaining on me, gaining on me.

Time to think of something else, Danny.

There comes a point past which running is useless. I saw an intersection ahead of me and could have jagged to try to throw off pursuit, but my body decided otherwise, streaking instead for the shelter of an alley. I burst into noisome darkness, no Power left to make a shield to ward off the smells of human death and decay. Iron burned against my palm as I leapt over a dumpster, shoving it back in the same motion. The end of the alley was what I'd hoped for, a blank brick wall, and I twisted in midair, boots thudding against it, and completed the motion by leaping lightly down facing back the way I'd come, ready now, my sword singing as it clove the air. My lips peeled back from my teeth. If I was going to die, I was going to die in combat, face-on, with my back to the wall.

My ribs flared with deep panting breaths. Adrenaline soared and sang through me, pushing me past rational thought and into the tearing-claw frenzy of an animal brought to bay and prepared to go down fighting.

He stood less than ten feet away, the darkness burning around him with a sound like voices whispering, chattering, sneering. My heart slammed into my throat, I dropped into guard, my blade suddenly glowing with harsh, hurtful blue light. The mark flared against my shoulder, soft velvet heat scoring into my nervous system.

His eyes. Anubis et'her ka, his eyes.

His eyes were like Lucifer's, piercing intense green. And his aura, the diamond-twisting black flames of a demon; he was the same as he had been the very first time I'd ever seen him on my front step.

Tierce Japhrimel was a demon again, and the look on

his face froze my blood. My heart smashed against my ribs, my sword blazed blue-white, every nerve in my body sang with the furious urge to kill.

I dug my heels into the concrete and prepared to sell myself dear if he came for me.

18

*J*aphrimel cocked his head, watching me. His face was shuttered, blank, only the terrible burning fire of his eyes to show he was something more than a statue. I swallowed copper. I knew how eerily fast he could move. My heart threw itself against my ribs as if it intended to explode and save everyone involved the trouble of killing me.

We stood like that, Fallen-no-more and *hedaira*, for about thirty of the longest seconds of my life. My blade, the weapon of a Necromance, spat blue flame, my head was full of the rushing noise of combat. I was set on lase-trigger, dialed up to ten, and just aching, *aching* to fight.

My patience broke. "If you're going to do it," I rasped, "*do* it, don't make me wait for it!"

A fleeting shadow crossed his face. He looked puzzled.

"What nonsense are you speaking now?"

I was relieved. He didn't sound like the soft evil voice that had crawled up from the bottom floor of the ruined apartment building. I was so relieved that he sounded like he always had—flat and ironic—that I actually let out a sharp breath, my swordblade dipping slightly. More thunder walked through the sky, the smell of rain turning thick and cloying. Whatever weather was crossing the city, it was very near.

Relief turned to whipsawing fear and irritation, riding just under my skin. I hadn't eaten, and I'd expended a *hell* of a lot of Power. My shields trembled once, snapped back into place. The mark on my shoulder pulsed, another hot wave of Power soaking into the mass of exposed nerves I was fast becoming. *Get it while you can,* I thought in a lunatic singsong. *Get it while it's good.*

"Dante?" He didn't move. His eyes flicked down my body, took in my feet in ready stance, the blue-glowing blade, came back up to my face.

"What happens now?" My breath jagged in my throat. My swordblade dipped even further, blue flame glowing, my rings flaring with golden sparks. "What *now*, Tierce Japhrimel?"

Comprehension lit his face. In that one moment he looked completely human despite the lasers of his eyes. My chest gave a horrible squeeze. His eyebrows drew together again, and I braced myself for it. *This is going to hurt. This is going to hurt worse than Jace, worse than Doreen, worse than anything. Oh gods, I've been wrong, he is planning on making me human again, he's going to tell me... how is he going to tell me? Japhrimel, please—*

"If you think I am about to fight you, Dante, you are exceedingly stupid." Now his voice held a faint note of disdain, or was it anger? Irritation?

I wished I could tell.

My throat closed. "Oh." I braced myself. "Are you sure?"

He made a curious little grimace, sighed. Clasped his

hands behind his back, his inky hair falling over his forehead, longer than it had been the first time I saw him. His shoulders relaxed infinitesimally. "Someday, Dante, I will discover how your mind works. When I do I will be able to live content, having solved one of the great mysteries of Creation."

What? "What?" I blinked. My shoulders relaxed. It was going to be all right. He was here.

But the red bath of instinct under my skin wasn't so sure. The animal in me wanted to *fight*, wanted hot blood and a deathscream, and I was so twitched-out on adrenaline and fear I wasn't sure I could stop myself.

"Have you lost your senses?" Definite anger, reined in, controlled, and burning out through his eyes. When had he learned to wear such a human face, the expressions flitting over his expressive mouth plain as day to me? "I *told* you I would come for you."

"There's a lot that expression can mean." My stupid mouth bolted like a runaway horse. "You told me to stay inside the house. They cracked the shields, if I hadn't gotten out of there the reaction fire . . . and the imp, there was an imp, and back there—"

"Ah." He nodded thoughtfully. "I see."

Silence again, crackling against the alley. My breathing began to smooth out. Slowly, so slowly, the tension and bloodlust faded, my pulse slowing down, and he made no move. I was still on the fine edge, pushed almost past rationality by the crazed burst of relief and fresh fear, I had just *escaped a demon* and now here was another one in front of me, and even though I knew him, I still felt pretty *damn* nervous. Each moment he just *stood* there scraped my nerves raw.

My nerves were jagged enough. I hitched in a breath. "Don't just *stand* there!" I shouted at him, twitching as if I meant to attack, sword dipping slightly.

He didn't even move. Just examined me, his hands behind his back and his shoulders straight.

"God*damm*it—"

"Hush." He shook his hair back, a quick flick of motion. "You must come with me, now. It isn't safe here for you."

"You're telling me." The sky lit overhead with a few thrown bolts of light. More thunder, seeming to send hot prickles through my aching, strained body. "I thought...I thought you would..." I couldn't bring myself to say it. My heartbeat slowed, but each pounding beat felt thick and heavy.

"Whatever you thought, I am here now. I am losing patience, Dante. Come."

My sword dipped the rest of the way. The blue fire along its edges spattered briefly, went out. The sudden darkness stung my eyes. Even the wristcuff had gone dark, and that was some comfort. It had been warning me of other danger, not of Japhrimel. I took a deep, lung-searing breath. My hands shook.

"You promised not to doubt me." Silken, the reminder. "There would be unpleasant consequences to breaking a promise to me."

What the bloody fucking hell are you talking about? I have just had one fuck of a bad week, and I'm a little twitchy, so just give me a minute. I am so fucking frightened right now I don't care who comes for me, I'll kill them. Kill. I bit the words back. Settled for a choked,

"Why didn't you tell me you were going to do that? Huh? Why didn't you *tell* me?"

"There are more pleasant ways to pass our time than this." He took a single step forward, the Power cloaking him pressing against me. "I returned as quickly as I could. You bear my mark, I am still yours."

My brain struggled with this, chewed it, and spat it back out. "You're a *demon* again. What happens *now*? What are you going to do to me?" I sounded scared to death, and not exactly in my right mind.

Amazing. For once I sounded exactly how I *felt*. I was too fucking panicked to be very coherent.

He took another step. "I am *A'nankhimel*, but given back my Power as a demon. I believe the term the Prince used is *abomination*." His eyes glowed. "And if you do not come with me now I will force you, and that will be unpleasant for both of us."

I dug my heels in against the compulsion in his voice, the pressure to do as he said; it was harder to resist than Lucifer's chill weight of command. Was it because Japh had so much more Power now, or because his mark was burned into my skin? "Don't. Just give me a minute, okay, and tell me *why*. That's all I'm asking. That's reasonable, Japhrimel. It really is. Just fucking tell me. I *need* to know." My voice broke, spiraling up into a jagged half-gasp, and wind brushed through the alley, bricks groaning uneasily behind me as Power jittered at the edge of my control.

He studied me for a moment. My sword hung to one side, loosely, and I was sure he could see me shaking like a Chillfreak. With each breath I dragged in I calmed down a little more, but not nearly fast enough.

All things considered, I am handling this very well.

"I took a risk, my curious. I thought it likely Lucifer needed us far more badly than he would admit. I could not warn you; he is far better at reading you than you may comprehend. Your reaction convinced him he could drive a wedge between us, cause trouble. Perhaps he was right." He paused. "I am sorry."

I measured his face, he let me. The mark still burned against my shoulder, waves of Power teasing at my skin. Sinking in, caressing, cajoling.

"You promised to trust me, and not to doubt me." His tone was kind, very soft, and familiar.

I didn't need the reminder. I set my back teeth, then slowly, slowly, sheathed my sword; heard the click as the blade slid home. Thunder rumbled in the distance. The storm was closing in. "I know." My voice was harsh, clipped. "You have exactly ten seconds to explain what the *fucking* hell just happened. Slowly. In great detail."

"It will take slightly longer." No hint of irony in his voice, just simple quiet reasonableness.

"I've got time," I shot back, and slid the sword all the way home with a click. "Lead on, lord demon."

Was it my imagination, or did he flinch? He stepped forward, deliberately, and approached me, each footfall silent but distinct. I didn't move, just shut my eyes. My lungs burned, I kept breathing. When his hands met my shoulders I sagged, and he pulled me forward, into the shelter of his body. "Do not, *hedaira*." His breath was hot in the tangled, chopped mess of my hair. "What I have done, I have done to protect you. Have faith in me. Just a very little, that is all I ask."

"I do," I whispered against his coat. "I knew you'd come."

His arms tightened, briefly. He kissed the top of my head, and some of the skittering panic rabbiting under my heartbeat eased. Just a little. "We must go. It is not safe for you here."

Funny, this seems like the safest place in the world to be. But I said nothing, just set my jaw and stepped away when he reluctantly let go of me.

19

We walked together under the rumbling sky, Japhrimel with his hands behind his back and a familiar thoughtful expression on his face. I kept my hand on my swordhilt and tried to look everywhere at once, the sour taste of fear in my mouth and all my nerve endings scrubbed raw and bleeding. Japhrimel didn't look at me, but he seemed intensely aware of our surroundings. Rain pressed low in the clouds, restless spatters touching the pavement and steaming away from the diamond glow of his aura. He was bleeding heat into the air, which made me think that maybe he wasn't as calm as he wanted me to think.

Of course, being a demon and having the resources of Hellesvront—the deep, wide net of agents and financial assets Lucifer had created on earth—Japhrimel had a suite in a high-rise hotel in the Novo Meste. True to form, he simply ignored the fawning of the hotel employees when he appeared with one tired and battered Necromance in tow.

The hotel was a pile of glittering plasteel and plasglass, soaring above the Rijna na Prikope. Here in the Novo Meste, hoverlimos drifted under steely orange clouds and the buildings were clean and high, like the financial district of Saint City. It was in the Staro Meste that the trash piled up and the bordellos rollicked all night; that would have been the part of town I was more comfortable in. This just felt too exposed.

Of course, my nerves were so jagged I would have felt naked anywhere.

I had to swallow harshly when Japhrimel stopped in the lobby, half-turning to consider me with those new, awful glowing-green chips of eyes. "Are you able to take the elevator?"

I nodded slightly, my chin dipping. "Fine." My voice was a battered husk, still velvety with a demon's seduction. "You still haven't explained a damn thing." *That's okay, I'm not in a mood to listen. I need to fight someone, anyone, but if I start now I'll go crazy and I won't stop until someone's dead. Or sex. That would be good too. Come on, sunshine. Take a deep breath. Calm the fuck down.*

It was impossible. I wasn't going to be calm anytime soon.

"Patience, my curious one." He made a slight movement, as if reaching for me. His hand fell back to his side when I shied away, my bootheel scraping the immaculate floor. It wasn't him I flinched from. It was that the elevators were very close and he obviously expected me to get into one, my hands threatened to start shaking again at the thought. My breath came hard, harsh, my ribs flickering. "Soon enough."

The normals in hotel uniforms drew back as he stalked through the lobby. I suppose a wild-haired, wide-eyed Necromance with a white-knuckle grip on her sword and the static of bloodlust and rage following her like a cloud wasn't exactly their usual clientele. The lobby was nice, I supposed—red velvet couches in baroque style, synthstone glowing white, a statue of a woman in a traditional Czechi costume with water pouring from her bucket into a rippling pool below. I tried to ignore the sudden swirling of fear and worry in the normals, followed Japhrimel's back. The tattoo on my cheek shifted.

One of the elevators opened as we approached. It was empty. It stayed open, and Japhrimel stepped inside.

No. Please, no.

I couldn't back down. I *had* promised, I'd said it was fine. Backing down now would be weak.

So I stepped into the elevator and fought down the hot sourness that rose in my throat as the doors slid closed. All the air seemed to vanish. I couldn't close my eyes to shut out the terrible feeling, so I stared at Japhrimel's feet, pressure building behind my eyes. The push of antigrav helped by pulleys made the bottom of my stomach drop out.

"Japh?" I sounded about a half-step away from panicking, my voice breathless and cracked.

A long pause. "Yes."

"Could you...is it possible for you to turn me back into a human?" *I have to know. I won't get any peace until I know. It's just one of those questions I have to ask. Just...I have to know.*

His boot-toes didn't shift. "Would you want to?" Was that *hurt* in his voice? Wonders never ceased.

"Will you just tell me? I need to know." *Had* to know. *Sekhmet sa'es*, he was a demon again, with all a demon's Power.

Did he still want me?

It's not that he's back to his old self. I stared at his boot-toes. *It's that I have no control. He could make me do whatever he wants. He could do anything he liked to me, and I wouldn't be able to stop him. That scares the hell out of me. How am I supposed to deal with that?*

"Even if I wanted to, I could not grant you mere humanity again." His tone was so chill the air cooled a perceptible five degrees. "The changes have settled in, and you would not survive such a thing. You will not escape me that easily."

You know, I would have settled for a simple yes or no, Japh. I sighed, my shoulders hunching with tension. The air inside the elevator was beginning to run out, precious little oxygen left. I needed to breathe. I *had* to breathe. My throat began to close, my hand cramped on my swordhilt. *Anubis et'her ka. Se ta'uk'fhet sa te vapu kuraph.* The prayer rose, and a blue glow rose with it inside my mind. I could have cried with the relief. My god had never denied me comfort, even before I'd passed through my Trial to become an accredited Necromance.

That, of course, reminded me of my altar and the shape of fire behind Anubis as he laid the geas upon me. I had studied geas in Theory of Spirituality classes, the gods asking of a specific service; they were rare even among Necromances. Gods, demons—*everyone* was messing with my life now. I tried to remember what the gods had asked of me. Couldn't.

I just had to wait. But the thought of *that* waiting didn't fill me with terror. I didn't think my god would ask me for anything I couldn't do.

The door opened and I bolted from the close confines,

searching for a wall to put my back to. Japhrimel stepped out, soundlessly, and waited. He knew better than to touch me, but his aura did what he refrained from, wrapping around mine in an almost physical caress.

When I looked up and nodded, taking in harsh gulps of blessed air, he led me down a quiet, red-carpeted hall and opened a pair of double doors. Once I followed him through, they sighed closed behind me on maghinges.

The suite was done in gold and cream, and a large mirror hung over the nivron fireplace, which was cold and empty except for a fire screen decorated with peacocks. And I wasn't alone in the room with Japhrimel. I caught a confused sense of movement and threw myself away, my back meeting the wall with a thump between a bathroom door and a tasteful, restrained end table made of spun plasglass.

Lucas Villalobos looked over from where he leaned against the mantel, his lank hair lying slick against his forehead. "Relax, *chica*," he said in his softest voice, but he was grinning like a maniac. Thunder rang under his words, the expensive plasglass windows shivering in their seatings. I could feel the building sway underfoot. "You're among friends."

"Friends?" My own voice cracked. My nerves were too jangled for me to be polite to anyone right about now. I was slowly, slowly coming back from the edge. "If these are *friends*, I'll take my enemies."

I didn't mean it. My mouth just bolted like a runaway hover.

Villalobos laughed, the crackling wheeze I was beginning to be uncomfortably familiar with. I had no idea when he started to find me so fucking funny.

Four other men and a woman watched me. A Shaman, a Magi, a Nichtvren—and two men without the glow of psions, but who weren't normals either. They weren't werecain, or kobold, or swanhild, or Nichtvren. I took this in as Japhrimel held perfectly still, his glowing eyes on me.

"Introductions." Lucas sounded maniacally calm. "Danny Valentine, meet everyone. Everyone, Danny Valentine."

Thanks, Lucas. That really helps.

The Nichtvren rose, a tall male with a shock of dirty-blond hair and the face of a holovid angel, his eyes curiously flat with the cat-sheen of his nighthunting species. Below the shine, they were a pale blue. He wore dusty black, a V-neck sweater and loose workman's pants, his feet closed in scarred and cracked boots. I had only seen this kind of Power once before in a Nichtvren, a heavy blurring onslaught of a creature built to be both a psychic and physical predator. He felt like Nikolai, the Prime of Saint City. "Tiens," he said.

I blinked.

Prickles of almost-gooseflesh touched my back. Nichtvren don't make me as nervous as demons do—but anything that fast, that tough, and with that much Power made me nervous enough. "What?" I managed, blankly.

"I am Tiens." He smiled broadly, showing white teeth; fangs retracted to look like ordinary canines. No wonder he'd been Turned—Nichtvren were suckers for physical beauty. I guess immortality was easier when you could collect pretty toys. The rolling song of a different dialect tinted his voice, it sounded faintly like Franje or Taliano. "At your service, *belle morte*."

"Nice to meet you," I lied. "Look, I don't mean to—"

"I'm Bella Thornton. I worked for Trinity Corp." The
female was a Shaman, her tat a curved symmetrical thorn-
laden cruciform. It shifted, stabbing her cheek. "Seem to
remember you cracked us once." She had wide dark eyes
and a triangular Neoneopunk haircut, her bangs falling
in her face. Her rig was light—only carrying four knives
and a scimitar. The sword lay across her lap, in a beautifully made leather scabbard, not reinforced by the look of
it. I would have bet hard credit the steel inside was only
decorative.

"Might have been me." It *had* been me, if she was talking about the corporate espionage I used to do with Jace.
I'd done Trinity a few times. "I hear Trinity had the best
shields in the biz while you were there." It was a lie—I'd
been before her time, and I knew it. She couldn't be more
than twenty, so unless she was working as an intern there
I wouldn't have cracked her shields.

She preened a little under the compliment and jerked
her chin toward the Magi, a thin, intense-looking young
Asiano man whose muddy hazel eyes sharpened as he
took me in. "Ogami, my partner. He doesn't talk much."
The Magi's tattoo was a Krupsev, bearing the trademark
swirls; he carried a longsword that reminded me of Gabe,
and from the way his hand rested on the plain functional
hilt I thought maybe he knew how to use it.

This is absurd. I shot a glance at Japhrimel. He watched
me, the green light from his eyes casting shadows further
down on his golden cheeks.

"Pleasure," I rasped. Rain began to smack the window
in earnest, driven by a restless wind. A harsh spear of
lightning flashed in the distance.

The other two, both spare, rangy men, watched me.

Japhrimel finally stirred as the sound of thunder reached us again, a low grinding counterpoint to the tension in the air. "Hellesvront agents." His voice stroked the air with Power. "Vann, and McKinley."

Vann was brown, from his chestnut hair to his rich warm eyes and tanned skin. He even wore brown—a fringed leather jacket and tough construction-worker's pants, a pair of supple, soft moccasins. *That* was a surprise; most people I met in my line of work wore boots, especially if they were, like him, armed to the teeth. Knives, guns, plasguns, spinclaws…even the butt of a plasrifle stood up over his right shoulder. I was surprised he didn't jingle when he shifted his weight, his eyes meeting mine and flicking away.

"Hey," Vann said.

"Hey." I sounded choked even to myself. *I've had a hell of a night, two demons and a goddamn elevator. Now I'm supposed to be polite?*

McKinley, on the other hand, was dark. Glossy crow's-wing hair, dark eloquent eyes, pale skin, and unrelieved plain-black clothing. Only two knives I could see. The only color on him was the sparkle of a strange kind of metallic coating on his left hand. He stared at me for a few moments, then lifted himself from the couch.

He moved like oil. I set my back against the wall and returned his stare, the back of my neck prickling.

He approached me, slowly, one step at a time. When he was almost past Japhrimel my sword leapt up from the scabbard. Four inches of bright steel peeked out. I swallowed. I didn't know who the hell he was, and the way he moved made me uneasy. "Don't come any closer." *If you*

come near me, I'm not going to be able to stop myself. I
am not safe right now, kiddo. Not safe at all.

McKinley studied me for a long moment. His eyes
flicked down to my left wrist. He glanced at Japhrimel,
whose eyes had never left my face. When Japhrimel didn't
move, the pale man nodded. "Impressive." His voice was
almost like a Necromance's, low—but not whispering.
Just quiet, as if he never had to raise it to get something
done.

"Glad you approve." Lucas heaved himself up from beside the fireplace. "I'm going to bed. G'night, kids."

"Lucas—" For a moment, I actually considered appeal-
ing to him for help. Then I regained my senses. "What the
hell is going *on*?"

"Isn't it obvious?" Villalobos didn't even look back
as he paced from the room. "Your green-eyed boyfriend
made good on your promises. Consider me paid and on
the job. 'Night."

"Tomorrow," Japhrimel said, and they took it like a
prearranged signal. They filed past me to the elevator,
while Lucas slid into another room, shutting the door and
immediately almost vanishing even to my senses. McKinley edged past me, gave me a long look before stepping
through the maghinged doors, and I shuddered at the
thought of being in an elevator, unable to fight, unable
to breathe.

Japhrimel stayed where he was. Watched me. The elevator door slid closed, the maghinged doors closed too,
and I let out a mostly unconscious sound of relief. I was
beginning to feel a little silly pressed against the wall.
Rain-heavy wind moaned against the windows. "I'm still
waiting for that explanation," I informed him. My hands

were still trembling, just a little. *What did you pay Lucas? How did you find him?*

"And yet, here you are." His eyes traveled down me once, the mark on my shoulder responding with a flare of heated Power, staining through my shielding. My entire body ached with unspent tension under that caress. Lightning flashed outside the window, the sharp jab of electricity echoing in my shielding.

Sparks popped from my rings. His eyes sharpened, and he looked straight through me. "I came out of Hell to find our home burning and my *hedaira* vanished. The smell of a scavenger overlaid your trail, and when I tried to locate you, I felt resistance. I thought you taken or tortured, or too weak to respond."

What happened next surprised me. He actually snarled, a swift brutal expression crossing his face. "Do you know what it is *like* to search for you, thinking you taken or worse?"

I jammed my sword back home in the sheath. "Were you hoping another demon would find me before you did?"

I have never had his gift for dry irony, it surprised me to hear something so horrible come out of my own mouth. It had sounded funny inside my head, but not so funny now hanging in the air between us.

Japhrimel took a single step toward me, his eyes burning. The air turned hot and tense, the plasglass table next to me beginning to sing softly, one trembling crystal note stroking the air. I considered slipping my sword free again. The storm outside settled into its predetermined course.

"Go ahead," he said softly. "Draw. If it will please you."

"I don't draw without reason." *So help me, I am so close to the edge now. Don't push me.* "Just fucking give me a few minutes, Japh."

"You're angry." He didn't even have the grace to sound ashamed.

"Of *course* I'm fucking angry!" Why did I sound like a hurt child? My voice hadn't broken like this since my first social worker had died, knifed by a Chillfreak for an antique watch and a pair of sneakers. "You pulled one *hell* of a bait-and-switch on me, and I just got chased and—"

"I did what was necessary. You may keep your precious scruples, because I did so." Dismissive. His eyes half-lidded, the green glow intensifying—as if that were possible.

I couldn't believe this. I was so happy to see him, and yet I was shaking with the urge to punch him. As if it would have mattered; I didn't think I could have hit him anyway, he was too fast. I searched vainly for a way to hold onto my temper. "My 'precious scruples' worked for you once," I said tautly. "I finished dealing with Lucifer. And if I hadn't burned my house down, you'd still be a pile of ash. Right?"

He shrugged. "I would have come back to you, one way or another. You know this."

Why were my eyes watering? He *had* come back, he had searched Saint City to find me and helped me destroy Mirovitch's leprous blue *ka*; he had spent so much patient time nursing me through the effects of the psychic rape Mirovitch had inflicted on me.

The anger went out of me. I could almost feel it go with a helpless snap. There are some things even I can't fight, and I was being ridiculous. No sleep, no food, and being chased by demons was not guaranteed to leave me in a good mood, but he didn't deserve the sharp edge of my temper. My muscles began to ache, a sure sign I was coming down from the raw edge of homicidal fury. "I'm just...gods. I could have done without this, you know. I *really* could have done without this. That's all. Can you just...I don't know, give me a little credit for *not* being mad at you but at the goddamn motherfucking situation Lucifer's trapped me in?"

"Dante." He took another step, approaching me cautiously. I glanced past him, toward the window running with rainwater, showing the sky jabbed with spears of light whose holoflashes showed the bridges over the Vltava. Reinforced plasglass. I would be able to leap, but I didn't know what *this* fall would do to me. The thought flashed through my head and was gone in less than a second. "I am sorry." More thunder underlaid his words. The magscan shieldings on hovers glowed with coruscating whirls as the craft disregarded the storm, whipping between high buildings.

I let out a long breath. "Me too." I didn't mean it to sound so sharp.

He repeated himself patiently, as if I was being an idiot. "I am sorry if you ever thought I could abandon you. Do you think I am *human*? Do you think I would throw away Hell for you, then tire of your company?"

For the sake of every god that ever was, I'm trying to be conciliatory here, for once in my goddamn life. Will you just quit it? "Well, you got Hell back, didn't you?" I responded ungracefully.

Japhrimel tipped his head back, closing his eyes. It took a few moments before I realized his jaw was working as his fury circled the room like a shark, looking for an out-let. It took about thirty seconds for his hold on his temper to come back. I stared, fascinated. It was like watching a reaction fire trying to contain itself. I had never seen this level of frustration in him.

"Were I to go back to Hell," he informed me, his tone dead level, "I would be shunned. I am abomination, an *A'nankhimel* who has bargained with Lucifer for a de-mon's Power. Every moment I spent there would punish me even more thoroughly. I have removed myself irre-vocably from Hell, and I have done it for an ungrateful, spiteful child."

I'm trying *to be* nice *to you!* Guilt twisted my heart as if a hand had reached into my chest and squeezed. *Why won't you* tell *me these things?* "Good for you." My hands were back to shaking. "Do you want a cookie or a pat on your widdle demon head?"

He shook his head, as if beyond words. I recognized the gesture—Jace used to make one like it when he'd reached the point of speechless rage during an argument with me. Then he took a deep breath, the crackle of Power dyeing the air around him with black flame.

"Punish me with sharp words if you like." He opened his eyes and regarded me. "Your time would be better spent laying plans. There is a demon to this city, one who thinks it would be tactically sound to kill Lucifer's new Right Hand before she can capture him."

"Great. Another thing that's my fault." *Come on. Lose your temper, Japh. I know you want to.* I could hardly breathe, both from the weight of Power in the air and my own self-loathing. Why did I have to taunt him?

Well, at least I know I have an effect on him. The

thought made me wince. I did feel strangely satisfied, as if by pushing him into losing his temper I could regain a little control over the situation. Gods above, I needed a little control.

"Not your fault. Mine. I was frantic, and too conspicuous in my search for you."

The admission took any remaining anger and drowned it. I slumped against the wall, my hand dropping away from my swordhilt. The wristcuff on my left arm warmed abruptly. "Lovely. More people who want to kill me." *I'm sorry, Japh. I know I'm not a nice person.*

"Is it any consolation that they are not 'people'?" Familiar dry irony. I sagged against the wall, my legs refusing to quite hold me up. I knew that tone in his voice, knew it all the way through my veins. It was the voice he used while we lay tangled against each other, his skin against mine, the most human of his voices. The most gentle.

"Why were you so frantic?" I tried not to sound as if it mattered. Tried not to sound like I wanted, *needed* to hear him admit to it.

He shook his head. Rain murmured and hissed behind him, I saw more jolts of lightning stabbing between heaven and earth. "You are not stupid, Dante. Why do you ask?"

Didn't he *know*? It took courage I didn't think I had to tell him why. "Because I need to hear you say it."

Long pause, moments ticked off in silence. The window was starting to look pretty good, rain or no rain. If I did decide to throw myself through it—just hypothetically, of course—how would I break the glass? And the fall, would it kill me? Could I lay the odds on that? I'd give myself three-to-one chances; I was pretty tough these days. I'd fought off an imp, hadn't I?

One lousy little Low Flight imp.

"I was afraid for you." Japhrimel turned on his heel. Stalked away from me, toward the wall of plasglass, trailing a streak of bright crimson across the air. He stopped, staring down at the lights of New Prague's Novo Meste underfoot, at the clouds crackling with stormlight. "You will not leave me to wander the earth alone, my curious little Necromance. I thought that was clear enough even for your stubborn head."

Oh, gods. He'd said that before, after Santino had shot me and Gabe dragged me back from Death. "You were afraid?"

"Yes." Just the one simple affirmation, no embroidery.

"*Sekhmet sa'es,*" I hissed, and watched his shoulders tighten. "I can't believe I…Japhrimel? Look, I'm sorry. I'm just…this just…."

He shook his head. "Not necessary, *hedaira.*"

"It is. I'm sorry. Okay? I'm sorry. I didn't know what to do, and I'm *scared*. You should have told me something! You should have—"

"Stop." He rounded on me, his fists clenched. Against the backdrop of the sky's theatrics, his eyes blazed and his black coat rustled. "Do you seek to drive me into a rage? You are safe, you are whole; well and good. You are angry that I used the Prince to gain a measure of safety for you, you are angry at me because I Fell, you hate me more than you can admit because I cannot be human, well and good. But *do not taunt me.*"

He thinks I hate him? How could he think I hate him? Where the hell did that come from? "I don't hate you.

That's been the motherfucking problem ever since I *met* you, hasn't it? I *can't* hate you. I keep treating you like you're human."

As usual when an uncomfortable truth is spoken, it hung reverberating in the air, unwilling to die. I looked down at my boot-toes, grimy from slogging through New Prague; the stains on my jeans from the puddle of slag I'd landed in after fighting off the imp. "I shouldn't have said that," I finished lamely, my left hand loosening so the scabbard slid through, lowering the sword. I wasn't going to use it.

Not on him.

"I should not have said that either," he said, from very close. His breath brushed my cheek. The velvet wash of his aura slid down mine, enfolded me. Then, slowly, he reached up, his fingers wrapping around mine where they rested against the swordhilt.

I didn't look up. I closed my eyes, the last few ounces of resistance leaving me. The touch of his skin on mine sent heat down my spine, wrapped me in comfort. I was acutely aware I hadn't really slept, that my body trembled on the edge of deep shock.

Please, Japhrimel. Help me. I can't do this on my own.

I let out a long trembling breath, the shaking in my bones intensifying until the scabbard of my sword tapped the wall behind me, a tiny embarrassing sound. No control left.

"You will do yourself damage if you do not cease your struggling." His breath ruffled my hair. "That will be uncomfortable for both of us."

How much more do you want from me? Why don't you

understand? "Japh?" I leaned into him, and his free hand slid up my right arm and around my shoulders. I rested my forehead on his chest, the terrible aching under my ribs easing. The shakes came in waves, passing through me and draining away as my nervous system struggled to deal with ramping up to such a high pitch and having nowhere to spend the energy.

"What, my curious?" Was that relief that made him shake, or was I shaking so hard I was jostling him?

Did I care?

"What demon was it? Back there? Which one?" My voice cracked again, husky with invitation. I couldn't help myself, I always sounded like a seduction, like rough honey and damp skin. Why couldn't I sound cold and ruthless, like a demon?

He shook his head, a movement I could feel even through my trembling. "Later." He kissed my cheek, then my mouth; I melted into him. Relief cascaded through me. He would make it *stop*—the jittering in my hands, the helpless rabbit-pounding of my heart, the sour taste of terror.

When he led me into the bedroom, I didn't even protest.

20

I wish I could say I made him work for it, but I was too relieved. He took his time with me, as usual; sex was the only language we truly shared despite all our time together. Even when he was talking Merican we had precious little common vocabulary. I can't ever remember being frustrated to the point of tears by my inability to *explain,* before he came along.

I had a sneaking suspicion he felt the same way.

He didn't let me tell him what had happened until we lay tangled against each other in a hotel bed, my leg over his hip, his fingers in my hair, his mouth against my forehead. I told him the entire story, pausing occasionally while he lifted sweat-damp strands of my hair and combed them with his fingers, his shoulder tensing under my cheek as I yawned. Softness draped against my hip, my back, his wing closed protectively over me.

I finally felt as if I'd survived.

Japhrimel turned slowly to stone as I explained about the reaction fire and the cracking of the house shields, and I could feel a fine humming tension in him when I told him about the hovertrain. He listened thoughtfully to the story about the reactive and the imp. His wing tightened, lying along my skin like a sheath around a knife.

He in turn told me of descending into Hell and of Lucifer's granting of his request only in the briefest of terms. He had come back to collect me and explain, found the house burning and the hoverlimo that had carried me part of the wreckage, an imp's trail mixed with mine. He had traced me to the hovertrain, taken one himself, lost my trail and caught it again, and arrived in New Prague shortly after the other hovertrain—the one with the huge hole torn in its back—had been remarked but before I rode into town. Hellesvront had been alerted, the two agents sent and set to finding a Magi worth the trouble of recruiting. Japhrimel started combing the city for me— and when Lucas Villalobos had started making inquiries, Japhrimel had gone to meet him personally, heard of the bargain I'd made, and had come to bring me in.

They found the door to Lucas's sanctum hacked open but no sign of a demon; the hidden escape-hatch hadn't been found. It looked like an imp just came in, found I wasn't there, and left to go topside to track me. From there it was a race to get to the end of the tunnel I'd slipped and slithered through. Then my flare of Power had brought all sorts of fun to the table.

"Do you know who it was?" I asked. "Which demon, I mean? Either of them?"

He shrugged. The movement tightened his wing against me. "I am not sure; he fled as soon as I arrived. I was too busy weeding through the human shields to find you."

"Human shields?"

"And a few imps. They may have been mercenaries to buy him time to escape—or to overwhelm a tired *hedaira*.

I do not know, I left none alive." Japhrimel's voice chilled. "Enough of that. We have other matters to attend to."

"Why not let Lucifer drown in his own stew? I know, I know. We've made a bargain." I yawned again, rubbed my cheek against his shoulder. My body sparked pleasantly, languidly, comfort wrapped around me.

"Sleep, my curious." His voice was soft, he pressed a soft kiss onto my forehead. "You attract far too much trouble for my comfort."

"Hm. Would have been more trouble if not for the bracelet." It felt good to be still, to not lay there cataloguing every sound and feeling my skin twitch with alertness.

"The bracelet." He didn't sound particularly happy about that, I wondered if I'd violated another arcane demonic protocol.

I forced one eye open to see him examining my face, his eyes two chips of light in the darkness of the hotel room. It didn't smell like home; but Japhrimel's scent and mine dyed the air, a soft psychic static. "It was in the hover. I thought it was from you." I wriggled a little to free my left arm from under me, bent my elbow, and lifted the wristcuff to his examination.

Japhrimel touched it with one golden finger, his eyes luminous in the dimness. "Ah," he said. "I see. . . . So."

"So what?" I yawned again. He touched my left hand, curled his fingers around it, lifted it to his mouth. Pressed his lips against my fingers, one at a time, each touch a star in the darkness. Thunder shook the sky, but it was warm and quiet under his wing.

"Tomorrow is soon enough to begin. Sleep."

"But what is this thing, if you didn't give it to me?"

The darkness was closing in, I was about to fall. He was the only truly safe haven I had ever known.

"I suspect it is Lucifer's comment on you, Dante. Sleep."

I slept.

21

When I woke, the bed was empty. Weak rainy sunlight fell in through the windows, outlining Japhrimel as he stood, hands clasped behind his back, looking out onto the Freetown. The light ran over his long black coat and the darkness of his hair—slightly longer now, falling softly over onto his forehead instead of a flat military cut. I liked his hair longer, it made him look a little less severe.

I pushed myself up on my elbows, the back of my neck naked without the heavy weight of long hair. I gathered the sheet, held it to my chest. Saw the glitter of the wrist-cuff, my rings sparking as another rushing wave of Power slid over me. It was nice, I decided. Maybe a side effect of him being...whatever he was, now.

Demon. Again. But still Japhrimel.

Still my Fallen.

I scrubbed at my face, my rings scraping. Ran my fingers back through my hair, wincing a little as chopped strands rasped against my skin. It was so silky the tangles would come out fairly easily, but so thick that combing promised to be a frustrating process. I looked at Japhrimel's back, and the rest of the night crashed back onto me.

As if he felt my gaze, he turned away from the window. I felt the humming in the walls—he'd shielded this room so well it was almost invisible. His eyes scorched green in the gray light, his face was just the same otherwise. Except for the faint line between his charcoal eyebrows, the way one corner of his mouth pulled down slightly, and the odd shadow over his cheeks.

"'Morning," I yawned.

He nodded. "More like afternoon. How do you feel?"

I took stock. Hungry, still a little shaky from the adrenaline surge of last night, and still not sanguine about getting through Lucifer's newest game in one piece. "Not too bad," I lied. "You?"

He shrugged, an evocative movement.

We both studied each other. Finally, I patted the bed next to me. "Come on, sit down."

He approached the bed soundlessly, dropped down. I touched his shoulder through the coat, rubbed my palm over the velvet-over-iron, trailed my fingers up the back of his neck, slid them through his hair. Touched his face— he closed his eyes, leaned into my fingers with a silent sigh. I brushed his shadowed cheek, smoothing away the wetness.

I hadn't known demons could produce tears.

I touched his cheekbone, the wonderful winged arch, teased at his lips with a fingertip until the bitter little grimace went away. Then I traced the line between his eyebrows until it eased out. Brushed my thumb over his eyebrow. His eyes half-closed, burning against their lids.

"What does that feel like, to you?" I whispered, my heart in my throat.

There it was, that slight tender half-smile he used just for me. "It's quite pleasant."

"How pleasant?" I found myself smiling back.

"Pleasant enough, *hedaira*." He submitted to my touch, his face easing. His aura enfolded mine, stroked up my back as I soothed him.

"Japhrimel."

"Dante." His mouth shaped my name, softly. He leaned slightly into my fingers, a small movement that managed to make my heart, trapped in my throat, leap.

"Why did you ask Lucifer to give you back a demon's Power?"

His expression didn't alter. "It was too good an opportunity to miss. Why did you cut your hair?"

"Camouflage. I don't think I could use skinspray, and if I used a glamour psions would get curious." I paused, acknowledging his wry expression. He appeared to find that extremely amusing. "I'm sorry. I was on a hair-trigger last night." I offered it in the spirit of conciliation. I had to admit, a full-fledged demon on my side dramatically improved my chances of getting through this.

"I am not some faithless human, Dante. I *fell;* I am Fallen, and my fate is bound to yours. It disturbs me, that you forget it." His eyes were still closed. He tipped his chin up, exposing his throat, I ran my finger down the vulnerable curve under his chin and he shuddered.

Oddly enough, it was that little shudder of reaction that convinced me. Did I need convincing when I'd slept next to him again? Shared my body with him again? "If you'd just talk to me about this, I wouldn't get so tangled up. Is that so much to ask?" *I think it's reasonable, Japh. Far more reasonable than anyone who ever knew me might think I was capable of being. I'm not known for forgiving people.*

"You promised not to doubt me." His voice was low, rough honey.

That's beside the goddamn point. It's because I trust you that I'm asking you this. "If you'd *tell* me what's happening when people are trying to kill me, I'd have an easier time," I repeated, but without my usual fire. "You just spun a complete one-eighty on me in front of Lucifer—how was I supposed to feel?"

"You had to appear shocked. It was necessary." He said it so kindly, so reasonably, that I felt like an idiot for still pressing the point. His eyes glowed green, a shade that reminded me of Lucifer's eyes even though they lacked the inherent awfulness of the Devil's gaze. I couldn't say exactly *how* it was different, but he looked more...human. Even with the glowing force of his eyes and the strangeness of his face, harshly balanced between severity and beauty, he still looked more human than he ever had.

"Necessary." I didn't like the way my hand shook. "Gods, Japhrimel. Don't ever do that to me again."

"Can you not simply trust in me?"

I never thought I would live to hear a demon plead. A new experience to add to all the other new experiences. They were coming thick and fast these days. The oldest curse in the book: *may you live in interesting times.*

"Listen." I tried another tack. "You've got all this power, you can make me do whatever you want. Can you understand that I might feel a little uneasy? I don't like being jerked around. Being *forced*. You know that, it's been there since the beginning. You know everything about me, but you won't tell me a single thing about what you've made me, or about this whole goddamn situation. I do trust you, I trust you more than I've trusted anyone else in my whole *life*, but you've got to help me out here."

His mouth turned down at the corners, almost bitterly. If I had to guess at the expression on his face, I would have called it frustration. Why couldn't he understand something so eminently reasonable?

"Let's bargain," I said finally, when I could talk around the lump of ice in my throat. "I'll do whatever you think's best if you promise to *talk* to me. Don't spring things like that on me. Deal?"

"I cannot, Dante." He sounded sad, now. Another first. His mouth actually *trembled* instead of being pulled into its habitual grim line. "There are things you must let me do. One of them is act for your safety."

"How is asking Lucifer to turn you into a demon again safe for me? How is any of this *safe* for me?" I kept a firm hold on my rising irritation. The ice slid down my throat and into my chest, like the creeping numb chill of Death.

"I am not demon, Dante. I am *A'nankhimel*, a Fallen with a demon's Power. There is a *difference*."

If you would just bloody well talk to me, I would know there was a difference. I thought this over, playing with the rough silk of his hair. "Gods." My breath hissed out. "I'm warning you, Tierce Japhrimel. You pull another one of those and I'll. . . ." I wasn't used to speechlessness. What *could* I do to him?

Another tremor slid through him, shocking in someone so controlled. "Fearing for your life is punishment enough, *hedaira*."

I decided to let it rest and touched his collarbone

through the coat, he shivered again. "I suppose you hired all those people?"

"Hellesvront. If we are hunting demons, if makes sense to use the resources available. There will be more if we need them." He looked like he wanted to say more, his eyes opening wider and a short breath inhaled. I waited, but nothing came out.

I ruffled his hair affectionately, he smiled again. An unwilling smile touched my own mouth. *I'd do anything you wanted if you just explained it to me, Japh. It's not that hard.* "I don't work well in groups, Japhrimel."

"Neither do I, my sweetness. Neither do I."

I let it go then. He had never called me that before.

22

"You're kidding." I braced myself on my hands as I leaned over the table. "This is *all*?"

"All we really need." Vann leaned back in his chair. "Just the nameglyphs for three of them."

"Oh, *Sekhmet sa'es*," I hissed. "What good is that?" How were we supposed to track down demons with only three runes? Not even their complete names, just the demon version of nicknames, shorthand. Demons kept their truenames a closely guarded secret, which is the reason for all those stories of a quick-thinking Magi solitary using a name to stop a demon.

I've always suspected those stories aren't anywhere close to the truth. I have difficulty believing a simple word will stop a demon, and I'm a Magi-trained psion. I work my magick by enforcing my Will on the world through words and will, so I of *all* people have a healthy respect for the magic of names. But still...*demons*. If you can't kill it with cold steel, hot lead, or a plasgun, I have a little difficulty believing a simple name spoken by anyone will stop it.

I never wanted to put it to the test, either. It was one of

those questions I could go my whole life without answering definitively. Funny how the older I got, the more of those I had.

"We know how to deal with demons, ma'am. We have a Magi," Bella pointed out. "Give Ogami the glyphs, let him work."

I threw up my hands. "Great. Just great. Have I mentioned yet how *useless* this is?"

"Many times," Lucas wheezed, looking over some magscans of New Prague. There were a couple of places with enough interference to hide a demon, mostly in the Stare Mesto. "Pointlessly. At great length. Shut up."

I subsided. He was probably the only person on earth other than Gabe who could have gotten away with that, if only because I had a healthy respect for him. I might not fear him as much as I had when I was human—but a man who couldn't die was a bad enemy to make. Lucas had a reputation for professionalism. If he told me to shut up, it was because I was being ridiculous.

Vann handed the file folders over to the Asiano, who gave me a long dubious look and retreated to a chair next to the fireplace. Japhrimel stood where he had for the last hour, in front of the rain-spotted window, his hands clasped behind his back. He seemed to be ignoring the rest of us, uninterested in events.

The storm had blown itself out, and the rain was dying in fitful gasps. I poured myself another cup of coffee. The Nichtvren had gone to ground and wouldn't be up until nightfall. Hell, *I* didn't even want to be up until nightfall. Thirty-five years of being a night-walking Necromance was a hard habit to break even after years as a *hedaira* and only needing sleep every third day or so. My body-clock was all shot to hell, and I was suddenly conscious of time passing in a way I hadn't been since the hunt for Kellerman Lourdes. I'd grown used to days that ran endlessly into each other, spent with Japhrimel's steady attention and my books. Now, suddenly, I was in a hurry again.

I didn't like it.

The other nonhuman agent—McKinley—was gone on some errand for Japhrimel. The two of them freaked me out—not human, but no other species of paranormal I'd ever seen before either. They didn't even *smell* human, which irritated me on a very basic level. They smelled like burning cinnamon and a faint tang of demon. And McKinley was seriously creepy; he just rubbed me the wrong way.

The rest of them were getting on my nerves too. I was still scrubbed too raw, all hyped up on adrenaline with nowhere to go. Sex had taken the edge off, true...but I was still twitchy.

As soon as I realized it, I tapped on my swordhilt, my claw-tip nails making a clicking sound. "Is there a sparring room in this pile?"

Silence met my words. Japhrimel turned away from the window. "You need combat?" It was a shock to see his eyes glowing green again. I'd grown so used to a human darkness in them.

An A'nankhimel with a demon's Power. All the Magi shadowjournals and demonology texts I'd read had never spoken of such a thing. If I *was* Magi, I'd have a better chance of knowing or guessing. I couldn't even do what a Magi might and call up another imp to answer my questions. I never wanted to see another damn imp ever again.

"I think I'd best get out of the way." I left my coffee cup on the table as I straightened. *A waste of good java, I'm too keyed up to even enjoy it.* "The only demon I hunted down was Santino, and I already had his trail from Abra. Until we get a direction to go in, I'm just going to fret and pull my hair out. Besides, I think better when I'm moving. Sparring qualifies as moving."

Bella glanced at me, her eyes widening. Then she cast a look at Vann, who shook his head slightly. As if cautioning her to keep her mouth shut. That irritated me far more than it should.

I'm tight-strung enough to hurt someone accidentally. That bothered me. If I hurt someone, I want it to be meant.

"There's a sparhall near here," Lucas said over his shoulder. "You could find something there. Lot of bounty action, psions. Rent's reasonable, ten New Creds an hour."

Relief smashed into my breastbone. A sparhall full of psions—I could rent a cage or a circle and get some action or just work through a few katas. "Thank the gods. Which way?"

"Due west, gray building on the Prikope. Can't miss it, got a cage hanging from the side." Lucas appeared to forget all about me, studying a map of New Prague. He was absorbing this with an incredible amount of equanimity. Than again, he hadn't batted an eye the time he'd seen Japhrimel with me in Rio. I wondered just what Lucas knew about demons, and how soon I could get him alone to pick his brains.

Vann's sad brown eyes flicked from me to Japhrimel

and back again, for all the world as if asking for direction. Japhrimel's face didn't change.

"I will accompany you," Japhrimel said. "It is not perhaps quite safe for you to go alone."

As if I was stupid enough to want to wander around alone with demons out looking to kill me. "Sounds good. Let me get my bag."

Japhrimel nodded. I headed for the room I'd slept in last night.

"My lord?" I heard Vann say quietly. "Does she intend to continue—"

Japhrimel said nothing. I ducked inside the room, grabbed my bag and Jace's coat, and made it out just in time to see Japhrimel shake his head.

"No," he said. I got the feeling I'd missed something. "I will not."

"But—" Vann flinched as Japhrimel's eyes rested on him. "Forgive me, my lord."

Japhrimel nodded. "Be at peace, Vann. There is nothing to fear."

Ogami, his eyes wide, stared from his chair. I caught him examining me as if I was a new and interesting type of bug.

"What's up?" I asked. Lucas was apparently absorbed in the maps, as if he wasn't listening. I didn't believe it for a moment. *I think you and I are going to have a little chat, Villalobos.*

"Nothing," Japhrimel's eyes met mine. "Vann thinks I am too forgiving of your disobedience."

I looked at the brown man. I could almost feel one of my eyebrows quirk. Time to get everyone on the same page about Danny Valentine. "Really? Let me clear everything up right now, then. I don't *obey*. I haven't since primary school." For a moment, my skin roughened, remembering Rigger Hall. The phantom scars across my back didn't burn, and I was grateful for that. Maybe I was starting to heal.

Maybe. "I'm generally reasonable when I'm *asked* instead of *told* what to do. But let's just get this straight: I don't take orders well. You got a problem with that?"

Vann's brown eyes widened as if I'd called his mother something unspeakable. "No ma'am," he said hurriedly, his gaze flickering over to Japhrimel, who merely looked bored and ever so slightly amused, just the smallest fraction of a smile tilting a corner of his lips up. "Not at all."

"Good. I'm going to go and get my head cleared out. When I come back, we'll try this again."

Outside the room, I stalked for the elevator. I had the odd feeling someone wasn't telling me something, but I chalked it up to being tense and decided to revisit the whole chain of thought once I was cleared out from some hard sparring. I *was* getting paranoid.

Then again, paranoid would help keep me one step ahead of the game, wouldn't it? *Paranoid* meant *careful*, and careful was good. I jabbed at the button for the elevator.

Japhrimel moved closer. I sensed crackling static in the air as his aura covered mine again briefly, a caress. The mark on my shoulder burned, a soft velvet flame. The elevator dinged and opened. I stepped in, familiar nausea and breathlessness rising. Japhrimel followed me, waiting until the doors closed to curl his hand around my shoulder. "Easy, Dante. There is enough air."

Says you. I couldn't spare the breath to say it aloud.

There was *never* enough air in small spaces. It was like some sort of thermodynamic law. Small space plus no windows equals no goddamn *air*, equals me gasping in panic. What a blow to my tough-girl image.

His hand slid up and around, warm fingers touching my nape. It helped, but not nearly enough. "I am with you."

I swallowed, closing my eyes. "Yeah. For how long?" My voice sounded gasping, panicky. *I didn't mean to say that, I didn't. Oh, gods.*

"As long as you allow it. And perhaps after."

I can't imagine that. I leaned against his fingers. "I wish I could go slicboarding," I muttered. That would work all my fidgets out.

"Do you truly wish that?" A curious, husky tone; my stomach flipped as the antigrav floated us down. He leaned closer, his solidity comforting.

I shrugged. "It's okay. I know you don't like that. I was just talking." *Just shooting my mouth off to keep from screaming, that's all.*

"If it would please you, I would learn to live with it."

I opened my eyes, saw him leaning close and examining my face, his fingers hard and warm against the back of my neck. His eyes glittered green, casting shadows under his cheekbones and drowning me in emerald light. I had always tried to avoid looking him in the eye before, when he'd been demon instead of Fallen. "Too dangerous," I said finally, as the elevator fell to a stop. The chime rang, couth and discreet, and I bolted out of the cage and away from his eyes.

Why am I so scared? It's only Japhrimel.

That was like saying it was only a hungry tiger. Living

with him had only brought home how much more than
human he was, and now that he had a demon's Power
back he was something else again. I had been pretending that he was only a man. Bad idea when it came to
anything nonhuman. But still, I couldn't think of him as
anything *other* than human. I couldn't stand to think of
living in a world without his quiet, dry humor and steady
hands. Go figure—the one guy I had a bad case for, and it
was a demon who had already proved he wouldn't necessarily tell me things I *really* needed to know. Here I was,
still hanging out with him. How was that for crazy?

I wasn't thinking clearly. I couldn't throttle back the
irritation I felt, steady low-burning irritation that was buried rage trying to work itself free. When you live your life
on the edge of adrenaline and steel, you can get really jittery. It's best to clean it all out with exercise, cleanse the
toxins from the body and clear the mind.

I stalked through the hotel lobby, ignoring the normals—guests and employees—scattering out of my path.
Japhrimel fell into step behind me, close as my shadow.
Just as he had since he'd met me. "You're running away,"
he said in my ear as I gave the door a push and stepped
out, blinking, into the pale watery sunlight.

I didn't dignify the obvious with a response.

Cracked pavement and a crowd of normals greeted me.
I glanced up to get my bearings and turned to my left,
heading generally westward and lengthening my stride.

New Prague is old, having been settled well before the Merican Era. The buildings are an odd mix of
new plasteel and old concrete, as well as some biscuit-
colored stone. The shape of the buildings is different from
Saint City's, echoing a time before hovers and plasteel, a

time before accredited psions, even though Prague had been a town known for its Magi and Judic Qabalisticon scholars.

It is also a town full of history. Here was where Kochba bar Gilead's last Judic followers had been killed by laserifle fire in the overture to the Seventy Days War, and where Skinlin had first learned the process of creating *golem'ai*, the semisentient mud-things that were a dirtwitch's worst weapon. This town was *old*, and I wondered if Japhrimel had ever been here before on Lucifer's business.

I wished I could find a way to ask.

One of the *good* things about being a Necromance is that even in a Freetown people get out of your way in a hell of a hurry when you come striding down a sidewalk with your sword in your hand and your emerald flashing. Many Necromances only use their blades ceremonially— there's nothing like good edged steel to deal with a hungry ghost or to break the spell of going into Death. The ones who, like me, deal with bounties or law enforcement are combat-trained. There's also a subculture of Mob and freelance psions who are generally very tough customers. Most normals are more frightened of a psion reading their mind than they are of the weaponry we carry, something I've never understood.

Jace had been Mob freelance. He'd been very good, but I'd had to hold back sometimes while sparring with him.

Thinking of Jace, as usual, made a lump of frustrated grief and fury rise to my throat. I slowed down a little, Japhrimel's soundless step reverberating behind me. He was demon, and all but shouted it now that I was *hedaira* and peculiarly sensitive to him I could feel the harpstrings

of Power under the physical world thrumming in response
to his very presence. Part of it was sharing a bed with him,
my body recognized him.

But that wasn't it, was it? I frowned, trying to figure out
why it felt so different. Was it just because he was a full
demon again? I stalked along the sidewalk, one little corner of my mind focused on tagging the people around me,
cataloguing their various levels of dangerousness. There
weren't a lot of psions out on the streets—of course, it
was during the day. Hard to find a psion in the morning,
unless you spot one heading home to bed.

I still hadn't figured it out by the time we reached the
sparhall, a large gray building due west of the hotel with
the universal signs of violence-in-training—magscan and
deep combat shielding, a twisted sparring cage dangling
from a hook bolted into the side of the building high
enough that slicboarders could tag it and make it rock,
slicboards racked along the front of the building, and the
blue psychic haze of adrenaline and controlled bloodlust
waving like anemones in the air.

Oh, yes. This was what I wanted—effort, maybe
enough to sweat, a few blessed seconds where I wouldn't
have to *think*, only move. No memory of the past, no
thought for the future, only the endless *now*.

Japhrimel said nothing as I stepped inside, but his
golden hand came over my shoulder and held the door
open for me. I tapped my swordhilt with my fingernails
and met the wide blue eyes of a Ceremonial behind the
front desk.

Her tat curved back on itself, she wore a rig with more
knives than I'd ever seen before. Propped next to her
against the desk was a machete with a plain, functional

leather-wrapped hilt. I measured her, she measured me, and her hand leapt for her blade.

"Whoa!" I lifted my hands. "I'm here to hire, not to drag anyone in." I didn't blame her one bit, I was popping with almost visible twitchy lasetrigger anger, and I looked like a demon to otherSight. Not to mention the fact that I was being followed by a very tall *definitely*-demon.

Her hand paused. I felt Japhrimel's attention behind me, drew myself up and leaned back into him. He was wound just tight enough to go for her if she twitched. I didn't like to consider how I knew *or* my instinctive response both to soothe him and to keep him away from her. I wasn't sure I could stop him if he started, but keeping myself in between them seemed like a *really* good idea. I'd never seen him in this mood before, not even during the hunt for Santino.

I heard the faint sounds of a sparhall behind sound-muffling—little sounds of effort, the clang of metal, the clicking of staves.

The Ceremonial eyed me, said something in Czechi.

Oh, damn. She doesn't speak Merican?

Japhrimel replied over my shoulder in the same language. *I am really going to have to learn a few new languages,* I thought as I caught a flicker of motion.

The roll of New Credit notes landed on her desk as Japhrimel said something else, short and harsh. I felt the air pressure change, and knew without looking back that he now wore a small chilling little smile.

I'd seen that smile before, and I hoped my reaction was less visible than hers. She paled, the inked lines of her tattoo suddenly glaring on her cheek. Her aura flared with fear, the air full of the rough chemical tang of it. The smell was pleasant, not drunkening like a sexwitch's fear but still enough to make my breath catch.

She reached slowly for a communit on the desk, spoke into it. I heard the ghostly tones float through the rest of the building as she made an announcement in Czechi.

The sounds of metal clashing and heated exclamations trailed off. I restrained the urge to look back at Japhrimel, instead watched the Ceremonial's right hand as it hovered near the hilt of her machete.

She relaxed a bit, scooping up the roll of notes and riffling through them. She glanced up at Japhrimel, jerked her chin up fractionally at me, and rose. She picked up her machete, carefully keeping her fingers away from the hilt. She said something that sounded vaguely conciliatory, then backed away to put her shoulders against the wall.

I didn't blame her one bit. I'd had that reaction before too.

"We may go in," he said behind me.

"Great. You're making friends all over, aren't you."

"It must be my personality," he replied, deadpan. I actually laughed, surprising myself.

I went past the desk to a pair of heavy airseal doors, pushed at them. They opened easily, the whoosh of airseals and the chill of a sparring room's climate control washed over my skin, roughening the smooth gold. *Hedaira* don't often get goosebumps—but I felt awful close for a moment.

The air swirled uneasily. If there was a place to find psions during the day, this was it.

Several Shamans, each of them holding a staff and eyeing the door uneasily. Three more Ceremonials, males each with edged steel, gathered around a watercooler, sweat gleaming on tats and wide shoulders. A few Skinlin and one Magi were scattered around. At the far end of the room a heavy bag shuddered as a double oddity—a male Necromance, with the trademark spatters of glitter in his aura—worked it low and dirty, throwing an occasional elbow, paying no attention to anything else. I took all this in with a glance.

The building was an old warehouse, the floor fitted with shockgel and full-spectrum lights boiling down from the ceiling. Shafts of sunlight lanced down from windows overhead, and weapons were racked in stasis cabinets along two walls. Dueling-circles were painted into the shockgel flooring, I finished my inspection by testing the magscan and combat shielding. Nice and deep, laid with skill and reinforced punctually.

Lucas was right. This was a good place.

"How long do we have?" I slipped my bag over my head and hung it on a peg near the door next to several similar bags, all glowing to Sight with different defensive charms. I shrugged out of my coat, unbuckling my rig at the same time and hanging both up over my bag. Flicked my fingers, my obsidian ring sparking slightly. A keep-charm blurred in the air, settling over my bag and coat to keep them safe from prying fingers. Not that I worried much—the very last place you'll usually find a pickpocket is in a sparhall. Few thieves are *that* suicidal.

"As long as you need." Japhrimel's eyes finished their own circuit of the room. The thuds from the Necromance working the heavy bag didn't diminish. "It seems we will have an audience."

So *he* was going to spar with me. I thought I'd have to find a psion partner and hold back. "Fine by me." I was hard-pressed to keep my tone businesslike, my pulse rose in my throat to choke me. I stepped out onto the shockgel, my right hand curling around the hilt. "You going to use a blade?"

"Not unless it becomes necessary." Was it just me, or did he sound amused? "I think I am equipped to handle one angry *hedaira*."

It was the first time he'd ever goosed me before a sparring match.

It worked.

I turned on my heel, my eyes coming up and meeting his. We stood like that, demon and *hedaira*, his eyes burning green, a spatter of golden sparks popping from my rings. "I think I'm angry enough to give you a little trouble." My voice was so harsh it sounded as if Lucifer had tried to strangle me again, and I was grateful I didn't sound like a vidsex queen right now. "I'm wound a bit tight."

Just a little tight. Just like Lucifer's a little scary.

He shrugged, spreading his hands. "I expected no less."

"Are you sure you want to do this?" It was my last-ditch effort to give him a graceful way to back out. I needed to work off my adrenaline, true—but I could spar with someone else, couldn't I?

Couldn't I?

No, I realized, as the Power began to shift between us, straining. We were heading for something, some shape of an event already lying under the surface of the world. There was a collective in-breath from the assembled psions. The steady thudding of the Necromance's fists against the punching bag paused. A few more good solid hits, then the sound stopped altogether.

Japhrimel nodded. Never one to use words when a single gesture would do.

I half-turned, walking sideways, keeping Japhrimel in my peripheral vision as I headed for the center of the warehouse.

I don't just want to spar to work my nerves off. I want to make him pay for making me afraid. Gods, I'm not a very nice person. I want to fight him, I have to fight him, to prove I'm not afraid.

The realization shook me. I looked down at my hand wrapped around the swordhilt.

"Dante," Japhrimel said softly, "you cannot hurt me."

That did it. *We'll just see about that.* I drew the blade free, the slight ringing sound of steel slicing thick air. Heat bled away from my skin, the demon-fed heat of a *hedaira*, it would make the climate control start to strain after a while.

I saluted him with the shining length of steel. Blue fire began twisting in the metal depths, runic patterns slipping like raindrops down a window, sparkling. I must really be upset for my sword to be reacting this way, usually blessed steel didn't react to his presence. It hadn't since he'd Fallen.

But he's demon again, isn't he? And so much more powerful than I could ever be. My rings crackled. I shook my head a little, forgetting my hair was a chopped-short mess.

"All right," I breathed. "If we're going to do this, let's do it. Come and get me."

23

*H*e paused for just the briefest moment before moving in, deceptively slow, his feet soundless against shockgel. My sword flicked, he slapped it aside. I used the momentum, whirling, shuffling back as he moved in; I darted forward and almost caught him. He actually had to take two steps back, bending slightly to the side to escape the whistling arc of my blade.

I blew out through my teeth. Held the scabbard in my left hand, resting it along my forearm to act as a shield. The sword kept moving, painting the air with blue flame. I learned long ago not to keep the blade still when sparring with him, he could take it away easier if I did.

We circled, Japhrimel's boots soundless, mine shushing, his hands actually, maddeningly, clasped behind his back again. His eyes burned green. His face wasn't set or angry. The only expression I could decipher was indifference with the faintest trace of amusement, his combat mask. Anger rose, tightly reined in and stuffed to the back of my mind. If I got angry this would be over far too soon.

I didn't want that. I *needed* to work this off, get the

poison of adrenaline out of my system so I could think again.

I moved in on him, slashing and feinting, he melted away from each strike with impossible grace. His hand blurred, his claws nearly tearing the sword from my grip. A loud clang shot through the air, sparks spraying from my rings as our shields locked together, a psychic engagement as well as a physical one.

He'd never done that before either.

My throat went dry. "You're serious, aren't you."

"You're holding back," he said quietly. "Come at me, Dante. You feel I betrayed you in some fashion. Make me pay for it."

It didn't sting that he was right about my holding back—but it *did* sting that he guessed I wanted him to pay.

I should have come alone and contracted a cage. Or taken a slicboard. Goddammit.

I used to love slicboarding, especially after a Necromance job. But Japhrimel didn't like it when I was on a board; it would be too easy to tip me off and since I had the mark, he said, it would be uncomfortable for him if I died or was injured.

I wondered just *how* uncomfortable.

I showed my teeth, a feral smile. "I just want to spar, Japhrimel." It wasn't precisely a lie—I had thought that was all I wanted until I got here and realized just how furious I still was.

"Then spar. You are wasting time."

"Oh, do I *bore* you?" My voice rose, took on an edge as he batted the sword away again. It doubled back on itself, hilt floating up, I cut overhand and struck with the scabbard in my left hand at the same time. He slid away from both strikes and we went back to circling, my breath beginning to come deep and fast. "I *bore* you. Maybe you want something more *interesting*—a nice little Androgyne copy of Lucifer to keep you warm instead?"

Even I couldn't believe I'd said that.

The only warning I got was Japhrimel's eyes narrowing before he blurred toward me, and I saw the bright lengths of knives reversed along both forearms. He'd gone to blades without warning me.

Another first. Well, wasn't this a day for surprises.

Knife-work is close and dirty, and his speed and strength gave him an edge. But my katana kept him just out of reach, scabbard flickering in to dart at eyes or to smack at his wrist; wall coming up fast and I was losing ground, giving way under the slashes. Parried a strike, metal ringing, hurt like hell and would have broken a human's arm, my sword followed the path laid out in front of it, blurred up in a solid arc and we separated, Power crackling as he pushed at me and I shunted the energy aside.

A thin line of black blood kissed his cheek before it sank in, sealing away the wound, golden skin closing over itself. Perfect. Flawless.

I had rarely been able to touch him, before. Was anger giving me speed to match his? If so, it wouldn't last.

I backed up at an angle to give myself more room. My sword-tip moved in precise little circles.

"You see?" Japhrimel said, both knives laid along his forearms, left arm in guard position, right hand held oddly, low and to the side. "I even let you wound me." His voice stroked along the edge of my defenses, a physical weight. I was overmatched and I knew it. He had too *much* damn speed. I was harder to kill now that I was *hedaira*—but I was no match for a Greater Flight demon.

Not even one that was being kind about it.

Fuck that. I licked my dry lips. *I killed Santino.*

But Santino had only been a Lesser Flight demon, brought to bay by Japhrimel. Killing him had almost crippled me.

Almost killed me.

"Don't do me any favors," I spat, and moved in on him.

Speed. Pure speed. Sword flashing, clanging off knife-blades, heard Jado's voice yet again. *No think! Move!* Scabbard ripped out of my hand, my wrist momentarily numb, sword whistling as I slashed in return and caught air, ducking under his arm and striking in, forcing him *back*.

My left hand closed around my katana's hilt under my right, my ribs flaring with deep breaths. We circled again. I don't usually fight with two hands on my sword—being smaller than most mercenaries meant I was at a distinct weight disadvantage while I was fully human. So I trained to use every ounce of speed I could get as well as the de-fensive measure of my scabbard.

But since I'd lost the scabbard and gained some demon strength I might as well make every stroke count.

He darted in, I took the only move I had at that point, leaping back like a cat avoiding a snake's lunge, sword streaking blue fire, chiming against a knifeblade, whip-ping down with all my weight and speed behind it in a solid silver arc. He faded away from under the strike then came back, slashing for me, my boots landed on the shockgel. Parried one strike, coiled myself, and *leapt*.

Tumbling, boots thocking down again, whirling to ward off another strike, now I had the entire length of the warehouse to retreat before I had to think of something good.

Breath coming tearing-hard, body alive and crackling, smashing aside a stroke of Power along the front of my shields. Adrenaline singing, clatter of metal against metal, his eyes narrowed and glowing behind the silver gleams of knifeblades streaking the air. One slash after another, each one just barely batted aside, giving ground but making him work for it, every single inch he gained paid for with effort. His shields locked with mine, shoving, an engagement no less psychic than physical. The entire Freetown could have gone up in reaction fire and I wouldn't have noticed, my entire world narrowing to the man in front of me with his knives and his habit of fading away under my strikes.

The idea came, laid inside my brain like a gift. I didn't hesitate. Breathing harsh, feet stamping the shockgel, I blurred forward. The *kia* rose from the very depths of me, a scream of rage and despair lifting from a smoking destroyed part of me, metal clashing and shivering and I slashed, he ducked—

—and my blade tore through the air as my foot stamped down again, following unerringly the path of his retreat, and kissed his throat.

Just as his knifeblade blurred in and touched my own pulse beating high and wild and frantic in my neck.

I stared at him, his eyes glowing green. A single trickle of black blood eased down from the corner of his mouth. He'd bitten his bottom lip, sharp teeth sinking in. Oddly enough, that made me feel like I'd won.

His aura wrapped around mine, enclosing me. The mark on my shoulder flared to life, burning through layers of shielding, my body tensing.

Ready to push the blade home.

The bright length of my katana rose over his shoulder, the razor edge about five inches from the hilt against his tough golden skin. I could fall backward away from his knife and slash, twisting my wrist through the suction of muscle.

I *could*.

"Give?" I asked, without any hope that he would.

"Of course," he answered without hesitation, his eyes locked with mine. "Anything you want, *hedaira*."

I felt a second prickle. His right-hand knife, against my floating rib. He could open my belly with a flick of his wrist.

He'd won.

Then why had he conceded?

The knives vanished. He clasped his hands behind his back and looked down at me, my blade still tucked under his chin. My hand shook slightly. I could push the steel in, step forward and twist, all momentum boiling down to one simple, undeniable movement.

I was no longer bloodthirsty enough to do it.

I took a step back. Coughed rackingly. My throat was dry. I could feel the back of my neck crawling. "Why do you make this so hard?"

"I will do what I must to protect you," he answered, inflexibly.

"Even if it means losing me?" Like there was any way in hell I was going to walk away from him. I was in too deep, and I knew it.

He smiled, the amused tender expression that made my breath catch. "We have nothing but time, my curious one."

It didn't satisfy me. My sword lowered, rose into second guard. I examined him. He tilted his chin up slightly, a subtle movement. Offering his throat.

The air was hot and still. I barely noticed the other psions against the walls, shields gone crystalline, the perfume of human awe and fear staining the air. Even other psions were afraid of me. Or afraid of Japhrimel first, and me only by association.

The blade blurred as I reversed the katana, dropping the tip and ending the movement with the blade tucked behind my arm, blunt edge against my shirt and the hilt clasped in my hand. I wasn't sweating—demons don't sweat and neither do *hedaira* without a *lot* of effort—but my ribs flickered with deep heaving breaths and my entire body hummed like a reactive mill. But I felt oddly cleansed. I'd got what I wanted, after all.

"We have demons to hunt." Now his voice was back to flat, with a tinge of... what? Gentleness? Pity?

No, not pity. Didn't he know how I *hated* pity? I would call it gentleness, from him.

I swallowed dryly. "Four demons. Then what?"

"Then we see what pleasures the world holds for us. Seven years is not so long."

Not for you, maybe. "Is there anything else you want to tell me?" I wasn't holding out any particular hope.

He shrugged, a fluid movement. I *hate* demons' shrugging. His coat ruffled a little, his wings settling completely.

I shook myself, like an animal shedding water. Blew my hair out of my eyes. "We'd better get back."

He nodded. I cast a glance around the sparhall.

The light had changed slightly. I met the human eyes locked on us. Bright eyes, accreditation tats shifting on human cheeks of every shade. Then I saw the other Necromance.

He leaned against the wall, his dark hair slicked back with sweat, unshaven cheeks hollow. Dark eyes over high balanced cheekbones. His tat was circular, thorns twisting in a yin-yang symbol; his emerald sparked a greeting and my cheek burned, answering it.

He nodded, lifted his left hand. He carried a katana too. He wore a Trade Bargains shirt over the tank top he'd been working the heavy bag in, and his boots were scarred from long use. He looked faintly familiar, but I'd never worked with him. I couldn't quite place the face, which was a first for my Magi-trained memory. Everything about him shouted "bounty hunter."

The nod was an invitation to spar.

I felt my eyebrows rise. Looked at Japhrimel, who had gone utterly still. "I think someone else wants a match with me."

"Be careful." His eyelids dropped fractionally. Did he look angry? Why?

The mark on my shoulder flared suddenly, heat rising to my cheeks. "I think I'm done." I lifted my sword and my right fist, bowed correctly to the Necromance, honoring him and respectfully refusing his offer. "We've got work to do, anyway."

Then I turned on my heel and stalked away from all of them. Sparring was supposed to make me feel better—

and I did. Clearer, cleaner, with the fidgets worked out. But most of what I felt was something hot and deep and squirming behind my breastbone.

It was shame. For a moment I'd thought of hurting him, and he'd offered his throat to the blade. Made himself vulnerable to me.

How could I have doubted him?

24

_J_aphrimel said nothing as we hit the street outside. Rainy sunlight still fell down, but darker clouds were rolling and massing; I smelled wet heaviness riding the air. That was worth a nose-wrinkle, and I wondered if another storm was moving in. I walked with my head down and my left hand holding my sword, my eyes fixed on the pavement and only occasionally lifting to check the crowd and the sky above.

Urban dwellers learn quickly to be peripherally aware of hover and slic traffic. Practically all Freetowns have realtime AI traffic controllers just like Hegemony and Putchkin cities. Freetown New Prague was no exception. The distinct swirls of hover traffic with slicboards buzzing in between were almost complex enough to use for divination.

The thought of hovertraffic divination made me smile. I glanced up again, my eyes tracking the patterns, my nape tingling.

Why was I so uneasy?

This is too easy. If there's a demon in New Prague who knows I'm here, why hasn't he thrown everything but the

*kitchen sink at me? Just a lone imp and one attack in a ru-
ined building doesn't qualify as a real battle. Either he's
more frightened of me than is possible…or he's laying
plans.*

Another, more interesting thought occurred to me. Why
would Lucifer bargain to have me as his official Right
Hand and not Japhrimel? What purpose did that serve?

Maybe the sparring *was* what I needed to shake my
thoughts loose. I cast around for a likely place and saw a
noodle shop, its door half-open.

Lunch and some heavy thinking. I ducked out into the
street, dodging a swarm of pedicabs. There was some
streetside hover traffic too, but the hovers were in a crush
of pedicabs and people and had to move at a creep, antigrav rattling and whining, buffeting people out of the
way.

Making it across the street in one piece, I slid into the
noodle shop. The smell of cooking meat and hot broth
rose around me; I had made it almost to the counter when
Japhrimel's hand closed around my upper arm.

"This is unwise," he said. I hadn't quite forgotten he
was with me, but I was so deep in thought I hadn't even
spoken to him. Taking it for granted he would follow me,
understanding my need for serious contemplation of this
problem.

I set my jaw. "I'm hungry, and I need to think." My
tone was sharp enough to cut glass. "Something about
this smells."

Amazingly, he smiled. "Now this is revealed to you?"

I swear, he could sound caustic as carbolic when he
wanted to. I scanned the interior of the noodle shop—plas-
covered booths, the counter with three Asiano normals be-

hind it, two staring at me and another one chopping little bits of something that smelled like imitation crabmeat. Holostills of Asiano holovid stars hung on the walls. The ubiquitous altar to ancestors sat near the front door with a small plashing antigrav fountain floating above it, coins shimmering underwater in its plasilica bulb just like miniature cloned koi.

"You're getting testy." I tried not to smile. The jitter of adrenaline bloodlust was gone, I felt like a new woman.

He gave a liquid shrug. I hate a demon's shrug; it usually means he won't answer your questions anyway. "I will not deny a certain frustration."

You're not the only one. I indicated a booth with a flick of my swordhilt. "Fine. Sit, eat, talk, relax. Just like old times, right?"

He shrugged. *Again.* "We should go back to the hotel."

"Not only do I hate the goddamn elevator, but all someone has to do is drive a hover through the windows and there goes our entire team," I said acidly. "We should go to ground. Somewhere safer, and somewhere without a goddamn elevator."

At least he didn't immediately disagree. A curious expression crossed his face, half thoughtful, half admiring. "Where?"

I slid into the booth. "The red-light district. Enough static and interference to hide most of our team—except for you and me. And that's where a demon's going to do his recruiting if he's fresh out of Hell and needs human hands. Ergo, it's where we're going to hear the most whispers and gossip."

Japhrimel slid into the seat across from me. His back

was to the door, mine to the back of the restaurant—as usual. We had fallen into that habit during the hunt for Santino, him courteously allowing me to put my back to the wall. My eyes flicked over his shoulder and checked the front window. People passing by, the soft roar of a crowd of normals, the staticky heartbeat of the city. New Prague smelled like pedicab sweat and paprikash, a spicy unique smell tainted with stone and the effluvia of centuries of human living. With a dash of burning cinnamon over the top of it.

The smell of burning cinnamon was demon. Two demons and a *hedaira* in a city, and the whole place started to smell. Something about that bothered me, but I couldn't quite wrap my mental lips around *what*.

It'll probably come back to bite me in the ass pretty soon. I should have told Lucifer to go fuck himself again. Should have told him that and taken my chances the first time.

It was empty bravado. I'd needed revenge on Santino, I couldn't have walked away from the deal even if I could by some miracle have fought off Japhrimel, Lucifer, and the rest of Hell *and* made my way back to my own world.

"Anyway," I continued, "Lucas is one of our biggest assets, and he's best on the shadow side—has a lot of connections. I've also got a nasty thought, Japh. Why isn't this demon throwing everything but the kitchen sink at me? And why did Lucifer ask for *me* to be his Right Hand instead of you? You're the one he can count on here."

One of the Asianos came to the table. She bobbed her dark head, smiling at Japhrimel and casting a little sidelong glance at me.

He ordered in a clicking tongue that sounded like Old

Manchu. I frowned at the shiny plasilica tabletop, tapping my right-hand fingernails with little insectile ticking sounds. The problem boiled and bubbled away under the conscious surface of my mind, sooner or later I'd hit the answer. Half of any problem, especially for a psion, is simply trusting intuition to do its work.

Of course, sometimes intuition only kicks in too goddamn late and you figure everything out as you're neck-deep in quicksand. I winced inwardly at the thought.

The Asiano bowed slightly and hurried away, her slippers hushing over the slick linoleum. Japhrimel's glowing eyes met mine. "The Prince can trust you, Dante. You are honorable. I, however, have bargained with him in the past. I am known to be somewhat...unruly."

Lucifer can trust me? I thought my eyebrows couldn't get any higher. "You? Unruly?"

"I won my freedom, did I not? And I am Fallen. That means I am dangerous."

"Why? What's the big deal? You won't tell me anything about the Fallen, and you complain when I try to research it on my own. Why are you suddenly so dangerous to Lucifer?" *Just one little shred of information, Japh. It won't kill you.*

"Why do you think he destroyed the original Fallen? They were a direct threat to his supremacy on earth. It was only a matter of time before a Fallen and his *hedaira* conceived an Androgyne. Then...who knows?"

Oh. I swallowed dryly. Lucifer controlled reproduction in Hell, and the Androgynes were the only demons capable of reproducing. Santino's creation of Eve had been a blow to Lucifer's power, one he couldn't cover up or simply ignore. Hence Lucifer's throwing me into the snakepit the first time.

The waitress came back with heavy real-china teacups, poured us both fragrant jasmine tea with shaking hands. She set the pot down and retreated in a hurry, her bowl-cut black hair shining under the fluorescent lights.

"Why didn't Lucifer kill us both when you...Fell?" I didn't expect him to answer.

He surprised me once again. "I suspect he thought he might have further use for us. In any case, I know better than to try to breed." Japhrimel's eyes dropped to the tabletop.

The steam rising from my teacup took on angular, twisting shapes. I cleared my throat. There had only been one time in my life that I'd even *contemplated* having children, and that time was long past. Still.... "What if *I* wanted to breed?"

I felt his eyes on me, but I looked at my teacup. Silence stretched between us.

"Never mind," I said hurriedly. "Look, let's just focus on one problem at a time. We should get everyone out of that damn hotel and into a safer place. Then we can start figuring out which demon's here in New Prague and what he's likely to be planning."

"Do you want children, Dante?"

He could turn on a red credit's thin edge. No more sarcasm. Instead, his tone was quiet and level. Of all the varied shades of his voice, I liked this one best. I stared at my teacup, willing the lump in my throat to go away.

"No," I said finally. "I have enough trouble trying to deal with *you*."

That made him laugh, a sound that chattered the teacups against the table. I stole a quick glance at him; looked back down at the table. I knew every line and curve of his face, almost every inch of his skin. It wasn't enough—I wanted to know what was going on behind those glowing green eyes, under that perfect poreless golden skin, behind that face that wasn't as gorgeous as Lucifer's but somehow enough for me, beautiful the way a katana's deadly curve was beautiful.

I wanted *inside*. I wanted to crawl inside his head and know for sure that he wouldn't abandon me.

"Japhrimel." My voice cut through his laughter. "What gave you the brilliant idea to bargain for a demon's Power again?"

He sighed, shaking his head. His hair was almost longer than mine now, falling over his eyes in a soft shelf. "I wanted it for one simple reason. To protect you, Dante. A *hedaira* is only as safe as her *A'nankhimel* can make her." It had the quality of a proverb, recited more than once.

Way to seize the moment, Japh. "I thought you said there weren't many demons who could threaten you, even Fallen."

"After we are done killing for the Prince, he may find us expendable." Japhrimel's tone had turned chill. "If that happens, I want every iota of Power I can possibly gather. I will not give you up. Not to Lucifer, not to your own folly—and not to your precious Death either. Therefore, I saw a chance and took it. It was not premeditated."

I stole another glance at his face. He looked over my shoulder, his eyes moving in a smooth arc. His right hand, resting on the table, had curled into a fist.

"Oh." I certainly couldn't argue with my own continued survival. "Well. That was a good idea, then, I guess."

He said nothing, but his eyes met mine. It was just a flash, but I could have sworn he looked *grateful.*

The woman arrived with the food—beef and noodles for me, a plate of something that looked like egg rolls for Japhrimel, who thanked her courteously. I scooped up a pair of plasilica chopsticks and set to with a will.

He didn't touch his food.

I looked over his shoulder, through the windows at the street. Marked traffic. Uneasiness returned like a precognition, swirling around me. I finished a mouthful of noodles, took a sip of tea. "So what do you think is going on? You have any ideas about these demons? Anything that might be useful?"

He moved finally, spreading his hands against the tabletop. "Enough to begin hunting, and enough to understand there is another game being played here."

I caught a bit of beef with my chopsticks. It was a relief to be able to eat with my right hand again. And it was nice to be in a Freetown, where you could be reasonably sure the meat wasn't protein substitute. Substitute is a good thing, but it leaves me still hungry, as if I haven't eaten real food. "What kind of game? Lucifer seemed to blame me for not knowing he was asking for me, too. What was that all about?"

"You were vulnerable. He could have broken you, Dante." Japhrimel paused. "He still might."

It was time for a subject change; not only was he *not* answering the question I asked, but he was telling me something I already knew. I lifted up my left hand, the wristcuff glittering in a stray reflection of light from the street outside as I took another slurping mouthful of noodles. "Mind telling me what this is?"

He shrugged, his eyes dropping back down to his plate. I didn't think he was going to eat any of the eggrolls—after all, he didn't need human food—but I was wrong. He picked one up, bit into it. "A demon artifact," he said after he finished chewing. If I hadn't thought him incapable of nervousness, I would have thought he was actually stalling.

I waited, but that seemed all he would say. "Meaning what? What does it do?"

His tone was quiet. "I don't know what it will do for you."

Or to you. The unspoken codicil hung in the air.

I looked down at my soup. It was the damnedest thing. I'd have sworn I was hungry. Ravenous. But all of a sudden I'd lost my appetite. A chill prickled down my back. "Do you have a datpilot code for any of the others?" My eyes flicked over the front window, tracking a stray dart of light; it was a reflection off an airbike's polished surface. I looked back at Japhrimel, uneasiness turning my stomach over.

He didn't look surprised. "You wish to contact them?"

"I want to tell them to get out of there now. I don't like this. My neck's prickling."

Japhrimel reached under the table, for all the world as if digging in a pocket. If I didn't know what his coat was made of, I would have believed the pretense. He extracted a sleek black datphone from under the table, pressed a button, and lifted it to his ear.

I looked back over his shoulder. The unease crystallized as I heard him murmur in what sounded like Franje. A true linguistic wonder, my Fallen.

I slid out of the booth, gaining my feet in one smooth

movement. My thumb clicked the sword free of the sheath's embrace. I heard a gasp from a normal behind the counter, ignored it.

Japhrimel looked up, his hair falling over his eyes. "Dante?"

"Are they getting out?"

"Of course. I respect your instincts. I suppose this means we won't finish lunch?" Damn him, he was back to sounding amused.

"I'll pay." I meant it, too; but he rose from the booth like a dark wave, tossing a few New Credit notes down. Of course, money means less than nothing to a demon, he never seemed to need it but it appeared whenever there was any question.

"My pleasure. What do you sense?"

"I'm not sure. Not yet." *But I will be soon.* The precognition rose through dark water, aiming for me...and passed by, circling. If I could just relax, the vision would come to me. Precog isn't my strongest talent; it's only spotty at best. But when it comes it's something to be reckoned with, for all that it usually comes too late.

The first dark, rain-heavy clouds slid over the sun. Shadow crawled over the street, hoverwhine rising and settling in my back teeth, the vision of something about to happen jittering under my skin. I didn't need to look down at the wristcuff to know it was glowing green. Me and the fashionable accessories. My skin crawled at the thought that Lucifer had given this to me and I had blindly put it on.

I met Japhrimel's eyes for a long moment. It was a relief that I still could, despite their radioactive green. "Out on the street, Japh. Move low and silent." I thought about it for a second. "And kill anyone who moves on us," I added judiciously.

"Of course." He sounded calm enough, but the mark on my shoulder flared again, velvet smoothing down my skin as another wave of demon-fed Power pulsed through the air between us.

I really wish I could decide if I like that.

A few desultory spatters of rain pawed at the crowd as we made our way slowly down the sidewalk, heading on a winding course back to the hotel through the Stare Mesto's narrow, ancient streets. I wanted to give the others plenty of time to get the hell out of there, I didn't want any of them catching blowback from a strike aimed at me.

That was mostly why I work alone. I don't want anyone else paying for my fuckups. Hell, *I* don't even want to pay for my fuckups.

Too bad that's part of living.

I would have liked a long, leisurely brooding lunch over some beef soup, but that wasn't meant to be. We were halfway back to the hotel when I stopped in the middle of the sidewalk, the hair raising on the back of my naked neck, something wrong I couldn't quite figure out until I glanced up instinctively, checking the hovertraffic.

And the big, oddly silent silver hover bearing down on us.

Well, isn't that creative. Smash us with a hover.

Then I thought of something else—the imp, screaming as it turned into a bubbling streak on the greasy slide of reactive paint. What would the thick glowing layer of reactive on the bottom of a hover do to Japh?

My heart thudded into my throat, lodged there. I glanced

back at Japhrimel, who was looking up with an amused expression on his face, opening his mouth to speak just as I gathered myself and leapt, my boots connecting solidly to kick him back, sending him flying as a plascannon bolt smashed into the hover and the soundless white flare of reaction fire exploded against my eyelids.

The burning tore through my entire body. I hoped I'd thrown Japhrimel clear enough that the reactive wouldn't affect him.

25

$\mathcal{G}$ray. Everything gray. Shot through with veins of white flame.

The burning. Everywhere, burning. Creeping fire. Every inch of skin, inside my eyelids, the sensitive canals of my ears burning, burning, my mouth burning. Teeth turned to molten chips. *Burning.*

Screaming. A raw agonized voice I barely recognized, breaking on a high note of suffering.

My own.

Cheek on fire. *Emerald. My emerald.* But no blue fire, no hovering of Death.

Wasn't I dead? At last?

"Hold that." Quiet, a male voice I didn't recognize, breaking through my agonized cry. "Goddammit, *hold* it, she's not dead. Don't know where she is, but she isn't dead yet."

Power, flaring out of my control. Sound of smashing plasglass. No blue glow. Only a ragged chant, nailing me in my body, a voice I didn't recognize.

Funny, every other time I'd been this hurt I'd gone into Death and begged the god to take me.

How hurt was I?

It hurt. It *hurt*. It tore along every nerve, worked inward, creeping up my arms and legs like the slow icy crawl of Death. But something fought it—my left arm, braceleted and shoulder-torn in agony, sending out waves of fiery cold, fighting with the other pain for control of me. Back and forth, tearing at me until I screamed, thrashing.

Caught. Held, my arms and legs stretched as I convulsed again.

"Stop." Japhrimel's voice was ragged. "Give me another unit."

A splash against my skin. A collective gasp. "More. As your gods love you, if you do not wish my wrath, *more*."

Chanting, a Necromance's chant; I didn't recognize the voice behind it. But I wasn't dead. No blue fire, no god of Death. Nothing but the ragged breathless male voice chanting, and the agony, tearing at my skin, working inward, collecting in every joint and rending tender tissues. Motion, spiked air dragging against my nerves, I was being taken somewhere. Or was the world just spinning away underneath me?

Flesh moving on my bones, literally crawling. Crawling as the chant melded with Power to knit together shattered and burned skin and muscle. Warmth, then, forced down my throat. Someone massaging my neck. Making me swallow. It burned all the way down, fire exploding out from the inside now as well as burrowing into my skin from the outside.

"More," Japhrimel said again. His tone had smoothed out. He no longer sounded ready to kill. That was good, I felt queerly unable to move, couldn't talk to calm him down.

Rich wet scent of rain. Was I outside? No, the air was too still. Another storm approaching?

There always is. A deep voice worked its way up through my racked brain. The voice of my instincts, quiet and sure.

"She'll live." The colorless voice that had been chanting, slow and slurred now. Tired, with a weariness that drew down to the bone.

"Help him, Tiens. McKinley?" Japhrimel's voice, chill and hurtful, impossible to disobey. He'd never spoken like that to me, and I was grateful.

"Here." McKinley's voice, soft and respectful.

"Question the humans. Get even the smallest piece of information. Do not fail me."

"Of course not." McKinley's low voice. I struggled, thrashing weakly, a hand closed around my wrist. Sharp inhale.

My body convulsed, a small weak sound torn from my lips.

"The Magi. What does he have?"

"He says it's close. That's all." Bella's voice, quivering. *She sounds so young. Did I ever sound that young? What is she doing involved with this?*

"Not enough. Go back to work."

"He needs sleep, he's exhausted. The countermeasures are—"

"Take what you need, but beware. Time is of the essence. Go." Dismissive. Again, a tone he'd never used on me.

Footsteps retreating. "Gods." I heard my voice crack, hoarse and shattered. It sounded like it belonged to someone else. "Gods. What *happened*?"

"First time I've ever seen a woman take on a hover," Lucas said, his voice wheezing and terrible with amusement. "It was *loaded* with reactive. Lovely. We're going to have the Freetowners crawling up our ass."

"The damage was contained," Japhrimel snarled. "What more do they want?"

Lucas was silent. Probably wise of him.

"More blood," Japhrimel said, his voice stony. Light pierced my eyes. It hurt.

I whimpered.

"Easy, *hedaira*." Something stroking my burning forehead. Ice-cold fingers, painful but also strangely comforting. Thank the gods, his voice was softer now, no trace of that chill hurtfulness. He sounded like himself again. "Let me work. You will not be scarred."

"The hover—reactive—*Japhrimel*—"

"Just because it affects an imp does not mean it will affect *me*. Now lie still."

"Japh—" I struggled with my unwieldy body. The reactive—the vision of the imp bubbling and screaming into a grease stain on the reactive rose again. "*Japhrimel*—"

"I am well enough. Ease yourself."

Relief. I collapsed, hearing a slight whistling sound as I let my breath out. "I'm not hurt," I managed, despite the awful burning sensation. It was no longer blind white agony, only a hard, sharp weight against my nerves. Like the touch of sun on already-burned skin. Or the awful creeping rash of slagfever. "The others?"

"Safe. They left the hotel in time. I must admit your instincts are finer than mine." A warm wave of Power, something else splashing against my skin and sinking in.

Something gelid and spicy like demon blood. "You *are* hurt, Dante, but not badly. Lie still."

Another voice. Tiens. Was it night now, the Nichtvren up and about? "The human's locked in a room."

"Feed him, keep him close. He is not a prisoner." Japhrimel sounded chilly again, used to command. Why had I never heard this tone from him before? "Tell him he has my thanks."

"Is she—"

"She will live, Tiens. Do as I say." Thin razor-edge under the command. Japh might be calmer but he was still on a lasetrigger.

Tiens apparently didn't consider it a big deal. "Of course, *m'sieu*. More blood?"

"No. I have enough. Get out."

Blood? That means Japhrimel's feeding. He never wanted to feed on blood in front of me, he preferred to visit slaughterhouses or feed on sex. I didn't think I'd be up for any bedgames for a little while. "Japhrimel?" I sounded delirious, wondered why. *Is he all right? The reactive...he sounds all right. I hope he's okay.*

"Be still, now. Let me work." Power, pulsing along my abused nerves. Coating them with honey. A crackling sound, then a chill as something peeled away from my flesh. Air hitting damp skin, cold and full of knives but still somehow better than the burning.

Peeling away. Fingers in my hair, stroking gently, spinning out the silky strands. A low humming sound of Power sinking into my skin, swirling and dyeing the air green; diamond-black flames twisted over me, working down toward my bones. Shadows began to form, coalescing against the bright white light. "Am I blind?"

"No. Let me work."

Now that the furious pain was gone I could *think* again. "My emerald—"

"Still there. Still alive with your god's presence. Be quiet now."

The strength ran out of my arms and legs. I felt something hard under me, Japhrimel's arms around me. A tickling touch over my face, down my throat, over my breasts, flowering down my body. A different type of tension stirred in me, my hips jerked forward. I heard a low moan—my own.

What, I'm a sexwitch now? The thought was panicked and dark, laden with uncomfortable hysteria—not at all like my usual self. Power had *never* evoked a sexual response in me.

Never.

It ran out my toes, a crackling tide of burning leaving me molten and shaken. I blinked several times, something fine and dusty falling from my eyelashes. Closed my eyes, still blind. Let my head tip back like a heavy fruit on my limp stem of a neck.

I still had eyelashes? Had someone said a hover laden with reactive? I'd been too busy trying to get Japhrimel out of the way to think about anything else.

Reaction fire. What was it with these people chasing me and the reaction fire?

Is it any consolation that they are not "people"? Japhrimel's voice, deep and amused, sounded in my memory.

Had a demon tried to smash me with a hover? It didn't seem like them, I somehow got the sense that demons liked to do their work a little more up-close. When you've got eternity to play in, bloodsport needs to be personal; anything else is just too boring. Or so I think, having studied what I can of demons.

Something else is going on here. Lucifer winds me up and sets me in motion—but he also takes the chance and makes sure I'm separated from Japhrimel. Someone sends an imp after me—but any Greater Flight demon would guess I would be almost capable of taking care of an imp. It was just to keep me running. And a hoverload of reactive—if it won't kill Japhrimel, it might not kill me, but it will slow us both down. So someone needs time to do something.

But demons had all the time in the world. Lucifer only contracted me for seven years. The *smart* thing to do was lie low and wait until I was no longer the Right Hand. Seven years was an eyeblink for a demon.

Someone was trying to throw me off the track. Someone wanted me to chase my own tail.

Or someone was using me for another purpose, bait or distraction.

Lucifer? An escaped demon? *Who?*

All of the above?

I opened my eyes. Saw darkness. Blinked, saw glowing green eyes. A familiar face.

"Japhrimel," I breathed. My body felt made out of lead, my mouth strangely numb.

His fingertips stroked my forehead. "Dante," he breathed back. "Did you think to protect me?"

"As a matter . . . of fact, I did." I blinked again. "Someone's trying . . . to delay . . . us. Or . . . use. . . ."

"Now this is revealed unto you?" He stroked my forehead again, bent to press a kiss onto my cheek. "Think no more on it. Sleep, and heal."

I fell into darkness, still trying to think through the soup my brain had become.

26

The next time I woke, it was to find myself in a small, cheap room in Freetown New Prague. Thick curtains were pulled tightly over blind windows. Day or night? I didn't know.

I rolled up, pushing aside the softness of Japhrimel's wing. Examined my hands. Thin tendrils of hair fell forward, brushed my cheeks. It was too long, past my shoulders, as if I'd chopped it months instead of a few days ago. Hair? I'd been in the middle of a reaction fire, I shouldn't have any hair left.

I shouldn't have any *skin* left. Not to mention bones, muscles, or blood.

My hands looked like mine. My shoulder looked like mine, with the scarring decoration of Japhrimel's mark. Even my legs were familiar, down to the velvet hollows behind my knees. Even my feet were mine.

I made it up to stand, unsteady. Japhrimel lay on his back, motionless, one arm flung over his eyes, his wings a soft darkness, one draping off the bed, the other curled close to his side where I had pushed it. The blankets were pushed down to his hips—he didn't like anything cov-

ering his wings when he lay next to me. He was warm
enough I didn't mind.

A slice of light showed from a white-tiled bathroom.
I bolted for it and scrambled inside, blinking against the
sudden assault of light. Found the mirror, stood trembling
in front of it, my fingers curling around the lip of the porcelain sink.

The same face, a ghost of my human looks bleeding
through the lovely golden features. My mouth pulled
down at the corners as I examined myself, dark eyes moving over now-familiar arches and curves. For the first
time, I felt relieved to see the marks of what Japhrimel
had made me in the mirror.

My accreditation tat showed sharp and strong against
the golden skin of my left cheek. The emerald glittered,
spitting a dart of light. My hair wasn't as long as it had
been—but it wasn't a chopped-short mess either. It
brushed my shoulders in silky disarray.

And so much simpler than going to a salon, the voice
of merry unreason caroled inside my head.

I closed my eyes, my fingernails driving against
the porcelain with a small screeching sound. Tried to
concentrate.

It didn't work, so I dropped down on my knees. Rested
my forehead against the porcelain.

It took a few breaths, but it finally came. My jagged
gasping smoothed out, I drew in a few more deep circular breaths and dropped below conscious thought, into the
space where a pulse other than my heart thrummed.

*Blue crystal walls rose up around me. The Hall was im-
mense, stretching up to dark starry infinity, plunging down*

below into the abyss. I walked over the bridge, my foot-falls resounding against the stone. My feet were bare—I felt grit on the stone surface, the chill of wet rock. The emerald flamed, feeding a bright cocoon, kept me from being knocked off the bridge and into the well of souls. The living did not come here—except for those like me.

Necromance.

On the other side of the bridge the sleek black dog sat back on his haunches, waiting, his high pointed ears focused forward. I touched my heart and my forehead with my right hand, a salute I would give to no other god, demon, or human. Only Death ruled me. Anubis. My lips shaped the other sound that was the god's personal name; That Which Cannot Be Spoken resonating through me.

What would you have of me, my Lord? *A thread of meaning slid through my words, laid in the receptive air of the hall like a glittering silver strand.* I am Your child.

He cocked His slim head, warmth flowing through the not-air. A thin vibrating elastic stretched between us, my emerald sparking as my rings did, a shower of sparks. Each spark a jewel, each jewel a tear on the cheek of infinity.

The god spoke again.

The meanings of His word burned through me, each stripping away a layer. So many layers, so many different things to fight through, each opening like a flower to the god.

The geas burned at me, the fire of His touch and some other fire that moved through him combining. I had something to do—something the god would not show me yet.

Would I do what the god asked? When the time came, would I submit to His will and do what He asked of me?

I bowed, my palms together; a deep obeisance reaching into the very heart of me. My long stubborn life unreeled under His touch. How could I resist Him?

I am Your child, *I whispered.*

The god's approval was like sunshine on my back. Then He spoke again, the Word that expressed me in all its complexity, and I had to go back. I was not even allowed fully over the bridge, to touch the god and feel the weight of living taken from me for one glorious moment. Instead, the god closed me away from Death gently, allowing me to see the well of souls, the bridge, the blue crystal walls—and the shape of Death shifting like ink on wet paper as He raised one slim paw—a hand, laden with dark jewels. No, it was a woman's hand, with a wristlet of bright metal that ran with green fire.

Wait. The god of Death had never changed for me; a psychopomp was coded into the deepest levels of a Necromance and didn't change. Ever. No Necromance's psychopomp had ever changed. At a Necromance's Trial, she suffers the initiation of the mystery of Death and the psychopomp appears. Unlike other disciplines, Necromances have to be accredited, have to pass a Trial and face the ultimate abandonment of control in the face of that most final of mysteries, the passage into the clear rational light of What Comes Next.

I could not even ask a question. My god's voice rang in the blue crystal hall as He spoke one more word, this one sadder than the last, so sad I found myself fleeing the terrible burning sorrow, blindly lunging back toward my body and the familiar pain of living.

*   *   *

I surfaced, my forehead against chill, slick porcelain. Japhrimel's hands circled my wrists, he pulled me into the shelter of his arms. I collapsed against him, gratefully. He pressed a kiss onto my forehead. Said nothing.

The shudders eased. Warmth rushed back into my fingers and toes. "Something's wrong," I said into his shoulder. "None of this makes any sense."

"It rarely does in the beginning stages. This game is deeper than I thought."

"Great," I managed. "Why don't I find that at *all* comforting?"

A low laugh. He kissed my forehead again. "Am I forgiven yet?"

I shrugged, feeling the slippery weight of hair against my shoulders again. Tipped my head back so I could see his expression. "We've got to work on our communication."

"Is that a yes, or a no?" How could a voice so flat sound so amused? He watched my face as if the Nine Canons were written there, his eyes bright and depthless with their demon glow.

Why does he even ask me that? I'm still here, aren't I? "Forgiven for what? Yes, sure. Now can I get dressed, or did my clothes burn off me?" I tried not to notice the way my heart leapt as his wrist brushed my skin, as he watched me with the intensity he seemed to have only for me.

A faint smile touched his lips, and I swallowed dryly. I knew that look. "Your clothes are beyond repair, but I managed to save your sword. And your bag."

I eased away from him. He stroked my shoulders, let me go. "Guns?" *I need firepower, the more the better. No time for games, Japh. Though I have to admit it's tempting.*

"Of course." He nodded. Thin tall demon, green eyes glowing in the face I knew. I reached up, traced his cheekbone with one fingertip, my black-lacquered nail brushing his skin. Winged eyebrows, a straight mouth, his jaw set but not clenched. "You do not have to protect me," he murmured finally.

I tried to stop myself, but I sighed anyway, rolling my eyes. My hair slid against my shoulders, a caress as gentle as his hands. "It wasn't exactly like I was thinking, Japhrimel. I saw what the reactive paint did to that imp. If anything happened to you I'd...."

"You would what?" If I thought his look was searching before, it was scorching now. I half expected his eyes to turn into industrial lasers.

He had been ash, after Rio. Cinnamon-smelling ash in a funeral urn, left either as a cruel joke or a hint by Lucifer. I had thought him dead, destroyed his urn as a penance; I had faced the idea of a world without him. The empty yawning abyss of that world wasn't anything I even wanted to even *think* about ever again. "I thought you were dead once. Once was enough. Now can I get dressed? We've got a demon to hunt, and I think I'm beginning to have an idea."

"May all the hosts of Hell protect me from your ideas, *hedaira*." But he smiled. Not the smile of invitation, but the warm smile I liked almost as much, wry amusement and irony combining.

I levered myself to my feet, glanced down as he rose, his boots scraping against the small white pebbly tiles. "Clothes, Japhrimel. And get the others together."

"What if I like you better unclothed?" A slight quirk of

his eyebrow. I folded my arms over my breasts, hoping I wasn't blushing.

An uncomfortable heat rose in my cheeks. "You can give me my sword, too."

He laughed, dropping his chin in a nod that managed to convey the impression of a respectful bow. I was actually a little disappointed when he took me at my word and went to find me some clothes.

27

*H*e not only brought me clothes—a new Trade Bargains microfiber shirt and jeans, socks, underwear, and my sword—he also had a new rig for me, supple oiled leather that might have been custom-made. New projectile guns (9 mm; anything less is useless when you're facing a determined foe) and a new plasgun, a reliable SW Remington in the 40-watt range. Some bounty hunters use 60-watt, but the chance of blowing up your own hand if a core overheats is exponentially higher with a 60. Give me a good 40 any day—what you lose in power you more than make up for in reliability.

Along with the guns were a new set of knives, even a thin fine polyphase-aluminaceramic stiletto to slip into my boot. The main-gauches were beautiful blue steel, sharpened to a razor edge and with a strange dappling in the metal. I tested the action of each knife and was impressed despite myself. It was nice that Japhrimel understood good gear. Of course, one couldn't expect any less from the Devil's assassin. The curtains rustled slightly, I glanced nervously at them and shrugged myself into the rig. I wanted to find something to tie my hair back, too.

As soon as I suited up and had a look at my slightly-charred but still-whole messenger bag I started to feel much better. Then Japhrimel flicked his wrist, and Jace's necklace dangled from his hand. "This I saved also. I have repaired some small damage to it, but it seems largely unharmed. It is . . . fine work, really."

I dropped down on the bed, all the strength running out of my legs. "Oh." My voice was a wounded little whisper. I looked up at him. "Japhrimel—"

He carefully bent over, his fingers gentle and delicate, slid his hands under my hair to fix the clasp and settle the necklace in its familiar arc below my collarbones. He even frowned slightly while he did so, a look of utter concentration that sent an oblique pang through me. His hair fell in his eyes, and his expression reminded me of a boy at his first Academy dance, pinning a corsage on his date. "I do not think," he said, his fingers lingering on my cheek, "that I understand you well enough. My apologies."

My heart hurt. It was an actual, physical, piercing pain. "Japh . . . it's okay. Really, it is. I . . . thank you." *Thank you. That's the best I can come up with, two silly stupid little words. Goddammit, Danny, why can't you ever say what you mean?* I caught his hands, held on as he looked down at me. "I'm sorry I can't be . . . nicer." *Nicer? I'm sorry I seem to be utterly incapable of anything but raving bitchiness. You're better than I deserve. I love you.*

"You are exactly as you should be, *hedaira*. I would not change you." He squeezed my hands, gently, and let go, pacing across the room and picking up a familiar slender shape.

"I wouldn't change you either." The words burst out of

me, and the moment of silent communication as his eyes met mine was worth anything I owned.

He presented me with my sword as properly as Jado might have, the hilt toward my hand and a slight respectful bow tilting him toward me. I accepted the slender weight and immediately felt like myself again. "It is the strangest thing, but your sword seemed unaffected by the fire."

"Jado gave it to me." *Did he give me a blade that can kill a demon? I certainly hope so, I might need one soon.* "Japh, the reaction fire. How did you—"

"My kind are creatures of fire," he reminded me. "No flame can hurt me, even a flame humans unlock from atoms. Steel, wood, lead, fire—none of these things will harm me in the slightest." He clasped his hands behind his back.

I wish I'd known. "Fine time to tell me." A sharp guilt I hadn't even been aware of eased. I finally felt like we understood each other. I didn't like fighting him, I wasn't any good at it.

"I have told you I will not bother you with trifles; I considered that a trifle." He paused, thoughtfully. "I thought it would alarm you to speak of it. If it will ease your mind to know such a thing, I will tell you."

If he had jumped up on the dresser and announced his intention to become a half-credit unregistered sexwitch trolling the sinks of Old Delhi, I would have been a little less surprised. "Good enough." I popped my sword free, looked at four inches of bright metal. Japhrimel was right—the sword was unaffected. I could see no weakening in its blue glow, no unsteadiness that would warn me the steel had become reaction-brittle. I probed delicately at it with a finger of Power, encountered exactly the right amount of resistance.

"I wonder who you really are," I said, not knowing if I was talking to my sword, my Fallen lover, or the demon we were chasing.

Or to myself.

The old Dante would have fought to escape from Japhrimel, would have tried over and over to push him away, would never have forgiven him one omission, one misleading statement. Would never have listened to his explanation, never mind that it was a good one. Dante Valentine, the best friend in the world—as long as you don't betray her. I had cut people completely out of my life for less.

Then again, I had forgiven Jace. Any lie he told me, every omission he made, had eventually not mattered when weighed against his determination to protect me. Or against the debt I owed him for his quiet, stubborn, careful love of a grief-crazed part-demon Necromance—and his love for the damaged, brittle woman I'd been. I had forgiven him, even though I'd sworn I never would.

Was I getting soft? Or just growing up?

And the strangest thing of all: if it hadn't been for Japhrimel, I wouldn't have learned to forgive anyone, least of all myself. A demon, teaching me about forgiveness. How was that for bizarre?

Japhrimel's soft voice interrupted that chain of thought. "I am your Fallen. That is all you need remember. Are you ready?"

"To try and figure out who's been trying to hit me with a hover? More than ready." At least I *sounded* like myself again, there was no betraying tremble in my voice. All in all, I was dealing with this really well.

Wasn't I?

"Dante...." He let my name hang in the air as if he wanted to say more. I waited, but nothing came. Instead, he stood with his hands clasped behind his back, his eyes glowing and his hair softly mussed. His coat moved slightly, settling around him, and I saw his face change. Just a little.

"What?" I bounced up off the bed and jammed my sword home. "I'm ready."

He shook his head, then turned to lead me from the room. "Hey," I said. "Thank you. Really. For saving the necklace. And my sword." *But most particularly, for saving me.*

Did his shoulders stiffen as if I'd hit him? He nodded, his hair moving ink-black above the darkness of his coat, and continued out of the room.

I didn't have time to wonder about that, just followed him.

28

The suite was on the third floor of a cheap hotel in the middle of the worst sink in New Prague, and that was saying something.

This section of New Prague's Stare Mesto had been the Judic Quarter, back in the mists of pre-Merican history. During the Awakening it was here that the first Skinlin had been trained by Zoharic and Qabalisticon scholars in their words of Power and the secret of making *golem'ai*. After the Seventy Days War and the absolute genealogical proof of the extinction of the line of David, the backlash of disbelief had risen against the Judics; their prewar alliance with the Evangelicals of Gilead had only sealed their fate. There were plenty of genetic Judics all over the world, but the culture they had kept alive so successfully foundered under the double shock of the miscarrying of their prophecies and their alliance with the Evangelicals—and, oddly enough, with the Catholica Church. War makes strange bedfellows, but even the most incisive of scholars could not explain why the Judics had allied with both factions of their old enemies. The Gilead records might have offered a clue, but they'd been destroyed in the War. The only theory was that Kochba bar Gilead had been persuasive, and quite a few—psions and humans alike—had believed him to be a messiah, if not *the* Messiah.

Curiously enough, most Judic psions turned out to be Ceremonials, gifted with using their voices to sing the Nine Canons and alter reality. The only remnant of Judic culture left was the Skinlin's pidgin mishmash of their language used to sonically alter plant DNA with Power wedded to voice. That, and the *golem'ai*.

If I'd been a little less worried about a demon trying to kill me, I might have gone looking for some historical sites of interest, especially the corner of Hradcany Square where the last of the Judic followers of Gilead—the stubborn band that had shown its hand too soon against Merican StratComm's final wrenching of political power away from Kochba's old guard—had been mown down by laserifle fire. As it was, scholarship would have to take a back seat to figuring out who the hell was trying to kill me now. On the bright side, I could always come back.

If I survived.

It was obviously night, since the Nichtvren leaned against the wall by the door, his arms folded. He wore the same dusty black sweater and workman's pants, but a new, shiny pair of boots. "There she is." He sounded lazily amused, the catshine of a night-hunting predator folding over his eyes. "You look better now, *belle morte*."

I heard rain pattering on the sides of the building, stroking the windows behind his words. No thunder, though. The storm had passed.

"I should." I stripped my hair away from my face. I *really* had to find something to tie it back. "Last time you saw me, I'd just been hit by a hover. Where's Lucas?" I wanted a little tête-à-tête with him, to touch gravbase and also—more importantly—to ask him what they talked about when I wasn't in the room.

"Gathering information." The Nichtvren inclined his head, his gaze flowing slow and gelid over my body. "I would have loved to Turn you, *cherie*."

That was a high compliment from a Nichtvren, but I never want to hear a bloodsucking Master contemplate any of *my* vital fluids.

"Thanks for the compliment." I settled for a shrug worthy of Japhrimel. My eyes flicked over the room, full of heavy pseudo-antique furniture. Drapes pulled tight over the windows, a nivron fire in a grate. The room was done in red and brown, a graceless slashed painting of a bowl of fruit hung over the fire. Two tables, a collection of heavy chairs. Bella crouched by the fire, her eyes closed. The Asiano Magi hunched over a table spread with papers, his sword close at hand. Today he wore a Chinese-collared shirt and a long brown coat, as if he was cold. He also looked extremely nervous. He was pale under the rich color of his skin, and his hair was sticking up like a crow's nest.

Vann peered out the window, tweezing the ancient curtain aside. He held a very respectable Glockstryke laserifle, with an ease that told me he knew how to use it. "McKinley should be back by now," he said darkly.

I looked past him—a fire escape going down to a dark alley. A good escape route, or a good way for an enemy to sneak up on us. I shook my head, backing away from the window. My hair fell in my face again, I pushed it back.

"He can look after himself," Japhrimel replied. "Do not worry on his account."

The Necromance I'd seen in the sparhall tipped me a lazy salute from a chair set in a dark corner, his long legs outstretched. His emerald spat a single spark, my cheek burned again in answer, the inked lines of my tat running under my skin.

Gods above. "What the hell are you doing here?"

"Nice way to thank a man who saved your life," he answered in a low, clear voice. "I was following you; saw you get hit with that hover. Your...ah, demon there, he shunted the reaction fire straight up and repaired the damage. Damnedest thing I ever saw." He rose easily; he was tall when he wasn't hunching. Dark eyes, dark hair, unshaven cheeks blurring his tat a little. Nice mouth. Lines around the eyes—he wasn't young. "I'm Leander Beaudry."

My jaw didn't quite drop, but it was close. "*The* Leander? The Mayan reconstructionist?" *I knew he looked familiar. What's he doing here, and why isn't he laser-shaved according to the Codes?* It was time to measure him out.

He grinned, the corners of his eyes crinkling. I'd seen that smile on holovids, no wonder he looked familiar. He'd made his professional name sorting out the skeletal remains of ancient Centro and Sudro Merican sacrificial victims, in some cases raising their apparitions so linguists and anthropologists could question them; then he'd moved to Egypt and worked on the tombs there. I hadn't heard any gossip about him for a while. "And you're Danny Valentine. I'm honored. I'm working Freetowns." He indicated his fuzzy cheek.

Ah. No Necromance codes out here. He was trained Hegemony, but he works bounties. Probably not very good at following orders, been doing freelance for a while. Nice to know. "I read about Egypt. Raising Ramses for the Hegemony Historicals. Nice work—I saw the holovid." *You kept his apparition up for a good forty-five minutes, very nice work indeed. I heard you're pretty good with an edged weapon, you brought in Alexei Hollandveiss alive and trussed up like a Putchkin Yule turkey. That's right, you specialize in cold-case bounties.*

He completed the psionic equivalent of dogs sniffing each other's rumps by meeting my eyes. "Well, mummies are easier than cremains. You're the one who raised Saint Crowley the Magi. And the Choyne Towers."

That managed to make me shudder. It was one of the jobs that had made my reputation as the best Necromance in the world, one capable of raising apparitions from bits of bodies instead of the whole corpses, the fresher the better, that other Necromances needed. A Putchkin transport had failed and crashed into the three Choyne Towers, and I'd worked for weeks raising and identifying the dead—all but the last ten, who must have been vaporized. *Thanks for reminding me.* I looked down at his hands, scarred and bruised from swordfighting and working the heavy bag. "Why were you following me?" A faint tone of challenge.

"Not every day I see a tat I recognize on the face of a holovid angel. Was curious. Did a few stunts with Jace Monroe in Nuevo Rio before he went solo. He always talked about you."

"Did he." I looked away first, down at the floor. My chest tightened. He'd talked about me? What had he said? "Well, you've fallen into bad company."

"Looks like you've got a hunt going. I want in."

Everything I'd ever heard said he was direct. "Ask Japhrimel." I tipped my head back. Japh had gone still and silent behind me, the mark on my left shoulder turned molten-hot. I paced over to the table the Magi was hunched over and pulled out a chair, dropping down and presenting the Necromance with my profile. "I normally don't work in groups, but it seems I'm overruled." I looked down at the papers, started shuffling through them. Maps of New Prague, magscans, sheets covered with cramped, crabbed Magi codewriting. I glanced at the Asiano, who said nothing. His eyes glittered at me, and I saw how tight his hand was on his swordhilt.

He's afraid of me. Why? My left hand tightened on my scabbard as I stared back at him. The room had gone hot and tense. "What do we have?"

The Asiano shifted in his seat, said nothing.

I heard Leander move, leather boots creaking. "If you're hunting demons, you'll need every hand you can get. I'm trustworthy, I've got a reputation to protect just like you do."

The Asiano handed me a blue file folder. The mark on my shoulder crunched with heat, another flush of Power tingling along my skin. "Fine." I glanced up at Leander, flipped the file open. "I told you to ask Japh. I'm not the one in charge here."

"Could have fooled me," Leander muttered. He turned on his heel, facing Japh. "What do you say, then? I've done bounties in every Freetown on earth, and I'm bored. A demon should be a nice change."

"If you like." Japhrimel sounded chill and precise. Why? It wasn't like him to care about something like this.

"You are here on Dante's sufferance, then, Necromance. Since you rendered her aid."

Amaric Velokel, I read. Then a twisted, fluid glyph—the demon's name in their harsh unlovely language. The glyph had lines scratched out and redrawn, obviously the Magi was working on figuring out if there was more to it. A combination of divination and codebreaking, feeling around for a demon's Name, sidestepping countermeasures and protections that the demon would use to keep its identity a secret.

I felt the familiar thrill go through me, shortening my breath and prickling at my skin. A new hunt.

All the shutting myself up in a library hadn't managed to change the way I felt about bounties. Sure, they paid well—most of the time. But the real reason I took them was for the hunt. The feeling of pitting myself against an enemy both strong and fierce; just like a sparring match and a battlechess game all rolled into one. The year that Japhrimel spent dormant I had flung myself into bounties, working one after another after another, always feeling nervous and edgy if I didn't have a hunt started or under way. Gabe called it "bounty sickness."

I hated the danger of bounties—they had almost killed me more than once—but I'd grown to need it. Almost addicted. Hate and love, love and hate, and need.

I had said all I wanted was a quiet life. Had I been lying? Or was it just that I was angry now, being jerked around by demons once more?

I turned the page over. More conversation in the room, but I closed it away. I turned over the next sheet too and looked down at a drawing, finely shaded in charcoal. A face—round and heavy, square teeth that still looked sharp, cat-slit eyes that seemed light-colored. The face wasn't human, for all that a human hand had drawn it. The eyes were too big, the teeth too square, and the expression was...inhuman.

This was the first demon, then. Was it the one hiding out in New Prague?

I spread my left hand over the picture, looking down at the wristcuff. Heard a slight sighing sound. Glanced up.

Ogami stared at the wristcuff, before his dark eyes flicked up to my face. He was pale under the even caramel of his skin, his thin mouth drawn tight in a grimace.

Bingo. We've hit a Magi that recognizes something about this. Maybe I can get him alone and ask a few questions.

I looked back down at the wristcuff. It flared with green light, the lines twisting back on themselves. Was this thing like a Magi tracker? It seemed to react to demons. Was that why Lucifer had given it to me? Why didn't it glow when Japhrimel was around?

Well, no time like the present to ask. "Does this cuff work like a tracker? Is this the demon in New Prague? 'Cause it seems like this thing lights up whenever a demon's prowling around looking to kill me."

Long pause. I looked up. Vann's eyes were fixed on me, his mouth slightly open. Ogami stared too. Bella, crouched by the fire, had craned to look back over her shoulder. Her hair was mussed, and the triangular haircut didn't suit her. Her chin was too sharp.

The Nichtvren leaned back against the wall, his eyes half-closed and his fangs dimpling his lower lip. I hoped he'd visited a haunt and was well-fed. A chill traced up my spine—I had never really dealt with Nichtvren in my human life. They didn't like Necromances much. I suppose bloodsuckers who prize their near-immortality—and all of them do—might not look too kindly on Death's children.

Japhrimel approached me soundlessly. Leander dropped back down into his chair, his katana placed at a precise angle across his knees. He was staring at me like I had grown another head. Why? I hadn't *done* anything.

"It is certainly possible." Japhrimel's hand curled around my shoulder. "Given the reaction of the Gauntlet, it's likely he's close."

Okay, finally. A usable piece of information. "So who is this guy? And what's the Gauntlet?"

"Velokel is of the Greater Flight." His hand tightened on my shoulder. "In an earlier age he was called the Hunter. He hunted the Fallen and their brides, and killed many."

A lump rose in my throat. "Great." I looked down at the wristcuff. "So what is the Gauntlet?"

"The Gauntlet is what you're wearing," Vann said quietly. "It's a mark given by the Prince. It means you're his champion, and any demon who doesn't bow to his authority is your enemy."

Oh, yeah. This just keeps getting better and better. I twisted in the chair to look up at Japhrimel. "When were you going to tell me about this?" *Why does everyone else seem to know more than I do? You'd think they'd be falling all over themselves to tell me everything they possibly could.*

He shrugged, his coat rustling. "It provides you with some protection."

The fact the Lucifer had given me the bracelet made

my bones feel cold and loose inside my skin, but I had other fish to heatseal at the moment. "He hunted *hedaira*? This Velokel guy?"

"He did. Nor was he the only demon who did so." Japhrimel's hand slid up my shoulder, curved around, and rested intimately against my nape. Heat rose up my neck, and I hoped I wasn't blushing. "But the *A'nankhimel* were only Fallen, no more." He paused. "They did not have the luxury of bargaining to regain their place, as I have."

"Great." *I can't tell whether to feel comforted or doomed.* "So what can you tell me about this guy, Japhrimel?"

"Intelligent. Resourceful. A good foe." Japhrimel paused. "He hates Fallen almost as much as he hates Lucifer, but I would have thought him too wise to leave Hell."

I looked down at the drawing, then met Ogami's eyes. "You drew this?"

The Asiano nodded. His eyes were so eloquent it was hard to believe he didn't once open his mouth.

"Good." I said. "Give me a full-body one. And write down in Merican what *you* know about this guy."

29

I pored over the magscans again as Ogami drew. Tiens stirred against the wall. I had almost forgotten he was there—he was that still and quiet. "The Deathless approaches." He moved gracefully aside from the door. "Rather quickly, too."

I heard the footsteps, light and shushing. Lucas's distinctive almost-shuffling gait—when he wasn't as silent as a knife to the kidneys, that is.

"Get all this together," I said, my neck prickling. Bella began shuffling the papers together. "Hurry. If Lucas is running, it's bad news. You." I pointed at Vann. "Watch the alley. *Anything* out of the ordinary, yell. Nichtvren, slip down to the foyer, take a look. Make sure Lucas isn't being followed. Get those papers together *now*."

Thankfully, none of them glanced at Japhrimel to make sure they were supposed to do what I said. I gained my feet with a single lunge, the chair scraping back. "Leander, I want you to hang out with Bella and Ogami. You're protection detail for our Magi."

"Gotcha." He levered himself up out of his chair, the trademark glitters swirling in his aura. If this Velokel was half as canny as Japhrimel said, he wouldn't think twice about taking out the Magi. And there would go my best link to him.

How well could a demon hide, though? They were huge magickal smears on the landscape of Power. Shouldn't Japh be able to track him better than a human Magi?

My eyes snagged on the magscans again. Intuition clicked into place as the answer I'd been searching for burst out like colors under full-spectrum lighting, shapes falling and locking together to create a picture. *Oh, crap. Right in front of me.*

Lucas opened the door and half-fell inside. Tiens had vanished, a slight shimmer leaching out of the air. The chill returned, touching my back—he must be old, and obviously a Master. A Nichtvren performing that trick in front of humans was something I'd never seen before, though I'd read accounts of it and taken the standard Paranormal Behavior classes at the Academy.

I wondered just how trustworthy a Nichtvren working for the Devil's agency on earth would be.

Lucas's hair was wildly disarranged. A splash of blood painted one yellow-pale cheek. His left hand was buried in his stomach—or what remained of his stomach, it was a mess. My entire body went cold. "I got hit, there's a net out there," he rasped, then glanced over at Leander and grimaced. "What the hell is he still doing here?"

"What do you have, Lucas?" I wanted his eyes on me, started forward. He needed a healcharm, something to stop the bleeding, and I wanted to take a look at the wound. "You look like shit."

He flung out his free hand, fingers splayed, and I stopped dead. "Keep the fuck away from me, girl. I got gutshot. It'll mend. Got a name around the sinks—Kel. The Hunter. He's lookin' for you just as actively as you're lookin' for him."

I opened my mouth, but Tiens blurred into being right inside the door. "Time to leave this charming place, *n'est-ce pas?*"

"I threw the pursuit, but the net was already here." Lucas doubled over, shoving his hand even further inside the ragged mass of his belly. My gorge rose, and I started forward again. I wasn't a *sedayeen*, but Necromances were the next best thing when it came to healing a serious combat wound.

A net? Thinking to sneak up on us, and Lucas comes back just in time. I sent up a silent prayer of thanks, my mind starting to click through alternatives, my pulse spiking. I tasted metal against my palate, the nervous excitement of a fight approaching.

"*Stay the fuck away!*" Lucas's voice scraped awfully as he backed up two shambling steps, his hand still outstretched to stop me. "I ain't fuckin' safe right now, bitch! Stay off and get the rest of these fuckin' nacks outta here!" He doubled over again, going ashen, and my heart trip-hammered in my chest.

"Out the window," I snapped over my shoulder. "Tiens, Japh, you first, clear the alley for the rest of us."

"You should go with Vann," Japhrimel said, as if I hadn't spoken.

I half-turned, grabbed his shoulders, and shoved him toward the window. He moved, shaking my hands away. "I'm safer up here until you clear that goddamn alley. I'll be right behind you—just *go!*"

Japhrimel made a slight movement, tipping his head,

Tiens nodded. For all the world as if I hadn't just told them what to do.

Goddammit, if there's one thing I hate, it's being ignored in a situation like this. Why even have me along if he's not going to listen to what I say? That was an interesting thought, but one I had no time for.

Vann pulled the window up, helped the limping, bleeding Lucas out. Villalobos was moving much faster than I'd expect a gutshot man to move, and I filed this away for further thought. He said he wasn't safe, but Vann—

Think about it later, Dante. Cover their retreat now. You'll have plenty of time to ask questions later. I whirled back toward the door, shoving my sword into the loop on my belt. My hands curled around the projectile guns. "Tiens, how many?"

"Four that I saw, *belle morte*," he said over his shoulder, ducking out the window. Bella followed, and Ogami.

Leander actually blew me a kiss before he ducked out, a knife glittering along his left forearm. His sword was thrust through his belt, and he looked fey. I promptly shoved Lucas and the Magi out of my thoughts—if they couldn't make it through with that kind of protection there was nothing I could do now. My job was to stop whoever came through the door and give them time to get to cover.

Japhrimel's eyes met mine, glowing green and suddenly much more frightening. "This is dangerous," he said softly. "Stay with me."

"Why aren't you listening to me? I told you to clear the alley." I ghosted across the room and put my back to the wall on the other side of the door, right where Tiens had been leaning. The hammers of the projectile guns clicked easily as I pulled them back, I settled against the wall and made it a point to breathe deeply, calmly. My heart pounded. A net, Lucas said, an encirclement. Expensive, and meant for capture or elimination, most likely the latter. And they'd managed to hurt the Deathless.

Lovely.

"Vann and Tiens are more than capable of protecting the humans." He went utterly still, his eyes flaring.

I shrugged. Listened.

Demon-acute senses are useful most of the time. Since Japhrimel had finally taught me how to control them, they had become even more so. I heard slight shuffling sounds—human feet. Two sets of soft padding footsteps that weren't quite human; the back of my neck wasn't just prickling now. It was flat-out *crawling*.

What the hell is that? I looked at Japhrimel, my eyebrows raising.

He clasped his hands behind his back, watching the door. I almost pitied the sad sonsabitches coming through, human or not.

Wood snapped, groaning, and something slammed into the wall at my back.

Of course. Imps don't need to use doors, Danny. I flung myself away from the wall.

Japhrimel made a short sharp sound of annoyance and moved forward as I rolled. I ended up on my side, hitting the table with a sickening *crack*. Another impact shattered the wall, splinters flying, dust smashing out. I squeezed the triggers, tracking two shapes that skittered away from the coughing roar of the guns. I clipped one human done up in assault gear—nightvision goggles, Kevlar, edged metal and an assault rifle. No plasgun I could see.

Two humans—no, three. Four. And two imps.

Why didn't I hear the other humans? Why didn't Tiens tell me there were imps? Goddammit. Made it to my feet, wood cracking again as I leapt up, boots slamming down hard on the groaning floor. Right hand moving, holstering gun and closing around swordhilt. Japhrimel moved, blurring between me and the two imps. They looked just like the other ones—babyfaces, sharp snarling teeth, black teardrops over their glittering eyes. I promptly forgot about them—Japh could take care of it.

I had other problems. The humans were just *crawling* with illegal augments, twitched out on neurospeeders and muscle spanners to make them quicker and deadlier than human even as it shortened their lives. Even a psion would have a hard time four-on-one with these guys; not only were they augmented, their gear was also top-of-the-line. Whoever sent them was making money no object.

Great. Time to dance.

My sword left the sheath with a long sliding metallic sound. Half-step forward, blade moving in a complicated whirling pattern; one man went to one knee by the door, raising his assault rifle. My left hand came up, gun roaring; he dropped. Smell of cordite, of blood, the man I'd clipped leapt for me, rifle reversed to use as a battering weapon. *Fast for a human, goddamn neurospeeders.* I ducked, my blade whooshing down in a half-circle. *Where's the other one, don't see him, where is he?* Sword flickering, slicing through Kevlar as my *kia* split the air, intestines falling in a shimmering wet slither, a human sound of pain. More movement boiling into the room, slippery padding demon movement; I ignored it. I had *enough* to deal with.

Whirling, feet slipping in bloody mess. Two other men, both moving in, one lifting the rifle to his shoulder. Shot him, recoil jolting up my left arm; moved forward so quickly I collided with the last one as I ran him through, twisting the katana to break the suction of muscle against metal, tearing it free from between his ribs as the smell of death assaulted me. Blood exploded as I jammed the gun under his chin for good measure, saw blond stubble on his cheeks, smelled human sweat and effort.

Anubis, receive them kindly. I squeezed the trigger.

Blood steamed in the air. I turned in a tight half-circle, sword whirling up as something streaked for me—clashing as an imp's claws rang off the blade, an impact jolting all the way up my arm. *Holy fuck! Where's Japh?*

No time. Backing up along the wall, sword a streak of blue flame as the imp lunged for me again, soft cheeks smeared with gleaming saliva as it champed and foamed, its claws clanging off the sword with a grating shock, its breath hot against my cheek as it drove forward. I smashed my back foot down and *lunged,* shoving it back from the corps-a-corps. That gained me a few moments and freed my sword. I gulped down air, almost backed into the corner next to the fireplace. If it came for me again what was I going to—

The imp chittered at me—and squealed, black blood exploding as Japhrimel's claws tore through its belly from the back, twisting up through its chest. He carved through demon flesh as if it was water, finishing with a single swipe that opened the thing's throat. Its squeal died on a burbling rush of black blood. Japhrimel flicked his fingers and the imp turned into ash, white flame flickering through it in a strange veined pattern before it exploded in a cloud of grit. "Dante?"

He sounded furiously, coldly calm. I'd never seen such a casual use of Power from him before. The grit sifted to the floor in with a soft pattering sound.

"I'm good." My breath came harsh and tearing in my throat. The humans had been tricked out for serious night work—the nightvision goggles alone were worth a fortune. Not to mention the augments. "Any more?"

"Downstairs." He straightened, impeccable, hands clasped behind his back again. His eyes glowed, not an inky hair out of place. I swallowed. I could never be prepared for how spookily *fast* he moved; my own speed was scary enough, but his was flat-out terrifying.

I was suddenly, appallingly, completely glad he was on my side.

"There's one wounded." I pointed out into the hall. My breath came fast but even, and I holstered my left-hand gun. Slid my sword back into its sheath. There was a *lot* of that fine, sparkling ash on the floor, swirling through the air. Just how many imps had come? None were left. "I just shot him once. Question him?"

"No need, the imps told me everything I need to know. Quickly. Out."

I didn't stop to argue. Ran for the window, wrenched it open—

—and ducked back as bullets chewed at the wooden frame, splintering the glass. Cursed savagely, Japhrimel's hand closing around my arm.

"This way."

Now this is more like it. I can see a demon doing this—but smashing me with a hover? No. "What did the imps tell you?" Dappled green light flared from my wristcuff, I held it up as Japhrimel pulled me out the shattered door, turning right, stepping over the moaning, bleeding man I'd shot. Japh didn't quite drag me down the hall, but I had a hard time keeping up with him. His hand had turned to iron on my arm; he didn't hurt me but I couldn't have broken free if I'd tried.

"Enough that I see the wisdom of leaving this place *now*," Japhrimel said. "Later, Dante. For right now, let us go."

He didn't have to tell me again.

Up the stairs. I heard something—thundering footsteps. Claws *skritching* against wood, a chilling glassy squeal. It didn't sound human, whatever it was. Memory replayed itself, matched the sound—I'd heard it in the abandoned building, only that time it had been a sort of snarl. What was chasing us? More imps? But they didn't sound scratchy, they sounded soft, padding, and almost wet, like strangling fingers in the dark.

One flight. Two. Three. It was getting closer, smashing against walls. It sounded *big*, and I smelled heat. Tang of smoke against my nostrils. The wristcuff squeezed my left arm, a terrible wrenching pain that made me gasp; the mark on my left shoulder flared in response. Japhrimel's face was set, his eyes glowing so fiercely they cast shadows under his cheekbones, spots of green light flickering as he checked each hall.

Sixth floor. No more stairs, he whirled and headed down the hall, his boots soundless against threadbare carpet. I was too busy trying to keep up to ask him what the hell he was doing. I certainly hoped he had an idea, at least, because I was fresh out. He kicked another door open, my nose filling with the smell of dust and human desperation. I caught a quick flash of a room—done in green instead of red, a cheap table and four chairs, the remains of takeout cartons scattered on said table—before he pivoted and aimed for the window. "Brace yourself."

I grabbed his shoulder, his other arm circled around me. *What do you mean, brace myself?*

He launched us both out the window, plasglass shattering and bullets screaming past. Fire dug into my right shoulder, and Japhrimel twisted, Power burning incandescent in the darkness. Clattering gunfire, a yell from high up on my left, the sound of a falling body. Whoever the sniper had been he was now dead—Japhrimel had shot him.

Anubis, this is going to hurt.

Impact. Too soon, I wasn't ready, the breath driven out of my lungs in a long howling gasp. Japhrimel hauled me up, his fingers slipping in black blood dripping down my right shoulder. Orange citylight glinted off the gun in his hand. My breath plumed in the chilly air. Desultory rain steamed as it met Japhrimel's aura. He literally *burned* with a mantle of Power so intense it was like looking into a furnace of black diamond flames. I had to blink fiercely to screen out my otherSight and see the real world.

It wasn't the street below, but another rooftop. He finished pulling me to my feet as easily as I might have picked up a piece of paper. *Well, that was wonderful; can't wait to do that again; gods, what* was *that thing?*

I gasped again, this time dragging a breath in as the hurt in my shoulder sealed itself away. Fine drizzling mist kissed my cheeks. "*Sekhmet sa'es,*" I hissed. "Warn me next time, will—"

He pushed me behind him so hard I skidded across concrete rooftop, my back slamming into a climate-control unit. I found myself squeezed between him and the unit's plasteel side. He went suddenly motionless, both arms up, two shiny silver guns in his hands. His aura spread over me, hazing and sinking in through my skin. I blinked furiously, trying to *see*, relieved when otherSight retreated. He was damn near blinding me with that trick.

I swallowed. He so rarely used a weapon it was almost shocking. If he had both guns out like this instead of one, it was *bad*.

"Dante," he said quietly, "if I tell you to, *run* down the fire escape on the other side of the roof. Do you understand?"

"What is it?" I whispered. "It didn't sound like an imp."

"It is not an imp." His voice was so chill and sharp I could feel cold air touch my cheek. "As you love life, *hedaira*, do as I tell you this once. Will you?"

I gulped down another breath, lungs burning. My pulse pounded in my throat. "What is it?" *It doesn't hurt to ask, does it?*

"Hellhound." Steam rose, twisted into angular shapes. "Be still, now."

Hellhound? That doesn't sound good. That doesn't sound good at all. I froze, barely even breathing. Watched the gaping hole in the building we'd just burst out from. The moisture wasn't even enough to qualify as rain, more like a heavy mist, tapering off. It steamed away from Japhrimel's aura, and I wondered why I felt so cold. "They're going to try to flank us," I whispered. "Japhrimel—"

It bulleted out from the hole in the side of the hotel, a low, streamlined lethal shape. I forgot about being quiet and screamed, the mark on my shoulder squeezing, my bloodslick right hand closing around my swordhilt. Japhrimel moved forward, the guns speaking in his hands, fire puffed out in small bursts from the side of the building as he tracked it. It moved with the same eerie speed he did, its eyes glowing unholy crimson. My sword sang free of its sheath. Blue fire crested, spilled free of the blade, the steel's heart flamed white.

It was shaped like a leaner version of a werecain, low and four-legged with hulking shoulders and long claws that snick-snacked as it landed on the rooftop and snarled. It was made of *blackness*, a dark so deep and fiery it burned. A vapor trail followed, its heat scorching the water in the air.

So this was a hellhound. None of the Magi texts had ever mentioned anything *close* to it.

I'm going to have to tell the Magi a thing or two. Just as soon as I get out of this alive.

Teeth made of obsidian snapped, Japhrimel faded aside; he shot it twice. Watching him fight was always strange, he moved with such speed and precision it was impossible not to be impressed. He kicked the hellhound, a sound like a watermelon dropped on a scorching-hot sidewalk. It howled, a long screeching sound, and its eyes swept across the roof, locking on me.

My sword flamed blue-white, etching shadows on the roof. My rings sparked, a cascade of gold; the emerald on my cheek burned.

The hellhound let out an amazing screeching yowl. Its claws scrabbled.

Japhrimel hit it from the side again, his booted feet connecting solidly. It rolled, twisted on itself, and streaked for me.

"*Dante! Go!*" Japhrimel bolted after it.

I set my feet in the concrete, my sword dipping, sudden knowledge flaring under my skin. I would *not* run, I would *not* let him face this thing on his own, no matter how good or inhumanly hard to kill he was. "*Anubis!*" I screamed, my cheek suddenly flaming with pain as the emerald answered, I leapt forward—

—and was knocked aside by a solid weight slamming into me, rolling in a tumbling mess of arms and legs, me trying to keep my sword from splitting my own flesh. I hurled a curse at whoever had hit me, got an accidental elbow in the face—a brief, amazing starry jolt of pain.

The hellhound streaked through where I had been standing, crashing into the casing. Sparks flew, hissing steam as the climate control circuits blew. Blue-white sparks fountained up. I cried out, throwing up a hand to shield my eyes, the light searing through dark-adapted pupils. Heard more snarls, more claws, and a curse in the spiky hurtful language of demons that made my blood run cold.

McKinley rolled free, gaining his feet in one fluid movement, I spat blood. Shook the dazing impact out of my head. There was a massive crunching sound, another scrabble of claws. *Sekhmet sa'es, it sounds like more than one of them, oh please, Japh, don't get hurt, I'm on my way*—

McKinley, dark eyes blazing, held up his left hand. The oddly metallic coating on it sparkled like quicksilver. "Come on," he said, low and taut. "Come *on!*"

Who the hell is he talking to, me or the hellhound?

The hellhound snarled—and Japhrimel, his coat flaring behind him, shot it twice in the head. Japh descended on the thing. I levered myself painfully up, watching as he moved gracefully, avoiding the thing's dying clawswipe as he tore the life out of it. Then he gained his feet, black blood smoking from his hands, and spat a single word I covered my ears against, the hilt of my sword digging into my temple. There was another low slumped shape—a second hellhound, lying twisted and broken on the rooftop. *Where the hell did that one come from? Anubis et'her ka,* two *of those things?*

The bodies twitched, convulsed, and began to rot right in front of me. Noisome fluid gushed out of slack-jawed mouths, streaming between the sharp glassy teeth. The smell smacked into me, I took two steps back, cement gritty under my boots. They were literally melting in front of my eyes.

I swiped at my face with my free hand. Blood from my nose crackled as I scrubbed it away, resheathed my sword. Japhrimel looked at me.

"Are you hurt?" His voice was so cold I half expected the foggy air to freeze between us despite the steam wreathing him, twisting into angular shapes like spiked demon runes. I gasped, unable to catch my breath, looking down at myself. I didn't *think* I was hurt.

"N-no." I glanced at McKinley, who had a gun out and trained on the closest body as it rotted. His black eyes blazed, and the metallic coating on his hand shifted a little, settling back into his skin. *Where the hell did he come from?* "Where did you come fr—"

"Time to go," McKinley said. "Transport's waiting. There are more on the way."

"Human, or otherwise?" Japhrimel's eyes swept the roof. Where had the second hellhound come from? They were so goddamn *fast*.

"Yes." McKinley's dark eyes flicked over me once. He went back to watching the hellhound's bubbling body. "My lord?"

"Come." Japhrimel arrived at my side, grabbed my arm, and gave me a once-over, nodded briefly to himself. "Leave it, McKinley. It's dead."

The Hellesvront agent holstered his gun. "Fire escape." He pointed.

"I told you to run." Japhrimel's voice was the color of steel. His eyes were furious, and his mouth a thin line. The mark on my shoulder turned hot, melting into my skin.

"I couldn't leave you to face that thing alone." I yanked my arm free of his hold. He let me, his fingers opening as if I'd struck him. "Let's go."

30

I closed my eyes, leaning against Japhrimel's side. Subway lights flickered as the hovertrain tore down reactive-greased tracks. McKinley watched the interior of the car from where he slumped in a seat, scowling. His crow-black hair was wildly mussed. We were alone on a New Prague subway train, fluorescent light buzzing overhead.

Japhrimel pressed his lips to my temple. He hadn't spoken, guiding us down through subway tunnels and finally onto this train. McKinley said nothing, too. I shuddered again, Japh's arm tightened around me, another wash of Power burning through my nerves as my eyes flew open. It was pleasant, and it kept me out of shock—but I was beginning to wonder if Japhrimel even realized he was flooding me with Power. It was an uncomfortable thought.

"That's not something I ever want to do again," I whispered finally. *Where did the second one come from? I didn't even see it. Gods.*

He kissed my temple again. "I told you to go. McKinley was waiting to cover your retreat while I dealt with the hellhounds," he murmured.

Goddammit. Just like a demon. "That was awful." I contented myself with a noncommittal reply for maybe the first time in my life.

"I prize you, my curious. I would not lose you." He spoke this into my hair, his breath scorching-hot.

"You won't." I tightened my right arm around him, my left hand aching as it squeezed the scabbard. "You killed it. Both of them."

"Hellhounds for a *hedaira*. They could have killed you." He sounded like he was just realizing it. I leaned into him a little more, suddenly very, very glad he'd found me. I had been extremely lucky not to run across any of those things on my lonesome.

"You were there. So everything's okay." *I sound like a drippy heroine on a holovid. But it's true.*

He wasn't mollified. "If we face another, you *must* do as I say. Do you understand me?"

The train rocked, bulleting through the underground tunnels. McKinley closed his eyes. He didn't look sleepy. Maybe he was giving us some privacy. Polite of him. I still had no idea what the hell he was, or how he had appeared out of nowhere and knocked me down—or why, when I looked at him, I felt the rasp of irritation and distaste rise under my breastbone. I just instinctively didn't like him.

"Dante? If we face another hellhound, you must do as I tell you." Japh repeated it slowly, as if I was an idiot.

I suppressed another flare of irritation with a healthy dose of fear. The thought of Japhrimel taking on those things alone chilled me. Even though I knew he was capable and was glad he was there … still. "I'm not going to abandon you," I said finally. "Don't ask me to do that."

"You *must* live, Dante. While you live, I live." He

stopped abruptly, as if he'd intended to say more and changed his mind.

"If I run, another one of those things might be lying in wait. We've got a better chance if we stick together." I didn't think he'd go for it, but he sighed, his face still in my hair. It was comforting, I decided, my body beginning to finally believe I was still alive. My shoulders went loose, thankfully. I blew out a long breath, leaning into the comfort of Japhrimel's warmth. I was alive, we were relatively safe, it was time to ask a few questions. "You said the imps told you something. What?"

"The hellhound might be Velokel's trick. He is the Hunter, and rode with hounds when your kind was not even a dream in the Prince's agile brain." Japh paused as the train bulleted around a bend. I felt his attention flare, scanning our surroundings. Finally, satisfied, he continued. "We may not be the only hunters the Prince has contracted. This was...not unexpected, but something I thought unlikely."

I absorbed this, worked it around inside my head, and tested it against the flash of insight I'd had while studying the magscan maps. It was worth saying out loud, at least. "The Hunter, right? He might be looking to take me out first, and you think Lucifer may have sent someone else too." I worried gently at my lower lip with my teeth. "All right. I've got an idea."

"Save me from your ideas, my curious. What is it?"

I wanted to look up at his face, but his arm was like a steel bar. The tension thrumming through him warned me; I didn't struggle. Instead, I rubbed my cheek against his shoulder. *Calm down, Japh. You scare me when you're like this.* "Try this hover for float, Japh. Lucifer wants these demons dead—but he doesn't trust either of us, especially after you pull your stunt. So what does he do? He smacks me with a few hovers and an imp, making as much noise as possible to distract and draw out whatever demon is around; then he sends another group of hunters in to do the real dirty work. Only this Velokel is a few steps ahead of Lucifer, shows up in New Prague just after me—because I've made a hell of a lot of racket with the imp on the hovertrain—and he takes to the underground, because the earth will hide him better than the red-light district. Lucas had his hidey-hole underground, there's a *reason*. Lucifer never said anything about us being the *only* ones after these demons, and he may have even wanted to clean us up as loose ends." *Though that wouldn't explain why he gave you back a demon's Power. Unless that doesn't matter to him, unless he can easily take it away or kill you anyway.*

My imagination just worked too goddamn well when it came to the possible perfidy of the Prince of Hell. Japhrimel was silent. His thumb stroked my arm.

"Well?" I persisted, as an automated voice speaking Czechi blared from the loudspeaker grilles. We were coming up to a stop. "What do you think?"

"It explains much of the chain of events. And yet...."

Right. And yet. I'm missing some crucial piece, a piece you probably have. Help me out here, okay? "It makes sense to paint a big target on my back and send me out. The demon in that building called me *Right Hand*. Even if he mistook me for you because we smell alike, how could he know you were working for Lucifer again so soon? Unless Lucifer made a *point* of leaking the information. If I was him, looking to get rid of me in the most efficient way possible and still use me for maximum benefit, that's what *I'd* do." *But I'm not Lucifer. I wouldn't ever do this to someone, use them in a trap to catch a bigger predator.*

"Indeed." He sounded grudgingly admiring. The train began to slow, resistance clamping down. I leaned into him. He kissed my temple again. "I would not want to be your enemy, *hedaira*."

"Huh." I manfully restrained from pointing out that he'd probably thought of all this before me. "Good. I'd hate to have to hunt you down."

McKinley swung up to his feet. Japhrimel's arm loosened on me. I breathed in deeply, shaking my hair back. I was almost beginning to feel like I'd survived again.

"There will never be a need." Japhrimel managed to sound, of all things, amused. He braced me as the train slid to a stop. McKinley swung out the door as soon as it opened, scanning the station.

Fluorescent light ran wetly over pre-Hegemony yellow tile, and a framed picture of a jowly, scowling man with a thick black moustache was set behind plasglass. Some kind of muckey-muck who had negotiated the Freetown's charter, probably. Permaspray graffiti tangled over tiles that hadn't been sonicwashed on the last maintenance run-through. The station was deserted; I had little idea of where I was, since this was underground. "Where are we?"

"The outskirt, near Ruzyne Transport," McKinley said, blinking his black eyes once. "I don't think we were followed."

I rolled my shoulders back, checking my rig. It was good gear, and had just come through its first engagement with flying colors. "I don't think so either. Where do we meet the others?"

Japhrimel shrugged. I looked up at his face, noted that he had a vertical line between his dark winged eyebrows. When he did that, pulling the corners of his mouth down, he looked even more grim and saturnine. He didn't immediately answer me.

Finally, he sighed. "Vann will take the others from the city. From here, the hunt is mine."

I felt my own eyebrows rising. "Um, hello?" I snapped my fingers in front of his face. McKinley frankly stared, his jaw dropping; it was the first sign of surprise I'd ever seen from him. "Excuse me, but I believe *I* was contracted for this hunt, Japh." A new thought struck me, one so terrible I almost choked.

My heart began to pound as I stared up at him, my hand frozen in midair. "They were simply bait, you wanted the Magi to draw out the demon so you could see it." I couldn't believe I had been so blind. "You're not surprised by any of this. You wanted me to go with the others so they could drag me clear of the blast zone, and you wanted me to run to McKinley so he could....You arrogant *bastard*." My stomach flipped over. No wonder Bella had looked so frightened, she'd figured out she and her partner were bait and my assumption that they were hunters instead of support staff must have scared her silly.

"I am concerned more with your safety than your wounded pride." He caught my hand in his, pushed it down to my side. "It makes no difference. I prefer you where I can see the mischief you intend, anyway. I expected you would not accede."

"I have *so* many problems with this," I muttered. *Would*

*it kill you to share a little information with me? And I will
not be a party to using other people as a lure, Japhrimel.
I won't do it.*

"I counsel you to caution." His eyes blazed. "I am no
longer your familiar, I am your Fallen—not bound to
obey, only to protect. You would do well to be silent, my
temper wears thin."

I closed my eyes and tipped my head back, feeling my
jaw work as I struggled to bite back the words rising toward the surface. When I was fairly sure I had my *own*
temper under control I gave him a level glare, bringing
my chin back down and half-lidding my eyes. "I *suggest*
you go a little easier on the autocracy, Japhrimel. I don't
like being ordered around and kept in the dark. What do
you think I am, some kind of idiot you can just—"

I barely even saw him move. The next thing I knew, I
was pinned against the tiled wall, his fingers twisted in
my rig and my feet a good half-meter in the air. He held
me up by the leather straps one-handed, as negligently as
a mama cat might dangle a kitten, his arm fully extended,
his lips pulled back from his teeth and his eyes green in-
fernos. I kicked, struggling, my fingers sinking into his
hand; he simply shook me, my head bouncing. He gauged
it carefully—my skull didn't hit the tile.

Then he sighed, fluorescent light running through the
inky darkness of his hair. I couldn't even grab for my
swordhilt, I was too busy sinking my right-hand fingers
into his hand, trying fruitlessly to get him to let *go*.

"I have been endlessly patient with you," he said softly,
each word crisp and distinct, "but we cannot have any
more of this. If you will not do as I ask without question,
I will shackle you, give you to McKinley, and continue

alone." He didn't even shift his weight as I kicked again, somehow he avoided the strike without moving, his eyes never leaving mine. "There is something in this game I do not understand, and until I understand fully I will not allow further disobedience. The Prince means to kill you with this errand despite his oath, and someone has almost succeeded in his desires twice already. I am *through* with playing. Do as I ask, and you can force a penance from me later at your leisure. But for the next seven years, *hedaira*, you are under my guard. Make it easier for both of us, and simply *obey*."

"*Stop it!*" My voice bounced off the tiles, smashed and echoed, the straps of my rig dug into my flesh. "Goddammit, Japhrimel, *stop it you're scaring me!*"

He shook me once more, maybe just to drive home how he could keep me if he wanted to, and dropped me. I landed hard, the shock jolting from my heels all the way up to my neck. I rubbed at my sternum where his knuckles had pressed, rubbed it and rubbed it. Had I been human, I'd have been bruised. *This puts a whole different complexion on things.* My eyes instinctively flicked toward the stairs leading to the surface. If I—

He caught my chin, cupping delicately, his fingers gentle but iron-hard. I caught a flash of McKinley standing with his arms folded, a study in disinterest though his eyes had a gleam I didn't like. "Don't even think of it." Japhrimel's tone was oddly tender. "It is for your own good, my curious. You *will* do as I say."

I jerked my chin free of his hand. "You didn't have to do that." My pulse beat high and frantic in my throat, and I sounded breathless even to myself. I pushed myself back, the tiled wall meeting me with a thump. He stayed where he was. The snarl on his face was gone as if it had never existed. My head was full of rushing noise; the mark on my shoulder flared with heat sinking all the way down through my chest, spilling through my bones.

He was still for a long moment, his face expressionless. He moved as if he would touch me, but I flinched back from him, the tip of my scabbard striking the tiled wall, scratching along like a blunt claw. My right hand closed around the hilt, and I stared at him as if he was a stranger, my mouth suddenly dry and the noise inside my head much worse.

Japhrimel stopped. His eyes dropped, taking in my stance and my white-knuckled hand on the hilt. "I am careful with you," he said, softly, still in that oddly intimate tone, the one that made him sound more horribly human. "I am so very careful. Can you imagine what would happen, were you caught by a demon who did not care for you?"

I swallowed dryly. It was one thing to be afraid he would use his strength and speed to force me into whatever he wanted. It was a completely different thing to have him actually *do* it. My chest ached. My cheek stung as the emerald spat a single glowing spark; my rings spiked and swirled with Power. "You shouldn't have done that," I told him, numbly.

"I will do what is necessary to protect you. Have I not proved it?"

"You shouldn't have done that." I could think of nothing else. Tears rose behind my eyes, a hot blurring weight of water. I swallowed them, set my jaw.

He sighed, shaking his head, the fluorescent light running wetly over his hair and the long fluid severe lines of his coat. His aura closed around me, a touch I tried to push away, couldn't. "This serves no purpose."

"How could you?" I whispered, rubbing at my sternum again. He hadn't hurt me, not physically, not yet. But I still rubbed at the spot where his knuckles had pressed. "How could you do this to me?"

"I do what I must." He grabbed my arm and dragged me away from the wall. "Come. We have a transport to catch."

Oh, gods. Anubis, help me. "Where are we going?" I could barely force the words out through numb, shocked lips. I didn't precisely fight him, but I did resist just enough to make him work for it. He cast me one extraordinarily green glance, but it was McKinley who answered.

"Another Freetown," he said, grinning. I didn't like that grin—it was too wide, too white, and too satisfied with current events. McKinley looked very happy to see me put in my place. "The Sarajevo DMZ."

Sarajevo? But why? They don't allow humans in there.

I could have dug my heels in and made him carry me, but the thought made me feel sick. I felt nothing more, except maybe a disbelief so huge it swallowed me whole, a disbelief only broken by a single phrase caroling through my head. *How could you, Japhrimel? How could you?* And under that, an even simpler phrase, repeating over and over again.

I trusted you.

31

New Prague had a transport dock—Ruzyne—on the outskirts. Japhrimel simply walked through security. McKinley and I did the same, and I found myself ushered aboard a sleek gleaming-black hover. My skin roughened—I hadn't had much luck with hovers lately. I couldn't even bolt for freedom on the dock—McKinley led us, and Japhrimel followed me, one hand on my shoulder. Exquisitely gentle, his thumb occasionally stroking my nape, but I'd just gotten an object lesson in how fast he was when he wasn't playing nice. It would be ridiculous to try to escape him.

Besides, if there were more hellhounds out there, I didn't stand much of a chance anyway.

I dropped into low black pleather seat, laid my katana across my knees, and proceeded to stare out the window at the lights of New Prague. No wonder Bella and Ogami had been frightened. No wonder Japhrimel hadn't seemed worried with the group's progress—he'd just been waiting for the enemy to show himself. Just playing patty-cake with me in the meanwhile, callously using the humans as bait. The fact that he'd sent them out with Vann and Tiens didn't excuse the pitilessness of the action. No harm done, but still.

I'd been a *part* of it. He'd made me a part of it. If it had gone bad, I would have been partly responsible.

Now I also knew why he'd been so damn close-mouthed about the Fallen. If I'd had any intimation that he was no longer bound by the rules of a demon familiar, I might have dug my heels in a little more and *demanded* he tell me everything. If I'd had any *warning*.

I hadn't had any warning. I hadn't even known the Devil was asking for me, hadn't even had a clue. Japhrimel hadn't acted guilty, or as if he was hiding *anything*, he had spent every waking moment with me. That led me to an uncomfortable wondering about just how often I'd been left alone while I slept, lulled into defenseless un-consciousness and abandoned while Japhrimel met with Lucifer. It could have happened easily. I'd *trusted* him.

He'd changed plans midstroke, bargained with Lucifer for a demon's Power, and dumped me in the hover to be flown home just like a kid. *Never mind about Dante, she's so easily led. So easily manipulated. Only a human, after all.*

I closed my eyes, searching for calm and an idea. Neither came.

McKinley took the hover's controls while he held a murmured conference with Japhrimel. I shut my eyes, opened them again, staring at the lights. Floating streams of hovertraffic threaded between the glowing cubes of high-rises.

The nagging sense of something wrong had gone away. Something hadn't jelled, hadn't seemed right—and this was why. Japh had never had any intention of letting me do what Lucifer's Right Hand was supposed to do.

The thought that I wouldn't have minded playing second fiddle on a hunt like this if he'd just *explained* to me what was going on wasn't very comforting either. Demons were nasty, tricky, and mostly too strong and fast for even a *hedaira*. Never mind that I'd killed an imp. If it hadn't been for the reactive paint things might have been very different indeed. And the hellhounds...my skin chilled, roughened into actual goosebumps. I most definitely wouldn't mind backup when facing *them*.

Most chilling of all was the logical extension to my line of thought—Lucifer had been angling to snare Japhrimel, use me for bait or distraction, and possibly kill Japh all along. If by some miracle we succeeded, we would still have to deal with the machinations of the Prince of Hell. Chances were if this plan failed, there would be another one. And possibly another after that.

I didn't think the Devil believed in giving up easily.

Japhrimel lowered himself into the seat opposite me. I stared out the window, my fingernails tapping at the hilt. He'd been holding back while sparring with me the whole time. The *whole time*. He'd even let me cut him once or twice.

Just to make me feel better?

Silence. Hoverwhine settled into my back teeth. A lump rose in my throat, I pushed it down. My sternum hurt, but that was because I kept rubbing it, reflexively, unconsciously.

He stirred, went still, and moved slightly again.

As if expecting me to say something.

I held my tongue. I was tempted to scream. Should

have screamed. Should have busted out the hover windows and thrown myself down. Gone limp. Nonviolent resistance. *Something.*

Anything instead of just sitting there.

What you cannot escape, you must fight; what you cannot fight, you must endure. An old lesson, my first true life lesson—but I wasn't enduring. I was simply unable to *do* anything. I was in a glass ball of calm, a type of shock insulating me from the world. He had used his strength on me, something I'd thought he'd never do. He was going to force me to do what he wanted. I was trapped, by the very last person I'd expected to trap me.

"I do not require you to forgive me, or to understand," he said finally. "I demand only your cooperation, which I will get by any means necessary."

"You should have told me." Point for him, he'd made me talk. I didn't recognize my own voice—none of my usual half-whispering. I said it as if I was a normal discussing dinner plans, the velvet weight of demon beauty in my voice taunting me. "I asked you. You should have *told* me all of this."

"You would not have agreed to any of it." Quiet, silken. "Especially my request for you to retreat while I deal with things beyond your strength."

Gods damn you. You might be right. "We'll never know now, will we."

"Perhaps not." A small tender smile. I could barely stand to see that expression on his face, his eyes softening and his mouth curving. Didn't he understand what he'd just *done* to me?

I couldn't help myself. "I could really hate you for this." *You asked me to trust you, I did, and this is what I get? You hurt me, hold me up against a w-wall*—I could still feel the casual strength in his hand as he held me helpless, my legs dangling, his knuckles digging into my chest.

"You will outgrow that." He still smiled, damn him.

I don't think I will. I shut my eyes again, closing him out. The hover banked, my stomach flipped. "You shouldn't have done it. You shouldn't have done that to me." *I sound like a broken holodisc player. Come on, Dante. Snap out of it.*

"I will do what I must. I am your Fallen." He didn't sound contrite in the least.

That would mean something to me if you hadn't just held me up against the wall and admitted lying to me. "I only have your word for that." It wasn't true—I had Lucifer's word as well as my own experience. But if I couldn't hurt him with steel, all I had left were words. The darkness behind my eyelids was not comforting, I could still see him, the black diamond flames that meant *demon*.

Was it just me, or did he seem to pause uncertainly? "I only wish to keep you safe. You are fragile, Dante, for all that I have given you a share of my strength."

I'm strong enough for some things, Japh. Go away. "Leave me alone."

"I will not." Flat, utter negation. I had rarely heard him sound less ironic and more serious.

"I mean it, Tierce Japhrimel. Leave me alone. Go finish your goddamn hunt and play patty-cake with Lucifer." I wanted to pull my knees up, curl into a ball, and wait for the tearing pain under my breastbone to go away. I didn't think it would go soon, but I needed to find a nice dark quiet place to hide in for a little while. "I want to go home."

Wherever that is. The whine of hover transport settled in my back teeth. My stomach roiled. I hadn't felt this unsteady, this *defenseless*, since … since when?

Since I'd been about twelve, that's when. My twelfth year, when the man who had raised me since infancy had been knifed by a Chill junkie. Losing Lewis had left me adrift in a world too big for me, and I felt the same way now, my breath choked and my fingers and toes cold as if I'd just gone treading into the hall of Death, my skin far too sensitive for the brutality of the world.

I felt very, very small.

Of course, he knew the thing to say that would hurt me the most. "Do you have a home, Dante?"

I hunched my shoulders. *Saint City's close enough. That's where I lived most of my life before you showed up to ruin it. Ruin everything. Dragged me into Hell, turned me into an almost-demon, died and left me alone, come back and finished off by … by …* I couldn't finish the thought. Still felt the tile, cold and hard against my back, and his fingers gone hard instead of caressing. *I thought you were my home, Japh.*

My skin crawled. I'd shared my body with him, let him into private corners of myself I had let no other lover access. Even Doreen, who had taught me to have a fierce pride in my body and its needs again, her gentleness opening up whole new worlds to me.

Even Jace.

The thought of Jace made the glass ball of calm numbness closed around me crack a little. I set my jaw, determined not to break.

I will not break. My teeth ground together, my hands tightened on my sword, my emerald spat a single defiant spark.

He sighed again. "Our legends warn of the price of becoming *A'nankhimel*. I cannot be human, Dante, not even for you. Can you not understand?"

What was it in his voice that hurt so badly? Pleading. He was definitely pleading.

Fury rose inside me, my right hand curling around my swordhilt. My eyes flew open. He'd just held me up against the wall of a New Prague subway station, and he wanted me to *understand*? "Understand you? I thought I did! I thought I—I thought *you*—" I seemed to lose all capability of speech, though I didn't splutter. It was close, though.

He nodded, leaning forward, elbows braced on his knees, fingers steepled together. "Rage at me, Dante. Be angry. Extract your vengeance later; I will allow it. As long as you will have me and after, I am yours. There is no escaping it, not now."

I shook my head, as if shaking away water. "I would have done anything you asked if you were just *honest* with me," I said miserably, tears welling up. I hated myself for crying. I hadn't cried through the hell of Rigger Hall, I had rarely cried afterward. It was the tone he used, I think, the gentle tone my body responded to. More than the softness in his voice was the betrayal. It was the betrayal that hurt the most.

Or was it the softness? I couldn't tell. I found myself rubbing at my sternum again, my knuckles scraping against my shirt under the diagonal leather strap of my rig. *I thought I knew you.* The lump in my throat swelled bigger each passing second, as if I was trapped in a windowless room.

"You are still in the habit of being human, Dante. It will take time." He didn't even sound sorry. At least when a *human* guy beat his girlfriend up, he makes a show of being contrite afterwards.

A hot tear rolled down my cheek. I couldn't even *fight* him, he was too strong. "I could hate you," I whispered.

"I warned you that you would. But you will outgrow that too."

I glared at him. *Jackshit I'm going to outgrow hating you. How could you, Japhrimel?* My eyes narrowed slightly, I dropped my right hand with an effort, tapped my swordhilt. Said nothing.

"You are contracted for seven years to the Prince. I will make sure you survive them. If I must chain you to my side I will." His jaw set and his eyes glowed. I believed him.

Oh, I'll survive all right. I'm good at surviving. And if I die I have nothing to fear, my god will take me. Maybe you won't follow me there.

I closed my eyes again. Leaned my head against the back of the seat. It was actually very comfortable. Nothing but the best for the Devil's henchmen.

"You do not have to forgive me," he repeated. "But I *will* have your cooperation."

"You know," I said, keeping my voice level, "you could really teach the Devil a thing or two." The blackness behind my eyelids was tempting. Unfortunately, I could still see him, the tightly controlled black-diamond flames of his aura, still reaching out to enfold me, the mark on my shoulder burning softly, Power spreading down my skin like warm oil. Soothing, like fingers stroking my skin, working out the knots in my muscles, easing away tension.

There was a faint rustle as if he'd moved, his coat shifting with him. "I am the lesser evil, *hedaira*. Remember that."

There was nothing I could say. If it was either the Devil or Japhrimel, where did that leave me?

Screwed, that's where. Painted into a corner by a demon.

Again.

32

Demilitarized Sarajevo is still almost-contested territory. It took two Nichtvren warlords and a whole cadre—seven Packs—of werecain to restore order after the nightmare of genocide following the Seventy Days War. Nowadays, it's the kind of place where even psion bounty hunters don't go—because human bounties don't either.

The northern half of the city is the Demilitarized Zone itself, where most nonhuman species have their enclaves; the southern half is patrolled by werecain whose only boss is the Master of the territory, a Nichtvren named Leonidas who was the final winner of the scramble for power. It's one of the four nonhuman Freetown territories in the world, a zone from the Adriatic to the forward border of Putchkin Austrio-Hungaro, bordered on the south by Hegemony Graecia. The last humans fled after the final Serbian uprising was put down by Leonidas and a werecain alpha named Masud about a century after the War, and the Hegemony and Putchkin negotiated absorbing the ethnic minorities and resettling them in the cultural areas that most closely resembled their former home. Linguists and culture-historians were busy for years sorting the tangles out.

Leonidas, probably understanding that even a Nicht-vren can't argue with joint Hegemony-Putchkin thermo-nuclear attack, made sure most of the surviving humans were released unscathed.

A few humans tried to go back, but nobody ever heard from them again. For a while there was a movement to reclaim the territory, especially the psychic whirlpool of the Blackbird Fields, but in the end the Nichtvren paid off whoever they had to and the whole issue became a moot point. Any human dumb enough to go into DMZ Sarajevo was either dead or Turned within twenty-four hours—and that went for psions too. Even accredited psions with combat training and bounties under their belt don't go there.

There are rumors, of course, of people desperate enough to go into Sarajevo and bargain to be Turned. There are also rumors of indentured servants and slave trading—but those are only whispered in dark corners. The Hegemony and Putchkin largely paid very little at-tention as long as Leonidas kept order and nothing ther-monuclear was smuggled out of the territory.

I'm actually in Sarajevo, I thought with dazed wonder, looking out the hover window.

"We've got clearance." McKinley looked back over his shoulder. "They'll meet us at the dock."

Japhrimel merely nodded. He had sat there the entire flight, watching me. After a while I had dropped all pre-tense of sleeping and instead had studied the darkness outside slowly falling under the hover. A faint grayness had begun in the east, the herald of dawn. I saw fewer lights than most cities, slices of complete darkness in certain districts north of the river, lots of neon as we banked over the DMZ, McKinley piloting the hover with a sure, deft touch.

"My lord?" McKinley asked.

Japhrimel finally stirred, swinging the seat to look toward the front of the hover. "Yes?"

"Is she...." It sounded like he couldn't find a polite way to phrase it. What was he asking? If I'd been taught my place yet? If I was all right? If I was still alive? Why the fuck should he care?

"That is not your concern." Nothing shaded Japhrimel's voice except perhaps a faint weariness.

"Yessir." McKinley turned back to the front. After a few moments, I saw the console begin to flash as a hover-dock AI took over. McKinley eased himself out of the seat and stretched, joints popping. The metallic coating on his left hand shone dully with reflected light.

He didn't look at me. I was happy about that.

Japhrimel turned back to me. "Your cooperation, Dante. I want your word on it."

That managed to wring a laugh out of me, a jagged sound that made the air shiver. "You sure you want to trust my word, demon?"

"You will give me little else." The mark burned on my shoulder, velvet flame coating my nerves. The sensation had once been pleasant. Comforting.

Now I hated it. The feeling of my skin crawling with loathing under the Power was new, interesting, and awful. It was the way I imagined an indentured servant would feel, helpless impotent loathing and rage. My sternum still throbbed with raw pain, maybe because I'd kept rubbing it, scrubbing it with my knuckles, trying to scour away the helpless feeling of being trapped and betrayed at once.

"I will make you pay for this," I whispered. My throat was full, my eyes hot and grainy. *You shouldn't have done that, Japhrimel.*

"No doubt. Your cooperation, Dante. Full and *complete* cooperation. Your word on it."

"Or what, you'll kill me?" I tried to make it sound like a challenge. "Hold me up against a wall again? Maybe you'll beat me up a little. Slap me around. Teach me my place."

A muscle in his sleek golden cheek twitched, but his voice was still soft and even. "I can think of more pleasant things to do with you, my curious. Your word."

I glared out the window, faintly surprised when the plasilica didn't crack. *You're going to regret this, you bastard.* "Fine. You have my word. I'll cooperate." *Cooperate with what and who, though? That's the question.*

He studied me. I let him have my profile, kept my gaze out the window. "You will cooperate with me for as long with our bargain with the Prince lasts."

"You get seven years from the day I negotiated with Lucifer," I returned tautly. *The first chance I have I'm ditching you, I can "cooperate" from anywhere in the world.*

The bravado was pure reflex, and I knew it. If I left him, how long would I last on my own?

"I have your word?" Damn him, he was pushing me. I could tell from the faint shadow of carefulness in his tone that he had probably gauged just how *far* he could push me without me snapping and trying to run him through.

If I did leap at him now, what would he do? Take my sword away? Cuff me with plasteel cuffs or the shackle of a demon's magick? *I am no longer your familiar; I am your Fallen. I am not bound to obey, only to protect.*

To a demon, "protection" might not mean what it meant to me. He was being careful, but he could force me to do just about anything. I had the same chance of escaping him as a stuffed and cuffed bounty has of escaping a good hunter.

In other words, no fucking chance at all unless I got a little creative and *very* lucky. But even if I managed to pull anything, what then? "I already said so." I bit off the end of the sentence. "Don't fucking push me."

McKinley didn't look at me, but he flinched. That was interesting. I had the not-so-comforting idea that the agent thought Japhrimel was still playing nice with me. Or that I was recklessly suicidal. Welcome irritation began to flow back into me like a tonic, giving me the strength to take a deep breath and measure Japhrimel with open eyes and defiantly lifted chin. *Even if you can force me to do anything you want, I'm still going to fight. I can make this difficult for you.*

Maybe he'd get tired of it after a while. I hoped so.

The hover descended. My ears used to pop every time a transport sank. Now I just felt a funny sinking sensation in my stomach. *Hedaira* don't usually throw up unless poisoned—I knew that much—but I was feeling pretty sick. It was anybody's guess whether that was from the hover or from recent events.

Japhrimel still wasn't done. "Be careful what you make of me."

As if I was somehow responsible for him treating me

like this. As if it was *my* fault. Just because he was stronger than me didn't give him the right to do that to me, did it? I set my jaw, looked down at my sword. The thought—*did Jado give me a blade that could kill the Devil?*—circled through my brain.

Then, like a gift, an idea began to form.

Are you crazy? my practical, survival-oriented half screeched. *It doesn't matter if he's a goddamn demon, he's still your best chance of staying alive! What happens if you run across another hellhound?*

A deeper voice full of stubborn determination took shape in the middle of my chest, right under the scraped and throbbing spot between my breasts. *It doesn't matter. 'Tis better to die on your feet than live on your knees, Danny. Rigger Hall taught you that. Santino taught you that. Every goddamn thing in your life that tried to break you taught you that. If you don't fight this, you're going to lose all the goddamn self-respect you've ever earned.*

I looked up at Japhrimel. "You have no right to treat me like an indentured servant," I said softly, shaking my head. A tendril of ink-black hair fell in my face, I blew it away with a short sharp whistling breath. "Just because I'm human doesn't give you the right to manipulate me or scare me into doing what you want."

I rocked up to my feet and stalked toward the front of the hover, looking down at the control deck. It would have been satisfying to smash it—but instead, I simply stood there with my head down, looking out the window and scanning the dock we were headed for. Japhrimel said nothing. It was gratifying to get the last word, for once.

Nichtvren, clustered at one end. A couple of werecain hulking behind them. I marked one Master, a large geometrical stain of Power; several Acolytes with their own shields depending on the Master's like satellites, and a few human thralls. I suppose the thralls didn't quite qualify as human, but still…it gave me a pause to see them there.

McKinley glanced at me, his back set against the partition between the cockpit and the rest of the hover. I was close enough to slip a knife into him.

The temptation was almost overwhelming.

I said nothing while the hover docked, the AI landing us with a slight thump. I closed my eyes briefly, reaching out—

—and retreating back behind my own demon-strong shields. The air outside was alive with creeping Power, like the House of Pain back in Saint City. No wonder they didn't let humans in; this many paranormal species in a city that had been soaked with pain and suffering made for a charged psychic atmosphere.

Charged like a reaction fire. I winced, wishing I could stop thinking about reactive.

Okay, Dante. Imagine you're held by enemies and in DMZ Sarajevo. Keep on your toes, stay loose, and look out for opportunity. He can't pay attention to you every single moment of the goddamn day.

At least, I hoped he couldn't. All it would take was a momentary lapse of attention and I'd have a chance to at least make Japh work for it, if not escape outright.

The good news was, if I could by some miracle get away from Japhrimel, I might be able to find someplace to hide and try to come up with a half-assed plan that would leave me alive.

The bad news was, if I ran across another demon, or even another hellhound, I might end up dead anyway.

It was looking more and more likely all the time.

33

The Nichtvren Master was none other than Leonidas himself, a spare, slim, blandly beautiful man only a little taller than me, with oily black hair elegantly corkscrewed and hanging down his back. He is the only person I've ever seen wear a microfiber toga with a broad purple stripe and sandals strapped to bare caramel-colored feet. One of his Acolytes held a parasol overhead. I was too busy checking out the lay of the land, so to speak, and so I missed most of the elegant bow he swept to Japhrimel.

His greeting, however, smacked me into full attention.

"Well. If it is not the Eldest Son and his beloved. Welcome to my humble city." He spoke, of all things, passable Merican—probably more because it was the language of trade than in deference to my limited linguistic capabilities. His voice was soft, smoothly accented, and carried enough Power to set off a plasgun charge. He wasn't as eerily, creepily Powerful as Nikolai, the Prime of Saint City.

But he was close.

Very close. Which was surprising, since by my guess,

Leonidas was the older Nichtvren. Age usually, but not always, means power among them.

If I'd still been completely human, I would have been frantically searching for a wall to put my back to. As it was, I didn't reach for my swordhilt only because Japhrimel's left hand circled my right wrist, a casual movement as effective as a spun-steel manacle. My rings rang with light, though they didn't spark. I kept myself as tightly reined as a collared telepath, almost shaking with the urge to draw my sword.

Japhrimel nodded. The Nichtvren's Power was a candle flame next to the reactive glow of his, but I still felt more uneasy about the bloodsucker than I did about the demon.

Go figure. Though Japh was rapidly catching up, wasn't he? The raw spot on my chest twinged, the pain fading. I wanted to rub at it again, quelled the urge.

"My thanks for your kind welcome. I am here to hunt, young one, and I am not in a mood for trifles." Japhrimel sounded bored, but McKinley grinned on my other side, a twitchy dangerous grin. I was the shortest person on the dock. One of the Acolytes, a massive blond man, showed his fangs when he caught me looking at him. Blue lines swirled over his face, tattoos from before he was Changed. Nichtvren skin doesn't scar.

At least, I don't think it does, not from what I could remember in my Paranormal Anatomy courses at the Academy. The blond wore what looked like moth-eaten wolf skins slung together in a kind of tunic. His eyes were dead pools, tarns that could suck a whole struggling human in to drown in their depths. The Power here smelled deliciously, mustily wicked, of Nichtvren with a sharp,

nose-cleaning tang of werecain that faded in and out—
reflecting the peculiar qualities of 'cain pheromones in
most species' nasal receptors. Over that was the flat copper scent of blood dried in fur, an alien smell that made
every human instinct in me scream like an unregistered
hooker caught holding out on her pimp. This was Power
that could eat a psion alive.

But I was no longer fully human, and instead of eating
me, the Power-well tickled deeper recesses in my psyche,
bathed me in a chill bloody weight of seductive whispering. *Get a hold on yourself, Danny.* I gave myself a sharp
mental slap, scanned the dock again. I couldn't afford to
sink into the atmosphere. The channels responsible for
circulating Power through my body tingled, fluxing; it
took me a little longer to adapt to the sheer amount of energy in the air. I shivered, and Japhrimel's thumb caressed
the underside of my wrist again. It was probably meant to
be comforting.

Watch. Wait. Sooner or later, Japh or McKinley would
slip or be distracted. I'd given my word, true—but I'd
given it under duress, I hadn't promised to stay nailed to
Japhrimel, and after what he'd done I was sure it didn't
count anyway.

Are you really sure? Unease rippled up my back. *It's
your word, Danny. Your* Word. *Anyone who uses magick
can't afford to break their word. Your magickal will depends on your word being truth.*

*But I only promised to cooperate. I didn't promise to
stay with him. I can cooperate from a distance just fine.*

I suppose dealing with demons rubs off on you after
a while. I would never have dreamed of wriggling out of
my word before.

It was also stupid. How long would I last on my own?

"Very well. But I have a message to give you, El-dest." Leonidas's heavy-lidded eyes closed like a lizard's, opened again. "There is one who wishes audience with your pretty companion. A demon with a green gem to match hers."

That could only mean one thing. *Lucifer wants to see me? Again?* The pit of my stomach was suddenly full of cold metal snakes, my heart thudding dimly in my chest.

Japhrimel was utterly still for a full five seconds, enough time for me to nervously check the entire dock again. I was fairly sure I could take the Nichtvren and I'd killed werecain before, but McKinley was a question mark. I didn't even know *what* he was. He wasn't demon, but he wasn't human either.

And Japhrimel? I had no chance. So I had to find something to distract him, to throw him off-balance. But what if—

What-ifs won't keep you alive, woman. Focus! It was a familiar male voice, laden with impatience, Jace's tone when he felt I wasn't paying proper attention during a sparring match. I was getting used to hearing Jace's voice in my head telling me to stay cool. Or maybe I was just talking to myself and using his voice. It's an occupational hazard for psions, the voices in our heads sometimes change into the people that matter most to us—or frighten us.

"When and where?" Japhrimel finally asked.

"The Haunt *Tais-toi*. Neutral ground. Tomorrow night, midnight. Alone." Leonidas grinned, exposing his fangs, Japhrimel's fingers didn't tense on my wrist but the mark on my shoulder went live again, a honeyed string of heat pressed into my flesh. "I will vouch for her safety, Eldest. There have been assurances given."

"By whom?"

That made the Nichtvren shake his blond head, clucking his tongue. "Now, can I tell you? I suspect your business lies with another demon, though."

"Perhaps. I am here on another errand. I wish to speak to the Anhelikos." Concrete groaned slightly, taking the weight of Japhrimel's voice. Most of the Acolytes stepped back, and the Master paled under the even caramel of his skin.

Anhelikos? What the hell is that?

Leonidas spread his expressive, slender hands. I wasn't fooled. Nichtvren have amazing strength, the older ones can shatter concrete with a negligent blow from a frail-looking hand. No wonder they're pretty much the top of the heap when it comes to paranormals. "I am neutral." But there was a definite glint in his black eyes. "Try not to destroy too much of my city, eh? I have been a good friend to you."

"Of course you have." Japhrimel nodded. "Very well. My thanks, Leonidas."

The Nichtvren seemed to find that funny. "He thanks me! Very generous. Well, dawn is coming. You will excuse us, I hope?"

I searched for something to say, found exactly nothing. Japhrimel stood still and silent as the Nichtvren faded into the darkness; the werecain loped away and vanished down a concourse that probably led to a hovertrain system to take visitors into the city. I glanced back over my shoulder—yes, dawn. A little more pronounced than before, a definite graying in the east.

We were soon alone on the hoverdock, cold air sough-ing gently through the cavernous half-shell structure.

"Well," Japhrimel said. "What do you make of that?"

"Don't send her alone," McKinley replied immedi-ately, as if he'd been dying to say it. "It's a trap."

"What *kind* of trap? That is the question." Another shade of grim amusement to Japh's tone. He'd never spo-ken to *me* like that.

I was beginning to get that there was a history between these two—and another history between Japh and Leoni-das. Curiosity pricked me, but I bit the inside of my cheek and studied the dock one more time, what I could see of the concourse and the half-shell roof supported with huge plasteel struts.

McKinley was no longer grinning. "A green-gemmed demon. Either the Prince or an Androgyne, which is the same thing. Here in the same city as the Anhelikos Kos Rafelos. I don't like it."

The whoosis whatsis? I wondered pointlessly if the Hellesvront agent knew anything about *hedaira*, and how I could trick him into telling me if Japhrimel left us alone. Unfortunately, if Japh left me alone with him I might be tied up or worse, unable to make an escape attempt.

"It is not technically a summons." Japhrimel looked down at me. "What do you think, Dante?"

I swallowed bitterness, hearing him say my name so calmly. *What the hell is an Anhelikos? Do I want to know?* "I'm not here to think," I said flatly. "Only to *cooperate*."

McKinley stared at me, his dark eyes wide. "My lord—"

"Quiet." Japhrimel's voice made the entire dock groan

softly. I set my jaw and stared at my boot-toes. "We shall seek the Anhelikos, then shelter."

McKinley nodded. He shut up too, which was a pity. I would have liked to hear what he had to say about me.

Just wait, Danny girl, Jace's voice murmured inside my head. I moved forward obediently enough when Japhrimel did, mulling over this new turn of events. So Lucifer wanted to see me again. I was getting mighty popular with the denizens of Hell nowadays.

And what was the Anhelikos? Looked like I was about to find out.

I put my head down so that my hair fell forward, hiding my face. My lips moved silently, shaping a prayer to Anubis. It was habit, when I found myself in a hopeless situation, to pray. Even a combat-trained part-demon Necromance is human enough for *that*.

Sarajevo is dark, its cracked streets faced with old sloping, crumbling buildings that look deserted except for the curious lack of broken windows and graffiti. The wind is drenched with the stinging, fading-and-returning reek of werecain, as well as the dry feathery smell of swanhild and the musty delicious perfume of Nichtvren, dyeing the air in ripples. The darkness itself seems alive.

Not to mention hungry.

McKinley followed as Japh made turns seemingly at random, my footsteps echoing in the eerie silence between a demon and a Hellesvront agent. I walked, my right wrist still caught in Japhrimel's gentle but inexorable grasp, stealing little glances now and again to fix the city in my Magi-trained memory. The darkness here was deeper than in human cities, where orange light from hoverwash and freeplas reaches up into the sky; the streetlamps here were mostly dark though not broken. It looked like paranormals don't go in for breaking plasglass the way humans do.

The Power in the air stroked my shields, teased at me even through the heavy weight of Japhrimel's aura over mine. It was the end of that long dark time of early morning that is late afternoon for psions, when the normals have gone to bed and the streets unroll like ribbons alive with secrets, the time when old people in hospitals die smoothly and silently. Here in Sarajevo the air moved soundlessly, crackling with force and full of the peculiar music of a thriving city, strangely hushed but still audible. I heard a few hovers, faraway sirens, and the indefinable sound of conscious beings moving around. The faint grayness of dawn was growing stronger, but sunrise was still a way off.

Japhrimel finally stopped on a corner, looking down one more featureless Sarajevo street. I could smell the river when the explosive furry reek of werecain vanished from my overloaded nasal receptors. I could also smell a faint, delicious smell I had to think about before I could identify—bread baking, with a drier tang. Like feathers.

"We are visiting a . . . being." Japhrimel's voice took me by surprise. His fingers were gentle around my wrist, but I didn't bother to try to pull free. "McKinley will wait outside for us. You will not be in any danger."

Well, isn't that comforting. I stared at the pavement, letting the spiderweb cracks blur as my eyes unfocused. *Would you tell me if I was?*

That was unfair, but I wasn't feeling too fucking charitable right at the moment. I settled for holding my tongue, taking refuge in childish silence. I wondered who or *what* he was visiting. It could be anything from a *gaki* to a ko-bolding, I'd already seen werecain and Nichtvren. I wondered where a demon would go for information, and what Japhrimel was likely to be asking, and who he was likely to be asking it *of*.

Wild werecain wouldn't have dragged the questions out of me.

He didn't add anything to that, just led me across the street. My bootheels clicked against the pavement, I could hear McKinley now, soft footsteps echoing mine eerily. I got the idea he was doing it deliberately, whether as a comment or a joke I didn't want to guess.

I looked up when Japhrimel paused. There was a high wall, older stones set in smooth concrete and humming with Power. The smell of werecain returned, stinging my nose. The shielding over the wall was something I'd never seen before, a violet haze that looked strangely diaphanous but still sparked and hummed as Japh drew near. There was a small, narrow wooden gate vibrating slightly, moving back and forth like the oscillation of a heartbeat. I couldn't see what was behind the gate, and the hazy shielding was enough to make me hinky. I had never seen this type of defense before. *Unknown* was synonymous with *possibly dangerous* when it came to magick, especially shielding. I stiffened, and Japh actually stopped.

"There is no danger," he said, as if I was a primary-school kid scared of the dark. I didn't bother replying, just took a step forward, tugging against his hand.

Now I had to act like I wasn't frightened.

McKinley stepped to the side, leaned against the wall, and folded his arms. The metallic glow over his left hand sparked with a flush of pale purple light that deepened to an indigo glow as he seemed to sink into the smooth surface, his eyes turning even darker. My jaw threatened to drop as he almost vanished, not only to my physical but also to my psychic senses. Japhrimel set off again, I stared at where McKinley had literally blended with the wall. *How did he do that? What the hell* is *he?*

Japh tented his fingers against the gate and pushed it open. I hung back as far as I could, then passed through the hazy shield. It slid over the edge of Japhrimel's aura, sparkling gold as it interacted with the scorching mark of a demon in the landscape of Power. My rings swirled uneasily, my sword rattling inside its sheath. I inhaled, found myself still alive and under the cloak of Japh's aura. Cautiously decided maybe I was all right.

Inside the wall was a garden. The persistent smell of werecain and Nichtvren died, replaced by the scent of damp earth, rosemary, and lilies. The pungent breath of sage touched my face; the breeze inside the walls was warm and full of the smell of spicy, lush growth.

The walk underfoot turned to flagstones. I saw an oak tree in full leaf, its trunk as big around as an illegally augmented Family bodyguard, and nasturtiums with leaves the size of small pizzas trailed over a stone bench. Nightblooming jasmine scented the air, and I smelled honeysuckle and the sharp tang of rue. A persistent breath of dry, oily feathers drifted by, making the garden even sweeter. It didn't smell like the very beginning of winter, nor was it as chilly as it had been outside the wall. It felt like summer, a perfect summer night in a flawless garden.

It reminded me of Eddie's garden in Saint City, of sitting on the lawn chairs and smelling the *kyphii* Gabe liked to burn, drinking old wine or Crostine rum-and-synth ly-

chee while Eddie fussed over the antique synthcoal barbe-
cue and Gabe's soft laughter drifted over the immaculate
beds. I'd taken both Doreen and Jace over to Gabe's at
different times, so I could remember Doreen sending
little flickers of Power dancing through the fireflies, making them chase each other in complex runic patterns. I
could also remember Jace searing steaks or reclining on
the lawn, shaping the smoke from Gabe's synth-hash
cigarettes into marble-sized globes drifting through the
yard, Gabe lazily flicking her fingers in stasis-charms and
freezing them into ash. They were good memories, and I
found myself wearing a completely unfamiliar smile.

Rising above the garden was a temple, high and narrow with a Novo Christer symbol—an uneven *tau* cross—
worked into the pre-Merican Era stained glass over the
front door. I shivered, thinking of the Religions of Submission and their war on psions. Stone steps eased up
from the flagstone walk, and I was almost up the steps
before I realized I was still grinning foggily.

Wait a second. I'm smiling. Why am I smiling?

The air was soft as silk, laden with good memories,
Gabe and I weeding a plot of feverfew together on a mellow spring evening, Eddie and I practicing with staves,
Doreen in a wide straw hat turning earth in the garden
she'd planted, Jace with a bandanna tied around his golden
head and muscle moving under his skin as he helped me
lay shingles on the roof. . . .

"What the hell is this?" I whispered as Japhrimel set
his foot on the first step.

"Anhelikos." He glanced down at me, his mouth turning down at the corners. "Is it pleasant? The beginning
stages usually are."

That doesn't sound good. I struggled to think clearly. "What is it?" *What have you dragged me into this time?* But looking up at him sent another cascade of memories through me—offering him my wrist after he'd soothed me out of a nightmare during the hunt for Santino, his gentle refusal. His voice as we lay in bed, my cheek against his shoulder, his patient work repairing the gaping holes in my psyche after Mirovitch's *ka* had almost killed me, Japhrimel stroking my back as I dialed Gabe's number, our linked hands swinging between us as we walked down a dusty Toscano road.

He stopped, his fingers gentle on my wrist. "Only a side effect, part of its lure. It will fade."

"Would it kill you to tell me what's going on?" I couldn't muster any anger, though I knew I *should* have been angry. It was odd to *expect* to feel it, but to be so curiously removed from any anger, as if a reflex circuit had been disabled. The breeze caressed my hair, touched my jeans, seemed to swirl around me.

"Watch, and wait." But he let go of my wrist, sliding his fingers down to lace through mine. "Come."

34

Inside, mellow candlelight played over the soaring interior. All unnecessary interior walls had been taken out. The choirloft was an empty space, and the belltower had no steps anymore. The floor was stone, polished to a low shine by centuries of foot traffic. The path up the middle toward where the altar would have been was still visible, and the pattern of darker stone where pews would have marched in ordered rows. Up on the dais, thick white pillar candles crouched on holders of every shape, their drenching, flickering glow burnishing every surface with mellow gold. I heard a soft, deep whirring, and it landed softly on the floor.

I say *it*, because it was strangely sexless. Lucifer had his own brand of pure androgynous beauty that was nevertheless tinted with absolute masculinity. This being lacked the hurtful razor edge of the Devil's golden immaculateness. Pale skin feathering into platinum hair, winged colorless eyebrows, slim bare shoulders and a long white silken vest; it wore loose fluttering trousers and had shapely bare white feet. Its eyes were bleached but glowing, a blue that reminded me of the winter sky in certain parts of Putchkin Russe on sunny days when the wind comes knife-edge over the permafrost and slices straight through the best and warmest synthfur. That blue is as intense and fathomless as it is cold, a faded color that nevertheless looks infinite and manages to drench everything underneath it with eerie, depthless light. The eyes were set in a face that could have shamed every gene-spliced holovid star by comparison, a marvel of delicately flawless architecture.

Japhrimel stopped. I wanted to look around, take in the territory just in case, but the creature looked at me and its wings ruffled.

Did I mention the wings? Much taller than the creature, who towered a head and a half above Japhrimel; the wings were soft white and feathered, wide and broad like a vulture's. It actually mantled as it landed, bare feet soundless on stone floor. The smell of feathers mixed with a deeper, sweeter fragrance I couldn't place, a warm breeze redolent of baking bread and that sweet smell kissing my face. I stared, I'll admit it. I gawked like a primary schooler arriving at Academy for the first time.

It examined us both. Its mouth moved, and a low sweet sound filled the air. The voice sounded like bells stroked gently, a melody against my ears that eased aches I hadn't even known I was carrying. The meaning arrived complete in my head without passing through my ears, as if the speaker was a class 5 telepath.

My greetings to you, Avarik A'nankhimel. And to your bride.

"Greetings, Anhelikos Kos Rafelos." Japhrimel spoke in Merican, maybe for my benefit. The winged being's eyes didn't leave my face, I noticed a slender hilt at its side, attached to a long slim sword-shape. Who would want to fight this creature? It was tall but thin, and looked fragile. "I trust your wings have not faltered."

Not yet. Nor your own, Kinslayer. You are not the first of your kind to come to me lately. The bell-like tone drifted through my head, leaving a sense of lassitude in its wake.

"Ah." Japhrimel tilted his head to the side. I tore my eyes away from the Anhelikos, looked at him. The candle-light touched his face, slid over it kindly, and I was surprised by a jolt of starry pain lancing through my chest. It didn't matter, nothing mattered but his fingers in mine, warm and solid. I began to feel distinctly woozy. "I wondered if that might not be the case. Has the treasure left your keeping, then?"

The wings mantled again. Soft white feathers scattered, the redolent breeze ruffling my shirt and fingering my hair. *It has left my keeping, but not in the way you imply. It has gone on its ancient route to the Roof of the World, as was agreed between your Prince and our kind. How did you come to regain your pride after Falling? You do not seem weakened.*

Japhrimel didn't dignify the last question with a reply. "Who else came, Rafelos?" His voice was harsh and clipped compared to the music of the Anhelikos. Harsh, but somehow cleaner. I frowned, trying to figure out just what I was feeling. Relaxed, very relaxed…but also un-settled. Deeply disturbed. Like a fly struggling in a nar-cotic web, tiring itself as it thrashes.

I pushed the mental image away with an exhausting effort.

I can so rarely tell you apart, Kinslayer. But this one

hunted the A'nankhimel and their brides. I recognize him from the fall of the White-Walled City and the Scattering of the Fallen. The creature's eyes met mine again. Wooziness spilled through me, ignited inside my head as if I was human again and drunk. The only other time I'd felt this inebriated was when I'd questioned a terrified sexwitch during the hunt for Kellerman Lourdes. Did this creature also flood the air with pheromones so strong they could turn me inside-out? How could I fight *that*?

The creature's slim fingers tapped at the bone sword-hilt at his side. Hanging a sword off the belt is not generally recommended, it's best to have the blade to hand if you think you might need it. Barring that, the best place to have a sword is strapped to your back, easier to draw and less likely to bang on things when you turn around. But having wings probably made things a little different. I swayed, Japhrimel's fingers tightening in mine.

The swirling disorientation poured through me. *Why does it feel so weird? Then again, weird is my life now. Why can't I be a normal psion?*

Has your Prince lifted his ban, then? The creature's hand caressed the swordhilt; I finally figured out what the look on its beautiful, feral face was.

It looked suspiciously like *hunger*.

My lips parted. "Japhrimel—" It was a whisper, I was barely aware of saying the word and wished I hadn't, because the thing's attention centered on me. *This scares me. Oh, gods, this scares me more than you do. Why did Lucifer pick me to inflict this on? I could have lived my entire life without getting this close to a demon or this... whatever it is. My entire, entire life.*

"Of course not." There was an edge to Japhrimel's

voice, grim satisfaction and sudden comprehension. Not to mention terrible anger. The kind of anger that could tear stone apart with a word. "*A'nankhimel* are under the sentence of death, wherever the Prince finds them. And if one cannot kill a Fallen, their brides are ever so fragile."

Ah, yes. So vulnerable. So trusting. The creature blinked, first one eye, then the other.

The mark on my shoulder crunched down on itself, a jolt of pain spearing through the languor wrapped around me. I found myself leaning against Japhrimel, our hands clasped between us, the butt of a projectile gun caught between my hip and forearm. The harder I fought, the more limp and relaxed my body became. I tried to stand up, lean away from Japh, *anything*. The strength spilled out of my legs, if I hadn't been propped against him I might have gone down in a heap.

The creature stared at me. A pale tongue flicked out, passed over its colorless lips. The blue eyes were hooded now.

"My thanks for your aid, Kos Rafelos." Japhrimel nodded briefly. "We will trouble you no more."

Oh, please. Just one little taste. They are so sweet, after all. Its mouth stretched into a lipless smile, showing a bloodless tongue and suddenly sharp teeth.

Japhrimel laughed. The sound sliced through the languid air, I gained my feet with a massive effort, bracing myself with his fingers laced through mine. Stiffened my knees, fighting, *fighting* to stay upright. "Not today, Kos Rafelos. This little one is not to your taste; she has a sharp spine. Good night, Anhelikos."

The creature's hand clasped around the hilt. I saw

the muscles in its thin, wiry arm tense, flickering under smooth pale skin.

My left hand jumped of its own volition, scabbard blurring, wrist flicked back, hand palm-upwards; fingers closed around the hilt of the sword and the hand snapping down, blade singing free as the inertia of the scabbard slid it from the sheath. Strength returned, flooding me like freeplas fumes, igniting in my head as I jerked against Japhrimel's hand. He didn't let go as I stepped forward, my knees unsteady, reflex brought the sword up and over in my left hand, held steady and slanting, a bar between the creature's pale gaze and my own level glare. The scabbard flew in a perfect arc behind us, striking the wooden door with a thin snapping sound. *Hope I didn't break it*, I thought, instinct pushing me away from Japhrimel, giving me enough room to fight without getting tangled in him.

"Draw that blade," I said, my voice slurring a little but still steady, "and you'll have more goddamn trouble than you can handle, wingboy."

The voice of self-preservation made its appearance, as usual, a good two seconds too late. *Danny, what are you doing? This thing is goddamn fucking dangerous and you're as drugged as a New Vietkai whore! Let Japh take care of this goddamn thing if it draws down on you!*

Japhrimel's hand was suddenly not clasped in mine, it was closed around my right shoulder. "Easy, *hedaira*." Did he sound, of all things, amused? Damn him. "There is no danger."

The creature's face *shifted*, from one moment to the next. Instead of sexless, transparent beauty, the jaw jutted forward and the nose turned to slits, the pale incandescent eyes bulging. It was only a flicker, there and gone so quickly I gasped, stumbling backward. Japhrimel dug his fingers in, holding me up.

The entire interior of the church rattled with a slow even hiss, the creature's supple body melting bonelessly into a serpent's fluid curve before it snapped back into a recognizably humanoid form. The wings ruffled, more white feathers boiling free, the smell of baking bread and sweet perfume turned cloying-thick.

A *hedaira* seeking to protect the Kinslayer. The thing's voice burrowed into my head, the bell-like tone suddenly gone brittle. Surely the time of reckoning is upon us now.

I wasn't trying to protect him. I was going to kill you if you drew, goddammit. I couldn't make my mouth shape the words.

"It makes no difference." As Japhrimel drew me back, I didn't look away from the creature. Its hand dropped from the swordhilt, wings smoothing as we retreated, step by careful step. The mark on my shoulder pulsed with soft, oiled Power. "If others of my kind come, you may tell them what you like. Only be sure to add this: as long as the Prince endures, my *hedaira* enjoys his protection. That means I am disposed to consider his...*requests*...most kindly."

My knees almost gave out on me again as I realized what I'd just done. The candle flames hissed. Japh dragged me out the door, the night air sparkling clean after the cloying interior of the temple. He somehow bent to retrieve the scabbard on the way out, too, though his hand never left my shoulder. He handed it to me as we stood on the top of the steps, the wooden door closing behind us. I heard another hissing, chuckling sound from inside as a wave of thick sweet clotted perfume belched

out through the rapidly narrowing crack between the door
and the jamb.

The Prince will not allow a *hedaira* to live, Kinslayer. Especially not your *hedaira*. You would do well to remember
the White-Walled City and the screams of the Fallen—

The door clicked shut. The garden rustled, leaves rubbing against each other with the sibilant sound of feathers
rasping. I coughed, the smell of dry feathers and bread
coating the back of my throat. My eyes watered, but I
could still resheathe my blade; the action was habitual
enough not to need sight.

Japhrimel pushed me down the steps. I stumbled and
he held me up. His arm came over my shoulders, but I
didn't care. I simply wanted to get *out* of this place as
soon as possible. My boots echoed on the flagstone path,
Japh's were silent.

*What was the White-Walled City? The roof of the
world? This thing was holding a stash of something and
now it's gone. What's Japh looking for? Goddammit.*
Frustration rose, fighting with the way my arms and legs
tingled numbly, clumsy. "Gods." I coughed again, wanted
to spit to clear my throat, didn't. "What the..." I couldn't
get enough breath to finish the sentence. Little bits of
plant life touched me—leaves, branches; they all felt like
tiny grasping fingers.

"Anhelikos." Japhrimel's tone was even and thoughtful. "They feed on anger. And hatred. You are perhaps
the first human to have seen one in almost five hundred
years." He pushed open the narrow wooden gate, the heat
of him cleaner than the thick clotted scent left behind us.
I shivered galvanically as we passed through the diaphanous shielding laid over the high wall. His arm tightened,

drawing me into his side, and my sword bumped my leg as it dangled in my nerveless left hand. "You are perhaps the only living creature to survive drawing steel inside one's nest. That was ill-advised."

"Sorry." I didn't sound sorry, wanted to shake his arm away, couldn't. My legs felt like I'd just run a thousand-mile marathon, and my head throbbed unevenly. "I feel sick."

"It is a thing inimical to you. The feeling will pass." He glanced at the wall, where McKinley suddenly reappeared.

"Any news?" The Hellesvront agent's black eyes flicked over me, I hoped I wasn't shaking visibly.

It feeds on anger, that's why I felt so drained. Gods. What is *that thing? I don't care, I never want to see it again. Gods above.*

"Some," Japh replied. "It has been moved, I expected as much. Someone came to fetch it, failed, and triggered the game." He stopped, glanced back over his shoulder at the high, smooth concrete wall. Then he looked down at me. "Did you think to protect me, Dante?"

No. I wanted to kill it before it drew. "It was about to draw, Japh."

"Unlikely." He paused. "I told you there was no danger."

I don't care what you fucking told me. "I wasn't exactly thinking clearly." *I don't even know why I did that. I hate you. I can't hate you. I wish I'd never met you.*

No, I don't. Gods. I was too confused and shaken to think straight. Stepping in front of him had just *happened*. I'd tried to protect Doreen, I'd tried like hell to protect Jace—but they'd been human. Like me.

Japhrimel probably didn't need me at all.

That thought hurt more than anything else.

"So it seems." He studied me for a few moments.

Sekhmet sa'es. I gave up. Leaned into his side, blinking as I stared at the pavement at my feet. My boot-toes seemed strangely far away. "Fine." My quads and hamstrings were starting to tremble, something I hadn't felt since before Rio. I felt about three seconds away from collapsing. "Whatever. Can I sit down somewhere?"

The silence stretched on for a good thirty seconds. I couldn't tell if they were looking at me or each other, didn't care. Finally, Japhrimel spoke. "The weakness will pass. Come."

He set off down the cracked and uneven pavement, I concentrated on putting one foot in front of the other.

Once again, I don't see how things could get any worse. I winced as I thought it. You'd think I would have learned by now not to say that, even to myself.

This being a nonhuman Freetown, the hotel was run by swanhild.

Swanhild, with their ruffs of white feathers and delicate long-fingered hands, are weak when compared to Nichtvren or werecain or even kobolding. But their flesh is extremely poisonous to most carnivorous paranormal species, and a variant of touch-telepathy means that a 'cain or a Nichtvren that kills a swanhild suffers a kind of psychic death in return. It's unpleasant to say the least, and as a result the 'hilds are the paranormal equivalent of Free Territorie Suisse. They function as message carriers and bankers, as well as several other kinds of service providers, for paranormal communities.

Swanhild don't like humans. Something about a pre-Merican Era prince who had trapped one, tried to marry her, and ended up killing her and committing suicide, I think. There used to be a very old ballai about it, but the swanhild campaigned so effectively it's hard to even get bootleg holos of old performances. Modern ballai companies won't perform it for audiences, either.

The hotel was a kobolding-restored building, with the characteristic fluid stone decorations carved into its facade. Inside, the lighting was dim, the windows UV-screened, and a collage of paranormals hung out in the hotel bar while McKinley checked us in. I saw—for the first time outside a textbook—a batlike Fumadrin, its snout buried in a bowl of what looked like whiskey but was probably paint thinner. I saw a red *gaki* with a long black drooping mustache talking to a blond man in a long black coat with a sword strapped to his back. The man looked human enough, but he had a crimson-black stain of an aura, which told me he was probably a host for something. A gaggle of swanhild gathered at one end of the bar, clicking and chirping back and forth; a single Nichtvren yawned as she paid her tab with a fistful of New Credit notes, wiping a red stain away from her exquisite lips. Two kobolding slumped in a corner, their table almost groaning under the weight of empty beer tankards; the bartender was a husky golden werecain whose yellow eyes flicked over the hotel lobby every now and again.

Japhrimel kept his arm over my shoulders, his thumb stroking my upper arm every so often. I kept looking down at the floor, though I was feeling a lot better. The languid, drained feeling had faded within a couple blocks of the Anhelikos's temple. I wasn't feeling a hundred watts, but

I was all right. Except for the way my chest hurt, especially the rubbed-raw little spot under the diagonal leather strap of my rig.

Thankfully, we didn't have to use an elevator to get to the third floor. McKinley led us up a long, sweeping red-carpeted flight of stairs lifting from the marble-floored lobby. A sharp right-hand turn past a glowering werecain guard, and I was ushered into a room that was dim and soft and luxurious, with antique blue velvet chairs and a silky cream-colored carpet I immediately wanted to foul in some way. A wet bar gleamed. There was even a canister of cloned blood in a stasis cabinet under the shelves of liquor. A plasma holovid player perched on a wide cherrywood dresser, and the beds were huge and looked soft enough to sink into.

There were, unfortunately, no windows. The walls were smooth and blank. A Nichtvren room, safe from daylight. Airless.

As soon as I realized this I looked up at Japhrimel, already feeling the air grow thick. "No. Please, no." My voice cracked, my throat closing with claustrophobic weight. If McKinley hadn't been right behind us I would have tried to backpedal. As it was, I tried fruitlessly to tear myself out from under Japh's arm, failed. "You don't have to do this. I'll be a good little prisoner and stay."

He shrugged, his fingers gentling but still iron-hard. I couldn't break his grip. "I am sorry."

"There's no goddamn windows. You know how I feel about—" I was about to start hyperventilating, I could *feel* it.

"This is *necessary*, Dante." His arm loosened, but I could feel his readiness. Even if I could bowl over McKinley, Japh would catch me before I got to the hallway. The fight went out of me. I could feel it leave, like a splinter drawn out of torn flesh.

"Fine." My voice cracked, making a picture-frame rattle against the wall. "Whatever." I tore away from him, stalked past the beds into the furthest corner of the room, and pushed the chair occupying it away. I put my back to the corner and slid down until I sat on the floor, my knees up, my katana across my lap, right hand clamped over the hilt, left around the scabbard. I leaned my head into the corner, closed my eyes, and struggled to breathe.

Japhrimel murmured to McKinley, I heard the room door open and close again. Peeked out from under my lashes to see Japhrimel walking softly around the end of a bed, approaching me. The familiar breathless feeling of demon magick rose as he warded the walls, demon defenses springing into being under the humming of the hotel's security net and magickal shielding. Cracking a kobold-constructed building run by swanhilds was a tall order indeed. We were probably safe, even if my heart hammered and my throat felt savagely constricted.

I took the only refuge I had left, shutting my eyes and breathing, reaching into the still quiet part of myself that had never failed me. "*Anubis et'her ka,*" I whispered. "*Se ta'uk'fhet sa te vapu kuraph.*" My mouth was dry, the whisper was cracked and imperfect. "Anubis, Lord of the Dead, Faithful Companion, protect me, for I am Your child. Protect me, Anubis; weigh my heart upon the scale; watch over me, Lord, for I am Your child. Do not let evil distress me, but turn Your fierceness upon my enemies. Cover me with Your gaze, let Your hand be upon me, now and all the days of my life, until You take me into

Your embrace." I breathed in again, tried it again. "*Anubis et'her ka. Se ta'uk'fhet sa te vapu kuraph.* Anubis, Lord of the Dead..."

The blue flame rose up before my inner eyes. I didn't see the hall of infinity, or the bridge, or the well of souls—but the blue light closed around me, and that was good enough. With a grateful sobbing breath, I gave myself up to the comfort of my god.

35

The room was twenty-four steps long from the blank
wallpapered wall to the door that led into a short entry
hall, with a huge bathroom off to one side. I know because
I counted the steps as McKinley paced it over and over
again. Japhrimel was silent, folded down cross-legged on
the carpeting a few feet away from me, his eyes closed.
Waiting. His coat spread behind him on the floor, a deep,
lacquered darkness.

Hours ticked away. I had plenty of time to think through
that long weary day, slipping in and out of a hazy blue-
flamed trance as I sought the comfort of my god over and
over again. My chest hurt. I could barely breathe, and I
was hungry, but I shook my head when McKinley asked
me if I wanted breakfast. Shook it again when he asked
about lunch. A third time when he asked about dinner.

Japhrimel sat, his spine straight, his face closed like the
room itself. Tears rose in my throat, pricked at my eyes, I
denied them. I would have liked to take a hot shower and
cry, but I was damned if I'd give them the satisfaction.
Instead, I studied Japhrimel's face, my fingers aching
around my swordhilt. I looked at the wallpaper, patterned

with gold fleur-de-lis. I examined the edge of the blue velvet bedspread. I looked at the nap of the carpet, found myself looking back at Japhrimel's face. How many times had I run my fingertips over his cheekbones, let him kiss my fingers, lain beside him and told him things I'd never told another living person?

What kind of inhuman patience had it taken to live with me for so long, keeping the fact of the Devil's asking for me to himself? All the presents, the sparring matches, his fingers gentle against my ribs, his mouth against my neck as he shuddered in my arms.

It couldn't all have been a game to him. It *couldn't* have.

I *knew* the Devil meant me no good. I knew other demons would want to kill me because of Lucifer's meddling my life. But I'd never questioned Japh since his resurrection. After all, he'd Fallen, hadn't he?

Hadn't he? Even Lucifer had said so. But neither the Devil nor Japh had told me very much about what *Fallen* really meant.

I didn't like the way my thoughts were tending. What did Fallen really mean? What had Japhrimel wanted to collect from the Anhelikos? Who was trying to kill me now, and why, and what was Lucifer's endgame in all this? I knew better than to think it was what he had originally presented to me—a straight, simple hunting-down of four demons, badda-bing, time served, Danny Valentine free of demonic manipulation.

Another thought rose, even worse than the first.

Let's just suppose Japhrimel has been ducking out to talk to the Devil while I sleep. Just for the sake of argu-

ment, let's say. What do they have planned? Was it all an act?

But Japhrimel had protected me, hadn't he? Tracked me down, found me, asked me to trust him, rescued me from the hellhounds.

That only means Lucifer has some use for you. Ten to one says you're bait too, Danny. It was a puzzle. I'd hunted down Santino for Lucifer, could that have made me an enemy or two? Santino had bred an Androgyne— the type of demon Lucifer was, the most rare and precious because Androgynes could breed. Santino—or Vardimal, as Japh called him—had thought he could create a puppet Androgyne to replace Lucifer on the throne of Hell, effectively crowning Santino as king too, if the Androgyne was malleable enough.

Maybe there were other demons who'd wanted a crack at Santino's patented process of creating an Androgyne, the shining path of genes even Lucifer with all his tinkering couldn't find. So, conceivably, they could want a little revenge for my interference, no matter that I'd been given no choice in the matter. So far this theory was holding up uncomfortably well.

If this was the truth, I was bait for any demons involved with Santino's rebellion. Lucifer had let Santino free to see what he could do, confident in his ability to recapture the Lesser Flight demon anytime he wanted to. Only Santino hadn't played along, had disappeared—and the Devil had started to scramble.

Which led me to another logical extension, chilling in its exactitude.

Try this on for size, Danny. Lucifer leaves Japh's ashes with me, thinking he can pick him up like a dropped

*toy whenever he wants to—whenever the demons allied
to Santino show themselves. When they do, he calls me
and plants the idea of resurrecting Japh in my head. I
don't listen, because I'm in the middle of hunting down
Lourdes. Japh wakes up and starts looking for me—and
Lucifer meets him, tells him to keep me alive and take
care of me, because I'm bait. Japhrimel does, I fall in with
the plan, and when the time is right and I'm ready for my
part, I'm called onstage. Only Japh slips in a mickey at
the last moment. After all, you can't trust a demon, and
he's got Lucifer by the short hairs. Which leaves me with
one question.*

*How far does Japhrimel's protection extend? How ex-
pendable am I?*

That was a distinctly uncomfortable thought. If Lucifer
gave the word, would Japh cut me loose? After all, he
had a demon's Power now. Maybe I couldn't be changed
back into a human, but maybe Japh could get his freedom
and his place in Hell back by bounty hunting these other
four demons and finishing it up by tying off the last loose
end.

Me.

*That's ridiculous, Dante. He's your Fallen. He's kept
you alive this far.*

Was that just because Lucifer had further plans for
me? I *knew* Lucifer was my enemy, was fairly sure any
other demon I'd come across at this point was an enemy.
Could my Fallen become an enemy too? Especially since
he wouldn't tell me what *Fallen* meant? He'd held back
during sparring, had kept things hidden from me—had he
also only *pretended* some kind of emotional link to me?

Or had he been amusing himself, as demons were wont to do in stories?

Do not doubt me, no matter what. I was busy doubting with all my little heart, now.

I considered him, sitting there with his eyes closed. My hand tightened on the swordhilt. I could draw and strike in a little under a second and a half while I was human; I was faster now. I wasn't fast enough to hit him. But what would he do? What could I get away with doing as long as I still had value as bait?

He could tie me up and leave me with McKinley. I shuddered at the thought. *He might, too, if I make any trouble.* I was fairly sure I could break my way out of pretty much any human bonds, given enough time and concentration. But a demon probably knew how to tie a *hedaira* up so she didn't escape. It was probably one of the things they learned in demon nursery school.

The thought of being tied up and having something like the hellhound attack was chilling, to say the least. McKinley's footsteps continued their even tread. My rings crackled uneasily, golden sparks pulsing in the air above them and winking out.

There was another problem, too. A green-gemmed demon wanting to see me at the Haunt *Tais-toi*, which from the name was probably a Nichtvren haunt. I'd been inside one—the House of Pain in Saint City—and I never wanted to see another.

So Lucifer wanted to see me again. What the *hell* for? To finish me off, now that I'd served my purpose?

Had I served my purpose?

The sense of some missing puzzle piece returned. Gods above, how I hate that missing-piece feeling. It always means I'm about to get deeper into trouble than even I can handle.

Between one moment and the next, Japhrimel's eyes flicked open. He studied me for a long moment, then stretched, the movement turning into a graceful rising to his feet. He offered me his hand. "Dinner first," he said. "An audience has been requested with you, *hedaira*."

How did he sound so bloody *calm*? Was Lucifer planning to kill me or subject me to some incredible new form of torture? Fury rose in me again, was throttled. I wanted to sound at least as calm as he did. McKinley halted. It was a good thing—the pacing was really starting to irritate me.

I made it to my feet on my own, bracing my left hand with my sword against the floor and levering myself up, my legs tingling briefly from forced immobility. I still felt a little shaky, but overall I seemed to have bounced back from the awful draining sensation. "I'm not hungry. I'll go to this meeting, though." My voice shook perceptibly. *Congratulations, Dante. You sound about as calm as a Necromance before her Trial.*

"It could be a trap." Japh's eyebrows drew together.

It's almost certainly a trap. But for who? "I doubt Lucifer wants to kill me. We haven't caught even one of the four demons he wants dragged in yet." *At least, not that I can tell. Though if he has other hunters out there, that might be inaccurate.* I took a deep breath, carried the thought to its logical extension. I was beginning to wish my brain and my imagination didn't work so blasted well. "If he does want me dead, he'll get me one way or another."

A swift snarl crossed Japhrimel's face, green eyes laser-burning. "He will not."

I shrugged. *Not until he's done playing with me and I've outlived my usefulness. If I'm bait, I don't have long to live.* "I'm a Necromance, demon. I'm not going to live forever." I brushed past him, intending to stalk for the bathroom. If I was going to meet the Devil again, I wanted to at least wash my face.

He caught my arm, his fingers gentle but inexorable. Was his hand shaking? Impossible. "Do not say such things to me, *hedaira.*"

"Don't call me that." I tugged my arm away from him. He didn't let me go, I set my heels and pulled, not caring if it hurt. "It's *Valentine* to you, demon. Let go of me. I've got a meeting with the Devil to get ready for."

Japhrimel shook me, gently, as if to bring home just how much stronger he was. How much *more*, even though he'd changed me. I tried to yank away from him again, almost feeling tiled wall against my back. Hearing a sudden roaring in my ears, the devouring feeling of helplessness as he held me still.

His voice turned cold. "Why must everything be a battle, with you?"

"Stop it." My breath caught in my throat. "*Stop* it. Let *go.*"

He did, and I stumbled, righted myself. My rings swirled steadily. I stalked away from him, past McKinley, who was staring at me again. I was getting tired of being stared at. All my adult life as an accredited Necromance I've been stared at. Too much of anything gets old.

I locked myself into the bathroom, twisted on the cold-water tap. There was a glassed-in shower floored with granite, the entire bathroom was done in kobolding-worked stone except for the deep bathtub and the porcelain stand-alone sink. No toilet—a Nichtvren room wouldn't need one, and I didn't either. That had been one of the harder things to get used to about no longer being strictly human—a female bounty hunter was *always* looking for a decent lavatory. You learned to take bathroom breaks when you could.

The mirrors reflected back a rumpled and tired *hedaira* whose black hair fell messily over her face in seemingly-choreographed strands.

I didn't feel a shock of nausea on seeing my own face, which must have meant I was finally getting used to it. I looked at myself critically, evaluating.

My own dark eyes, liquid and beautiful. Sculpted cheekbones, a sinful mouth now drawn down at one corner as I frowned, winged dark eyebrows. I touched my cheek, and saw the beautiful woman in the mirror brush her exquisite cheekbone, trace her pretty lips with a black molecule-drip polished nail. Japhrimel had made me demon-beautiful, but without the air of *alienness* demons exuded.

If I looked hard enough, I could still see traces of who I'd been in my face—my eyes were still mostly my own, and when I relaxed my mouth still quirked up habitually on one side as if I didn't quite believe what I was seeing. The little half-smile had always seemed welded onto my face before, a professional defense. If I was smiling, it couldn't hurt that bad, could it?

I brushed my hair back with wet fingers, washed my face. Scrubbed my skin dry with a towel. Shrugged inside my rig a little, tested the action of each knife. Checked my bag, scorched and battered but still mine. Extra ammo. I still had my plasgun, too.

I looked at myself in the mirror, the water still running into the bowl of the sink. I wiped the half-smile off my face, watched as the lovely woman facing me grew solemn, the tattoo on her cheek shifting slightly. The twisted caduceus ran its sharp ink lines lovingly over her skin. The emerald set high on her flawless left cheekbone flashed.

There was another green flash, and my eyes dropped. I lifted my left wrist, the breath slamming out of me.

The wristcuff ran with green light, fluid lines scrabbling with humming urgency. A warning.

I drew my plasgun. Left the water running. Edged for the bathroom door. Stopped, and looked at the shower. My eyes snagged on the bathtub, too. A low stone-tiled wall between the bathtub and the shower, only about three feet high. Probably for the plumbing. The bathtub was set in the floor, but behind it was the wall the room shared with the outside hallway.

I bet that wall isn't stone all the way through. It likely wasn't kobolding-made, which meant it wasn't as tough as the exterior wall.

The wristcuff squeezed, a bolt of pain firing its way up my arm. My breath stopped in my throat. Demons. Whether from Lucifer or escaped from Hell, they certainly didn't mean me any good.

You've got to make up your mind, Danny. Let Japhrimel push you around or strike out on your own. Even if you won't last long without him, at least you won't have someone owning you. Forcing you. Lying to you.

Clear coldness settled over me. In the end, everything

boiled down to one thing—what I *had* to do. Even if I loved Japh, I couldn't be a slave.

I heard McKinley's voice, low and urgent. Then, a soft light rap on the hotel room's door. Demons, here and knocking at the door.

A static-laden silence smashed through the room. Then a crunching, smashing impact; the bathroom door rattled against its hinges. A low, coughing snarl—a hellhound.

Just before all hell broke loose, I took a deep breath, stepped back, and pointed my plasgun at the wall. Power spiked under my skin, and I squeezed the trigger.

36

$\mathcal{N}$ight lay thick and heavy over Demilitarized Sarajevo. It felt strange to be in a city of paranormals, but the static in the air was enough to hide even me for once. I crouched in the lee of a dark alley, listening to the snarling as two werecain engaged in a deep philosophical discussion about something out on the pavement across the cobbled square, right in front of the Haunt *Tais-toi* nightclub.

Nightclub is too kind a word. It was a Nichtvren haunt, communal feeding ground, and social gathering spot rolled into one. Instead of thick shielding to keep the hungry Power contained, this had only token barriers—after all, who would be stupid enough to attack a haunt in Sarajevo? And besides, there were no normals or psions around to keep away from the well of carnivorous Power because of the risk of Feeders.

This particular haunt had been a temple once, a twin-towered cathedral in the café section of Sarajevo, facing out onto a wide square now eddying with every conceivable shape and size of paranormal. Species I'd only read about in school lived here in their own enclaves, and night was the time they came out to play.

My shields shivered, demon-strong and flexible. I blinked a few times, feeling a purely human reaction uncomfortably like what any prey would feel in the presence of predators. Maybe I wasn't fully human anymore—but I'd been born one, and something blind and old inside me recognized that to these creatures, the Danny Valentine before Japh's alterations would be walking meat in Sarajevo.

My head still felt tender from the plasgun-plus-Power burst. True to my guess, the wall hadn't been pure stone, just plasteel struts and sheetrock with thin marble tiles. It had blown out nicely. I, on the other hand, had slid into the glassed-in shower. The single low stone wall between the shower and the bathtub provided perfect cover as I buttoned myself as tightly down as I could. My feet had crunched on broken glass from the shower door. The mark on my shoulder bit down with sudden pain as the demon attackers, followed by McKinley and Japhrimel, streaked out into the hotel. I heard a werecain's howl—the guard at the top of the stairs. Everyone thought I'd busted out and was running away—or was being *dragged*.

Jeez, not too bright, I'd thought, my breath still choked in my throat. Then I'd scrambled out through the hole in the wall, Power bleeding into the air from where my strike had smashed through Japhrimel's demon-laid wards. Any other demon's shielding, I probably wouldn't have been able to do so—but I wore Japh's mark, and his wards weren't meant to strike against or harm me.

Or so I'd hoped, and turned out to be right. Besides, the smashing against the front door meant the shields were automatically concentrating to throw back the force of that attack and were thus more vulnerable here.

Low and silent, I turned to the left and was around the corner in another hall before I heard the crashing chaos of a hell of a fight behind me. I didn't wait around. Instead, I kicked in a door, and—*thank Anubis*—found a room with actual windows. A swanhild room, actually, with a large round nestingbed full of feathery stuff. I didn't stop to apologize to the screaming swanhild trio that greeted me, feathers swirling around their shocked faces and narrow naked torsos. I simply dove out the plasglass window and was gone before the attacking demons had realized I'd outsmarted them. The drop hadn't been pleasant, but it hadn't hurt me much.

Finding the Haunt *Tais-toi* had been as easy as getting to a busy street and politely asking a passing swanhild, then following her careful directions.

The psychic interference was so intense I couldn't scan the place. Nichtvren poured in, and I spotted a whole pack of werecain—from an alpha in a long leather coat all the way down to a few teenage pups. A few swanhild decked out in silver chains, miniskirts, and not a lot else waltzed in the front door.

There wasn't a lot of hover traffic. I guess the paranormals around here didn't use them—who needed a hover when you could use the Nichtvren shimmer-trick, or when a werecain could cover ten blocks of city street in seconds? Swanhild were territorial and rarely traveled despite their messaging system, and kobolding hated to leave wherever they'd been hatched.

At least if there aren't a lot of hovers, I might not get hit with one.

I checked the street again. Too many shadows. Any one

of them could hold a demon, and the interference was intense enough I wouldn't know it in time.

I was pretty sure I'd shaken all pursuit, and the interference that would hide them would hide me a lot better, since I wasn't as big a disturbance in the Power flow.

Danny, what are you doing? You should be running as far away from here as you can, going as deep into cover as you can.

I couldn't run forever. If Lucifer wanted to kill me, he was welcome to try. I'd die fighting. Besides, why bother to schedule a meeting with me and send assassins for me? Far easier and more satisfying to do it himself.

Besides, this was the one thing Japhrimel couldn't *force* me to do. He was stronger than me, faster than me, more powerful than me. This was my chance to do something by myself.

I finally melted out of the shadows and walked across the street. My bootheels snapped against concrete and patches of cobbles. It was odd to be in a city where the sky wasn't dyed orange with reflected light; it was even more odd when I walked right up to the door of the Haunt *Tais-toi* and plunged into the red-neon thumping bass cave that was the second Nichtvren haunt I'd ever walked into in my life.

The music folded around me, I winced as reflex compensated for the demonic acuity of my ears. *One thing I can thank Japh for, he taught me how to turn the volume down.*

I'd spent so long with him in the forefront of every thought, even while he'd been dormant and I'd struggled unsuccessfully to go on with my life. I suspected I'd miss him for the rest of my life.

The rest of my life might be a very short time, I thought grimly, glancing around the haunt. The dance floor was crammed, prickles of Power racing over my skin from the throng. A bar ran down one whole side of the building, a low stage held four werecain and a Nichtvren. Two 'cain had guitars, one had a bass, another one fingered a Taziba keyboard; the stick-thin, red-haired Nichtvren sang in some language I didn't recognize. He wore leather pants and had his eyes closed, crooning, his voice cutting through the din with little effort, helped along by Power.

The music helped with the interference. I shouldered my way through a gaggle of swanhild and headed for the bar. I was early, according to the timefunction on my datband.

I hoped the Devil was early too. The sooner I could get this over with, the better.

Before, I'd just had to get too tired to care before I could face down the Devil. Now I was tired, hungry, missing Japhrimel, running *away* from Japhrimel, scared out of my mind, and heartbroken.

I was hoping it was enough. It might almost be a relief to have everything over with.

I got to the bar. The bartender was a rarity, a four-armed kobolding. Swanhild and kobolding like to drink, and Nichtvren occasionally take an alcohol chaser with their blood—it doesn't affect them but they like acidic tastes. I hear the stomach cramps are a bitch, though. There were various other stimulants and depressants for other paranormals, and the smell of synth-hash smoke wreathed around me. The thunderous fading-returning odor of werecain, the dry feathery sweetness of swanhild, the deliciously wicked smell of Nichtvren, smoke and stone for the kobolding, other assorted odors.

I let my eyes travel over the place as the Nichtvren's voice hit a new pitch that made my shields shiver. A thread of wonder ran through me. I wouldn't have been able to experience this if I was still human.

There were some things to be grateful for in this new body, however short a time I had left to enjoy it.

Danny, your imagination just works too goddamn well.

I ordered a double shot of Crostine rum and handed the 'tender a fifty New Credit note. My roll was getting pretty thin, I'd have to score some more cash soon. If I used my datband to draw on my accounts, I could be traced. I would have to find a bank and carefully plan a run. Get in, get cash from my accounts, get out and vanish.

Always assuming you live past tonight, sunshine. "Danny Valentine," I said to the bartender. "I've got a meeting."

The 'cain palmed the note and nodded over my shoulder. I whirled, my hand going to my swordhilt.

My heart leapt to my throat. Yellow eyes blazed in a scar-ruined face; Lucas Villalobos grabbed my arm, stopping only to gulp down the double shot and nod to the bartender. "You get into *more* trouble," he wheezed in my ear, his breath laden with rum and the dry scent of a stasis cabinet. He smacked the shotglass down on the bar. "This way."

"What the *hell* are you doing here?" I considered drawing my sword, discarded the notion. I was too glad to see him.

"I don't like losing track of my clients. Puts me in a bad

mood." Lucas scanned the building, his oddly flat aura moving like a revolving door. No wonder he was able to get into DMZ Sarajevo, he didn't look human at all on an energetic level. "There's someone you should talk to."

My heart plummeted, then leapt to pound in my throat. *Lucas? Working for Lucifer? No. Let's hope not.* "Great. Is he here?"

"Not *he*," Lucas said in my ear. He'd found a new dark-gray shirt but still wore the same bandoliers I'd always seen him in, his boots were the same rundown pair he'd always had. I wondered how often he got them resoled. "She. And you'd better hurry."

Lucas led me through the dance floor, press of immortal Nichtvren flesh on every side, a knot of werecain twisting in the corner, sweet synth-hash smoke wreathing in billows as a mated pair twined around each other, damn near copulating. I'd always liked dancing, shaking every thought out of my body. I hadn't gone in years.

Not since Jace.

I remembered Jace's hands on my waist, sweat dripping down my neck and spine, a short silken skirt swinging against my thighs as I raised my arms, the music slamming through my bones as I lost myself in one of the oldest communal ecstasies known to humanity.

I shook the memory away. I'd never asked Japhrimel if he liked to dance. Probably not—but he was so graceful. It would have been nice to dance with him.

Will you just quit thinking about him? You'll need all your wits for whatever's going to happen in the next ten minutes.

We reached a dark corner, and Lucas tilted his head at

the hulking orange-eyed werecain on its hindlegs in full huntform, a fringe of hair around its genitals. It didn't move as we went past. Lucas's pale hand spread against a door. It opened, disclosing a set of stairs. The reek of werecain faded as the receptors in my nose shut down. He pushed me in, and I went gratefully. The door swung closed behind us, shutting out the wall of music.

I sighed. "How'd you find me?"

"I squeezed the agent—Vann—until he gave up that McKinley had sent a communiqué, said he was headed to Sarajevo. Then I called in a favor and caught a smuggler transport out here. Listen, Valentine, your demon had orders in place that you were supposed to be kept out of the action once we ID'd the first demon. Leander's spittin' mad. He's recruiting in Cairo Giza. We're gonna catch a transport out of here in three hours, but you better hear this first."

"Hear *what* first?"

"I said Abra put me on your trail." He pushed me, the stairs were rickety and groaning under the bassbeat. "I lied. She only told me when to be in New Prague to find you. I was contracted to look after you *before* you showed up in that bar."

What? I pushed the door at the top of the stairs open and stepped into a dimly lit room with a blue Old Perasiano rug, a nivron fireplace full of crackling flame, two heavy mahogany chairs set across from each other—and a dozing hellhound lying against the wall under a small window half-hid behind a blue velvet drape.

My heart slammed into my mouth. Next to the hellhound, his shoulders broad and his catslit eyes glittering icy gray, the demon Velokel stood. His face was round and heavy, square teeth that still looked sharp, and those eyes glowing blue around the vertical slits deep and dark enough to swallow the scream struggling up through my throat. The cuff was quiescent on my left wrist, no dappled green light flaring.

A slim female shape standing by the fireplace half-turned. A flash of dark-blue eyes under a sleek cap of pale blond hair, and a glimmering emerald ringing a soft greeting from her forehead. Power blazed through her; the power of an Androgyne. She smelled like fresh bread, like spiced Power and musk, like....

Like Lucifer.

Anubis, my Lord, my god, watch over me. The prayer rose unbidden, and the thought after that was almost as intense in its supplication.

Japhrimel.

Why was I thinking of *him*? Couldn't I stop thinking of him?

Might as well ask yourself to stop breathing, Danny.

"Don't be afraid, Dante," she said softly. "I won't hurt you, and neither will the hound. Come in, sit down."

37

I swallowed bile as I eyed the hellhound. And the motionless Velokel, who all but thrummed with lethal power. I found myself absurdly comforted by a single thought, an instinctive weighing of every erg of Power this being possessed. *He isn't as strong as Japhrimel.* The comfort was short-lived. *He can still kill me. He can still easily kill me.*

"Relax, Valentine," Lucas said from behind me, pushing me none too gently. "I was contracted to keep your skin whole."

She wore a loose blue cable-knit turtleneck, khakis with a sharp crease, and a pair of expensive black Verano heels. Her breasts moved slightly underneath the sweater. Velokel didn't move. If he wanted to kill me, he'd had more than enough time. He'd had more than enough time as soon as I opened the door.

My hand dropped away from the swordhilt. Lucas closed the door behind us, leaned against it with his head cocked. "You're too old," I whispered. I sounded choked. My cheek burned, my emerald answering the green gem that flashed on her forehead. "Too *old*." She should still be a child.

She looked just like Doreen. Just like my *sedayeen* lover, dead on the floor of a warehouse while Santino giggled and snuffled happily to himself, collecting his "samples." My beautiful, gentle, wonderful Doreen, the lover who had given me my soul back. Who had given me *myself* back.

Eve smiled, one corner of her mouth quirking up. It was a familiar smile, but I couldn't quite place it. Doreen hadn't ever smiled like that. "A year in Hell isn't the same as a year on earth. Far from. Please, come in, sit down. It's good to see you."

I eased across the room, staring at her. Velokel might as well have been a statue. My skin crawled. "You...I...*you*—"

"I hired Lucas to find you as soon as I left Hell. It was difficult, but I wanted you to have the benefit of some protection. Someone you could trust. It took him a while to find you; the Eldest had you hidden well." She paused. "We could not locate you for a long time, and when we did, we could not approach. He was too...watchful."

Japhrimel, listening to a sound I couldn't hear. Taut and ready, perhaps sensing someone looking for me. Aware that I was in danger, knowing Lucifer was calling for me. That look on his face, that sense of him listening, hadn't been because he was dissatisfied with me. It had been vigilance, the type of protective attention I'd sometimes practiced while doing bodyguard duty but had never, *ever* thought I would be the subject of. So living in Toscano had been to hide me.

To keep me safe.

"You're in a dangerous game, Dante." She moved slowly, like oil, over to the chair that stood with its back to the hellhound. She sank down gracefully, crossed her legs. "Lucifer has contracted you to kill four demons."

I found myself lowering into the other chair, the katana across my knees. My heart beat thinly in my wrists, my ankles, my throat. In my temples. I swallowed, hearing my throat click. "Yes," I said cautiously. *One of them's standing right over there, pretending to be a block of marble.* I cast a quick nervous glance at him, wished I hadn't. His eyes were fixed on her, he hadn't shifted or moved a muscle but his entire being seemed to yearn toward her. *I can bet you're one of them too. No wonder Lucifer... gods. Oh, gods. Did Japhrimel know? Did he?*

She smiled again, that same half-quirk of her lips that seemed so familiar. "I suppose I'm one of them too, then. The Twins, Kel, and I have all escaped Hell." She leaned back into the chair, looked away from me. Doreen's eyes in her face, staring into the fire. "The fault is mine. I am... unique, it seems."

Then her eyes returned to me. Her gaze was so like Doreen's I was having trouble breathing. The demon and the hellhound were utterly still, Lucas just as still. As if the only two people in the room were Eve and me.

I was almost beginning to believe she was sitting in front of me. "Dante," she said, "listen very carefully. I am about to tell you something nobody else knows. Varkolak Vardimal created me from two genetic samples: one taken from the Egg, Lucifer's genetic material. The other sample was a *sedayeen*—your friend and lover. What Vardimal may not have known, and what the Prince of Hell certainly doesn't know, was that the second sample was contaminated with someone else's material." She paused, maybe for effect. "Yours. You are my other mother, Dante. When Vardimal bled the *sedayeen*, he somehow got your blood in the mix."

Memory slammed into me, swallowed me whole.

"Game over," he giggled, and the awful tearing in my side turned to a burning numbness as he slashed, I threw myself backward, not fast enough, not fast enough.

"Danny!" Doreen's despairing cry.

"Get out!" I screamed, but she was coming back, hands glowing blue-white, still trying to heal.

Trying to reach me, to heal me, the link between us resonating with my pain and her burning hands—

Made it to my feet, screaming at her to get the fuck out, Santino's claws whooshing again as he tore into me, one claw sticking on a rib, my sword ringing as I slashed at him, too slow. I was too slow.

Falling again. Something rising in me, a cold agonizing chill. Doreen's hands clamped against my arm. Warm exploding wetness. So much blood. So much.

Her Power roared through me, and I felt the spark of life in her dim. She held on, grimly, as Santino made little snuffling, chortling sounds of glee. The whine of a lasecutter as he took part of her femur, the slight pumping sound of the bloodvac. Blood dripped in my eyes, splattered against my cheek. Sirens howling in the distance— Doreen's death would register on her datband, and aid hovers would be dispatched. Too late, though. Too late for both of us.

I passed out, hearing the wet smacking sounds as Santino took what he wanted, giggling that high-pitched strange chortle of his. His face burned itself into my memory—black teardrops painted over the eyes, pointed ears, the sharp ivory fangs. Not human, *I thought,* he can't be human, Doreen, Doreen, get away, run, run—

Her soul, carried like a candle down a long dark hall, guttering. Guttering. Spark shrinking into infinity. I am a Necromance, but I couldn't stop her rushing into Death's arms....

I stared at her, my nape prickling and my mouth full of copper. It *could* be true. We'd certainly both bled enough when he killed her. But wouldn't Santino have known? A demon geneticist was perfectly capable of telling a contaminated sample from a pure one. There was no reason for him to even *keep* a contaminated sample.

Unless he'd guessed he might find a use for it.

She looked back at me. Her mouth curled up in that little half-smile again. "Vardimal may or may not have known. In any case, it was immaterial once he realized the value of what he had—a viable sample. A viable *fetus*." Now her mouth pulled down into a soft grimace, Doreen's little moue of distaste. It was damn hard to think with the smell of her filling the air. I shivered galvanically on the hard seat, my eyes flicking past her to the dozing hellhound and returning, compelled, to meet hers.

Doreen's eyes. My dead lover's eyes.

In someone else's face—a face that held an echo of Lucifer. I was responding to her, unfamiliar desire rising to swamp me. A thin trickle of heat purred through my belly. *Doreen. Oh, gods, Doreen.*

My heart slammed against my ribs. The mark on my shoulder was alive with heat, burrowing into my skin. "Why are you telling me this?" I still sounded choked.

I'm in a room with two demons, a hellhound, and Lucas Villalobos. Anubis protect me.

"I'm explaining." Her voice was soft, soothing. "Vardimal failed to keep me away from *him*. The call the Prince is capable of exerting on an Androgyne is…immense. We are of his kind and he is the oldest, the Prime. I had very little chance of denying him access to my mind when I was a child. However…the Prince, whenever he creates an Androgyne, also implants several commands before the Androgyne is hatched. One of them is obedience. I wasn't implanted until I was five human years old. The implant held until very recently." The half-smile was back. I realized with a deep chill that I recognized it because I'd seen it in the mirror. It was my own expression. "It seems I have inherited your stubbornness, Dante. That is the only explanation I can arrive at for why the Prince has been unsuccessful in his attempt to break me."

"Break you?" My voice seemed to come from very far away. My hands felt weak and unsteady, as if they were shaking. *What would Japhrimel think of this? Does he know? Did he?*

If Japhrimel had known, and hadn't told me…there was nothing, *nothing* that could make that omission less than a complete and utter betrayal.

Had he thought I wouldn't find out? Of course not. He was certain he was stronger than me, able to force me to do whatever he wanted.

Had he known? Would I ever get to ask him, and could I trust his answer if I did?

My chest split, cracking. *Now I know I have a heart,* I thought inconsequentially. *It's breaking.*

The thought managed to shock me back into rationality.

Eve. Here. In the world, free. Maybe not for very much longer, since Lucifer had contracted not only me and Japhrimel but possibly more hunters to track her down. No wonder I'd felt like bait. I *was* bait, a lure to draw her out. To betray her without even knowing it.

"I am the only Androgyne to leave Hell for many mortal years, other than the Prince." She blinked her dark blue eyes at me. Her face was clear, unlined, but mature. She looked like a woman on the cusp of twenty-five, except for the shadow of demon knowledge in her gaze.

She couldn't be more than seven or eight *human* years old. How long had she been out of Hell, if Lucifer had been asking for me all this time?

A year in Hell is not the same as a year on earth. How old was she in Hell years? Were they like dog years? How many to a human year, how old was she, how *long* had she been there, suffering under the Prince of Hell?

Bile rose in my throat, and rage under my ribs. Cold, vicious rage, of a type I'd never felt before in all my long and angry life.

This rage was different. It was pure unalloyed hatred.

My eyes flickered back to Velokel. Returned to Eve.

She continued, apparently thinking I was too stunned to respond. She was right. "I am in rebellion against the Prince. I am Androgyne, and I am determined to stay alive and free." She took a deep breath. "I want your help, Dante. I'm not bargaining, I'm only asking. You're capable of feigning to hunt me and mine, I'm asking you not to try too hard. Distract your *A'nankhimel*. Seven years from now your bargain with the Prince will be done, and I promise you all the protection and aid I can offer." She leaned forward, her eyes sparkling. "*Freedom*, Dante. I want mine, you want yours—together we can provide an alternative to the Prince and his stranglehold on both earth and Hell."

That was uncomfortably similar to Santino's cant about freeing everyone from Lucifer. But Santino had wanted to implant me with other Androgyne fetuses. He had thought he could rule Eve, and through her, Hell. I looked over her shoulder at the dozing hellhound, steam rising gently from its pelt. Velokel still stared at Eve, an expression on his round face I had no trouble deciphering. It was equal parts fierce concentration and protective tenderness, he didn't bother to disguise it. It would have been a human expression except for the blazing intensity in his catslit eyes. He looked obsessed with her. Velokel, apparently, was in love.

If demons could love. I'd seen that look before on another demon's face.

"Gods above," I rasped. "Are you *serious*?"

"I swear on the waters of Lethe, this is the truth. I ask you only for time. I won't twist your arm and try to force you like *he* would." It was obvious who "he" was, every time she mentioned Lucifer her pretty face twisted.

You know, I understand. What would it be like to live in Hell, to live with that goddamn viper that calls itself Lucifer? She's half human. Half Doreen. What part of her is mine? I took a deep, endless breath. *Let's get this straight.* "You want me to break my bargain with Lucifer. Set myself up against the Devil."

She nodded. "I do."

I blew out through my teeth. *Well, nice to know we understand each other.* "That's one tall order, sunshine."

Velokel stirred. Eve lifted her expressive golden hand,

and he stopped, subsiding against the wall. The hellhound didn't move. I snapped a glance at Lucas, who looked supremely unconcerned, leaning against the door. His bandoliers creaked as he shifted his weight, a small sound.

Eve lowered her hand. "Think on it, Dante. *He* fears you. You took the Right Hand and stood a very real chance of denying *him* access to me. Had you not returned to Nuevo Rio, *he* would have been forced to treat with you as a suppliant. Not so long ago, *he* tried to bargain with your Fallen to kill you. Theoretically, in return the Eldest would be restored to Hell. Such a thing is impossible, and well Lucifer knew it. Still, your Fallen refused, I heard it myself. The Prince was desperate to regain his Right Hand. His hold on Hell has been slipping for quite some time."

Wait a second. Back up. When did this happen? Maybe during the time Lucifer was asking to see me and Japhrimel was refusing? My heart leapt inside my ribs. Japhrimel had refused to kill me in order to go back to Hell. Never mind that it was "impossible."

How twisted was it, that I grabbed at that to feel better? But I had another question. "What about the demon who wanted to kill me in New Prague? The hellhound?"

"Kel wished to meet the Eldest and treat with him, but retreated when he realized the Kinslayer had misunderstood his attempt. The hellhounds in New Prague were not part of Kel's pack. Another demon might have rebelled and sought to strike before the Kinslayer could find him—after all, the Eldest is the demon most feared among those who would rebel against the Prince. There are other trackers and hunters after me as well, Dante. The world is full of peril." She tipped her elegant head.

Power stroked along my skin, as warm as Japhrimel's nonphysical caress. I was hard put to swallow a slight, betraying sound as my body flushed with heat. "Tell your Fallen this is Kel's pledge—he will not hunt you unless you threaten us."

Velokel seemed almost to leap without moving, his attention suddenly refocused on her. Eve's eyes dropped slightly, and a faint flush rose to her cheeks. Very interesting. I had the idea that this Kel was a little more intimately involved with Eve than he should be.

Good to know.

"Kel." My eyes met his for a long moment. The mark on my shoulder began to pulse, quietly. "The Hunter. The one who hunted *hedaira*?"

Eve tilted her head, her pale hair moving soft and silky. "He did so at the Prince's orders. Were you told who hunted the ones Kel could not?"

No, nobody told me about that. I met her eyes. "Let me guess. The Right Hand."

She nodded. "The Prince's Eldest killed more *A'nankhimel* and *hedaira* than Kel could hope to. He is not called *Kinslayer* for nothing."

My skin chilled. No wonder Japhrimel didn't talk about the Fallen, if he'd killed so many of them. He must have never expected to end up as one of them.

Oh, gods. Japhrimel. Did you know about this? About her?

I licked my numb lips. "I can't say for sure. But if it's possible, if can do it, I'll help you." Then I spoke the words. "I promise."

If she did manage to break Lucifer's hold on Hell, what would happen? Would there be uncontrolled demons roaming the earth? I was no Magi, but I knew enough about Hell's citizens that the prospect filled me with an uncomfortable feeling very close to terror.

But what else could I do? What the *hell* else could I do?

Eve opened her mouth to reply, but a thin growl rose through the air. I looked past her shoulder. The hellhound's head was up, its teeth bared. It didn't look at me, it looked at the door.

Velokel spoke, a single word, sharp and weighted with the consonants of the demons' strange, unlovely language. He was suddenly tense, his broad shoulders corded with muscle. He reminded me of a bull, powerful and slow, but I was willing to bet he had the same spooky, blurring speed as other demons.

"Time to go," Lucas said. "Come on, *chica*."

I made it to my feet like an old woman. One shock after another, I was starting to feel like a punch-drunk cagefighter. My hand fastened on my swordhilt as I stared at the hound. Oddly enough, I was more scared of the hellhound than of Velokel.

Eve stepped close to me. Her smell, the smell of an Androgyne, a scent that threatened to unloose my knees and spill me to the floor, caressed me. My head filled with heat, my lips parted. I'd never responded like this to Lucifer—I'd been too terrified to feel anything close to desire for him, even though he was beautiful and lethal. I had *never* had a sexual response to pure Power before, but she was heir to all Lucifer's crackling force and she wore Doreen's face like a sexwitch wears submission, like a perfume. The face of my *sedayeen* lover, the person who had taught me the prison of my body could be a source of joy as well as pain.

You feel everything, don't you? Doreen had asked me once. *But you don't like to show it. You keep that mask of a face up, and people think you don't care. But you do, Danny. You care.*

She had been the only person, *ever*, who understood that about me. She had been the only lover who hadn't asked more of me than I could give.

I had given her all I had.

What wouldn't I do, if only for Doreen's memory, if only to expunge the guilt of my failure to protect her?

"Don't decide yet. I'll contact you when I can." Eve's breath touched my cheek, warm and forgiving.

I nodded, beyond words. Was it true?

Did my blood mix with Doreen's? Was my genetic material part of Eve's?

Was she my child as well? My daughter, the only daughter I would ever have. I couldn't see myself breeding with Japhrimel. *Sekhmet sa'es*, no. Not now. Maybe not ever.

He refused to kill me. He turned Lucifer down. Gods. I stood frozen as she stepped away, beckoning to the hellhound. It got up, shook itself, and paced after her as she walked to the nivron fireplace. Then, wonder of wonders, she stepped *into* the fire, flame lifting to caress her body like a lover, and promptly vanished. A high squealing note of Power split the air, my rings spat and the wristcuff rang with green light. Velokel gave me one narrow-eyed, lip-curling look and followed. The hellhound looped on itself and leapt through the fire after them. Vanished.

What the hell, were we supposed to hunt her when she

can walk through fucking walls? Why didn't Lucifer mention that?

Of course he hadn't told me. I would never have agreed to hunt Eve, no matter what he threatened me with.

Japhrimel. Had he known?

He refused to kill me to go back home to Hell, and he'll at least keep me alive. I'm feeling pretty fucking charitable toward him right now. Except for the little matter of him possibly keeping this to himself.

Lucas was at my shoulder. "Don't stand around, Valentine. Somethin' tells me we better get out of here. We got a transport to catch."

"Gods," I said. "*Gods*. Did you believe a word of that?"

"Analyze later," he said, just as the mood of the building underneath—sex and feeding and music blurring together—tipped strangely. A single thrill of fear slid up my spine. "Move *now*." He flung the door open and began down the stairs.

"We're not going out the window?"

"Nope," Lucas flung over his shoulder. "Sheer brick wall straight down to a blind alley, we'll be trapped like rats. Come on, *chica*. I'm s'posed to keep you alive."

38

We jolted down the stairs and burst out into the music. The werecain guard at the door was gone. I checked my datband, lifting my left hand, weighted with my sword.

Quarter to midnight. I was beginning to think I might still be alive and not dead of shock. Power spiking in the air cleared my head, and I noticed the crotch of my panties was uncomfortably damp. I had *never* responded like that before. Never.

She was Doreen's child, and maybe mine. That I reacted to her was a shameful secret, nothing more. She did, after all, wear my dead lover's face. I wasn't attracted to her, I told myself. No, I was simply determined to keep Doreen's daughter from being dragged back into Hell or killed to salve Lucifer's fucking pride.

I've had just about enough of the Devil. My eyes found the wristcuff snugged above my datband.

The cuff ran with fluid lines of green fire, settling into a frozen, scratched rune, a backwards-leaning spiked H.

Danger.

Yeah, like I don't already know that. I was beginning to feel like myself again. If Japhrimel had known it was

Eve instead of Lucifer here…had he guessed? Why had he thought Lucifer wanted a little chat with me again? Leonidas hadn't named the demon wanting to see me, and I wondered about that too.

Forget it, Dante. Now it's time to move.

The dance floor still pulsed with writhing bodies. My awareness swept through the interior, and found the swanhild gone. That was interesting. Something feral stalked closer, if I could feel it the 'hilds certainly could, with their exquisite sensitivity to predators.

I took a deep breath tainted with synth-hash and followed Lucas's rigid, bandolier-crossed back through the press of Nichtvren flesh, was jostled by a werecain who snarled at me. The mark on my shoulder heated up again, a live brand pressed into my flesh. It hurt, scorching through the layers of gray numbness threatening me.

I almost welcomed the pain. I wished Japhrimel was behind me. Sure, he was a lying bastard—but right now I was feeling very much like I might not get out of this tangled web without him.

I can't believe I just thought that. He refused to kill me to go back to Hell. He gave up his home for me.

Yeah, and he just "forgot" to mention Eve was out of Hell and giving the Devil a run for his money. Sure he did.

We were halfway across the dance floor when Lucas veered, taking a course that would bring us out near the stage and a glowing green sign in Cyrillic that probably said *exit*. I kept my sword in both hands, left on the scabbard, right on the hilt. The back of my neck prickled, running chills sliding down the shallow channel of my spine. I felt cold even in the middle of the heat and flux of Power, desire draining away and leaving me aching, unsatisfied. A roar went up from the bar—some kobolding playing a drinking game. The kobolding bartender, however, had his back to the mirrored wall holding glass shelves of bottles and stasis cabinets for cloned blood and other things. His yellow eyes glittered as he sniffed. He scanned the place suspiciously, lifting his gray lumpen head.

The shadows thickened near the bar, and I caught sight of a familiar shape. Broad shoulders under a black T-shirt, a black leather Mob assassin's rig, a shock of wheat-gold hair. Recognition slammed through me, and instant denial.

It couldn't be.

I stopped dead on the dance floor, buffeted by moving Nichtvren on all sides. I stared, going up on my toes to get a clearer view.

The man—was it a man? Not in DMZ Sarajevo. But he reached out with one hand and touched a staff leaning against the bar. The staff stood taller then his head, and small bones tied to it with raffia twine clacked as his fingers touched it. That small sound cut through the music and welter of Power, spilling prickles through my veins. My nipples tightened, I gasped.

He swung around. Blue eyes flashed.

Jace Monroe regarded me across a throng of thrashing Nichtvren. He lifted his sword, and I realized I could see *through* him, as if he was made of colored smoke.

I am a Necromance, death is my trade. But I had *never* seen anything like this. Most ghostflits are pale gray smoke, not colorfully lifelike. And this was not where he had died. This was not where his ashes were, the cremains a Necromance could use to bring his apparition through to

ask questions—if she was powerful enough. This was not
a place Jace had haunted in life.

He should not be haunting it now.

The ghost grinned at me, raising his sheathed *dotanuki*, the same blade that had hung above the altar in the
Toscano villa, bent and corkscrewed with the agony of
his last strike and death still ringing in the metal. Only
his ghost held the sword as it had been, unbent, true and
familiar.

My right hand crept up to touch the shape of the necklace under my shirt.

He *winked* at me. Then his face grew grave, and his lips
shaped three words.

Run, Danny. Run.

The strength spilled out of my legs. I would have fallen
except for the press of Nichtvren flesh around me. The
ghost of my dead lover shook his head, the same way he
used to when I was too slow during a sparring session.

Go. I heard the word clearly, laid in the shell of my ear,
Jace's breath on my nape. My entire body tightened, heat
spilling into my lower belly again, my panties soaked as
if I'd been necking like a heated Academy teenager. What
the *hell* was wrong with me?

I. Am. Not. A. Sexwitch.

Lucas's hand closed around my upper arm again. He
made a spitting sound and hauled on me, and I went
willingly. We forced our way through the crush of the
dance floor, Lucas shouldering aside a pair of Nichtvren
Acolytes poured into matching red pleather outfits. We
freed ourselves from the press just as the entire building
shivered.

Lucas swore. He let go of me—I was thankfully able to

walk on my own now. His hands came up with a 60-watt plasgun in each. I jammed my sword into the loop on my belt, keeping my right hand on the hilt. I drew steel, and my newly freed left hand closed around my own plasgun just as all hell broke loose. Again.

39

I had a few seconds to decide what to do as the second hellhound crashed through the wall, bricks flying. The first hound was busy with four werecain who had unluckily been in its way, and the howling spitting mess crashed into the bar. Plasglass tinkled. Lucas grabbed my shoulder and hauled me back as the second hellhound bulleted forward.

These two were different from the others. Their eyes were green, a fierce glowing green instead of crimson. Heat shimmered and warped away from them all the way across the dance floor.

Lust vanished. Survival took its place, chill fury rising under my skin. The cuff on my wrist made a thin humming sound, like crystal stroked just right.

My sword finished ringing free of the sheath as the second hellhound snarled, a low, vicious sound tearing at the air. The music had halted, but a rising crescendo of screams took its place. Three Nichtvren burned like fatty candles, screeching as the hellhound brushed past them, hair and preternatural skin igniting. Paranormal creatures scrambled for the door, the crowd acting very human for all its Power and inherent danger.

Lucas fired at the hellhound streaking for me. A crimson streak of plasbolt clove the air, smashing into the beast, which snarled and shook its head, crashing to the floor. It literally shook the building. Dust pattered down, I heard the singing whimper of plasteel support struts flexing.

Sekhmet sa'es. It must be dense to rock the building like that. The dragging feeling of being trapped in a nightmare, arms and legs weighted down with sleep while a beast lunges for you, paralyzed me.

"*Go!*" Lucas screamed in his high whistling voice. Paralysis broke.

I backed up, unwilling to turn away from the things. A shattering squealing roar rose from the battle near the bar. Bottles exploded, glass and plasglass flying through the air with little deadly sounds. Alcohol and other fluids ignited, bursts of blue and red flame. Stasis cabinets shattered, and the stink of frying Nichtvren and frying blood filled the air. A line of fire swiped across my forehead, flying plasglass shards, black blood dripped into my eyes. The slice sealed itself before I could even flinch.

The mark on my left shoulder gave one livid burst of pain that almost drove me to my knees. The air was hot and still, popping sounds beginning as the wooden bar caught fire.

Lucas backed up. "I ain't gonna tell you again, Valen—" he began.

Then he was flung back as the second hellhound reached its feet and launched itself at him. It moved so quickly it seemed to simply flash through the intervening space.

"*Lucas!*" I screamed, and flung myself after it. My sword blazed blue-white, a rising song of bloodlust caroling out from the steel. My feet ground in broken glass, shattered brick, and other debris.

Then things began to get *really goddamn interesting*.

I reached the hellhound just as fresh screams started from the door and the air pressure changed. A wave of sickening Power roiled through the air as I chopped down, my *kia* taking on sharp physical weight.

The hellhound's head jerked up and it screamed as my blade, livid with Power, carved deeply into its back. Black blood boiled up, steaming as the glow of my blade made the acid drops sizzle and spatter like hot oil. *Oh, my gods, I actually cut it!*

It turned back on itself with a crackle of flexible bones, and I dropped flat as it flew over me, its momentum making it overshoot. It landed amid a pile of Nichtvren, who tangled and screamed as flame burst through them. Coiled itself, claws raking flesh and flooring both, and I found myself on my feet, the sword slicing down and around as I made sure I had free play in my right hand. It was a swordsman's move, easy and habitual, and the entire world narrowed as the hellhound snarled and launched itself at me again.

It didn't reach me.

A wall of huge Power crashed into my side and I flew sideways, my fingers torn from the hilt. *Wha—*

The hellhound squealed, a sound of glassy frustrated rage. I hit the wall, stone and brick shattering with an almost musical crash. Before I hit the floor he was on me, elegant golden fingers sinking into my throat and the entire world thrumming with the fury of the Prince of Hell.

"*Where is she?*" Lucifer demanded, his eyes glowing so brightly they cast shadows under his flawless cheekbones. His hair glowed too, a furnace of gold like the sun's own flame.

I couldn't have answered even if I wanted to. His fingers tightened, curling almost all the way around my neck. I heard something crackle in my throat—it sounded like a small bone—and did the only thing I could. I kicked, hard, and smashed at him with all the Power I could reach.

His head snapped aside, a thin line of black blood tracing up his beautiful cheek. The emerald set in his forehead spat one single, terrible spark of green so dark it was bloody.

The air chilled as I struggled. His fingers didn't give. Steam drifted up from his skin and mine in thin twisted coils. His hand was so tight I couldn't even tuck my chin to look down at him, instead I saw a rapidly darkening slice of the shattered burning bar opposite. The four-armed kobolding lay twisted and broken like a rag doll in the debris, its body smoking.

"You have meddled for the last time, Necromance," he spat, and I could feel it gathering, breathless electricity. Pain rolled down my skin, vicious little teeth nipping at me, darkness clouding the edges of my vision, struggling to *breathe*.

Oh, gods. I'm dead, I'm dead. I struggled even harder, achieved exactly nothing, darkness closing over my vision, no blue flame though. Lungs burning, burning, heart pounding, my eyes bulging, as if I was in a depressurized cabin and thrashing, struggling, *dying* to breathe.

Had Death forsaken me too?

No. My god would never forsake me.

Crimson light splashed against him, and he dropped me. I collapsed, too weak even to cough, my lungs burning. Whooped in a long gasping breath full of smoke and an awful crisped stench. Paranormal flesh burning: Nichtvren, kobolding, werecain. Ugh.

"You must be the Devil," Lucas wheezed. "Pleasetameetcha. Can you guess m'name?"

I coughed again, hacked, made a low, wounded noise. Frantically scrabbled in the wreckage and dust. *My sword, where's my sword, gods above and below give me my sword, I* need *my sword—*

"Deathless." Lucifer's golden voice stroked the word. I heard a hellhound snarl. A massive impact against my belly—Lucifer had kicked me, an afterthought. I was flung back, hit the wall, a short gasping sound jerked out of me. More plaster and stone shattered, dust poofing out. "You may leave. I have no quarrel with you."

I never thought I'd feel grateful to hear Lucas's grating laugh. There was a gritting sound—he had stepped forward, kicking something out of the way. "She's my client, *El Diablo*. Can't let you kill 'er."

The air chilled even more. Lucifer's attention shifted like a shark swimming through cold water. Brick and plasteel groaned, plaster dust filled the air.

The Devil spoke again. His voice tore the air, left it bleeding, and *hurt* me. "Leave now, or die."

Lucas seemed to find this incredibly funny. At least, he laughed—and fired at the Devil again. The world turned red and I heard the whine of a plasbolt; Lucifer's feet made a light sound as if stroking the surface of a drum.

I moaned. Made it up to hands and knees, coughing. My belly ran with razor fire. The sound of the rest of the world came back in a high towering wave, smashed into my sensitive ears. Crashing. Screaming, deep groaning coughs of werecain in distress. High chilling crystal screams from Nichtvren bleeding or burning.

I scrabbled away from the wall, coughing at plaster dust stuck in my nose. Had to hunch, it felt like Lucifer's kick had ruptured something and my belly ran with lava. *My sword, my sword*—My entire world narrowed to finding my sword. I was in shock, the world graying out, my left arm singing with agony and my throat burning.

More crashes, unearthly screams, and Lucas's laugh again. He was giving the Devil a run for his money, it seemed.

I don't care who hired him. My sword. I need my sword, if Lucifer's going to kill me, I want to die with my sword.

Then, like a gift, I spotted a black-wrapped hilt. My fingers closed on it just as Lucifer's hand sank into my hair and he pulled my head up. I managed to get my feet underneath me, but my spine curved as he yanked my head back, exposing my throat as my knees folded. I crouched, dangling from his hand. My choked cry slammed shut midway, a spear of pain rammed through my stomach.

"I will tear the secret of your talent for inspiring such loyalty from your screaming ghost," he said meditatively in my ear, broken plasglass and plaster grinding as he shifted his weight. Was the Devil crouching over me? "I will only ask once more, *human whore*. Where is she?"

I won't tell you. I will never tell you. Do your goddamn worst, you sonovabitch. I coughed as if choking. I probably was. I couldn't seem to get enough air in.

"*Where is she?*" He shook me.

I took a harsh tortured sip of air. Struggled to *speak*, to say what I had to.

I managed it. Two little words. "Fuck . . . you."

He made a sound like the earth itself ripping in half. The sword thrummed in my grasp. Hair tore out of my scalp as he hauled on me again, this time hissing in his demonic language. I'd driven the Devil to a sputtering fit of rage.

Huzzah. Lucky, talented me.

I had only one clear, crystalline thought. *Now or never.*

I stamped my feet under me, dug in, and pushed with all the strength in my legs, his hand pulling terribly one last time at my hair. Power sparked, flooded up my left arm, my sword burning white as I twisted, the sharp edge of the katana facing out and the blunt edge along my forearm. As I turned I flexed my wrist, dragging my sword's edge across the Devil's belly.

I felt the blade Fudoshin bite deep.

A tremendous sound, like every key on an ancient pipe organ hit at once and fed through feedback-laced speakers, slammed over the abused air. I fell over backward, my head hitting a pile of bricks and plaster with stunning force. Pain tore through me, something ripping loose inside my abused belly. But I kept my sword, heard metal chime against debris. My fingers were locked around the hilt.

Then I heard something I never thought I'd be so happy to hear again.

"Touch her again, *Prince*," Japhrimel said coldly, a pall

of freezing closing over the demolished interior, "and it will be your last act on Earth."

Silence like a nuclear winter. Ticking of time and plaster dust both falling through empty space. Lucifer spoke again, his voice killing-cold as a nuclear winter. "Did you just threaten me, Fallen?"

"No," Japhrimel said quietly. "I simply inform you of a consequence. It is not fit to treat your Right Hand so."

I dragged in a deep heaving breath, flinched as my gut clenched and broke open with hideous pain. I wanted to close my eyes and curl into a ball, let the world go on without me. So tired, so very tired. Exhaustion dragging down every nerve.

I braced my left hand against the floor. Pushed myself up. It took two tries before I could get to my knees, my left arm braced across my abused stomach. My sword dragged against metal and bricks, too heavy to lift. I coughed, rackingly. Spat black blood. My throat burned as if another reactive fire had been set off inside it to match the one in my middle, below my ribs.

"She was *here*," Lucifer snarled. He sounded almost speechless with rage, and for once his voice wasn't beautiful. "She—"

"She is your servant, wearing your trinket, and has already suffered violence because of it. Including attack from the other hunters you have sent." Japhrimel's tone was eminently reasonable, and colder than anything earthly. "Are you relieving us of the burden of your service, Prince? I can think of no other reason for such treachery."

Oh, gods above, Japhrimel, what are you saying? I

raised my head, muscles in my neck shrieking. It seemed to take forever.

Japhrimel stood in the middle of the wrack and ruin of the Haunt *Tais-toi*, his long wet-dark coat lying on his shoulders like night itself. Lucifer faced him, the Prince of Hell's lovely face twisted with fury, suffused with a darkness more than physical. Japhrimel's hand closed around Lucifer's right wrist, muscle standing out under Lucifer's shirt and Japhrimel's coat as the Devil surged forward—and Japhrimel pushed him *back*.

If I hadn't seen it, I would never have believed it possible. But Japh's entire body tensed, and he forced Lucifer back on his heels.

The Devil stepped mincingly away, twisting his wrist free of Japhrimel's hand. Retreated, only two steps. But it was enough.

Lucifer's aura flamed with blackness, a warping in the fabric of the world. They looked at each other, twin green gazes locked as if the words they exchanged were only window-dressing for the real combat, fought by the glowing spears of their eyes. The two hellhounds wove around them, low fluid shapes. Lucifer's indigo silk shirt was torn, gaping, across his midriff, showing a slice of golden skin—and as I watched, a single drop of black blood dripped from one torn edge. More spots of dark blood smoked on the silken pants he wore.

I'd cut the Devil.

One dazed thought sparked inside my aching head. *Jado must've given me a hell of a good blade.*

Then another thought, ridiculous in its intensity. *Here. Japh's here. Everything will be all right now.*

Childish faith, maybe, but I'd take it. If it was a choice

between my Fallen and getting killed right this moment, I'd settle for Japhrimel, no matter how much of a bastard he'd been recently. Funny how almost getting killed radically changed my notions of just how much I could forgive.

Japhrimel's eyes didn't flick over to check me, but the mark on my shoulder came to agonized life again, Power flooding me, exploding in my belly. White-hot pokers jerked in my viscera. My scalp twinged, I tasted blood and burning. My sword rang softly, the core of the blade burning white, blue runic patterns slipping through keen edge and painting the air. I managed to lift it, the blade a bar between me and the Devil facing his eldest son.

The red lights were still flickering, sweeping over the entire building in their complicated patterns, eerie because there were no dancers. "You would have me believe—" Lucifer started. Stone and plaster shattered at the sound of his voice, dust pattering to the wracked floor.

Japhrimel interrupted him again. I felt only a weary wonder that he was still standing there, apparently untouched, his long black coat moving gently on the hot fire-breeze. "We were told by the Master of this city—*your* ally and Hellesvront agent—that you wished to meet Dante here alone. Did you lure your Right Hand here to kill her, Prince? Breaking your word, given on your ineffable Name? Such would conclude our alliance in a most *unsatisfactory* fashion."

I could swear that Lucifer's face went through surprise, disgust, and finally settled on wariness. He studied Japhrimel for a long, tense thirty seconds, during which my throat burned and tickled but I didn't dare to cough.

Japh clasped his hands behind his back. He looked relaxed, almost bored. Except for the burning murderous light of his eyes, matching Lucifer's shade for shade.

I stayed very still, my left arm cramping as my belly ran with pain and my right trembling as I held my sword. A small part of me wondered where Lucas was. The rest of me stared at Japhrimel with open wonderment.

If I survive this, I'm going to kiss him. Right after I punch the shit out of him for lying to me. If he lets me. The nastiness of the thought made me suddenly, deeply ashamed of myself. He was here, and he was facing Lucifer. For me.

He had given up Hell. He had also taken me to Toscano and let me heal from the psychic rape of Mirovitch's *ka*, protecting me from dangers I hadn't had the faintest idea existed. He was loyal to me after all.

In his own fashion.

Lucifer finally seemed to decide. The flames among the shattered wreckage twisted into angular shapes as some essential tension leached out of him. "I rue the day I set you to watch over her, Eldest." The darkness in his face didn't fade, however—it intensified, a psychic miasma.

The tickling in my throat reached a feverish pitch. I *had* to cough, shoved the urge down, prayed for strength. *Anubis, please don't let me attract their attention. Both of them look too dangerous right now.*

Japhrimel shrugged. "What is done, is *done*." His voice pitched a little higher, as if he imitated Lucifer. Or was quoting him.

The Prince of Hell set his jaw. One elegant hand curled into a fist, and perhaps the other one was a fist too, but I couldn't see it. I think it was the first time I saw the Devil speechless, and my jaw would have dropped if I hadn't clenched it, trying not to cough. I took a fresh grip on my belly, trying not to hunch over. I wanted to see, *needed* to see. My sword held steady even though my hand was shaking, the blade singing a thin comforting song as its heart glowed white.

He finally seemed to regain himself. "You deserve each other," he hissed. "May you have joy of it. Bring me back my possession and eliminate those who would keep it from me, Tierce Japhrimel, or I will kill both of you. I swear it."

Japhrimel's eyes flared. "That was not our bargain, my lord."

Lucifer twitched. Japhrimel didn't move, but the mark twisted white-hot fire into my shoulder, a final burst of Power. The urge to cough mercifully retreated a little. I blinked drying demon blood out of my eyes. I wanted to look for Lucas.

I couldn't look away from my Fallen. He stood tense and ready, in front of the Devil.

"I am the Prince of Hell," Lucifer said coldly.

"And I was your Eldest." Japhrimel held Lucifer's eyes as the air itself cried out, a long gasping howl of a breeze coming from them, blowing my hair back. I felt the stiffness—blood and dust matted in my hair. I was filthy, and I ached. I stayed where I was. "I was the Kinslayer. Thus you made me, and you cast me away. I am yours no longer."

"*I* made you." The air itself screamed as the Prince of Hell's voice tore at it. "Your allegiance is *mine*."

"My allegiance," Japhrimel returned, inexorably quiet, "is my own. I Fell. I am Fallen. I am not your son."

One last burst of soft killing silence. I struggled to stay still.

Lucifer turned on his heel. The world snapped back into normalcy. He strode for the gaping hole torn in the front of the nightclub. Red neon reflected wetly off the street outside. A flick of his golden fingers, and the hell-hounds loped gracefully after him, one stopping to snarl back over its shoulder at me.

Well, now I can guess who sent the hellhounds. Probably Lucifer himself, to make sure I fulfilled my intended role as bait. You bastard. You filthy bastard. I sagged. My sword dipped, and the urge to cough rose again. It felt like a plasgun core had been dropped into my gut.

The Prince stopped, turned his head so I could see his profile. "Japhrimel." His voice was back to silk and honey, terrible in its beauty. "I give you a promise, my Eldest. One day, I will kill her."

Lucifer disappeared. Vanished. The air tried to heal itself, closing over the space where he had been, and failed. He left a scorch on the very fabric of existence.

Japhrimel was silent for a moment, his eyes fixed forward. He didn't look at me. I was glad, because his face was full of something terrible, irrevocable, and devouring.

"Not while I watch over her," he said softly.

40

I finally coughed, a racking fit that ended with me spitting more black blood. It felt like I'd been torn in half. My legs were made of insensate clay. I doubted I'd be able to stand.

Japhrimel knelt beside me, caught my right wrist and pushed my sword away with simple pressure. He said nothing, but immediately slid his other hand under my left arm, pressed flat against my shirt. His fingers burned.

A jolt of Power seared through me. I cried out, hunching over, and retched; a deep, amazing hacking sound. He swore, passionlessly, and I tipped into his arms as the awful tearing agony went away. *All right. Everything's going to be all right. He's here.* The ludicrous, childlike certainty welled up, I choked back tears.

Right then I didn't care what he'd done to me before. I was just damn glad he'd shown up in time.

He kissed my forehead, my cheek, hugged me. Spoke into my hair. "*A'tai, hetairae A'nankimel'iin. Diriin.*" His voice was ragged now. "Why, Dante? *Why?*"

What are you asking me for? I'm just trying to stay alive. I hitched in a breath. Another. It rasped terribly against my abused throat. What was it with demons and crushing my trachea? "Lucas," I rasped. "Took on Lucifer...is he—"

"Check for the Deathless," Japhrimel said over his shoulder. "Hurry."

Who else is here? The thought was very far away. Shaking. Shivers roaring through me. Why? I wasn't cold. "J-j-j-japh—"

"Be silent. You're hurt, and you need rest." His tone was clipped now. "Do not fight me, now."

"Japhrimel—" I tried to tell him. "I...I saw... *before*—"

He didn't listen. "No more of this."

I tipped into blackness, but not before I heard Lucas's wheezing voice.

"Goddammit, that *hurt*. Get your ass moving, we have a transport to catch."

Long hazy time of darkness. When I woke, slowly, I found myself on my side. Warmth closed over me, and softness. Power pulsed down my skin, sank in, ran along my bones. I heard Japhrimel's voice, quiet, saying something in his native tongue. Something stroked my forehead, a touch that sent a sweet gentle fire through my entire body. He traced my hairline, touched my cheek, ran his knuckle over my lips.

Hoverwhine. I felt the peculiar humming sensation of antigrav transport. Was I on a hover?

I don't think I like hovers anymore.

I opened my eyes. Dim light greeted me. I felt my swordhilt, both hands locked around it. The sword lay with me, its subliminal hum of Power good and right against my palms.

Japhrimel moved as soon as I looked up at him, straightening and stepping back. I was on a medunit table bolted to a wall behind a partition, and the curve of the plasteel walls told me it was a fairly good-sized hover. The table was hard, but I wasn't being strangled and I didn't feel ripped in half. I was still breathing, and I had all my original appendages.

It felt *great*. I closed my eyes, opened them again, and he was still there.

"Gods," I rasped. "I'm glad to see you."

He managed to look surprised and gratified at once, his saturnine face easing. "Then I am happy. You are well and whole, your friend Lucas has mended, and McKinley and Vann are no worse for wear. Tiens will meet us in Giza. The humans have gone back to their lives, except for your Necromance." His mouth turned down slightly at the mention of Leander.

I nodded. It was getting hazardous to hang around me, and humans were fragile.

I felt only a twinge of guilt for thinking that. After all, I'd been wholly human once, hadn't I?

Was Japhrimel right? Was it no more than a habit? I didn't want to think so. I was human *inside*, where it counted.

He leaned forward, his eyes still bright and green. I examined his face as he examined mine, something new in the silence between us.

He broke it first, for once. "He could have killed you."

I nodded, my hair sliding along a crisp cotton pillow-case. Where had the pillow come from? "He certainly wanted to." The question spilled out of me. "Did you hunt the Fallen, Japhrimel?"

He froze. I would never get used to his particular quality of stillness, as if his very molecules had slowed their frenetic dance. Then his face darkened. It was all the answer I needed.

"Why won't you talk to me?" It came out plaintive instead of angry. I was too emotionally exhausted to be angry. "If you would just *talk* to me—"

"I see no reason to tell you of every assassination I committed at the behest of the Prince." There was no mercy in his tone; it scorched with bitterness not directed at me. "Why will you not *trust* me? Is it so hard to do as I ask?"

You could make me do whatever you wanted; you could force me. You probably will. And I'll fight however I can, no matter how much I love you. You can't control me. "I *want* to trust you," I whispered. "You make it hard." I had one last question. "Did Lucifer offer you your place in Hell back if you got rid of me?"

He stared at me for an endless moment. Then comprehension lit his face, comprehension and savage anger. "Vardimal's Androgyne."

"She wanted to meet me." I opened my mouth to tell him the other half of it—that she'd said she was my daughter too—and shut my lips.

He didn't need to know that. That was private. That was human, between Doreen and me. It was *mine*.

"Ah. *Now* it makes sense." Japhrimel straightened, and turned away from me. His shoulders shook, stiffly. He tipped his head back, his inky hair falling away from his forehead, and I felt the slight tremor that raced through the hover.

"Japhrimel?" I didn't expect him to listen, but he did. "Please, don't."

His reaction told me everything I needed to know. He hadn't kept the knowledge of Eve's escape from me, he hadn't even known. I was willing to believe it.

Are you believing it just because you want to, or because it makes sense?

I didn't care.

The earthquake of his fury eased. I could barely tell anyone else was on the hover, it was so silent.

When he turned back to me, I almost flinched. His upper lip drew back, exposing his teeth; his eyes were incandescent. He looked far more lethal than Velokel the Bull. "An Androgyne out of Hell," he said tightly. "Of course. Of *course*. I suppose the Hunter and the Twins are in league with her?"

"I think so." I freed my right hand from my swordhilt, started to push myself up on my elbow. The softness—it was one of the new microfiber spaceblankets, warm and soft at the same time—crinkled as it folded down. He was immediately there, helping me; I felt clean, my clothes were soft as if freshly laundered. Probably cleaned off with Power; he knew how I hated to be dirty. I was vaguely surprised to find my sword had a new reinforced sheath, deep indigo lacquer. "Japhrimel, she asked me to distract you. To just wait out the next seven years and pretend we can't find her. She wants to—"

"She is in rebellion against the Prince." He stroked my hair back from my face with his free hand as he steadied me. "She cannot *possibly* win. She is young, untutored, without any support."

"She can win if you help her. You're..." I couldn't believe I'd said it, and apparently neither could he, because he set his jaw and looked away, a muscle flicking in his golden cheek.

"No." Just the one word, forced out through his lips.

"Japhrimel—" *Please*, I was going to say. I was going to plead, to beg if that was what it came to. Stopped myself just in time. Begging was weakness.

But she was part Doreen's, and part mine. It was worth any weakness if I could make him understand, if I could convince him to *help* me.

He spoke before I could muster the words. "You are asking me to endanger your life by throwing our lot in with a rebellion that cannot possibly succeed. No, Dante. I will not risk you."

"Lucifer wants to kill me anyway." It came out flat and hopeless. What chance did I have if the Devil wanted me dead?

"I can keep him from you." His hand bit into my shoulder. "Have I not kept him from you so far?"

Oh, Japh. Please. Help me out here. "She only asked, Japh. She didn't demand, she didn't manipulate, she didn't force me. She just *asked*."

That seemed to make him even angrier. "She's demon. We *lie*, my curious one, in case you have not noticed."

Oh, I've noticed. Believe me, I've learned to count on it. "What about you?"

He leaned in close, his nose an inch from mine, his eyes filling mine with green light just like the wristcuff's warnings. "Judge me by what I *do*. Have I not *always* kept faith with you?"

I opened my mouth to retort, but he had a point. All I had to do was breathe to understand the answer to that particular question. "The Master Nichtvren didn't say it was Lucifer, he just said it was a demon with a green gem. You *did* lie."

No response. My heart pounded. *You gave up Hell for me, and you just lied to the Prince of Hell for me.* "You lied to protect me from the Devil. And you pushed him back. You *stopped* him."

He shrugged, his coat moving with a whispering sound. Said nothing.

I reached up with my right hand, touched his face. He sighed, closing his eyes. Leaned into my fingers.

If he hadn't been so close, I might have missed the single tear that slipped out beneath his eyelashes and tracked down his cheek in the semi-darkness.

Oh, Japhrimel. My heart broke. I could actually feel it cracking apart inside my chest.

"What am I going to do with you?" I managed around the lump in my throat. "You tried to force me to do what you wanted. You *hurt* me."

His face contorted, I smoothed his mouth down with my fingers. "I am sorry," he breathed. He leaned into me, his lips brushing my skin so that he kissed my hand with each word. "I should not have, I *know* I should not have. I was afraid. Afraid of harm coming to you."

Oh, gods. I traced the arch of his cheekbone, the shape of his bottom lip. Felt the tension go out of him as I leaned forward, pressed my lips to his smooth golden cheek. "You idiot," I whispered, my lips moving against his skin. "I love you. Do you have any idea how much I love you?"

He flinched as if I'd hit him. "I am sorry," he whispered. "Do not doubt me."

He'd actually apologized. Miracles were coming thick and fast now.

I couldn't say anything through the lump of stone in my throat, but I nodded. I swallowed a few times.

When his eyes opened again, I almost gasped, their green was so intense. He studied me up-close, then pressed a gentle kiss onto my cheek. He made sure I was steady, sitting up, then straightened, backed up two steps and clasped his hands behind his back. "You're hungry. We land in half an hour."

Understanding flashed between us. His eyes said, *Forgive me. Teach me how to do this. You are the only one who can.*

My heart leapt. *Just trust me, and don't doubt me either. That's all I need from you.*

There was more, but I couldn't have put it into words. The softening in his mouth told me he understood. For that one split second, at least, we were in total accord. My heart twisted inside my chest and my cheeks flamed with heat. Whatever *Fallen* meant, Japhrimel loved me. Hadn't he proved it enough?

The rest could wait.

I nodded. Held up my sword. "Thank you. For the scabbard." My voice was back to rough honey, granular gold. Soothing.

That wasn't all I was thanking him for, and he knew it.

His slight smile rewarded me. Then he reached up,

opening a small metal stasis cabinet. He lifted down
something small but apparently heavy and took a single
step forward, handing it to me. I had to lay my sword
down to accept it. "A small gift, for my beloved."

He vanished through the opening in the partition as I
brought my hands down and found them full of a familiar weight. The statue was obsidian, glowing mellowly
through a scrim of heat-scarring from the fire that had
destroyed our house. The woman sat, calmly, Her lion's
head set firmly atop Her body, the sun-disc of hammered
gold still shining. I could see traceries of Power, careful
repair work, where Japhrimel had spent his demon-given
Power to repair the weakening of molecular bonds the reaction fire had caused. It would have taken unimaginable
Power and precision to repair the glassy obsidian, phe-
nomenal strength and inhuman concentration.

All for me. A gift, the only gift he knew how to give.
His strength.

Tears spilled hot down my cheeks.

I'd misjudged him, after all. Just as badly as he'd misjudged me.

41

$\mathcal{L}$ucas slumped in a chair, blood stiffening on his torn shirt. Sunlight poured in the hover windows, I pushed my hair back behind my ear and examined him.

He looked like hell, gaunt and sticky with dry blood everywhere except for a swipe on his cheek where he'd probably rubbed the dirt-dusted gummy crust off. He still held one 60-watt plasgun, tilted up with the smooth black plasteel barrel resting against his cheek. His legs stretched out, clad in shredded jeans. At least his boots had survived. His yellow eyes, half-lidded, were distant and full of some emotion I didn't want to examine too closely.

Something like banked rage, and satisfaction.

I lowered myself down in the chair opposite him. This hover was good-sized but narrow, with round porthole windows like a military transport. I didn't know where Lucas had gotten it, but it was taking us away from DMZ Sarajevo, and that was all I cared about.

McKinley and Japhrimel held a low conference up front in the pilot booth—this hover was old enough to have an actual booth instead of a cockpit—and Vann leaned against the booth's entrance, his arms folded. He scowled at Lucas. There were horrible livid bruises on his brown face, and one eye was bandaged.

I didn't want to know.

There was no smell of human in the hover. The agents smelled like dried cinnamon, with the faintest tang of demon, Lucas smelled like a stasis cabinet and blood dried to flakes, and Japhrimel and I...well, we smelled like demon. Of course.

I leaned back in the chair, my katana across my knees.

I have a blade that bit the Devil. Gods grant me strength enough to use it next time. I'm sure there's going to be a next time.

"Who are you really working for, Lucas?" My voice was quiet, stroking the air, calming.

He shrugged, his eyelids dropping another millimeter. "You," he said, in his painful whisper. "Since New Prague. I was contracted by Ol' Blue Eyes to meet you, look after you. Figured the two jobs tallied."

I nodded, my head moving against the chair's headrest. Thought about it. Decided. It was only fair, after all.

"If you want to go on your way, I won't blame you. You stood up to the Devil for me." *Gave him a bit of trouble, too. We might almost have had a chance.*

Not really. Not without Japhrimel.

He gave another one of those terrible, dry, husking laughs. He certainly seemed to find me amusing nowadays.

"Shitfire," he finally wheezed. "This's the most interesting thing I seen in years. Ain't gonna stop now. Four demons, eyes an' ears. Until the fourth demon's dead, *chica*, I'm your man."

I nodded. Braced myself. It was always best to pay debts before the interest mounted, and I owed him. If not for him,

Lucifer would have killed me before Japhrimel could reach me. "I told you the pay's negotiable. What do you want?"

"Your demon boyfriend paid me, Valentine. Consider yourself lucky."

Well, it was certainly a day for surprises. I shifted uneasily in the seat, then rested my head against the seat's high back.

"Do you think she was telling the truth?" I meant Eve. He'd been in the room, after all.

"Don't know. I ain't no Magi." He shifted a little in the chair, as if he hurt. "Explains a helluva lot."

"Are you all right?" It was a stupid question. We'd both gotten off lightly, for tangling with Lucifer.

"Devil damn near pulled my spleen out through my nose. It hurt." Lucas sighed. He sounded disappointed. "Guess even he can't kill me."

"Give him time." I didn't mean for it to sound flippant. Then I leaned forward, running my hand back through my hair. "Lucas, do you have any friends? I mean, real friends?"

An evocative shrug. His yellow eyes fastened on me.

"If you had a friend," I persisted, "and he lied to you but it was for a good reason, what would you do?"

Silence. Lucas studied me.

The hover began a stomach-jolting descent then rose again, probably to avoid a traffic stream. I folded my left arm across my belly; it wasn't tender, but I was still cautious.

Finally, Lucas hauled himself upright, leaned forward. Rested his elbows on his knees. "You askin' me for advice, *chica*. Dangerous." He rasped in a breath. "I seen a lot of shit on the face of the earth. Most of it pointless. The only thing I can tell you is—take what you can get."

I weighed the statement, wondering if it was any good. *Take what you can get.* Was that even honorable? "So you don't have any friends?"

He shrugged again.

I closed my eyes, leaning back into the chair's embrace. "You do now, Lucas." I paused, let the fact sink in. "You do now."

After all, he'd shot the Devil. For me. Who cared if it was just a job to him?

Take what you can get.

Eve wanted her freedom. Lucifer wanted her dead or captured—most likely captured, since he had used me as bait to draw her out. Lucifer also wanted me kept so busy with "hunting" down his escaped children that I didn't have time to find out it was Eve he was really after. Japhrimel probably wanted to keep us both alive long enough to figure out which was the winning side, and I didn't blame him. Lucas was curious, and he might have thought Lucifer could finally kill him.

Take what you can get.

What did I want out of this? I didn't even know yet.

We were going to land in Giza, meet Leander, and figure out what course to follow next. I had to decide if I was going to hunt down Doreen's daughter for Lucifer, or if I was going to risk my life—and Japhrimel's too—taking on the Prince of Hell.

Who was I fooling? I already knew what I was going to do.

The trouble would be talking both myself and Japhrimel into it.

Glossary

A'nankhimel: (*demon term*) 1. A Fallen demon. 2. A demon who has tied himself to a human mate. *Note: As with all demon words, there are several layers of meaning to this term, depending on context and pronunciation. The meanings, from most common to least, are as follows: descent from a great height, chained, shield, a guttering flame, a fallen statue.*

Androgyne: 1. A transsexual, cross-dressing, or androgynous human. 2. (*demon term*) A Greater Flight demon capable of reproduction.

Animone: An accredited psion with the ability to telepathically connect with and heal animals, generally employed as veterinarians.

Anubis et'her ka: Egyptianica term, sometimes used as an expletive; loosely translated, "Anubis protect me/us."

Awakening, the: The exponential increase in psionic and sorcerous ability, academically defined as from just before the fall of the Republic of Gilead to the culmination of the Parapsychic and Paranormal Species Acts proposed and brokered by the alternately vilified and worshipped Senator Adrien Ferrimen. *Note: After the* *culmination of the Parapsychic Act, the Awakening was said to have finished and the proportion of psionics to normals in the human population stabilized, though fluctuations occur in seventy-year cycles to this day.*

Ceremonial: 1. An accredited psion whose talent lies in working with traditional sorcery, accumulating Power and "spending" it in controlled bursts. 2. Ceremonial magick, otherwise known as sorcery instead of the more organic witchery. 3. (*slang*) Any Greater Work of magick.

Clormen-13: (*Slang: Chill, ice, rock, smack, dust*) Addictive alkaloid drug. *Note: Chill is high-profit for the big pharmaceutical companies as well as the Mob, being instantly addictive. There is no cure for Chill addiction.*

Deadhead: 1. Necromance. 2. Normal human without psionic abilities.

Demon: 1. Any sentient, alien intelligence, either corporeal or noncorporeal, that interacts with humans. 2. Denizen of Hell, of a type often mistaken for gods or Novo Christer evil spirits, actually a sentient nonhuman species with technology and psionic and magical ability much exceeding humanity's. 3. (*slang*) A particularly bad physiological addiction.

Evangelicals of Gilead: 1. Messianic Old Christer and Judic cult started by Kochba bar Gilead and led by him until the signing of the Gilead Charter, when power was seized by a cabal of military brass just prior to bar Gilead's assassination. 2. Members of said cult. 3. (*academic*) The followers of bar Gilead before the signing of the Gilead Charter. *See* **Republic of Gilead.**

Feeder: 1. A psion who has lost the ability to process

ambient Power and depends on "jolts" of vital energy stolen from other human beings, psions, or normals. 2. (*psion slang*) A fair-weather friend.

Flight: A class or social rank of demons. *Note: There are, strictly speaking, three classes of demons: the Low, Lesser, and Greater. Magi most often deal with the higher echelons of the Low Flight and the lower echelons of the Lesser Flight. Greater Flight demons are almost impossible to control and very dangerous.*

Freetown: An autonomous enclave under a charter, neither Hegemony nor Putchkin but often allied to one or the other for economic reasons.

Hedaira: (*demon term*) 1. An endearment. 2. A human woman tied to a Fallen (*A'nankhimel*) demon. *Note: There are several layers of meaning, depending on context and pronunciation. The meanings, from most common to least, are as follows: beloved, companion, vessel, starlight, sweet fruit, small precious trinket, an easily crushed bauble. The most uncommon and complex meaning can be roughly translated as "slave (thing of pleasure) who rules the master."*

Hegemony: One of the two world superpowers, comprising North and South America, Australia and New Zealand, most of Western Europe, Japan, some of Central Asia, and scattered diplomatic enclaves in China. *Note: After the Seventy Days War, the two superpowers settled into peace and are often said to be one world government with two divisions. Afrike is technically a Hegemony protectorate, but that seems mostly diplomatic convention more than anything else.*

Ka: 1. (*archaic*) Soul or mirrorspirit, separate from the *ba* and the physical soul in Egyptianica. 2. Fate, especially tragic fate that cannot be avoided, destiny. 3. A link between two souls, where each feeds the other's destiny. 4. (*technical*) Terminus stage for Feeder pathology, an externalized hungry consciousness capable of draining vital energy from a normal human in seconds and a psion in less than two minutes.

Kobolding: (*also:* kobold) 1. Paranormal species characterized by a troll-like appearance, thick skin, and an affinity to elemental earth magick. 2. A member of the kobolding species.

Left-Hand: Sorcerous discipline utilizing Power derived from "sinister" means, as in bloodletting, animal or human sacrifice, or certain types of drug use (*Left-Hander:* a follower of a Left-Hand path).

Ludder: 1. Member of the conservative Ludder Party. 2. A person opposed to genetic manipulation or the use of psionic talent, or both. 3. (*slang*) Technophobe. 4. (*slang*) hypocrite.

Magi: 1. A psion who has undergone basic training. 2. The class of occult practitioners before the Awakening who held and transmitted basic knowledge about psionic abilities and training techniques. 3. An accredited psion with the training to call demons or harness etheric force from the disturbance created by the magickal methods used to call demons; usually working in Circles or loose affiliations. *Note: The term "Magus" is archaic and hardly ever used. "Magi" has become singular or plural, and neuter gender.*

Master Nichtvren: 1. A Nichtvren who is free of obligation to his or her Maker. 2. A Nichtvren who holds territory.

Merican: 1. The trade lingua of the globe and official

language of the Hegemony, though other dialects are in common use. 2. (*archaic*) A Hegemony citizen. 3. (*archaic*) A citizen of the Old Merican region before the Seventy Days War.

Necromance: (*slang:* deadhead) An accredited psion with the ability to bring a soul back from Death to answer questions. *Note: Can also, in certain instances, heal mortal wounds and keep a soul from escaping into Death.*

Nichtvren: (*slang:* suckhead) Altered human dependent on human blood for nourishment. *Note: Older Nichtvren may possibly live off strong emotions, especially those produced by psions. Since they are altered humans, Nichtvren occupy a space between humanity and "other species"; they are defined as members of a Paranormal Species and given citizen's rights under Adrien Ferrimen's groundbreaking legislation after the Awakening.*

Nine Canons: A nine-part alphabet of runes drawn from around the globe and codified during the Awakening to manage psionic and sorcerous power, often used as shortcuts in magickal circles or as quick charms. *Note: The Canons are separate from other branches of magick in that they are accessible sometimes even to normal humans, by virtue of their long use and highly charged nature.*

Novo Christianity: An outgrowth of a Religion of Submission popular from the twelfth century to the latter half of the twenty-first century, before the meteoric rise of the Republic of Gilead and the Seventy Days War. *Note: The death knell of Old Christianity is thought to have been the great Vatican Bank scandal that touched* *off the revolt leading to the meteoric rise of Kochba bar Gilead, the charismatic leader of the Republic before the Charter. Note: The state religion of the Republic was technically fundamentalist Old Christianity with Judic messianic overtones. Nowadays, NC is declining in popularity and mostly fashionable among a small slice of the Putchkin middle-upper class.*

Power: 1. Vital energy produced by living things: prana, mana, orgone, etc. 2. Sorcerous power accumulated by celibacy, bloodletting, fasting, pain, or meditation. 3. Ambient energy produced by ley lines and geo-currents, a field of energy surrounding the planet. 4. The discipline of raising and channeling vital energy, sorcerous power, or ambient energy. 5. Any form of energy that fuels sorcerous or psionic ability. 6. A paranormal community or paranormal individual who holds territory.

Prime Power: 1. The highest-ranked paranormal Power in a city or territory, capable of negotiating treaties and enforcing order. *Note: usually Nichtvren in most cities and werecain in rural areas.* 2. (*technical*) The source from which all Power derives. 3. (*archaic*) Any non-human paranormal being with more than two vassals in the feudal structure of pre-Awakening paranormal society.

Psion: 1. An accredited, trained, or apprentice human with psionic abilities. 2. Any human with psionic abilities.

Putchkin: 1. The official language of the Putchkin Alliance, though other dialects are in common use. 2. A Putchkin Alliance citizen.

Putchkin Alliance: One of the two world superpowers, comprising Russia, most of Territorial China (except

Freetown Tibet and Singapore), some of Central Asia, Eastern Europe, and the Middle East. *Note: After the Seventy Days War, the two superpowers settled into peace and are often said to be one world government with two divisions.*

Republic of Gilead: Theocratic Old Merican empire based on fundamentalist Novo Christer and Judic messianic principles, lasting from the latter half of the twenty-first century (after the Vatican Bank scandal) to the end of the Seventy Days War. *Note: In the early days, before Kochba bar Gilead's practical assumption of power in the Western Hemisphere, the Evangelicals of Gilead were defined as a cult, not as a Republic. Political infighting in the Republic—and the signing of the Charter with its implicit acceptance of the High Council's sovereignty—brought about both the War and the only tactical nuclear strike of the War (in the Vegas Waste).*

Revised Matheson Score: The index for quantifying an individual's level of psionic ability. *Note: Like the Richter scale, it is exponential; five is the lowest score necessary for a psionic child to receive Hegemony funding and schooling. Forty is the terminus of the scale; anything above forty is defined as "superlative" and the psion is tipped into special Hegemony secret-services training.*

Runewitch: A psion whose secondary or primary talent includes the ability to handle the runes of the Nine Canons with special ease.

Sedayeen: 1. An accredited psion whose talent is healing. 2. (*archaic*) An old Nichtvren word meaning "blue hand." *Note: Sedayeen are incapable of aggression* *even in self-defense, being allergic to violence and prone to feeling the pain they inflict. This makes them incredible healers, but also incredibly vulnerable.*

Sekhmet sa'es: Egyptianica term, often used as profanity; translated: "Sekhmet stamp it," a request for the Egyptos goddess of destruction to strike some object or thing, much like the antique "*God damn it.*"

Seventy Days War: The conflict that brought about the end of the Republic of Gilead and the rise of the Hegemony and Putchkin Alliance.

Sexwitch: (*archaic: tantraiiken*) An accredited psion who works with Power raised from the act of sex; pain also produces an endorphin and energy rush for sexwitches.

Shaman: 1. The most common and catch-all term for a psion who has psionic ability but does not fall into any other specialty, ranging from vaudun Shamans (who traffic with *loa* or *etrigandi*) to generic psions. 2. (*archaic*) A normal human with borderline psionic ability.

Sk8: Member of a slicboard tribe.

Skinlin: (*slang:* dirtwitch) An accredited psion whose talent has to do with plants and plant DNA. *Note: Skinlin use their voices, holding sustained tones, wedded to Power to alter plant DNA and structure. Their training makes them susceptible to berserker rages.*

Slagfever: Sickness caused by exposure to chemical-waste cocktails commonly occurring near hover transport depots in less urban areas.

Swanhild: Paranormal species characterized by hollow bones, feathery body hair, poisonous flesh, and passive and pacifistic behavior.

Synth-hash: Legal nonaddictive stimulant and relaxant synthesized from real hash (derivative of opium) and kennabis. *Note: Synth-hash replaced nicotiana leaves (beloved of the Evangelicals of Gilead for the profits reaped by tax on its use) as the smoke of choice in the late twenty-second century.*

Talent: 1. Psionic ability. 2. Magickal ability.

Werecain: (*slang:* 'cain, furboy) Altered human capable of changing to a furred animal form at will. *Note: There are several different subsets, including Lupercal and magewolfen. Normal humans and even psionic outsiders are generally incapable of distinguishing between different subsets of 'cain.*

Lilith Saintcrow was born in New Mexico and bounced around the world as an Air Force brat. She currently lives in Vancouver, Washington, with her husband, two children, and a houseful of cats. Visit the official Lilith Saintcrow website at www.lilithsaintcrow.com

Find out more about Lilith Saintcrow and other Orbit authors by registering for the free monthly newsletter at www.orbitbooks.net

SUPPLEMENTARY MATERIAL

Excerpt from '*A Face for Death*'
Hegemony Psionic Academy Textbook,
Specialized Studies
By Fallon Hoffman
Sirius Publishing, Paradisse

In classical antiquity, the psychopomp was merely any god relating to death or the dead. The term narrowed with the advent of the Awakening and narrowed even further after the Parapsychic Act was signed into law. The psychopomp – defined as the god or being a Necromance sees during the resurrection phase of the accreditation Trial – is thus an ancient concept.

Necromances are unique among psions because of the Trial. Borrowed from shamanic techniques born in the mists of pre-Awakening history, the Trial is nothing more than a specific initiation, a guided death and rebirth for which every Necromance is carefully prepared through over a decade and a half of schooling and practice in other magickal and psionic techniques.

There is no such thing as a non-practicing or non-accredited Necromance. The nature of a Necromance's peculiar talent demands training, lest Death swallow the unpracticed whole. In pre-Awakening times, those gifted with this most unreliable talent usually ended up in mental hospitals or prisons, screaming of things no normal could see.

During the Awakening, it became much more dangerous and common to slip over the border into what any EKG will label the 'blue mesh,' that particular pattern of brainwaves produced when a Necromance triggers the talent and creates a doorway through which a spirit can be pulled to answer questions. Many nascent Necromances were lost to the pull and chill of Death, their hearts stopping from sheer shock. Unprepared by any schooling, meditation training, or Magi recall techniques, the Necromance faced death defenseless as a normal human – or even more so.

The solution – a psychological mechanism of putting a face on Death – was stumbled upon in the very early days of the Awakening. Unfortunately, we have no record of the brave soul who first made the connection between the psychopomp and a managed trip into Death, instead of the less-reliable techniques such as soul-stripping or the charge-and-release method. Whoever she is (for Necromances, like *sedayeen*, are overwhelmingly female), she deserves canonization on par with Adrien Ferrimen.

The reason the psychopomp is so necessary is deceptively simple. Death is the oldest, largest human fear. To create a screen of rationality between the limited human mind and the cosmic law of ending, the defense mechanism of a face and personality makes the inhuman bearable and even human itself. A psychopomp is no more than a graceful fiction that allows a human mind to grasp the Unending. It is the simplest and most basic form of god-making, hardwired into the human neural net. It is much easier to believe in a god's intercession than in a random mix of genetics and talent allowing what our culture still sadly views as a violation of the natural order – bringing the dead back, however briefly.

A psychopomp is unutterably personal, coded into the deepest levels of the Necromance's psyche. Gods are mostly elective nowadays, except for those rare occasions when they choose to meddle in human affairs. But to plumb the depths of mankind's oldest fear and greatest mystery, a human mind needs a key to unlock those depths and a shield to use against them. That key needs to be strong enough, and rooted deep enough in the mind, to stand repeated use.

The psychopomp serves both functions, key and shield. First, it gives the psyche a much-needed handle on the concept of Death. Intellectually, the human mind knows death is inevitable, that it visits every single one of us. Convincing the rest of the human animal, not to mention the animal brain, is impossible. Death is disproved by every breath the living creature takes, by every beat of a living heart. The psychopomp allows empirical evidence of the living body and of the non-space of Death to coexist by providing a framework, however fragile, to fix both concepts in.

Psychopomps also function as a defense against the concept of death itself. Necromances, when interviewed, speak of 'Death's love' – not the worship of Thanatos but an affirmation of Death as part of a cosmic order and the Necromance as a necessary part of that order, helping to keep the scales balanced. The idea of balance is intrinsically linked to any god dealing with Death, proof again of the psyche's grasping for reason in the face of the eternal.

Necromances speak, often at great length, about the emotional connection to their psychopomp. This is necessary, otherwise the fear reflex might crush even the most finely honed sorcerous Will. Indeed, the outpouring of emotion lavished on death-gods by Necromances is only matched by the propitiatory offerings made in temples by normals in hopes of Death passing them by. The idea that

Death can be reasoned or bargained with haunts humanity with hope.

The psychological cost of trips to the other side of Death's doorway shows itself in several ways, from the Necromance's common need for adrenaline boosts to the compensatory neuroses detailed in Chapter 12. Were it not for the useful concept of a god as guardian, gate-keeper, eternal Other, and protector, Necromances might still be going mad at puberty, which is when the talent commonly manifests itself. . .

Incident Date/Time/Duration: **/*/**** / Beginning approximately 1300 / 10 days (tentative)
Incident Prime Location: Nuevo Rio, Sudro Merica, Hegemony
Secondary Location(s): Inapplicable / Classified

Incident: Class 5 interaction with dimensional rift. Class 3 and suspected Class 5 interaction with nonhuman (sp: demonic) forces.

Abstract: Several sources claim subject has been 'transformed' by Class 5 nonhuman being (demon, level 1). Possible interference with sealed Hegemony Directive 2048-E (Project Eden) due to prior contact with FS source Prometheus (HSF-IW-002399Z) in the course of source's collection of viable samples for Project Eden. Project Eden met, of course, with a premature end after initial success. Two sources (codename: Vickers and Preacher) link subject to failure of Project Eden. However, neither source is considered reliable.

Detail: Subject exhibits radically altered genetic profile and has received large sums of hard credit from unidentifiable source. Sources claim a level 1 demon (codename: Starstrike) carried out genetic reshaping on subject in return for unspecified services relating to the interruption of Project Eden. However, the prime mover of Project Eden (codename: Veritas) has insisted subject be kept only under light surveillance. Given the training and background of subject, analysis agrees. Chance of unacceptable information dispersal if surveillance moves above "light" is calculated at an unacceptable 80% (+/- 2).

The incident in question centers around destruction caused to roughly 40 percent of Nuevo Rio's buildings, presumably by Starstrike in reprisal for an unidentified interaction between Prometheus and subject. The incident definition has expanded to include the destruction of Project Eden's laboratory and refuge (cross-ref, HFS-IW-*******) and the services of Veritas in tying off Project Eden.

Casualties in Nuevo Rio were kept to a minimum (critical loss estimated at less than 4 percent). Incident was declared a federal disaster zone, sealed and repaired within 83.6 hours, emergency funding dispersed under sealed Hegemony Directive 0003-A.

Damage done to diplomatic relations with Veritas has been contained. Information dispersal to subject (classified as slight) is considered acceptable, in light of overriding factors such as Starstrike's suspected interference and Veritas's claim of ownership of subject (pursuant to sealed Hegemony Directive 2048-F, ownership of human genetic material transformed by Class 5 nonhuman interference). Subject has been confirmed unsuitable for advancement of Project Eden.

Suggested Action: Continued light surveillance of subject. Consideration of recruitment of subject for high-level wetworking has been advanced several times, despite analysis of subject's psych profile providing high chance of deconstruction and high unsuitability for impersonal motivations for such activity.

Notes: Project Eden may be considered a limited success. Necessity of keeping diplomatic relations open with Veritas dictated a less-than-satisfactory endgame in relation to ownership of Project Eden's greatest success (codename: Omega). Monitoring of Omega is almost impossible due to dimensional interference.

Reclaiming Omega is of prime importance to the FS despite low chance of success.

Claims of Starstrike's demise are being investigated by Internal Watch, Division 5. (See HFS-IW-*******) Various methods have brought no conclusive proof. Chance of survival is calculated at 53 percent (+/- 40).

SAINT CITY SINNERS
EXTRACT

Cairo Giza has endured for a very long time, but it was only after the Awakening that the pyramids began to acquire distinctive etheric smears again. Colored balls of light bobbed and wove around them even during the daytime, playing with the streams of hover traffic that carefully didn't pass *over* the pyramids themselves, instead separating as if around islands in a stream. Hover circuitry is buffered like every critical component nowadays, but enough Power can blow anything electric just like a focused EMP pulse. There was a college of Ceremonials responsible for using and draining the pyramids' charge, responsible also for the Temple built equidistant from the stone triangles and the Sphinx, whose ruined face gazed from her recumbent body with more wisdom long forgotten than the human race could ever lay claim to accumulating.

Power hummed in the air around me as I stepped from the glare of the desert sun into the shadowed gloom of the Temple's portico. Static crackled, sand falling out of my clothes and whisked away by the containment field. I grimaced. We'd been on the ground less than half an hour and already I was tired of the dust.

One tired, busted-down half-demon Necromance, sore from Lucifer's last kick even though Japhrimel had repaired the damage done and flushed me with enough Power to make my skin tingle. And one Fallen given back the power of a demon pacing behind me, his step oddly silent on the stone floor. The mark on my left shoulder – *his* mark – pulsed again, a warm velvet flush coating my body. My rings swirled with steady light.

My bag bumped against my hip and my bootheels clicked on stone, echoing in the vast shadowed chamber. The great doors rose up before us, massive slabs of granite lasecarved with hieroglyphs of a way of life vanished thousands of years ago. I inhaled deeply, smelling the deep familiar spice of *kyphii* and feeling my nape begin to prickle. My sword, thrust through a loop in my weapons rig, seemed to thrum slightly even through the indigo-lacquered scabbard.

A blade that can bite the Devil, I thought, and a cool finger of dread traced up my spine.

I stopped, half-turned on my heel to look up at Japhrimel, who paused. His hands clasped behind his back as usual, he regarded me with bright green eyes glowing through the dimness. His ink-dark hair lay against his forehead in a soft wave, and his lean golden saturnine face was closed and distant as usual. He had been very quiet in the last hour.

I didn't blame him. There was precious little to say now. And in any case, I didn't want to break the fragile truce between us.

One dark eyebrow quirked slightly, a question I found I could read. It was a relief to see there something about him I could still understand.

'Will you wait for me here?' My voice bounced back from stone, husky and half-ruined, still freighted with the promise of demon seduction. I sounded like a vidsex operator, dammit, and the hoarseness didn't help. 'Please?'

His expression changed from distance to wariness, then the corner of his mouth quirked up slightly. 'Of course. It would be a pleasure.'

The words ran along stone, mouthing the air softly.

I bit my lower lip. The idea that I'd misjudged him was uncomfortable, to say the least. 'Japhrimel?'

His eyes rested on my face. All attention, focused on me. He didn't touch me – but he might as well have, his aura closing around mine, the black-diamond flames that proclaimed him as *demon* to anyone with Sight. It was a caress no less intimate for being nonphysical; he was doing that more and more lately. I wondered if it was because he wanted to keep track of me, or because he wanted to touch me.

I shook my head, deciding the question was useless. He probably wouldn't tell me the truth anyway.

Was it wrong, not to hold it against him?

I heard Lucas's voice again. *Take what you can get.* Good advice? Honorable? Or just practical?

Tiens, the Nichtvren who was yet another Hellesvront agent, would meet us after dark. Lucas was with Vann and McKinley; Leander had rented space in a boarding house and was recruiting. The Necromance bounty hunter seemed very easy with the idea of two nonhuman Hellesvront agents, but I'd caught him going pale whenever Lucas got too close. It was a relief to see he had some sense.

Then again, even I was frightened of Lucas, never mind that I was his client and he'd taken on Lucifer and two hellhounds for me. The man that Death had turned his back on was a professional, and a good asset... but still. He was unpredictable, impossible to kill, and magick just seemed to shunt itself away from him – and there were stories of just what he'd done to psions who played rough with him, or hired him and tried to welsh. It doesn't take long to figure out so many stories must have a grain of truth to them.

'Yes?' Japhrimel prompted me. I looked up from the stone floor with a start. I'd been wandering.

I never used to do that.

'Nothing.' I turned away from him, my boots making precise little clicks on the floor as I headed for the doors. 'I'll be out in a little while.'

'Take your time.' He stood straight and tall, his hands clasped behind his back, his eyes burning green holes in the smoky cool darkness; I could almost feel the weight of his gaze on my back. I shook my head, reached up to touch the doors. 'I will wait.'

The mark on my shoulder flared again, heat sliding down my skin like warm oil. The sense of being caressed by a sheet of demon-fueled Power returned.

He was Fallen-no-more. I would have wondered what that made me, now, but he hadn't even told me what I was in the first place. *Hedaira*, a human woman given a share of a demon's strength. Japhrimel kept telling me I would find out in time, when he told me anything at *all,* that was.

With Lucifer looking to kill me and Eve to save, I just might die with everything still a mystery.

I spread my hands – narrow, golden, the black molecule-drip polish slightly chipped on my left thumbnail – against the rough granite, pushed. The doors, hung on maghinges, whooshed open very quietly. More *kyphii* smoke billowed out, fighting briefly with the burning-cinnamon musk of demon lying over me.

I looked up. The hall was large, all space architecturally focused on the throned Horus at the end, Isis's tall form behind him, Her hand lifted in blessing over Her son. The doors slid to a stop, and I bowed, my right hand touching my heart and then my forehead in a salute.

I paced forward into the house of the gods. The doors slid together behind me, closing him out. Here was perhaps the only place I could truly be alone, the only place Japhrimel would not intrude.

Unfortunately, leaving him outside the doors meant leaving my protection too. I didn't think any demon would try to attack me inside a temple, but I was just nervous enough to take a deep breath and welcome the next flush of Power spreading from the mark down my skin like warm oil.

Another deep breath. Panic beat under my breastbone. I told myself it was silly. Japhrimel was right outside the door, and the god had always answered me before.

But ever since the night my god had called me out of slumber and laid on me a geas I couldn't remember, He had been silent. And losing that compass left me adrift in a way I'd never been before.

Cairo Giza had been Islum territory in the Merican era, but Islum had choked on its own blood during the Seventy Days War – along with the Protestant Christers and the Judics, not to mention the Evangelicals of Gilead. In a world controlled by the Hegemony and Putchkin, with psions in every corner, the conditions that had given rise to the Religions of Submission had fallen away. After a brief reflowering of fundamentalist Islum during the collapse of the use of petroleo, it became just another small sect – like the Novo Christers – and the old gods and state religions had risen again.

The single biggest blow to the Submissions had been the Awakening and the rise of the science of Power. When anyone could contract a Shaman or Ceremonial to talk to the god of their choice and spiritual experiences became commonplace – not to mention Necromances proving an afterlife existed and Magi definitively proving the existence of demons – most organized religions had died a quick, hard death and been replaced by personal worship of patron gods and spirits. It was, in all reality, the only logical thing to do.

Here in Egypt those old gods had returned with a vengeance, and the pyramid Ceremonials were starting to take on the tenor of a priesthood again. It was one of the biggest debates among psions, most of whom were religious only to the extent that the science of belief made Power behave itself. Necromances were generally more dedicated than most; after all, our psychopomps took the faces of ancient gods and acted a little differently from the average man's deities.

Part of that probably had to do with the Trial every accredited Necromance had to face. It's hard not to feel a little bit religious toward a god who resurrects you from the psychic death of initiation and stays with you afterward, receiving you into Death's arms when it is finally time.

The question still remained – could a Ceremonial be a priest or priestess, and what exactly did the gods *want* anyway? Only nowadays, people weren't likely to murder each other over it. Not often, anyway. There was a running feud between the priestesses of Aslan and the Hegemony Albion Literary College, who said the Prophet Lewis was a Novo-Christer, but only ink was spilled in that battle, not blood.

I turned to my right. Sekhmet sat on Her throne, lion-headed and strangely serene, heat blurring up from the eternal fire in a black bowl on Her altar. The heady smell of wine rose, someone had been making offerings. Past Her, there was Set, His square-eared jackal-head painted the deep red of dried blood. The powers of destruction, given their place at the left hand of creation. Necessary, and worshipped – but not safe.

Japhrimel's last gift to me before breaking the news that Lucifer had summoned me again had been a glossy obsidian statue of Sekhmet. That same statue of the Fierce One, repaired and burnished to a fine gloss, was set by the side of the bed in the boarding house Leander had found even now. *Please tell me She isn't about to start messing around with me. I have all the trouble I can handle in my life right now.*

I shivered, turned to the left. There, behind Thoth's

beaky head, was the slim black dog's face of my own god, in his own important niche.

I breathed in, drawing *kyphii* deep into my lungs. A last respectful bow to Isis and Her son, and I began to walk to the left.

Thoth's statue seemed to make a quick movement as I passed it. I stopped, made my obeisance. Glanced up the ceiling, lasepainted with the figure of Nuit stretching through the skies.

Plenty of psions worshipped the Hellene gods, and there were colleges of Asatru and Teutonica as well as the Faery tradition in Hegemony Europa. The Shamans had their *loa*, and there were some who followed the path of the Left Hand and worshipped the Unspeakable. The Tantrics had their *devas*, and the Hindus their huge, intricate assemblages, Native Mericans and Islanders had their own branches of magick and Shamanic training passed down through blood and ritual; the Buddhists and Zen-mos their own not-quite-religious traditions. There were as many religions as there were people on the earth, the Magi said. Even the demons had been worshipped at one long-ago time, mistaken for gods.

But for me, there had never really been any choice. I'd dreamed of a dog-headed man all through my childhood, and had taken the requisite Religious Studies classes at Rigger Hall. One of the first religions studied was Egypti-anica, since it was such a popular sect – and my nape had tingled from the very beginning of that class. Everything about the Egyptian gods was not so much learned for me as deeply *remembered*, as if I'd always known but just needed reminding.

And the first time I'd gone into Death, He had been

there; He had never left me since. Where else would I turn for solace, but to Him?

I reached His niche. Tears welled up, my throat full of something hard and hot. I sank down to one knee, rose. Stepped forward. Approached His statue, the altar before it lit with novenas and laid with offerings. Food, drink, scattered New Credit notes, sticks of fuming incense. Even the normals propitiated Death, hoping for some false mercy when their time came, hoping to live past whatever appointed date and hour Death chose.

My rings sparked, golden points of light popping in the dark. From the obsidian ring on my right third finger to the amber on my right and left middle fingers, the moonstone on my left index finger, the bloodstone on my left third finger; the Suni-figured thumbring sparked too, reacting with the charge of Power in the air. And the Power I carried, tied to a demon and no longer strictly human myself. I sank down to my knees, my katana blurring out of its sheath. Laid the bright steel length on the stone floor in front of me, rested my hands on my knees. Closed my eyes and began to breathe.

Please, I thought. *I am weary, and I hunger for Your touch, my Lord. Speak to me. You have comforted me, but I want to hear You.*

My breathing deepened. The blue glow began, rising at the very corners of my mental sight. I began the prayer I'd learned long ago, studying from Novo Egyptos books in the Library at Rigger Hall. '*Anubis et'her ka,*' I whispered. '*Se ta'uk'fhet sa te vapu kuraph. Anubis et'her ka.* Anubis, Lord of the Dead, Faithful Companion, protect me, for I am Your child. Protect me, Anubis, weigh my heart upon the scale;

watch over me, Lord, for I am Your child. Do not let evil distress me, but turn Your fierceness upon my enemies. Cover me with Your gaze, let Your hand be upon me, now and all the days of my life, until You take me into Your embrace.'

Another deep breath, my pulse slowing, the silent place in me where the god lived opening like a flower. '*Anubis et'her ka,*' I repeated, and the blue light rose in one sharp flare. The god took me, swallowed me whole – and I was simply, utterly glad.